D0275216

DEADLY WEB

Also by Barbara Nadel

Belshazzar's Daughter
A Chemical Prison
Arabesk
Deep Waters
Harem
Petrified

DEADLY WEB

BARBARA NADEL

headline

Copyright © 2005 Barbara Nadel

The right of Barbara Nadel to be identified as the Author of
the Work has been asserted by her in accordance with the
Copyright, Designs and Patents Act 1988.

First published in Great Britain in 2005
by HEADLINE BOOK PUBLISHING

10 9 8 7 6 5 4 3 2 1

Apart from any use permitted under UK copyright law, this publication may
only be reproduced, stored, or transmitted, in any form, or by any means,
with prior permission in writing of the publishers or, in the case of
reprographic production, in accordance with the terms of
licences issued by the Copyright Licensing Agency.

All characters in this publication are fictitious
and any resemblance to real persons, living or dead,
is purely coincidental.

Cataloguing in Publication Data is available from the British Library

ISBN 0 7553 2126 X (hardback)
0 7553 2127 8 (trade paperback)

Typeset in Times by Palimpsest Book Production Limited,
Polmont, Stirlingshire

Printed and bound in Great Britain by Clays Ltd, St Ives plc

Headline's policy is to use papers that are natural, renewable and recyclable
products and made from wood grown in sustainable forests. The logging and
manufacturing processes are expected to conform to the environmental regulations
of the country of origin.

HEADLINE BOOK PUBLISHING
A division of Hodder Headline
338 Euston Road
London NW1 3BH

www.headline.co.uk
www.hodderheadline.com

To Malcolm – a real star.

Thanks to all the usual suspects in Turkey and the UK. However, special mentions go out to Jim for his magical insight, to Alex for helping me with my occult connections, and to Malcolm for his computer expertise. Also special thanks to the Göreme 'gang': Pat, Ruth, Jeyda, Faruk, Hüseyin, Dawn and Caroline. Time spent amongst the 'Fairy Chimneys' allowed me to finish this book.

List of Characters

Çetin İkmen – middle-aged senior İstanbul police inspector

Fatma İkmen – Çetin's wife and mother to his nine children

Çiçek İkmen – Çetin and Fatma's eldest daughter

Hulya İkmen Cohen – Çiçek's younger sister, married to Berekiah Cohen

Balthazar Cohen – ex-police constable, father of Berekiah

Jak Cohen – Balthazar's brother, a wealthy nightclub owner, resident in the UK

Mehmet Süleyman – İstanbul police inspector, used to work for Çetin İkmen

Zelfa Halman – psychiatrist, Mehmet Süleyman's wife and mother to his son, Yusuf

Zuleika Topal – Mehmet Süleyman's ex-wife, married to Burhan Topal

Fitnat Topal – Zuleika's stepdaughter

Dr Arto Sarkissian – Armenian pathologist, Çetin İkmen's oldest friend

Dr Krikor Sarkissian – Arto's older brother, an addiction specialist

Commissioner Ardıç – Çetin İkmen and Mehmet Süleyman's boss

Ayşe Farsakoğlu – Çetin's female sergeant

İsak Çöktin – Mehmet Süleyman's sergeant – a Kurd

Kasım Çöktin – İsak's cousin

Metin İskender – young police inspector

Alpaslan Karataş – Metin İskender's sergeant

Maximillian (Max) Esterhazy – an English teacher and Kabbalist

Ülkü Ayla – Max Esterhazy's maid

Turgut Can – Ülkü Ayla's boyfriend

Gonca – a gypsy artist and fortune-teller

İbrahim Dede – antiquarian bookseller and dervish

Demir Sandal – a pornographer

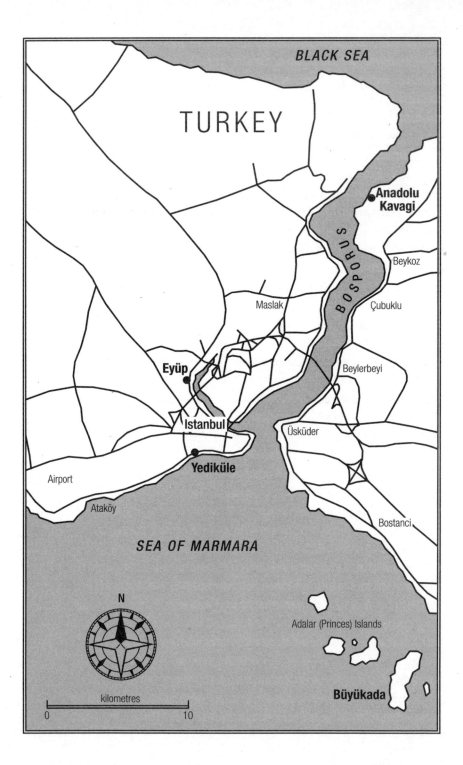

Chapter 1

She didn't walk on to the ferry, she skipped. The Bosphorus Tour –
a long, leisurely trip up the great waterway – tourists did it every
day. As she scanned the rows of seats on the lower deck for somewhere suitable, she smiled. Tourists, yes, there were a few, but there
weren't any young, single Turkish girls like her. She found a place
next to a couple in their thirties who spoke in a language she couldn't
even begin to fathom, and sat down. Just being stationary on the water
made her feel cooler. Summer had lingered on late this year, persisting in a fierceness that had left everyone feeling debilitated. It was
so nice to be both outside and cool.

The couple sitting next to her were poring over a guidebook to
İstanbul. She noticed that it wasn't written in the Roman alphabet.
The woman, all dazzling teeth and brown skin, looked up at her. The
man said something in the strange language that they shared, which
prompted the woman to speak to her in what she recognised as
English.

'Do you speak English?' the woman said.

She nodded proudly. 'Yes.'

The woman moved the guidebook over to show her. 'Can you tell
me where is the last place this boat stops?'

She looked at the map of the Bosphorus, studded with what looked
more like random odd marks than words. She pointed to the small
collection almost at the top of the Bosphorus and said, 'Is Anadolu
Kavağı, then the boat returns.'

'Ah. Thank you.'

The woman went to turn away, back to the man, but the girl, unable
to resist, continued, 'I am going there to Anadolu Kavağı to meet
someone.'

'Oh,' the woman said, probably imagining that she meant a

1

boyfriend of some sort. 'Have you been to the Princes' Islands?' she asked, flicking once more through the pages of her strange guidebook.

'Yes, but this is not the tour of the Islands,' the girl said. 'This is—'

'I know,' the woman replied. 'We go to the Islands tomorrow. There are some many Jewish people in the Islands, I think.'

The girl shrugged.

'We are from Israel,' the woman said, indicating that the man was included with her.

'Ah.' So that's what the strange marks in the guidebook were – Hebrew. The girl suddenly furrowed her brow. Once, quite a time ago, he had said that it was important to understand Hebrew, for some reason. But he hadn't mentioned it since. Perhaps that came later.

As the ferry sounded its horn and moved out into the sparkling blueness of the Bosphorus, the girl, smiling again now, closed her eyes.

He had been invited to the actual ceremony, but he couldn't face it. Not on his own. İkmen, although he hadn't actually said anything, had understood. When he'd said he could only make it to the party the inspector had patted him kindly on the shoulder and smiled. But then İkmen, both his friend as well as his colleague, *knew*.

The man sitting in the Pera Palas Hotel teashop, waiting to go to the wedding reception of the daughter of his friend Çetin İkmen, didn't look like a man anticipating a good time. At thirty-nine, Inspector Mehmet Süleyman of the İstanbul police was both thinner and sadder than he had ever been before. And although, as his mother never tired of telling him, he was still dazzlingly handsome, Mehmet was painfully aware of what his fears and anxieties were doing to him. Smoking almost continually, he took little nourishment beyond the tea he was drinking now out of an antique silver-encrusted glass.

He looked around the slightly down-at-heel, self-consciously 'Ottoman' tearoom and smiled. How well this place summed him up! The deep, brocade-covered tub seats, the ratty ostrich-feather fan suspended from the tall, dark hat stand in the corner. Faded artefacts from a past characterised by fezzes and fat odalisques, by consumptive

Turkish princes drinking crates of champagne while their Empire rotted around them. Spoiled, ignorant men, self-destructing to forget – like Mehmet's own princely grandfather. Like Mehmet.

How could he have been so stupid? To sleep with another woman when one was already married was one thing, but to sleep with a prostitute . . . He shook his head at the memory of it, disgusted with both the recollection of the act and his enjoyment of it. Whether or not he would have told his wife, Zelfa, about his unprotected liaison with the Russian whore if the girl hadn't been diseased, he didn't know. The reality was that she had been HIV-positive and so to conceal what he had done from Zelfa had never been an option. His first test had been negative, but as his doctor, Krikor Sarkissian, had told him at the time, it was the second test, three months after the 'contact', that would show whether or not he was infected. Not that Zelfa had waited around to find this out. Irish on her mother's side, an infuriated Zelfa Halman had packed up her elderly Turkish father, closed their house in Ortaköy and returned to Dublin. She had taken Mehmet's infant son, Yusuf, too. The memory of the little boy caused tears to gather at the corners of Mehmet's eyes. When would he see his son again? How would he, if he were HIV-positive, even begin to ask to see the child? Mehmet looked down at his left arm, recalling the sharp stab of the hypodermic needle in his vein. Dr Sarkissian had said that the results of the second test would take at least a week . . .

Mehmet took a sip of tea from his glass and lit yet another cigarette. When Zelfa threw him out, he'd had to return to his parents' house, live cheek by jowl with the man some still called 'Prince' – his weak aristocratic father, Muhammed, his snobbish, common mother, Nur, and, thankfully, his widowed brother, Murad, and his young daughter, Edibe. His old friend Balthazar Cohen had offered him a room in his apartment in Karaköy – Mehmet had lived there during the hiatus between his first and second marriages – but the place was already cramped and, with Cohen's son now married to İkmen's daughter, space was about to become even more scarce. And so Mehmet endured. People did – until one day they stopped doing that. Until, he thought, bizarrely in the case of the young boy he'd seen the previous week, they took their own lives. Young, intelligent and from a wealthy background, Cem Ataman had destroyed himself in a way Süleyman found hard to think about, even though he could all too easily empathise with it. After all, he – unlike Cem, with his money, his youth and his place at İstanbul University – had very little to look forward to. Now, with the results of his second HIV test looming, there was only looking back – to happy times, to his son, to the past security of his own body . . .

'Mehmet!'

He looked up at the familiar features of an attractive woman in her mid-thirties. Rising quickly to his feet, he offered the woman his hand. 'Zuleika,' he said with a small, tired smile. 'How good to see you.'

They shook hands and sat down. Zuleika arranged numerous bags around her feet as she sat, each sporting the name of an exclusive and expensive shop – Gönül Paksöy, Surreal Kılık İpek.

Mehmet tipped his head towards the bags and smiled. 'I see you continue to prosper.'

Zuleika smiled in return. 'Burhan is prosperous, Mehmet,' she said. 'I'm very fortunate.'

'Yes.'

'But then so are you,' she continued. 'How is little Yusuf?'

'He's fine,' Mehmet responded quickly. Although his ex-wife and also his cousin, Zuleika didn't know about the grim reality of his new existence. The official line from the older Süleymans was that Mehmet's wife and child were merely visiting relatives in Dublin. Just like his Ottoman forebears, 'Prince' Muhammed Süleyman preferred to keep his private life 'walled'.

As soon as the waitress arrived, Zuleika ordered tea.

'So what are you doing here?' she asked her ex-husband when the girl had left. 'I don't see this place as a haunt of policemen.'

Mehmet smiled once more. 'Çetin İkmen's daughter Hulya is getting married here in the hotel,' he said. 'I'll be going off to the party in a minute.'

'Oh?' Zuleika frowned. 'Very grand venue for someone like İkmen, isn't it? I'd have thought that with all his children . . .'

Zuleika had never liked Inspector Çetin İkmen. Even despite his being older than Mehmet, that İkmen was senior to him was something she had never understood. İkmen, though educated, was, to

Zuleika's mind, common. But then with nine children, a raffish apartment in Sultanahmet and a wife who covered her head, how could he be anything else?

'The groom's uncle is actually paying for the wedding,' Mehmet replied, his awareness growing with every passing second of all the reasons why he had left this woman.

Zuleika leaned across the table, assaulting Mehmet's nostrils with heavy, expensive perfume. 'Anyone we know?'

'I don't think so,' Mehmet said. 'The uncle, Jak Cohen, has lived in London for the last thirty years.'

'Cohen?' She frowned again. 'No relation to your old colleague, what was his name—'

'Balthazar,' Mehmet cut in, 'yes. Jak is his brother. Berekiah, Balthazar's son, is marrying Hulya İkmen.'

Zuleika sighed. 'Oh, well,' she said, 'I suppose if İkmen's wife has found it within herself to take a Jew . . .'

'Berekiah is a very fine young man,' Mehmet responded hotly. 'Anyone would be proud to have him join their family.' He then added acidly, 'Anyone with any sense, that is.'

Zuleika's tea arrived and, for a few moments, she sat back sipping it in silence. What a fool Mehmet still was! Forever fascinated by his working-class friends, wearing a watch she recognised as a street vendor fake. Burhan would rather die than be seen wearing such a thing! Burhan, her husband, with his many houses, his smart Şişli apartment, his cars, his yacht – his thin, grey hair, his teenage daughter . . .

'I'm sure they'll be very happy,' she said in a conciliatory tone.

Mehmet, feeling now that he'd won some sort of moral victory, sat up straight. 'Yes,' he said, 'so am I.'

How handsome he still looked! Especially when he was asserting himself – so upright, regal. The pale young girl dressed entirely in black who approached the table now also shared that view. Her eyes visibly dilated as she looked at him.

'Zuleika . . .'

'Oh, Fitnat.' Zuleika saw the twin lights of both desire and suspicion in the young girl's eyes. 'This is my cousin Mehmet Bey.'

'Ah . . .'

Mehmet rose to take the young girl's hand in his.

'Mehmet, this is my stepdaughter, Fitnat.'

'I'm very pleased to meet you, Fitnat.'

'Right . . .' She placed a large pile of bags on the floor, next to her black boot-covered feet, then sat down in the one remaining empty chair while Mehmet resumed his seat.

As soon as everyone was settled, Zuleika turned to the girl and said, 'So did you get some nice, light, pretty clothes, Fitnat?'

'Yes,' the girl smiled, 'lots. I'll show you at home. I'm sure Mehmet Bey doesn't want to—'

'Your father will be so pleased,' Zuleika cut in, and then turning to Mehmet she said, 'Fitnat has been going through a "Gothic" phase of late. Black clothes, heavy make-up, all that nonsense.'

Yes, Mehmet had seen the so-called 'Goths' in and around Taksim Square and İstiklal Caddesi – young black-clad kids, listening to dirges on their CD Walkmans, talking about suicide. Not that they ever, in his experience, were any more prone to it than others. Maybe even less so. Cem Ataman, whose blood had oozed into the shoes of the officers who had found him, only had, as his parents had put it, Gothic 'interests'. He hadn't, or so it appeared, been one of the actual black-draped brigade like this girl.

'But you're done with all that now, aren't you, darling?' Zuleika said as she put a hand out to stroke Fitnat's thick, artificially black hair.

'Yes . . .'

'She's still only very young, you see,' Zuleika said as she watched the girl watch her ex-husband's every move and gesture. 'Sixteen. Just a child really.' Fitnat, stung not so much by what had been said, as by the spite that was implied within it, turned to look at her step-mother. Zuleika smiled. 'And so in order that she might find a nice young man of her own age, she does need to take advantage of her prettiness,' she said, 'not hide it all under ugly black bags. Plenty of time for that when you're old, like Mehmet Bey and myself, Fitnat.'

The girl looked into the beautiful face of her stepmother with both lack of comprehension and not a little hurt.

*   *   *

No trip out to Anadolu Kavağı would be complete without lunch at one of the little fish restaurants clustered around the harbour. The Israeli couple, as well as a young Frenchman the Turkish girl had briefly spoken to on the ferry, thought so and went straight for it.

But she was too excited to eat. Even though the meeting wouldn't, couldn't take place until sunset, just the thought of it . . . Impulsively she hugged her arms to her chest, smiling, her features distorting when viewed through the steam rising from her tea glass. The other people at the çay bahçe – a fisherman, a middle-class woman and her daughter – thought she looked a little odd at the time. But then they didn't know what she knew, couldn't know what delicious torment she was in.

She'd saved herself for this day, deliberately and with what she now knew was joy. It hadn't been easy but then nothing that was really worth anything ever was – that's what she'd been told, that's what she had learned. That wasn't what her father had told her. But then what did he know? Nothing. Nobody knew anything because she'd been so good – just like a young bride should be. She smiled, finished her tea and, through dreamy half-closed eyes, she watched the street cats fight and play outside the tiny police station on the waterfront.

Apart from the accent, which was now, to İkmen's way of thinking, decidedly weird, Jak Cohen had changed little in the thirty-something years since he'd left İstanbul. Still, like his brother Balthazar, small and thin, Jak in middle age actually looked better than he had done during his hungry, semi-orphaned youth. When İkmen offered him a glass of champagne, which was one of the few contributions the policeman had made to the festivities, Jak declined.

'No, thank you, Inspector,' he said as he held one hand aloft to signal his refusal. 'I've never touched it and never will.'

İkmen shrugged, took a glass for himself and sipped from it with pleasure.

'If you remember my father . . .'

'Of course Çetin Bey remembers our father! Everyone remembers our father!'

Both Jak and İkmen looked down at the shrunken man in the

wheelchair clutching, as if for his life, on to a glass filled with white, cloudy liquid – the local anise spirit rakı, mixed with water.

'Yes, Balthazar,' Jak replied gravely, 'they do. Drinking yourself to death while neglecting your children does tend to attract attention.'

The man in the wheelchair cleared his throat. 'Ah, he had his problems. It was his way.'

'It was a bad way.'

'Yes, but—'

'But today we mustn't think of the past, only look forward to the future,' İkmen interjected quickly. He'd known the Cohen boys, Balthazar, Jak and Leon, since childhood, which, given that İkmen himself was now fifty-five, was a long time. He knew how, even now and despite Jak's generosity, disagreement could escalate between them.

'Your daughter and my son, mmm,' Balthazar frowned, 'a Muslim and a Jew to become lovers in this world filled with hate.'

'A Muslim and a Jew to show the way forward in this world filled with hate, I hope,' İkmen said as he lit cigarettes for both himself and Balthazar.

'You did agree to this marriage, Balthazar,' Jak began. 'I—'

'I agreed because I knew it was inevitable,' the man in the wheelchair retorted. 'I called you,' he looked up at his brother, scowling, 'because if it had to be done I wanted it done properly.'

'I am your brother. I love you. I'll do anything I can for you.'

'And I'm grateful, Jak. Just don't ask me to be happy, because I can't do that.' He placed the cigarette İkmen had given him firmly between his lips and began to wheel himself away.

In all the years that he'd known him, İkmen had only come across this side of Balthazar's character in recent times. Until the great earthquake of 1999, which had been responsible for putting him in his wheelchair, Balthazar Cohen had been the cheerfully adulterous Constable Cohen. A rather slovenly officer, he had sometimes helped and sometimes hindered İkmen in various investigations over the years. That he never exhibited any sort of religious sensibility had led İkmen to believe that he possessed few feelings about his origins. But then along came his own catastrophic injuries, coupled with the mental disintegration of his eldest son, Yusuf, and suddenly Balthazar was only too aware of his five-hundred-year-old heritage as one of İstanbul's ancient families of Sephardic Jews. Maybe it had to do with the fact that Berekiah, İkmen's new son-in-law, was Balthazar's only avenue into the future . . .

'Balthazar tells me that you work in the entertainment business over in London, Jak,' İkmen said, changing the subject for everyone's sake. 'You've done well.'

Jak laughed. 'I get by, Çetin,' he said with a shrug. 'I've a flat in Docklands, a house in Surrey and an ex-wife with expensive tastes. It costs me to keep Daniel, that's my son, at Cambridge. But, please God, when he does finally get his degree it will have all been worth it.'

'You know I'm very . . .' İkmen struggled with the words of gratitude he knew were neither expected nor required, 'grateful to you . . .'

'Your daughter is a very decent and beautiful girl, Çetin Bey,' Jak said, changing his form of address to the more respectful 'Bey'. After all, monied though he may now be, Jak could remember only too clearly when he and his ragged-arsed brothers had felt privileged to be allowed to play with Çetin and his brother, Halil – the İkmen boys, clever sons of the university lecturer Timur İkmen and his ethereal-looking wife, Ayşe, the Albanian, the famous witch of Üsküdar.

İkmen looked across the room at the slim, handsome young man hand in hand with his eighteen-year-old daughter. Resplendent in white and gold, Hulya İkmen, now Cohen, looked like a bride from a fairy tale. Beside the couple, standing a little distant from them, was another attractive female, somewhat older and, to İkmen's way of thinking, a little sadder than Hulya.

'I am very happy to welcome Berekiah into my family,' İkmen said, and then tipping his head in the direction of the young woman beside the couple he added, 'I just wish that my Çiçek could find someone.'

Jak, following the policeman's gaze, looked at the young woman and smiled. 'Oh, I shouldn't think you'd have too much trouble there,' he said. 'I mean, look at that fellow there. He's very attractive and he's moving in on your Çiçek, by the look of it.'

For just a moment, İkmen thought that perhaps some new and

exciting young man he'd never seen before had come on the scene. But when he saw that it was Mehmet Süleyman, he turned away from Jak and looked out of the open French doors across the terrace towards the Golden Horn and the great Imperial Mosques of the Old City.

'I don't think that he's entirely suitable,' İkmen said, more to himself than to Jak. 'He's got too much past.'

And then the music began, softly at first, echoing up into the marble galleries that lined the upper storey of the function room. The Pera Palas Hotel, built for the elegant passengers arriving in İstanbul on the Orient-Express, erstwhile residence of Atatürk, Agatha Christie, Jackie Onassis, various Ottoman princes – including now Mehmet Süleyman. Poor Mehmet, childless, wifeless, worried, talking earnestly to Çiçek – about something. İkmen shook his head as if to free worrying thoughts from his mind and went to join his headscarfed wife and her sisters out on the terrace.

The climb was steep and after a short while she began to pant. It wasn't so hot now – around 5.30 p.m. – but, though young, she was mildly asthmatic and so it was hard. The asthma, so her doctor said, was a nervous condition, brought about by her anxieties. He'd given her medication for it. That the condition persisted now that she didn't have any more anxieties, hadn't had them for a while, was strange. Perhaps the medication, had she taken it, would have helped. She climbed on, gasping, using, where she could, the stout trunks of the trees to support her.

Above, the Byzantine castle of Yoros loomed. At the height of summer, even this late in the afternoon, this area wouldn't be deserted as it thankfully was today. A combination of late season and rumours of an impending war between America and Turkey's neighbour Iraq had meant that İstanbul as a whole had done badly for tourists in recent weeks. In some quarters it was being said that perhaps this war could affect Turkey herself. Even İstanbul, some said, was close enough to Iraq to make gas or chemical attack a possibility. Her breath became more laboured, dizzying her head with lack of oxygen.

Before the Christian Byzantines built Yoros Castle, the site on which it now stands was a pagan shrine dedicated to Zeus. The Ancient Greek sailors who wished to pass safely through the straits would first make sacrifice here, pouring innocent blood into the earth for their god to take and use for his nourishment. That the 'new' religion of Christianity had appropriated this site was nothing unusual. Up-coming faiths often did this to old sites, stamping down hard on what had gone before, neutralising what had been 'evil' and making it their own. Up in the city, Aya Sofya, once a church constructed from the ruins of pagan temples, then a mosque, now a museum, was a perfect example. All this the girl with the swimming head had learned and understood.

Just below the castle, in a small clearing she had been taken to before, the girl stopped and sat down. Though still taut with excitement, she was beginning to feel hungry. But now was too late and, besides, there was too much to think about and do in the intervening time. Now she knew he had to be preparing to come to her. When the sun set he would arrive. She took her clothes off and piled them neatly in front of a tree. Then she sat down, legs crossed, and removed her crystal from her bag. She thought how beautiful it was as she stared into its transparent depths.

'People commit suicide every day,' Çiçek İkmen said as she put her cigarette out in a small, white ashtray.

Together with Mehmet Süleyman, she had moved from the main function room of the hotel and into the bar. Sitting at a distant table over by the hotel's front windows, they had both decided to sit out of the orbit of the huge mirror that hung like a vague threat over the old, darkwood bar.

'But then you, just like my father, must know that,' Çiçek continued as, in unconscious mimicry of Çetin İkmen, she proceeded to chain-smoke. 'Perhaps it was the boy's youth that so affected you.'

Mehmet leaned back in his chair and sighed. 'Maybe.'

'Or maybe the method . . .'

'I don't want to talk about that.' He too took a cigarette from his packet and lit up.

'OK.' She crossed one slim leg over the other and settled back to look at the ornate and archaic décor.

He couldn't tell her the truth. He couldn't tell anyone the truth. Besides, although he knew she was aware that Zelfa had left him, he didn't know whether Çiçek knew why. It was almost certain she didn't know the whole story. She was so normal with him. People weren't generally this casual when talking to those living under possible sentence of death. And HIV, Aids – it wasn't nice, not a comfortable death. But then two handfuls of the antidepressants he'd been prescribed plus half a bottle of rakı would fix it even before it began. Even taking the route the boy had taken ... No, that was far too upsetting, too messy, too much trouble for all of those left behind. It was, however, compelling, strangely attractive and just at this moment he wanted it with all of his soul. But he couldn't tell her that. Now smiling as her sister the bride entered the bar with their father, Çiçek was so obviously pleased that the young girl had got what she wanted. Tales of death were not appropriate here. He reined them in and forced a smile.

'My sister looks dazzling, don't you think?' Çiçek said as she raised her champagne glass up to her lips.

'You belong to an attractive family,' Mehmet replied.

'With one exception,' Çiçek joked as she flashed her eyes briefly in the direction of her father.

Mehmet laughed. Small, thin and rumpled İkmen might be but, as he reminded the man's daughter, her father had such charm and charisma that looks were largely irrelevant in his case.

'Well, I suppose that my mum must agree with you,' Çiçek said just after she drained her champagne flute. 'She's been with him for ever.'

'Yes.'

'Hey, you know Dad's engaged a gypsy fortune-teller out on the terrace? He knows her; she's supposed to be really good,' Çiçek said excitedly. 'Do you fancy having your cards read?'

Süleyman grinned. İkmen and his soothsayers, spiritualists and other assorted misfits! 'No,' he said, 'it's not for me. But you go.'

'OK.' She got up and left.

When she'd gone, just briefly Mehmet caught İkmen's eye and watched as the older man's features broke into a smile. He is, Mehmet thought, in a sense holding me close. He knows what I think and what my intentions could be. As the most successful and prolific homicide detective in the city he has a legal duty to protect me. And he is the son of a witch. And he loves me, I know, like a son. If I lay hands upon myself, he will stop me.

The sudden touch of a hand on his shoulder made him jump. İkmen, suddenly materialised at his side, took his face between his hands and kissed him hard on both cheeks.

The sunset call to prayer brought him just as he'd said. Wordlessly, from behind, he took her naked arms in his hands and entered her. It hurt. Terror briefly took over from desire and she just managed to stifle a scream. Big, hard and cold – as she knew it would be – slowly at first it moved inside her, agitating the pain. But then as the rhythm began to increase a curious thing happened – a sort of anaesthetic effect took hold, an absence of sensation that then suddenly blossomed into something she had never experienced before. A feeling somewhere between pleasure and pain, a glorious tightening of the senses. She gasped. Long, elegant hands reached around to pull and tease at her nipples and the girl let out a small, breathy scream.

Her body now moving in time to his, she took her hands away from the earth and kneeled up, her eyes closed. She'd been told about this moment, the one that was approaching with such ecstatic rapidity. She heard her chest wheeze as her body attempted to deal with the increased need for oxygen. He spoke now, possibly in Hebrew, and she, in response, began to gasp. The experience took him to another level, one that was so wonderful and yet at the same time so frightening for her that she screamed.

Let it finish, let it last for ever, she thought as the full force of orgasm broke across her.

And then with him still hard inside her, others, their faces hooded, came and touched her body too. Sharing their ceremony, his and hers. She didn't see the knife because her eyes were closed. But she felt it, plunging into her heart as great flashes of white lightning flew all around the clearing like a display of fireworks at a wedding.

Chapter 2

In spite of his father's protestations to the contrary, Nurdoğan wasn't convinced that he was right.

'She must have gone to a club; she's probably at Sırma's,' his father said as he took himself and his hangover out to his car.

But Nurdoğan knew that Gülay hadn't seen Sırma for months. She hadn't seen any of her old friends for quite a long time. He walked up the stairs to his mother's bedroom.

'Gülay's bed hasn't been slept in,' he said to the red-haired woman lying on the bed eating grapes and smoking a cigarette. Her considerable make-up was still, he noticed, plastered to her face from the night before.

'She's staying over with Sırma,' his mother coughed.

'I don't think she sees Sırma any more,' Nurdoğan replied as he lowered himself down on to his mother's slippery and, in his opinion, uncomfortable red satin sheets.

'Well, that's probably for the best.' She smiled briefly. 'Where's Kenan? Aren't you supposed to be at school?'

Nurdoğan's young face hardened. 'It's Sunday.'

His mother just raised her eyebrows in acknowledgement.

'Mum, it is eleven o'clock now and Gülay didn't take her pump with her. It's still by her bed.'

'She'll be OK.' The woman ground her cigarette out on the plate she was also using for grape pips. 'Why don't you go out on your bike or something? Gülay will be here when you get back. It's not that she hasn't stayed out before, is it?' she added tetchily.

She was always like this when she'd been out to the club with his father. The drink just seemed to carry on taking effect, blunting every real feeling she might possess. He was, he knew, supposed to leave her alone, carry on being in the care of Kenan and the small group

15

of young girls who worked in the house, until she felt 'better' again.

There wasn't really any great need to be worried about Gülay. Sometimes she did stay out, although not in recent months as often as she had. And, if Nurdoğan were honest, he would have to say that Gülay had been happier of late. But this time, for some reason he couldn't really articulate, he was worried about his sister. She used to tell him everything, still in fact said that she told him everything, but Nurdoğan was no longer sure about this. Sometimes she just went off without telling anyone and she'd taken to locking herself in her bedroom. Nurdoğan had always been close to his big sister, the two of them in a sense allied against their parents. It was an alliance that had survived all sorts of teenage 'phases' on Gülay's part. Only now, when she was 'normal' again, did there seem to be a problem.

Nurdoğan went downstairs and retrieved his bicycle from the garage. His father, who had taken his car out in order, apparently, to clean it, stopped talking to the large man Nurdoğan recognised as one of his club managers as he passed.

'If you're satisfied there are no signs of foul play, I'll release the Ataman boy's body for burial,' the small, round man said with a smile.

Mehmet Süleyman shrugged. 'I can't see any reason to hold back,' he said wearily. 'He took his own life. Not to any rational purpose but—'

'Yes, he did.'

The smile faded from the round man's face. Dr Arto Sarkissian had been employed as a police pathologist for all of his working life and had, during that time, seen most things that people could do to others and themselves. But premature, seemingly needless deaths like that of young Cem Ataman still shocked him.

'I'll contact the family and make the necessary arrangements,' he said, and then, as if putting Cem Ataman himself to one side, he moved the boy's notes to the edge of his desk. 'So what time did you eventually leave the party?' he asked, changing the subject to something far more pleasant.

'At about midnight,' Süleyman replied. 'I think everyone,

including Hulya and Berekiah, had had enough by then.'

Arto nodded. 'Yes. Weddings are tiring. Mine was. I would have stayed longer yesterday, but my wife doesn't thrive well in the heat. I think Çetin understood.'

'I'm sure he did.'

It was a safe assumption. Friends since childhood, the Turk Çetin İkmen and the Armenian Arto Sarkissian barely needed to speak now in order to know what the other was thinking. That Arto had been there to support his old friend at his daughter's wedding had, both he and Süleyman knew, been enough.

'I couldn't help seeing you talking to my brother,' the Armenian began.

'Yes,' Süleyman cut in quickly, 'but not about . . .'

'I realise that Krikor won't have your results yet,' Arto said, alluding to the second HIV test Süleyman had recently undergone at the hands of his addiction specialist brother.

'No.' Süleyman reached into his jacket pocket for his cigarettes and lit up. 'Çetin told me that Jak Cohen has bought the young couple a house,' he said, reverting to the lighter side of the İkmen/Cohen wedding once again.

Arto shook his head slowly from side to side. 'Yes. Amazing. In Fener and needing some work, I understand, which is why they'll be living with Mr and Mrs Cohen for a while. But to give them a house! I don't know what Jak Cohen does over in England but he must be very good at it.'

'I think he works in the entertainment business in some capacity,' Süleyman confided. 'His brother isn't exactly forthcoming on the subject, which I suppose could lead one to all sorts of rather unsavoury conclusions.'

The Armenian laughed. 'By which I take it you mean sex "work".'

'Maybe. But then if he runs strip or dancing clubs, so what? Such places are legal in Britain and so any money he earns from these pursuits would be "honest".'

'Nothing to disturb Çetin's sleep then,' Arto said.

'We all know that Balthazar and his brothers can be a little morally selective, to say the least,' Süleyman replied, 'but I don't believe that they're bad people, and I've lived with them so I should know.'

'Then all we can and should do is be happy for the young people.'

'Yes,' Süleyman agreed, 'that is all we should do.'

Hamdı Alan had been a police constable for only three years. Based at the small and really quite picturesque station on the waterfront at Anadolu Kavağı, he didn't get to experience much beyond the odd disagreement between drunken fishermen. Luckily Hamdı, whose main preoccupation in life was to find a nice Muslim girl, marry her and have children, liked it like that. No trouble meant more time sitting quietly in the sunshine, reflecting, or not, upon the meaning of life. However, this new situation – he didn't know what to call it yet – had already rattled his customary peace and thrown him rapidly into a world he neither knew nor wanted to know.

The body had been discovered by an elderly woman who'd been up at Yoros grazing her small family of goats. Not so much shocked by the blood, most of which had soaked into the ground, as by the girl's nakedness, she'd thrown her coat across the body in order to preserve the modesty of the deceased. Constable Fuat Ayla, who had offered, reluctantly, to accompany Hamdı up to the site, had pulled the coat away and then turned the body on to its back as soon as he arrived.

'Obvious what happened,' Ayla said as he stared down at the butchered body at his feet. 'Killed herself.'

'Yeah.' She'd taken off all her clothes to do it and laid them very neatly in a pile at the edge of the clearing. She'd even put a lump of what looked like crystal on top to hold them down. Hamdı frowned. Something similar had, he was certain, occurred somewhere else in the greater city area . . .

'Choosing to send her own soul to damnation.' Ayla stuck a cigarette into his narrow, fat mouth and shook his head. 'Can't understand it.'

'No.' Although, good Muslim lad that he was, it wasn't the dead girl's soul that was exercising Hamdı's mind at this precise moment.

Ayla, his large almost womanly bottom wobbling as he walked, stomped over to the pile of clothes at the edge of the clearing.

'All we can do is find out who she was, get a doctor to look at her, and then return her to her family,' he said.

And yet the way she had killed herself, if indeed that was what she had done, was so violent, so bizarre, and there was that other case, involving a boy, if Hamdı remembered correctly . . .

'No,' he said, holding his hand up to stop his colleague from disturbing the girl's clothes, 'no, I don't think we should touch anything, Fuat.'

'Why not?'

Hamdı shrugged. He didn't actually *know* why he felt so edgy about this suicide – Allah knew that he didn't want the aggravation – but there was something just too weird about it all.

'I think we should get help,' Hamdı said after a pause. 'I think we should get someone over here who knows what he's doing.'

The girl's identity card stated that her name was Gülay Arat. She was seventeen. Sergeant İsak Çöktin held it up for his superior to see, but Süleyman just flicked his eyes up at it without comment. Over by the trees the two local cops, the old fat one and the young sleepy-looking one, stared down at the site, smoking in that silent, concentrated fashion so typical of those raised away from the bustle of the city.

'I'll need a doctor to look at her before I make any sort of judgement,' Süleyman said as he rose, rather grey-faced Çöktin thought, to his feet, 'but I think it's the same as Cem Ataman.'

Çöktin, unaware of what his out-of-town colleagues should and should not know, lowered his voice. 'Stabbed herself through the heart.'

'She or someone did.' Süleyman took his mobile phone out of his pocket and searched through his directory for a particular number.

'How could she do it?' Çöktin said, shaking his head as he looked down at the blood-soaked corpse spread-eagled on the earth before him. 'She's only a little thing. You need to exert tremendous force to stab through the chest. What state of mind must she have been in?'

Süleyman shrugged. 'We'll need to get a team up here as soon as possible,' he said. 'I just hope that our local friends there,' he tipped his head in the direction of the two Anadolu Kavağı cops, 'haven't disturbed the site too much. The word as well as the concept of

19

procedure is, more often than not, unknown to people like them.'

'Right.' Çöktin, who didn't always share Süleyman's views about the ignorance of ordinary folk – he was, after all, a working-class Kurd himself – did grudgingly have to concur in this case. The two locals, with their scruffy uniforms and slow, country ways, did appear to be less than well informed.

'Ah, Dr Sarkissian . . .' Süleyman said into his telephone, turning aside in order to gain some privacy as he did so.

İsak Çöktin had attended the scene when Cem Ataman's body had been discovered in Eyüp Cemetery. Slumped behind the tall, uninscribed gravestones of several Ottoman executioners, the eighteen-year-old's torso had been folded over the arm carrying the knife that had taken his life away. And although his upper body was bare, he had been wearing trousers and underwear when he died. Cem, though not big, had been far larger and stronger than this tiny, naked girl.

'The doctor's coming straight way,' Süleyman said as he replaced his mobile in his jacket pocket, 'and I've called for a team to be dispatched. I'd like to find the weapon used.'

'I thought the doctor didn't work on Sundays,' Çöktin said in reference to Arto Sarkissian's nominal adherence to Christianity.

'No, he's on duty all day,' Süleyman replied. 'I've told him to rescind his order for the release of the Ataman boy's body.'

'That was suicide.'

'I thought so, yes,' Süleyman said as he moved away from the body and lit a cigarette, 'and that may still be the case. But this has raised some doubts.'

'What do you mean?'

'I mean that even taking into account the fact that this girl's death could be a case of copycat suicide, I think that two incidents of this nature in such a short space of time necessitates our further involvement.'

'Dr Sarkissian was certain that Cem Ataman took his own life. The boy left that note about—'

'Yes, and I'm not saying that he was wrong.' He beckoned Çöktin to come closer to him. 'I'm not even saying that I suspect foul play, but as Inspector İkmen taught me many years ago, two similar events could be the start of a pattern and violent patterns require our attention.'

'So if young kids are killing themselves . . .'

'We won't be able to stop that, but if young people are being encouraged to do so, that we can try to prevent,' Süleyman said, and then seeing the look of confusion on the younger man's face he added, 'I have read of instances, not in this country, where people have been encouraged to end their lives by others.'

'What for?'

'Sometimes a person is terminally ill and a friend or relative helps them to commit suicide.'

'Yes, that I can understand,' Çöktin commented.

'But there are other instances,' Süleyman continued, 'where self-destruction is encouraged for more sinister reasons. For instance, some families may encourage an unstable but wealthy relative to end it all, and then there are the truly sick instances of people doing it because they get pleasure from it. And Cem, as we know, was interested in some pretty dark stuff.'

'Yes,' Çöktin frowned. 'Mind you, sir, the method Cem used wasn't reported in the press. So a copycat—'

'Oh, I agree the possibility is remote. But maybe if this girl knew him and his family . . . But we're very much in the dark at the moment, so keep your mind wide open.'

'Inspector Süleyman?'

He looked across at the younger of the two local officers and said, 'Yes?'

'Er, what's happening? Should we move the body?'

'No, no.' Süleyman held up a staying hand. 'No, I've asked for an investigation team and a pathologist to attend.'

Constable Hamdı Alan's eyes widened. 'So, do you think she's been murdered then, sir?'

'I don't know, Constable,' Süleyman replied. 'That is why I've requested expert help.'

The two country policemen looked at each other with something between fear and excitement in their eyes. If it was murder then Anadolu Kavağı wasn't going to be as quiet as usual, which would, they both knew, be a mixed blessing. More visitors, more money,

21

more disputes to settle, many more sightseers, deranged murder ghouls they would have to try to keep away from Yoros.

'Oh, and I'll need to interview the person who discovered the body,' Süleyman said before turning back once again to Çöktin. 'Once the site has been secured you and I must contact this girl's family.'

'Yes, sir.'

They both momentarily looked back at the naked corpse upon the ground. Although Süleyman at least had dealt with giving similar bad news to Cem Ataman's parents, he didn't know how he might do that in this case. After all, Cem, though young too, had been strong, male and dressed. Allah alone knew how little Gülay Arat had managed to summon up the strength to plunge a knife into her chest, if indeed she had done so. Also, she had been naked and so the possibility of sexual assault was not to be ruled out. Maybe she'd taken her life after she'd been assaulted; maybe her family were very traditional and she just couldn't face telling them about what she had endured.

'I also want to re-interview the Ataman family,' Süleyman said as he put his cigarette out. 'I want to see if there are any connections between them and this girl's family.'

Çöktin shrugged. 'OK.' And then he wondered what, if anything, new he might learn from Mr and Mrs Ataman. He, *post mortem*, knew Cem better than they ever had. Finding similarities where, on one side at least, only a void existed was going to be difficult. Çöktin lit up a cigarette and watched his boss climb away from the site up towards the old castle. Wanting, if only briefly, to be alone. He did it a lot now. The rumour mill back at the station had it that his wife, who Süleyman himself said was on holiday, had left him. If she had, she'd taken their infant son with her.

Süleyman was sitting on the ground now, just below the castle, looking out across the startling blueness of the Bosphorus. Though still handsome, recent probably unintentional weight loss had made his features look sharper than before. In profile as he was now, he looked like a great, noble bird.

Chapter 3

The place seemed empty without her. Of course it wasn't. As usual, there were numerous people in, out or resting in the İkmen apartment. There were three other daughters, for a start. But in spite of whoever else was about, Çetin İkmen missed Hulya. For weeks she'd dominated activity in the apartment, running around with swathes of white material and pretty but uncomfortable shoes under her arms. Phone calls to and from her groom, Berekiah, and his Uncle Jak in London had happened sometimes on an hourly basis. The place had been mad and, OK, if he were honest, really quite irritating too, right up until they'd all left for the ceremony. Had that happened just yesterday morning?

İkmen put his head in his hands and tried to remember whether he'd taken his last dose of aspirin two or four hours previously.

'How's your hangover?'

İkmen looked up into the amused eyes of his daughter Çiçek.

'It's a very good one, actually,' he said as he moved across the settee to allow her to sit beside him. 'Pounding head, churning stomach.'

'Oh, all the symptoms,' she smiled. 'Maybe you should ask Sınan or Orhan to give you something for it.'

İkmen took a cigarette out of his pocket and lit up. 'Doctors, even if they are my sons, can't help me with this,' he said gravely. 'The spice merchants in the Mısır Çarşısı can say what they like about their disgusting so-called remedies, no living being has ever developed a truly effective cure for a hangover. It is one of the great mysteries of life that Allah, in His wisdom, chooses to conceal from us.'

'I don't think Allah has a great deal to do with overindulgence in alcohol.'

'No, He probably doesn't,' İkmen said. 'If I believed in Him, I'd say a prayer and ask Him, but since I'm an atheist, I'll have to just remain ignorant on that point.'

He was always tetchy after drinking sessions these days. Time was when Çetin İkmen would happily throw vast amounts of brandy in particular down his throat with no thought for anything beyond the pleasure that drinking gave him. But ever since his numerous stomach ulcers had started giving him pain a few years previously, drinking had become something for which a price was always exacted.

'You know that Berekiah let Hulya tread on his foot,' Çiçek said, alluding to the old belief that whoever manages to tread on the other's foot during the marriage registration will have the upper hand in the relationship.

İkmen shrugged. 'She's my daughter and he's a realist.'

Çiçek reached down into her handbag and took out a cigarette. 'Dad, do you think that Zelfa will ever go back to Mehmet?'

İkmen, not at all happy to address the Süleymans' marital relations, turned slightly away. 'I don't know.'

'It's just that he looks so lost . . .'

'Zelfa left for a reason, Çiçek.'

'Which, of course, you know all about.'

He turned to face her. Çiçek had always been very fond of Mehmet Süleyman, and he had no desire to undermine that fondness. But, given his colleague's track record with women, not to mention his current possible health troubles, he didn't want Çiçek getting any ideas about his elegant Ottoman friend. His daughter was, after all, nearly thirty, still unwed, beaten to the marriage register by her teenage sister. Çiçek was vulnerable.

'What I know and don't know about Mehmet is not your concern,' İkmen said sternly. 'That is his private business.'

'I'm only trying to—'

'I know exactly what you're trying to do, or rather find out, Çiçek,' İkmen continued. 'I saw you talking to him yesterday. Your eyes were glued to his face.'

Çiçek put her head down, just like she'd done when she was a little girl, caught out by her father in the pursuit of some prank or other.

'Your hot sergeant couldn't take her eyes off Mehmet either,' an amused masculine voice put in.

Somehow, without either İkmen or Çiçek even noticing, the latter's twenty-year-old brother, Bülent, had entered the room. Tall and skinny, he threw himself down on to one of the cushions on the floor and then proceeded to stuff pistachio nuts into his mouth.

'I'd prefer it if you spoke more respectfully about Sergeant Farsakoğlu, Bülent.'

'I'm only saying what I saw, Dad.'

And, of course, the boy was right and, of course, İkmen knew it. His deputy, Ayşe Farsakoğlu, had once enjoyed a brief affair with his friend some years ago, prior to Süleyman's current marriage. She'd never got over him. But then most of the women he seemed to come into contact with were like that. Not for the first time, İkmen wondered what it was that Mehmet Süleyman had that so fascinated and obsessed women of all ages and backgrounds. Bülent, young and also, famously within his family, tactless, offered up one theory for discussion.

'Perhaps he's some sort of sexual superstud . . .'

'That's enough!' İkmen, his head now pounding more violently than it had been when he first woke up, rose to his feet. 'If you can't at least fake some respect for your elders—'

'Dad, I was only joking! I like Mehmet!'

İkmen, suddenly deflated, sighed. 'Yes, we all do,' he said as he looked down at the sad face of his daughter. 'Some of us like him a lot. But he's got a few problems at the moment and so perhaps it's best if we don't discuss him and his business at this time.' He put his cigarette out in one of the ashtrays before muttering, 'I feel really bad. I'm going back to bed. Got to be at the station in the morning.'

He then left his now silent son and daughter and walked down the corridor towards his bedroom. Fatma, İkmen's wife, made a brief appearance as he passed the bathroom, distracted from her cleaning activities by the need to harangue him once again about his drinking. But he ignored her, closing the bedroom door behind him with a bang. He threw himself down on his bed and shut his eyes. However, as soon as he did so, his neighbour, Mr Gören, 'started', his raised voice, together with that of his adversary, Mr Emin, dragging İkmen's reluctant head back to full consciousness again.

Mr Gören, who had lived in the next-door apartment for the last six months, had a daughter about the same age as Çiçek called Halide. Plain but honest, Halide still silently mourned the Anatolian village she and her father had left to come and seek their fortunes in the big city. Unfortunately, her sadness had caught the attention, and inflamed the affections, of the owner of one of the small pidecis down below the apartment building on Divanyolu. Mr Emin, at seventy-six, was in love – it was something he demonstrated all the time via his daily shouting sessions with Halide's father.

'I'm a man of means, I'll provide well for her!' Mr Emin shouted through the closed front door of Mr Gören's apartment.

'My daughter is fully occupied looking after me, her father, thank you,' Mr Gören responded.

'But you must want your daughter to be married! It must be a worry for you! She is no longer young! An old maid . . .'

In spite of the heat, İkmen shoved his head under his pillow and sighed. Marriage, sex, sex, marriage – it was all he'd heard about, thought about for months. Young girls getting married, older girls not getting married. And now Çiçek, suddenly made aware of her age by the occasion of her sister's marriage, rekindling her teenage crush on Mehmet Süleyman. Poor Çiçek, İkmen's beloved 'old maid', glamoured by a man possibly infected with Aids . . .

Allah, but it would be good to get back to police work again in the morning! But what a shame it was that someone had to die in order for the adrenaline to really get going. Unless, of course, that person were either Mr Gören or Mr Emin.

'What do you mean, "what did he do"?'

'I mean, Mr Ataman, what were your son's interests? Who did he associate with?'

Giving the Atamans the news about their son's yet again delayed burial was proving, if anything, even more distressing than telling the Arat family that their daughter had been found dead. At least at the Arats' the girl's young brother had cried . . .

'You saw the note. Consorting with "devils", apparently.' Mete Ataman threw his long arms petulantly into the air. 'He was eighteen and chose to give his life, seemingly, to something entirely fictional!

What else do eighteen year olds do, Inspector Süleyman? You tell me.'

'If I hadn't been in my office day and night, we might have been able to stop him doing this terrible thing to himself.'

All heads turned towards the thin woman in black, sitting, dead-eyed, beside a window that looked out directly across at the Galata Tower.

Ataman, his face now red with fury, bore down upon her, one finger wagging violently into her face. 'You said you wanted to be independent, Sibel! I gave you that job, I made it happen! It's what you wanted!'

'I know! I know!'

'So don't pretend you would have enjoyed being around for your son—'

'I'm not pretending! I'm just . . .' She looked up at Süleyman, her eyes wet. 'So unhappy, my son! So morbid! You know, he used to cut his arms—'

'Sibel!'

'Yes, we do know that your son did harm himself, Mrs Ataman.'

'Just about cut the skin, you mean!' Mete Ataman put in acidly. 'All for effect! Like those so-called Gothic freaks up in town! All for attention!'

'Be that as it may,' Süleyman said, 'I would like your permission to search your son's room, Mr Ataman. I—'

'You've looked at his things!'

'In light of this other, similar incident, I would like in particular to have access to your son's computer . . .'

Only fifteen-year-old Nurdoğan Arat had had any idea what his sister, Gülay, liked to do. 'She liked her computer,' he'd said as his parents, two middle-aged socialites, reeking of alcohol, looked on blankly. 'She spent hours on it.' Locked into her room apparently, doing what Nurdoğan could only describe as 'something'. But it was a start. Maybe, via the computer, Cem and Gülay had come into contact with each other. After all, or so it would seem, they had at one time, at least, shared rather dark interests.

'He only played games on it.' Ataman threw himself down into one of his leather chairs and lit a cigarette. 'I tried to teach him how to use spreadsheets, preparing him for some level of responsibility in my business, but he wasn't interested.'

'Our son was a very . . . self-contained boy, Inspector,' Sibel Ataman said gently. 'He felt that our work was trite.' She turned her head and looked hard at the tower beyond the window. 'Which it is.'

Her husband first threw the back of her head a murderous glance and then looked back at Süleyman. 'As far as I'm concerned you can take anything you want,'he said, and then with his voice breaking he continued, 'My son is dead, I have no use for childish things.'

'Thank you, Mr Ataman.'

'Just let us know as soon as you can when we can bury him.'

'Of course.'

Süleyman and Çöktin stood up. Sibel Ataman turned back from the window to smile at them.

'Tell me, gentlemen,' she said softly, 'do you believe that our Muslim death traditions are indeed fact . . .'

Her husband put his head in his hands and groaned.

'. . . that the soul of the deceased is in torment until the body is buried in the ground?'

'Mrs Ataman, I can't really—'

'For the love of Allah, Sibel, will you stop?' Ataman, his face puce now with both rage and suppressed despair, shouted. 'Your son is dead, you're too old and too frigid to have any more children! Your son is dead! He's dead! He's gone! My son . . .'

And then he began to cry.

Süleyman and Çöktin removed themselves to Cem Ataman's bedroom, leaving his father weeping in his antique-stuffed living room. Sibel Ataman did not move to comfort or even look at her husband.

Night had fallen by the time Gülay Arat's body entered the mortuary. Her father, a hard, thuggish-looking man in his mid-forties, arrived to identify her formally, after which she entered the care of Arto Sarkissian. In spite of the lateness of the hour, he had decided to begin his examination of the corpse immediately. As he told Constable Hikmet Yıldız, who had accompanied the body from Anadolu Kavağı to the mortuary, 'Inspector Süleyman is very keen for me to compare this girl's body to that of the boy we found in Eyüp,' and then turning to one of his technicians he said, 'Ali, I'll need the subject in number five, please.'

'Yes, Doctor.'

The technician disappeared into another room from which, a little later, Yıldız heard grinding, metallic noises.

'I take it you're staying with us, Constable?' the doctor said as he arranged an alarming selection of instruments on a table beside the still-covered body of the girl.

'Until either Inspector Süleyman or Sergeant Çöktin arrives, yes, sir.' Süleyman in particular, praise be to Allah, always preferred to attend these things personally as opposed to letting some subordinate, like young Yıldız, do it for him. But he and Çöktin hadn't yet returned from either the Atamans' or the Arats'.

'Well, it isn't like you haven't seen anything like this before,' Arto said as he pulled the bloodied sheet from Gülay Arat's greenish-white body.

Yıldız swallowed hard. 'No, sir.'

The technician returned with the sheet-covered occupant of 'number five'. Thin tendrils of water vapour, from the refrigeration process he had undergone, rose from the anonymous lump that had been Cem Ataman.

'All right, Ali, uncover him, please,' Arto said with a smile.

The middle-aged technician did just that, and Hikmet Yıldız felt his lunch, which had been his favourite kokoreç (grilled sheep intestines) begin to move in an upward direction. If there was another colour beyond green, Cem Ataman's body was that colour. Yıldız looked away while Arto Sarkissian began his examination of the wound in the girl's chest whilst simultaneously referring to Cem Ataman's file.

'Unlike the Ataman boy, we have no weapon,' he said, 'and this body had been disturbed.'

He moved across to the other body and bent down low over the gaping wound in the chest.

'Cem, of course, was found slumped over the knife while the girl was, so we are told, originally spread-eagled,' he continued, 'but then the downward slope of the hillside would have caused that.'

'She fell over backwards.'

29

'Or was pushed.' He returned his attentions to the girl's body. 'As I said when we were at the site, I want to check for sexual activity. Forensic are of the opinion that others were present . . .'

A minute or two passed – Yıldız, his lunch threatening to rebel at any moment, wasn't counting – accompanied by the sound of dead flesh and bone being shifted around on the table.

'Well, there's some damage . . .'

'So she could have just had sex . . .'

'I think it's possible,' the doctor said, 'although I won't know until I've performed a full autopsy, which I'll do first thing in the morning.'

'Oh. Good.' Yıldız had thought for a moment there that he was in for the long haul. Full autopsy in the middle of the night, his tired stomach bubbling with undigested sheep's intestines. But then the doctor, as was evident, had to be too tired to perform such an arduous procedure effectively at this time.

'I'll just have a little preliminary look,' the doctor said as he tapped at Yıldız' shoulder in order to get his attention. 'Why don't you go and wait in my office? Have a glass of water.'

Yıldız, suddenly ashamed of what he imagined the doctor would perceive as a weakness, looked away from the small Armenian very quickly.

'You've gone a bit of a strange colour,' Arto whispered gently.

'Oh.'

Half an hour later, the doctor returned to his office where a much more healthy-looking Yıldız and now Süleyman were waiting for him.

'Well?' the older man asked as he rose to his feet at the Armenian's approach.

The two men shook hands and then sat down.

'Well, as I said to the constable here,' Arto said as he looked across and smiled at Yıldız, 'I can't make a judgement as yet with regard to cause. But the weapon used, as with the boy, was an unserrated dagger. It was very sharp. I should imagine it had been prepared in advance for just this purpose.'

'Anything else?'

'I can confirm sexual activity.'

Süleyman frowned. 'Which we didn't have with the boy.'

'No.'

'So, semen—'

'Oh, don't get too excited by that,' Arto said as he held up one hand to silence the policeman. 'When I said sexual activity, I meant that an act of sex had taken place, not necessarily with another person.'

'Ah.'

'Although another person was involved.'

'What do you mean?'

'I mean that the girl has been penetrated by something,' the doctor said. Yıldız, embarrassed and again a little nauseous, looked down at the floor.

'What?'

'I don't know yet,' Arto continued, 'but I don't believe that she was masturbating herself. She has bruises on her shoulders, consistent with fingermarks. The fingers held her from behind, which is where whatever entered her, a penis or, I believe, something larger and more, shall we say, unkind than that, came from. It bears out Forensic's contention that there were others present at the site.'

'When do you think you will know what this "thing" might have been, Doctor?'

'I'll have to get back to you on that, Inspector,' Arto said with a sigh. 'I've harvested some samples just now. Tomorrow I'll open her up and then we'll find out some more.'

Chapter 4

There was nothing sinister about any of the games so far. Youngsters liked computer games; they had, after all, been brought up with them. To be honest, İsak Çöktin wasn't averse to the odd afternoon shooting up aliens or driving a computer-generated Ferrari himself. Not that he got a lot of time to do such things. His own involvement with computers, outside of his police duties, was rather more business-orientated than that.

'Good morning, İsak.'

He raised his red, curly head over the top of the screen and, when he saw who it was, he smiled.

'Hello, sir. Did the wedding go well?'

İkmen beamed. 'It isn't often that one gets the opportunity to feel really proud in this life,' he said, 'but Hulya's wedding was one of those rare occasions.'

'I congratulate you, sir.'

'Thank you.' İkmen, attracted by the flashing colours on Çöktin's screen, moved in closer. 'Playing games on the department's time, İsak?' He shook his head in mock disapproval. 'Bad boy. What would Inspector Süleyman say?'

Çöktin laughed. 'Well done, I should expect, sir.'

'Oh?'

And then Çöktin proceeded to outline what had happened the previous day with the discovery of Gülay Arat's body and the possible connection between her death and that of Cem Ataman.

'I was aware of the Ataman boy,' İkmen said as he slipped down into a chair opposite Çöktin and lit up a cigarette. 'Inspector Süleyman told me it was suicide.'

'Which it was. The girl's death is still open to question, but . . .' Çöktin sighed, 'it's just that two such similar and bizarre deaths in such a short space of time is unusual.'

'People sometimes copy each other.'

'Yes, although the actual method Cem used to kill himself wasn't reported in the media.'

İkmen shrugged. 'Then perhaps Cem and this girl knew each other somehow.'

'Not obviously so,' Çöktin said. 'They didn't live close to each other. Gülay Arat was still at high school – a different one to the place Cem had attended – he was a student at İstanbul University. But there is a possibility they may have had contact via the Internet, which is why I'm looking at their computers.'

'At games?'

Çöktin looked up at İkmen's wry face and smiled. 'I've only just started. I'm just seeing what they've got on their machines.'

'I believe you.'

'Both of the youngsters spent a lot of time on their computers. If they shared anything, it was an interest in the dark, supernatural side of life. The girl, Gülay, used to be one of those Goth kids.'

'And their families?' İkmen put his cigarette out in one of Çöktin's ashtrays and then immediately lit another. 'What did they have to add?'

Çöktin shrugged. 'Not much. The boy's parents are both careerists, advertising sales. Gülay Arat's father owns a couple of those loud nightclubs out in Ortaköy – I think her mother's a drunk. None of them seems to have much of an idea about what their children did or were interested in. We only found out about Gülay's computer habit from her young brother.'

İkmen shook his head slowly and sadly. 'So many of these poor kids now, offspring of the nouveaux riches – they have everything except their parents' attention. It's why they dress in black, talk about vampires and exist only in their computers.'

'Yes, although quite a few working-class youngsters spend a lot of time on line too, you know.'

'By on line, I suppose you mean on the Internet,' İkmen said gloomily. 'Yes, I know. My youngest son keeps on pestering me about getting a computer so he can go on line. He says it will help him with his homework. He's only at middle school.'

'A lot of primary school kids have them these days, sir.'

İkmen shook his head and stood up. 'From what I can gather there's more rubbish and stupid chat on that Internet than anything else. It's like mobile phones. You know, my son Bülent spends a ridiculous amount of money and time calling and texting his friends. Even at work, because of this text messaging, he and his friends communicate all day long about nothing.'

Çöktin smiled. Like a lot of the older officers in the department, İkmen was a technophobe. Although he was now more accustomed to his mobile phone than he had been, İkmen still couldn't use the text function. The department had issued him with a computer some time ago, which he did use on occasion, although it was well known that his sergeant, Ayşe Farsakoğlu, was the real user of the equipment.

'But I must go now,' İkmen said as he walked towards the office door, 'leave you in peace with your virtual cars or whatever that is on the screen.'

'Yes, sir.'

He left and Çöktin returned to what he'd been doing before, which was, in fact, driving a Humvee at speed through the streets of Los Angeles.

Nur Süleyman looked across the table at her son and frowned. Ever since that foreign bitch had taken his son, her grandson, away, Mehmet's weight had dropped. He was always tired now too. Today, when she hadn't been able to rouse him until eight thirty, was a case in point. He had been due at work at nine and, although she didn't like his being a common policeman any more now than she had done when he'd started, she recognised that he needed to earn money. Unlike her husband who, she knew, was planning to spend the day as he always did – doing nothing.

'Mehmet, I think you should see Dr Birand,' she began.

'I've told you, I am seeing a doctor, Mother,' Mehmet said without looking up from his tea glass.

'I don't mean some police—'

'I've been to see a very good doctor, thank you, Mother,' he cut in, 'and I am fine.'

'No you're not!'

35

He looked up, angry now. 'I am. Under the circumstances, I'm really holding up very well.'

'Under the circumstances!' Nur flung her arms in the air and shook her head. 'Such circumstances! Our Yusuf gone with that baggage you would insist upon marrying! How that woman could leave you, I don't know! At her age, she should have been kissing your feet in gratitude!'

'Mother, you don't understand! There were faults on both sides. It wasn't just Zelfa.'

'Of course you will be able to marry again,' his mother continued as she poured out more tea for herself and her son. 'Women will be falling over themselves—'

'I'm still married at the moment.'

'Yes, but not for long,' Nur said with conviction. 'Get a divorce as soon as you can, Mehmet. I'll speak to Mr Bayar for you today.'

'When I need a lawyer I'll speak to one of my own choosing myself!' Mehmet, incensed, rose to his feet. 'I may be living at home for the time being, Mother, but I'm not a child! I'm nearly forty!'

'I still do everything for your father,' Nur responded nastily. 'What makes you think you're not like him?'

'Nothing, Mother.' Mehmet picked his cigarettes and lighter up off the table and put them into his jacket pocket. 'We're both useless!'

He then walked quickly out of the dining room before he said something even more inflammatory. Living back with his brother, Murad, and even his father, wasn't really that bad, but his mother was and always had been intolerable. He'd only been separated from his wife for a matter of days before he returned to his parents' house. But Nur had been on to him immediately: suggesting the names of women he might like to take out on a date, prattling on about how some people these days found their partners on the Internet. As if she knew anything about it!

How could he, in his position, even think about dating? He couldn't even think about sex at the moment. Not that he had been thinking about sex. Ever since the possibility of his being HIV-positive had become apparent to him, sex had been relegated to the status of things other people did. Sex was something that he came across sometimes during the course of an investigation.

Gülay Arat, so Dr Sarkissian had told him last night, had had sex prior to her death. Or rather, she'd had something, maybe not a penis, he thought, inside her vagina. Something large. What kind of brutal and sterile act was that? Where was the pleasure in using an inanimate thing on a woman? Sex, surely, was about two people connecting, flesh to flesh, achieving pleasure together. He loved the feeling of his skin melting into the skin of a woman. But then not everyone got their kicks in the same way. Perhaps whoever had put something inside Gülay got off on fucking women with dildos or whatever. Playing with sex 'toys' wasn't, after all, that unusual. What was more worrying was just when this person had done this. Naked on a steep hillside, Gülay Arat had either plunged a knife into her own chest or been killed by someone as yet unknown. Had that been before or after the person who'd been moving the thing inside her had achieved orgasm? Or had that happened at the moment of her death?

'I'm here for another two weeks and so I may as well help you get things moving.'

Hulya looked up at her husband and shrugged.

'If you're sure, Uncle Jak,' Berekiah said. 'You don't come home often. You must have better things to do.'

'You mean like listening to your father's list of complaints?' Jak sighed. 'Something we can all do without. True, I've got a bit of business here, but I'd like to help you kids get started.'

'It's very good of you, Mr Cohen.'

'Jak, please,' he said as he smiled broadly at Hulya, 'we're family.' Then, taking his mobile phone out of his pocket, he continued, 'Right, so I think if we get some people in to clear the garden first, that'll give the builders more space to put things when they come to do the structural stuff. Let me just go outside and see if I can roughly estimate the square meterage of the plot.'

He bounded out through the hole that was the kitchen door and disappeared into the bramble-and-bindweed-choked garden. Hulya and Berekiah looked at each other and then at the total chaos around them. As if defeated by the sheer scale of the problem that was his and Hulya's house, Berekiah sat down on the rickety floorboards and put his head in his hands.

'It was very nice of your uncle to give us this house,' Hulya said – the tone of her voice seeming to intimate that she was trying to convince herself of that fact.

'Yes,' Berekiah answered through his fingers.

'It will be perfect for a family.'

Berekiah raised his head from his hands and looked around again. 'For a family the size of yours, yes,' he said, 'but for us? I'll be an old man by the time we'll have finished paying for all the work this place needs. And, anyway, I thought we were only going to have two children.'

'Maybe.' She walked around, idly touching old, dust-covered pieces of furniture as she went. 'Your uncle seems very keen to help us.'

'Yes, but we can't let Uncle Jak pay for much more. It isn't right to take advantage and, anyway, Dad would go mad if he knew.'

'Your dad was quite keen for Jak to pay for our wedding.'

'Only because it was his only way of saving face,' Berekiah said. 'Çetin Bey was going to do everything. Dad would have been totally dishonoured. Not only is his son marrying a Muslim whether he likes it or not but he's too poor to pay for the bridegroom's suit! How would that have looked? He had to call Jak.'

Hulya bent down to look into a low cupboard. 'And now Uncle Jak has bought us a house . . .'

'He's bought us what is left of a house, yes,' Berekiah said as he rose quickly to his feet. 'I know you love the eccentricity of the place, Hulya, but it has been empty for years. Some really big, and expensive pieces of work will have to be done before we can move in.'

'I know.' She shut the cupboard door and then walked over to what had once been the kitchen fireplace.

'We may have to live with Mum and Dad for some time.' He followed her and placed his hands on her waist. 'Which means that we'll have to take every opportunity to be away from them that we can,' one of his hands moved up to her breasts, 'like coming up here, at night . . .'

'Berekiah!'

His other hand slid inside her skirt. 'I just keep on and on thinking about it, Hulya!' he whispered. 'How beautiful it was! If only Jak . . .'

After one quick look over her shoulder, Hulya took Berekiah by the arm and led him into what looked like an old larder or storeroom. 'Come on!'

He didn't protest then or when, a few moments later, she pulled him towards her.

'Oh, Hulya!'

She took his tongue in her mouth. Her hands began to move down his chest.

'Hulya dear, could you get a glass of— Oh . . .'

The two young people looked back into the room where Jak was standing together with a heavily bearded monk.

'Ah.' Berekiah whipped his hands away from his wife as if scalded.

'Brother, er, Constantine here has had a rather nasty shock,' Jak said.

'Desecration!' the monk said in a trembling voice. 'At the church!'

Hulya went to him and placed her hands on his shoulders. 'That's terrible,' she said.

'It's evil!' the monk whispered harshly. 'Godless!'

Jak, Berekiah and Hulya all looked at each other as the monk descended into tears.

It was the shock more than anything else that caused Sırma Karaca to burst into tears. She hadn't been close to Gülay Arat for some while. In fact the last time they had spoken properly, which was a good six months before, the two girls had fallen out. In retrospect, like a lot of things, their disagreement looked stupid to Sırma now.

'She said that she couldn't possibly go around with me any more because of my clothes,' she said as she rested her head against her mother's shoulder. 'She said she found them childish and embarrassing.'

Her mother reached across the coffee table to get her daughter a tissue.

'But she used to wear this stuff too,' Sırma said, holding up metres of thin black dress for her mother to see. 'She used to come with us to Atlas Pasaj. It was Gülay who first went there.'

'Yes, but Gülay . . . moved on . . .'

'You mean "grew up"!' Sırma turned her black, smudged eyes

39

furiously on to her mother's face. 'Why don't you say it, Mum? It's what you're thinking.'

'Sırma!'

'The way you worry about me is stupid!' Sırma said petulantly. 'I like going to Atlas Pasaj. My life would be nothing without the friends I've got there. And I like how I dress too.'

'Yes, darling, but in this heat . . .'

'You'd like me to wear pretty, summery dresses?' Sırma pulled away from her mother and scowled. 'I don't do that.'

Her mother smiled sadly. 'Oh, but Sırma, black is so depressing.'

Sırma wiped the tears away from her eyes with one of her long, cobweb-style cuffs and stood up. 'Right, and you're so worried about my depression, aren't you? But the way I am hasn't got anything to do with that. I like how I am, I'm happy like this! And anyway, I'm taking Prozac so I'm not going to kill myself, am I?'

'No . . .'

'No, it's Gülay who's dead, isn't it? Gülay, who left the scene for a much more grown-up life and pretty dresses.'

'Sırma, I know you're upset about Gülay.'

The girl suddenly lost all of her fight and began to cry once again. Her mother stood up and hugged her.

'I really used to like Gülay a lot you know, Mum,' the girl said miserably. 'Tanzer, Defne, Hüseyin and me – we've never been the same since Gülay went away.'

'I know.'

But then as quickly as her misery had started, so it finished, giving way to the flashing anger she had exhibited before.

'If anyone's to blame for Gülay's death it's her parents!' she snapped.

'Sırma!'

The girl pushed her mother away with a theatrical shrug and then threw herself back down on to the plush sofa she had been reclining upon when her mother came to tell her about her friend's death. As the thin black material settled about her, Sırma said, 'She had to get away from them. That's why she was here so often. They never had time for her.'

Her mother first reached for a cigarette and then sat down beside her daughter, a grave expression on her face.

'Sırma, you shouldn't say such things about Gülay's parents.'

'Why not?' Sırma sneered. 'It's the truth. Mrs Arat is always drunk and Mr Arat is a gangster.'

'Sssh!' her mother hissed. 'We—'

'Dad says he's a gangster and he doesn't care who hears him!' Sırma retorted in response to her mother's fearful reaction. 'He has sex with young girls. Gülay told me. He even used to come into her bedroom . . .'

'Sırma!' Nervously her mother first lit her cigarette and then wiped away the sweat that had gathered at her hairline. 'Sırma, you really shouldn't throw around accusations like that about people.'

'Yes, but it's true!'

'Maybe.' She took a moment to draw a calming breath before continuing, 'But if you only heard this from Gülay—'

'Of course I only heard it from Gülay! Her dad wasn't likely to tell me, was he? Or her stupid drunk mum.'

'No, but I think that out of respect for Gülay's memory you should keep that to yourself, Sırma,' her mother said sternly. 'The Arats are very influential people and I don't think it would be wise to make such accusations against them.'

'I'm only telling you,' Sırma said sulkily, 'so what does it matter?'

'Well, it doesn't. But don't tell anyone else, will you, Sırma?'

The girl, looking down at her black varnished fingernails, shrugged.

'Sırma?'

'No.'

'No what?'

Sırma rose from the sofa and began to walk wearily out of the room. 'No, I won't say anything to anyone else,' she said. 'Not that anyone's going to ask me anything about it anyway . . .'

Who would want to? According to Gülay, no one had ever been interested in the way her father made her feel before. Apart from Sırma she had once told her grandmother about it, but she'd just hit her and told her not to tell lies. Her mother, or so Gülay had told Sırma, knew what her father was like. But then so long as there was alcohol in the house, she didn't care about much else.

And people think I'm weird, Sırma thought as she slumped her way back up to her bedroom.

Mehmet Süleyman had just returned to his office when he received the call from Arto Sarkissian. As ever these days he hadn't actually eaten very much, but he'd enjoyed the company. His cousin Tayyar, who had been his lunch 'date', was a very amusing man who had spent much of his life travelling the world with little more than his wits for company. He was also very well acquainted with another of their cousins, Süleyman's ex-wife, Zuleika. Odd that both seeing and talking about Zuleika had occurred in less than a week. Sometimes months could pass without even a hint of her existence.

İsak Çöktin was still staring at the screen of Gülay Arat's computer when Süleyman arrived. The younger man was fascinated by machines of all types and hadn't so much as moved to get a drink since first thing that morning. However, the doctor's call quickly distracted Süleyman from his deputy's absorbed countenance.

'The Arat girl was penetrated by something with a sharp or rough edge to it,' the doctor said once he had completed the usual social niceties. 'Quite large. I think from what I've seen it was probably made of metal.'

Süleyman frowned. 'A metal what?'

'Something long and phallic, I can't really say any more than that,' the doctor replied. 'The rough or sharp edge could have been either an accident of manufacture or a deliberate flaw designed to evoke pain – I can't say unless I can see the item. I do, however, know that the girl was a virgin prior to the assault.'

'What about the timing of the assault with regard to time of death?'

'You mean was she assaulted before or after death?' Arto cleared his throat. 'Certainly before and maybe for a short while afterwards.'

'So at the point of death this "thing" operated by someone could have been inside her?'

'Yes.'

'What about the notion that she took her own life?'

'Almost impossible,' the doctor replied, 'now I've had a proper chance to look at her. The angle of the incision is all wrong for self-infliction. I think we must assume that unlawful killing has occurred.'

42

So she'd been murdered. 'Right. Thank you, Doctor.' And then looking over briefly at Çöktin, he said, 'Gülay Arat was murdered.'

'Ah.'

So involved was the sergeant in that computer he was barely breathing, let alone taking in what Süleyman was saying.

So when he'd finished his conversation with the doctor, Süleyman went to see what Çöktin was doing with the dead girl's computer. Looking at the screen, he watched as his deputy flicked through what looked like snippets of conversation. Much of it was, or appeared to be, incredibly inane.

'What's this, Çöktin?' he asked as he braced his hands against the back of the younger man's chair.

'Gülay Arat belonged to three newsgroups,' Çöktin said. 'She had an incredible involvement in one and less interest, but still quite a bit, in the other two.'

'Newsgroups?'

Çöktin looked up at Süleyman and smiled. 'Discussion groups, sir.' He pointed at the screen. 'This one is for fans of Brain Dead.'

'That's a band, I take it?'

'Yes, sir. They're a skate punk outfit, quite heavy and doomy.'

Süleyman drew a tired hand across his features. '"Quite heavy and doomy"?' he repeated. '"Skate punk"? What are you talking about, İsak?'

'It's a youth thing, sir. Metal music, you know.' And then seeing the look of incomprehension on his superior's face he added, 'If it's any consolation, I don't really understand it either. I'm too old.'

'Well, if you're too old, I don't know what that makes me,' Süleyman said darkly as he continued to peer at the screen. 'Are you sure this is actually about this band, İsak? Look there.' He pointed. 'Whoever that is is talking about kaymak.'

'Oh, they go off the point all the time,' Çöktin said, 'just like real conversations.'

'Yes, but kaymak!'

Çöktin looked up again at his now outraged superior. 'Why not?' he shrugged. 'In real conversations we talk about food. Kaymak is food. I like it with figs myself. Newsgroups like this are, in effect, little neighbourhoods. People converse, make friends, sometimes they even argue.'

43

'And you say that the girl was involved in several of these groups.'

'Yes, this one and another one dedicated to another skate punk band, Rashit. Then there's this other thing which calls itself "Theodora's Closet".'

'What's that about?'

'I've only just glanced at it so far,' Çöktin said, 'but from what I can gather it's about the Byzantine Empire. Aya Sofya, the Kariye – but mainly about, as you'd imagine from the title, the Empress Theodora.'

Süleyman put his hand in his pocket and removed his cigarettes. 'So Miss Arat had intellectual as well as normal teenage interests. Cigarette?'

'Thank you, sir.' Çöktin took a cigarette from Süleyman's packet and lit up. 'I don't think, from what I've seen of it, that Theodora's Closet is exactly intellectual. It's rather gossipy and a bit camp, actually. I should imagine that quite a lot of gay men post to that site, although I don't suppose young Gülay Arat realised it.'

'Mmm . . .' Süleyman, cigarette in hand, returned to his desk. 'What about these other "music" sites?'

'The one she posted to most frequently, Brain Damage, is typical of the skate punk movement.'

'Meaning?'

'Dark, depressing and without hope,' Çöktin replied. 'İstanbul skate punks are, to me, anyway, indistinguishable from Goths. We know that Gülay was a Goth at one time, don't we, and so her interest in Brain Damage, the Brain Dead newsgroup, is understandable.'

Probably like, Süleyman recalled, his ex-wife's stepdaughter. He couldn't remember her name, but he did recall that Zuleika had been very pleased that the girl was shedding her black weeds for a more 'normal' image.

'I'm going to look at all these sites in more detail,' Çöktin continued, 'although I am inclined to think that Brain Damage is where I should be concentrating my efforts. The sheer volume of her involvement could be significant and there are certainly allusions to death and violence on there.'

'Do you think that whoever runs this newsgroup or maybe someone who is significant within it could be manipulating these young people?'

Çöktin shrugged. 'It's possible. There have, as you know, sir, been some accounts of forces abroad intercepting paedophiles who have been what they call "grooming" children for sex over the Internet. I need to spend more time on it and I need to get to grips with the boy's computer in order to make a comparison.'

'To see whether they did similar things on their computers?'

'Yes. Similar games, newsgroups, things like that.'

'You know a lot about these things, don't you, İsak?' Süleyman said as he regarded his deputy with a frown. 'Do you belong to any of these groups yourself? I ask only out of academic interest.'

Çöktin felt all the hairs on the back of his neck rise. Hoping that his rather delicate pale skin hadn't reddened he said, 'Yes, I do a little bit of posting.'

Süleyman smiled. 'What topics do you discuss, İsak?'

'Music, films, you know,' Çöktin forced himself to return a smile.

'Ah,' Süleyman laughed, 'music for young people, I expect, eh, İsak? This African stuff I sometimes hear in Beyoğlu.'

'Something like that, yes, sir,' the younger man replied. And then he looked down at the screen and pretended to get absorbed into his work once again.

Chapter 5

İkmen had told his daughter not to worry unduly about the obscene graffiti on the wall of the Church of the Panaghia Mouchliotissa.

'It's probably the work of bored kids,' he'd said when she had, amid some embarrassment, described it to him. But Hulya hadn't been satisfied that he really understood what she'd described and so İkmen, if reluctantly, given the current heat wave, had gone over to Fener to see for himself. It had been an interesting trip that had resulted in a further excursion to Beyoğlu.

Simurg bookshop, which is on Hasnan Galip Sokaǧi, is actually two shops side by side. Both are owned by the same person and they stock a wide selection of books and sheet music, both new and old. It's a laid-back sort of a place, and one can browse Simurg's stock for hours if required, provided one is prepared to shift the shop's numerous sleeping cats from their literary beds. As both a book and cat lover, İkmen had a lot of time for Simurg and its regular clientele of argumentative old intellectuals – men not unlike his late father. Not that he had come for that unique Simurg ambience on this occasion. He'd come specifically to see Max, and Max always came into Simurg at around 6 p.m.

İkmen, who had positioned himself by the main entrance, which was currently being guarded by a barely sentient Angora, was looking at a copy of *Wuthering Heights* in English when Max appeared.

'Hello, Max.'

İkmen spoke in English and also quite loudly. Up there in the clouds where Max existed, those on the ground could be difficult to hear.

The tall, slim man in the doorway looked down and smiled. Max, though of indeterminate years, was, İkmen knew, about his own age. He'd always had grey hair, ever since İkmen had first met him in the

1970s. Quintessentially English, Max was nevertheless a much darker man than İkmen – something that had little to do with exposure to the Turkish sun over so many years. Max was just dark – in several different ways.

'Hello, Çetin,' Max said as he bent down in order to catch the smaller man in his embrace. 'How are you?'

İkmen replied that he was well, smiling as he observed Max go into his usual evening routine of feeding small and succulent pieces of fish and meat to his many feline fans at Simurg.

'I wondered if I could take you for a coffee?' İkmen said once the last cat had been fully satisfied.

Max's large green eyes lit up. 'What a great euphemism that is!' he said enthusiastically. 'Coffee! When you want a chat – coffee! Sex – coffee! Or, as I suspect in this case, information – coffee!'

'Well, not exactly information, Max,' İkmen said. 'Expertise is really more the word, I think.'

'Oh, spooky stuff.'

'Yes.'

'OK.'

They went to the Pia café on Bekar Sokak, a low-key haunt of artists and writers that İkmen knew Max liked. They took a table out-side and ordered two cappuccinos. After greeting several men İkmen thought looked like 1960s beatniks, Max lit up a long, thin cigar. İkmen took a Polaroid photograph out of his jacket pocket and laid it out in front of his companion.

'Do you have any idea what this is, Max?'

The Englishman squinted down at the image.

'I took it myself,' İkmen said, 'which is why it's not very good, I'm afraid. Can you make out what it is?'

'It looks like the Goat of Mendes to me,' Max said, 'although I've only ever seen him depicted with either one or two penises before. There have to be—'

'There are thirteen,' İkmen cut in, 'all with women ecstatically impaled.'

'How fascinating!' Max looked up. 'Where's the original?'

İkmen sighed. 'On the wall of the Church of the Panaghia in Fener. You know Hulya and Berekiah are renovating a place up there. They came across one of the monks, very distressed. He told them about it and then took them to see it. At first I thought it might be kids . . .'

'Who knows these days?' Max shook his head, his thin face bookish in its concentration. 'But this is definitely the Goat who, as I'm sure an educated man like you will know, is an aspect, a very sexual manifestation, of Satan. It's a very . . . Christian, a Western motif. Goya represented the Goat with witches and hags throwing themselves around him in an orgy of sexual desire. How long has it been there?'

'I don't know, but I think it must be very recent.'

Max leaned back in his chair just as the waitress came with the cappuccinos. At her approach, İkmen quickly stuffed the photograph back into his pocket.

When the girl had gone, Max said, 'And so the question is, I suppose, what is it doing there? And further, what might it mean?'

'Brother Constantine has interpreted it as an attack. An act of desecration.'

Max took a sip from his cup before continuing. As he lifted it to his lips, İkmen noticed that his hand shook. 'So someone got to the church, drew it, probably at night, and then buggered off. But why and what its purpose might be . . . ?' He shrugged. 'I'm afraid that I can't tell you, old chap.'

'So there aren't any . . .' İkmen searched for the right word, but Max beat him to it.

'Satanists in residence?' he smiled. 'There is, or rather was, a small group of very bored and boring English and American ex-pats over on the Asian side. I came across them a few months ago, or rather, they contacted me. Some gruesome Yank wanted me to replicate Aleister Crowley and raise the god Pan.'

'Aleister Crowley?'

'An early twentieth-century English magician,' Max explained, 'into heroin and fallen women. He tried to raise the god Pan in Paris and got into a bit of bother.'

'Ah.'

'So as you can imagine, I've never been keen to give Pan a go myself. A most destructive and mischievous force.' Max shuddered. 'I told our American friend to go about his business in no uncertain terms,' he laughed, 'but not before I'd taken a small sample of hair from his jacket to work with.'

'You cursed him?' His mother had always used either hair or nails in her more malignant spells, İkmen recalled.

'Not exactly,' Max replied, 'but I put a stop to their activities. I don't like Satanists – all that negative energy. And anyway, people always confuse people like me with people like them, which, quite frankly, gives me the pip!'

'That's the only group you know of who might be involved in such activities?'

'I've come across a few of you chaps, Turks, who meddle,' Max said, 'but if you don't mind my saying so, Çetin, Turkish Satanists are pretty bloody useless. In fact, quite honestly, I don't believe they exist at all in the conventional sense. I know you've come across it – some sick necrophiliac gets caught in a graveyard and says the Devil made him do it. But I've never come across one Turk in all the years I've been here who successfully worships and invokes Satanic forces. They get it all wrong. Maybe that's why your Goat is so very atypical.'

'Drawn by one of my ill-informed countrymen.'

'Maybe. But then perhaps your assertion that it was just a kids' prank does have some validity. There's so much information now, what with the TV, computers and what not, people are constantly bombarded with things they barely understand. I look at all these so-called Goth kids running around in black with pentacles at their necks and it makes my blood go cold. They have no idea what they are dealing with. I mean, I know that we all live in uncertain times, what with this situation in Iraq and the possibility of war involving the Americans, but wearing black and courting Beelzebub is not the answer. Not for them.'

İkmen could only, if silently, agree. His son Bülent was due to be conscripted into the army in 2003 and so if the Americans did decide to go into Iraq, possibly with Turkish support, it would include him. İkmen knew he would, if he could, do anything to change that situation – even maybe invoke 'dark' forces – assuming he knew how to do that and indeed felt desperate enough to do so. Though currently calm, these were anxious times. 'You say that this image is incorrect,' he said.

'In my experience yes,' the Englishman replied, 'but I'll check it out anyway, Çetin; speak to a few magical "faces", as we say back home.'

'I would appreciate it, Max.'

'Oh, it's no bother, old boy.' Max's eyes twinkled. 'I'll just add it to the list of favours I've done you over the years.'

'It hasn't all been one way, you know,' İkmen said gravely as he sipped some of his coffee and lit up a cigarette. 'I've done things for you . . .'

'Yes, except where women are concerned,' Max responded acidly. 'If that girl—'

'My daughter Çiçek is a big girl now with concerns quite outside what you call "spooky stuff", Max. Above everything, she wants a man at the moment.' İkmen's face resolved into a grim expression. 'If I'm right the man currently in question is somebody she shouldn't even be looking at.'

'You should let me train her in the arts,' Max said with a dismissive wave. 'She'd soon forget about men. I've only ever met one truly natural adept before and she was—'

'As I've said before, Max,' İkmen said firmly, 'my daughter for good or ill will stay as she is.'

'Oh, well . . .'

And that, temporarily at least, was that. For the remainder of their time together the policeman and the magician spoke of 'un-spooky' things and eventually parted company at just before eight.

As İkmen watched Max go he experienced that uneasy feeling the man always seemed to evoke within him. He liked Max. They'd met many years before when Max had come in to the station to report the theft of his wallet and a wand. Because he was a foreigner – and odd – İkmen had been called in to assist. The two men, as the Englishman later described it, 'clicked' immediately, and when İkmen did in fact manage to retrieve Max's possessions a slightly weird and sometimes troubling friendship was born. But then Max was a very powerful Western magician, a Kabbalist, an adept and a close acquaintance of both angels and demons – whatever they were. So, in the same way that İkmen, the insightful witch's child, had been both in love with and repelled by his magical mother, so he felt that a distance of some sort needed to be put between himself and Max. This was especially true when it came to İkmen's daughter Çiçek. Max, on meeting the girl quite by chance with her father on the street one day, had nearly fainted when he saw her. She was, he'd said, quite the most naturally magical creature he had ever encountered and he wanted to 'train' her, as he put it, desperately. Whether Çiçek was 'magical' in Max's sense of the word or not, İkmen didn't know. That she possessed the 'sight' attributed to her father and grandmother was something he didn't need some foreigner to tell him. But she'd never wanted to use it. Çiçek wanted to be 'normal', which was what her father was committed to making sure she was. And besides, there had been another pretty girl Max had wanted to train many years before and that had ended badly.

At the moment, however, İkmen's mind was rather more exercised by Çiçek's growing fascination with Mehmet Süleyman. Married, albeit only in name, he was a man who always had trouble with women. And love the man with all his heart as he did, İkmen didn't want such a man for a son-in-law. Women desired him far too much and every so often he would, İkmen knew, fall from grace. And just look at where his latest escapade, with a prostitute of all things, had landed him!

İkmen rose from his seat and started to make his way back towards İstiklal Caddesi. According to Hulya and Berekiah, the Greek brothers in Fener were keen to paint over that – what was it Max had called it? – Goat of Mendes thing. But İkmen felt that was probably not a good idea. Not yet. Not until Max had spoken to some of his magical 'faces', as he'd called them.

Süleyman finally left his office at just before nine. İsak Çöktin, still seemingly engrossed in Gülay Arat and Cem Ataman's computers, said that he'd be responsible for locking the door when he left.

Although he didn't have an appointment at his friend Cohen's place, Mehmet had promised to visit when he and Balthazar had spoken at Berekiah's wedding. And so he drove over to Karaköy and parked in front of Cohen's shabby apartment block. As he got out of his car, he was aware of a group of boys and girls walking up the hill towards him, but it was hot, he was tired and he didn't pay them much attention. It was therefore quite a shock when one of them, a girl, tapped him on the shoulder.

'Hello, Mehmet Bey,' she said as she placed one seductive finger up to her black-painted lips.

'Er, hello,' Süleyman began, for a moment quite unable to place her.

The girl laughed. 'You don't remember me, do you?' she said, clicking her tongue in mock disapproval. 'Naughty! We met at the Pera Palas, with my stepmother . . .'

'Ah . . .'

'Fitnat.'

'Burhan Bey's daughter,' Süleyman smiled. 'Yes, of course.'

'My stepmother has talked about you a lot since our meeting,' Fitnat said with innocent, downcast eyes.

Süleyman, well aware of what she was implying, said, 'We're cousins.'

Fitnat didn't reply.

'I see you've gone back into black,' Süleyman said, referring to her dark, ratty dress and macabre make-up.

'Oh, yes,' the girl replied breezily, 'I love it. I used to go to Atlas Pasaj all the time, but I don't go quite so often now. Zuleika doesn't like it and besides, I do have to be more serious about my studies – it's important. But my friends persuaded Daddy to let me come tonight because it's İlhan's birthday and he's going to get his eyebrow pierced.'

A tall, thin boy in the middle of the little group of Goths smirked.

'I take it,' Süleyman said, 'that Atlas Pasaj is where people who like dark clothes and—'

'It's where the Goths hang out, yes,' Fitnat laughed, and then, moving closer towards him, she said, 'Want to come along, Mehmet Bey?'

'Oh, I think I'm a bit too old for that, don't you?'

'Depends what kind of music you like,' Fitnat replied.

'What sort of music do you like, Fitnat?'

'Metal, skate punk . . .'

'Skate punk?' That was what Çöktin had said Gülay Arat had liked. Proper Goth music, apparently.

'Yes, we all like that,' Fitnat said as the little group behind nodded in agreement. 'Bands like Crunch are, as Zuleika would say, *de rigueur* for people like us.'

'And Brain Dead?' Süleyman said, citing the band that Gülay Arat had, it seemed, liked most.

'Oh, they're brilliant!' Fitnat brought her arms seductively up to her wildly tangled hair and said, 'Hey, Mehmet Bey, you know quite a lot about Goth music, why don't you come along?'

The boys and girls behind her turned away in order to laugh.

'I don't think so, Fitnat,' he said. 'I think you'll have much more fun with your friends.'

The girl shrugged.

'You can answer me a question, though,' he said as he placed his car keys into his jacket pocket.

'What's that?'

'Do these bands ever play live at the places you go to?'

'Not on Atlas Pasaj,' she said with a frown. 'You have to go up to Kemancı for that.'

'What's Kemancı?'

'It's a club on Siraselviler Caddesi. Brain Dead have played there. Why? Want to go?'

Süleyman laughed again. 'No.'

'Well, just don't raid it then, will you?' Fitnat said as she leaned across quickly to kiss him on the cheek. 'Stepfather.'

And then, giggling at her own naughtiness, she went back to her friends and they all ran up the hill towards İstiklal Caddesi.

What a little flirt! Zuleika would be horrified if she knew her stepdaughter had come on to her ex-husband. Which was why Süleyman resolved not to tell her. But it had been an interesting exchange from a professional point of view. As far as he knew Gülay Arat had been out of the Goth scene for some time – there certainly had been few black weeds in her wardrobe. But she had obviously still liked their music. Had she, he wondered, ever gone to Atlas Pasaj or the Kemancı? He imagined she must have done at some point. It had been tempting to drop her name to Fitnat, see whether the girl had known her. But not in front of her friends. Maybe later, when Çöktin had had more of a chance to get to grips with her computer files. After all, tribes like the Goths were notoriously secretive and he didn't want to compromise Fitnat in any way. Besides, he did, after all, know where she was if he needed to speak to her. He'd have to have someone else present if he did, though. Fitnat, with her eye for an older man, could, he felt, be quite dangerous.

'Thirteen penises?'

'Oh, you understood that, did you?' Max put the telephone down and turned around to look at the young girl hunched over her book in the corner.

'Yes.'

'My, but your English is improving, Ülkü.'

The girl laughed and then put her book down on top of the replica Egyptian sarcophagus beside her.

'You talk about "spooky" things, Max Bey?' she said, using his own, typically British expression.

'Yes, but not too much to you, Ülkü,' Max replied a little sternly. 'I promised your mother I'd teach you English, not spooky stuff.'

'Who you talk to today about thirteen penises, Max Bey?'

'Never you mind,' the Englishman said, touching his nose with the tip of one long, thin finger. 'A friend, someone you don't know.'

'Oh.'

Ülkü, who at no more than sixteen still wore the thick peasant clothes indigenous to her village, walked barefoot across the old tattered kilim on the floor and stood in front of her mentor.

'Would you like me to do anything before I go, Max Bey?' she said, her eyes down-turned.

'Have you finished your translation?'

'Is on the table,' she replied, pointing to the top of the sarcophagus. 'I have clean bathroom and toilet very good.'

'I have cleaned both the bathroom and the toilet to a high standard,' Max corrected.

'Yes.'

'Well, repeat it then, Ülkü.'

She did.

Max took a large hardback book from one of the shelves in front of his desk and opened it with a satisfied sigh. 'You can go now,

Ülkü,' he said, 'but if that Turgut starts to get sexy, I want to know about it. He should show you respect, remember?'

'Yes, Max Bey.'

'And no mixing with all the mad people up on İstiklal Caddesi.'

'No, Max Bey.'

Her boyfriend, Turgut, was just outside the door, waiting, listening. But then Max knew that; he'd said what he had for a reason.

'Off you go then,' he said, and turned once again to the book on his desk.

Ülkü and Turgut walked the kilometre in complete silence from Max's dark, book-lined apartment to a room containing one small, greasy bed. Once Turgut had shut the door behind them he took his clothes off and, sitting on the bed, he drew Ülkü down to sit beside him.

'Suck it,' he said breathily as he attempted to push her head down towards his crotch. 'Like a city girl!'

'No!'

'My cock is bursting!'

'No!'

Still fully clothed and looking away from Turgut as she did so, Ülkü took his penis in one hand and began to masturbate him.

Suddenly mollified, Turgut closed his eyes. 'So,' he said as with a sigh he resigned himself to sex without her mouth. 'What did Max Bey have to say today?'

'There was talk of a creature with thirteen of these,' Ülkü said as she looked down briefly at his penis. 'Max Bey laughed on the telephone as he spoke about it.'

Turgut Can, in spite of what she was doing to him, frowned.

Chapter 6

He couldn't sleep because of the heat and so İkmen eventually got up and went into work. It was only 5 a.m. when he arrived and there wasn't much happening in the station, with the exception, that is, of Inspector Süleyman's office.

'Have you been home, Çöktin?' he asked a very sweaty and smoke-grimed individual as he put his head round the door.

'No, sir.'

'Why not?'

'I've been looking at these machines,' he said, indicating the two computers on top of his desk.

'Still?'

'Yes.' And then İsak told him about the newsgroups he'd found on Gülay Arat's computer.

'And what about the other machine, the boy's?' İkmen asked as he lit up his fourth cigarette of that day.

'Cem was into newsgroups too,' Çöktin said as he rubbed his reddening eyes with his fingers. 'Not the same ones as Gülay, unfortunately. His interests were far more academic than hers. However, there is a kind of a connection between this Byzantine site, that Gülay liked—'

'Theodora's Closet.'

'Yes, and this Christian thing.' He peered hard at one of the screens. 'The Blood of the Lamb.'

'Sounds a bit gruesome,' İkmen observed.

'From what I can gather it's all to do with the Crucifixion and Jesus shedding His blood in a sort of sacrifice. There's some description of their rituals.' Çöktin looked up and smiled. 'I don't really understand Christianity that well, sir.'

'Fair enough. But what's the connection, Çöktin? Apart from the obvious about the Byzantines being Christians?'

'It's words, sir,' Çöktin replied. 'Not many and only posted by a couple of people, but in both of these sites there are foreign words.'

İkmen walked over to the machines and leaned down to look at their screens.

'Are they up now, these words?'

'Yes, sir.' Çöktin pointed with one hand at each screen. 'See here and here.'

İkmen frowned as he read, smoking in a deep and focused fashion. After a few moments he said, 'I can see what you mean, Çöktin. They seem to be the same. Here, this word "madi" appears on both machines. Some of the others . . . I don't know what any of them mean. Can't even guess at the language.'

'No. But on Cem's machine you have these words being used by someone who calls him or herself "Communion", while on Gülay's Theodora site the user is called "Nika". I don't know whether Nika and Communion are the same person.'

'Does anyone ever reply to these people in this language you have discovered, Çöktin?'

'No, that's what's so odd, sir. Nika and Communion exclusively use these words. No one else ever asks what they mean and yet they all seem to be able to understand and reply to them.' He sighed. 'I've not, as far as I know, found anything sinister on any of these sites apart from the fact that Nika was the last person Gülay Arat communicated with by computer before she died.'

'What did Nika say?'

Çöktin did what to İkmen was some arcane things with the computer before he read out, 'Nika – "I guess you must really be looking forward to becoming a haş gagi."; Gülay as "Empress I", which is her newsgroup name – "Yes, I can't wait to tell you all about it."'

'When did this Nika communicate with the girl?'

'The day before she died.'

'Doesn't sound like she knew she was about to die, does it?'

'No, sir,' Çöktin replied, 'sounds far more, to me, as if she's going to go off and do something enjoyable, then come back and tell this Nika all about it. Perhaps it was the sex? Maybe she was looking forward to it?' He frowned. 'If only we knew what a haş gagi was or is.'

58

İkmen shrugged and then moved across to Süleyman's desk and sat down.

'Can't you trace this Nika through the Internet?' he said. 'I mean, if you know that Gülay called herself Empress I, which I assume must be Irene, then you can surely contact Nika.'

'No, I can't, sir.'

'You've identified Gülay.'

'Only because I have her machine.' Çöktin leaned back in his chair, yawned and then lit a cigarette. 'People hide their identities – not necessarily for sinister reasons.'

'How do they do that?'

When nothing but silence greeted his question, İkmen looked up. Çöktin's pained expression told him everything he needed to know.

'I wouldn't even begin to understand, would I, Çöktin?'

'No, sir,' Çöktin murmured, but then he cleared his throat and added, 'And neither would many people, including Inspector Süleyman, if that's any consolation.'

İkmen smiled. It wasn't that he didn't want to learn about computers, the subject was just simply beyond him. Even reading and writing e-mail was a trial – Ayşe had been obliged to show him numerous times before he got the gist of it. And if something out of the ordinary happened he was helpless. People talked about what they did on their machines all the time, but to İkmen it all just sounded like so much gibberish.

'So if this Nika has hidden his or her identity, what about all of the other people involved in this group?'

'They all use these pseudonyms.'

'Don't they ever meet?'

'What, in the flesh?' Çöktin smiled. 'I doubt it, sir. Newsgroups aren't like chat rooms. People don't generally go on to them to look for a date. Newsgroups are about sharing information and exchanging ideas. Some of the debates can get quite heated and people usually want to protect their identity just so that they can express themselves without fear of ridicule or retribution.'

'Sounds weird to me,' İkmen grumbled.

'I mean, there's days of this stuff,' Çöktin said as he turned his attention back to the machines once again, 'arguments, chat, information. I don't know how long it would take me to sort through it all.'

'Well, you'll need help,' İkmen said. 'Inspector Süleyman will have to request assistance.'

'I'm not sure that will help actually, sir.'

'Why not?'

'Because,' Çöktin said, 'it's as I've said before, sir, complicated. If you want to hide your identity, there are plenty of ways in which this can be done with ease. I don't really understand it myself, but I do know that there are ways of routing data that render it well-nigh untraceable.'

'So this line of enquiry is hopeless?'

'Maybe, or at least it will be unless I can find a way to contact someone,' Çöktin said darkly.

İkmen, leaning forward now across Süleyman's desk, frowned. 'Contact who, Çöktin?'

The Kurd shrugged. 'If I knew the answer to that, sir, I'd have contacted whoever is Mendes a long time ago.'

'Jak! Jak!'

With what Estelle Cohen felt was a very teenage-style sigh, Jak Cohen turned round to look down at his brother.

'What?'

'Where are you going at such a mad hour of the day?' Balthazar said from his huddled position in his chair next to the kitchen door. He'd slept in the chair all night. Sometimes it was more comfortable for him than his bed. But as often happened these days, he'd lost track of time.

'It's nine o'clock, Balthazar,' Estelle said. 'Jak has a meeting in Beyoğlu.'

'A meeting?' Balthazar pushed himself up on his elbows and rubbed his eyes with his fingers. 'Who with? When? You're driving me to the hospital at two.'

'Yes.'

'So if you've got a meeting how—'

'My meeting, Balthazar, is this morning,' Jak said, his teeth gritting against the aggravation his brother was causing him – it had been pretty much constant since he'd returned to İstanbul. 'Your appointment is this afternoon. I will take you to it, as I promised.'

He then turned to retrieve his briefcase from the floor.

Balthazar, mollified, lit a cigarette. 'So who you going to see in Beyoğlu then?' he said through a welter of coughing.

'A business associate.'

'Yeah, but who?' Balthazar smiled. 'Remember, I know a lot of men in your line of business in this city, Jak. I've arrested a lot of flesh traders in my time.'

'And used their wares,' Estelle put in, looking down disgustedly at her husband as she did so.

'I'm not a pimp, Balthazar,' Jak said evenly as he watched his sister-in-law retreat miserably out to the balcony. 'I run dance clubs where beautiful women dance for men. There's no touching, no meeting after the show . . . The men pay, the women dance. It's perfectly legal.'

'You didn't bring one to dance for me, did you, you bastard?'

'No.'

'So maybe you can get me one from your business associate here?'

Jak straightened his tie. 'I don't think so.'

'Why not?' Balthazar pouted. 'Don't you want to give your poor crippled brother a little happiness?'

'I thought I'd done that when I paid for your son's wedding.'

'Oh, throw that in my face!' Balthazar scowled. 'Pornographer!'

Jak leaned down and braced his hands against the arms of his brother's chair. 'I run legitimate clubs and shops selling sex aids and literature,' he said firmly. 'I don't touch any weird stuff – children or animals. Ask the British police about me and they'll tell you I'm a legitimate businessman.'

'How can I ask them?' Balthazar threw his arms theatrically into the air. 'I've never been to Britain! You've never invited me!'

'Then why don't you ask your friend Mehmet to ask the British police to check me out? I've got to go!'

Jak pushed himself away from his brother's chair and stood up.

'Go where? To see who?' Balthazar reiterated.

'To see a man.'

'Who?'

Finally worn down by his brother's questioning, Jak said, 'He's called Demir Sandal. I'm going to see him about belly dancing costumes for my girls. I want to do this Middle Eastern-themed thing. Why are you laughing?'

Balthazar, wheezing through many years' worth of mucus, nearly choked.

'Because,' he breathed, 'Demir Sandal makes the filthiest video tapes I've ever seen. Now he *is* a pornographer . . .'

'Well, he may be,' Jak continued, unabashed by what his brother had just said, 'but I'm going to see him about costumes. God, Balthazar, what kind of idiot do you think I am? If I want smutty tapes I can get them at home without the aggravation of taking the fucking things through customs!'

'I came into possession of one of Demir's tapes once,' Balthazar said – almost, Jak felt, dreamily. 'Girls, with each other, you know.'

'Lesbians.'

'It opened my eyes,' Balthazar laughed. 'I had to have some of that and I did. British girls – they'll do anything.'

'My son is British, Balthazar,' Jak said as he finally managed to tear himself away from his brother. 'Be careful what you say.'

And then he left.

Balthazar leaned back into his chair once again and closed his eyes. His interesting interlude with the two British girls had been, now he thought about it, longer ago than he had originally recalled. It had to have happened back in the late eighties. God, but that had been good. Money well spent. Demir Sandal had to be getting on in years now – he'd been knocking out cheap photo books and videos for years. Balthazar wondered, idly, what the old pornographer was into now. Something, no doubt, of an extremely exciting nature. Balthazar smiled.

Süleyman had joined them now, sitting in his chair, frowning. İkmen, who had brought a chair in from his own office, sat beside him, his face a picture of confusion.

'Mendes is a hacker,' Çöktin said. 'He can get into and out of systems and you and I don't even know that he's been there. He, or she – it could be a woman, after all – is a legend.'

'Hacking is illegal,' Süleyman said sternly. 'How do you know about this?'

'I know because Mendes is sometimes discussed on some of the newsgroups I post to.'

'Music groups?'

'Some, yes.' Çöktin turned away.

'Some?'

İkmen, who had, as was his wont, been considering more arcane aspects of what they were being told, cleared his throat. 'You know the Goat of Mendes is a European Satanic figure. I don't know much about it, but I do have a friend who has an interest in—'

'Max—' Süleyman began.

'Yes,' İkmen nodded. Max did, like all Englishmen, have a surname, but that wasn't something he wanted Süleyman to share with anyone, not even Çöktin. 'Do you think that this Mendes might be involved in some sort of Satanic practice, İsak?'

Çöktin could feel his face redden. And although he was turned away from his superiors, he knew that they could see it. But in spite of the fact that everyone in the room knew it, Çöktin's religion was not something any of them could or would talk about. An adherent of the native Kurdish Yezidi faith, Çöktin wasn't comfortable with talk about Satanists. Known as the 'Devil Worshippers', Yezidis believe in a benign and restored version of Satan they call 'The Peacock Angel'. Consequently, they are frequently misunderstood and confused with the Western conception of Satanists and the dark deeds those people perform.

Realising that this was obviously proving difficult for Çöktin, İkmen added, 'Not, of course, that you would know anything about Satanism . . .'

'No, sir.'

'But it is thought, is it not,' Süleyman interjected, 'that some of these kids who assume the "Gothic" lifestyle are interested in things Satanic? I met a little group last night. I know of a young person who goes to their clubs and bars. There is a place, what is it, Kemancı – they all go there to listen to that skate punk you told me about, İsak. Maybe there's a tie-up between this Mendes, the newsgroups and these children?'

'I don't think so, sir,' Çöktin said, 'or at least I would be surprised if there were. From the little that I know of Mendes, I think he's been around too long to be a teenager. And anyway, nobody knows where he is. He could be anywhere.'

'But he is Turkish?'

Çöktin shrugged. 'Maybe. I've never communicated with him. I don't know anyone that has directly. All my information is anecdotal. It is said that he communicates in several languages including Turkish, but—'

'In view of what you've found on these machines, I may get some of the younger officers into these Goth places,' Süleyman said. 'See if anyone can remember a Gülay Arat or a Cem Ataman.'

'Gülay hadn't been involved for some months,' Çöktin said, 'and, dark as he was, we've no evidence that Cem Ataman was actually part of the Goth scene.'

'That's true,' Süleyman agreed, 'but I feel it's worth checking. I'm going to ring that friend of Gülay's her brother told us about today too. You know, the one she fell out with.'

'Sırma . . .'

'That's it.'

İkmen, his mind still relentlessly upon the arcane, said, 'There is another connection here too.' And then he told his colleagues about what he had seen at the Church of the Panaghia and Max's partial explanation of it.

'Thirteen penises!'

'Max says that strictly there should only be, at the most, two,' İkmen said.

'I've never heard anything sexual about Mendes,' Çöktin said. 'As I said before, we don't even know what sex Mendes might be.'

'And yet you know people who have made contact with this entity?'

'Yes,' Çöktin looked down again, 'but it's a bit like, do you remember that American series on TV some years ago, *The A-Team*?'

'Yes,' Süleyman replied, 'what of it?'

'Well, sir, they used to say on that that if you had a problem that no one else could help you with and if you could find them you could hire the A-Team.' He smiled. 'It's exactly like that with Mendes. He isn't good, he isn't bad, but he is invisible.'

'But you know people—'

'Mendes, sir, can only be a legend if he retains his anonymity. Working for us could threaten that and it could also destroy his credibility.'

Süleyman looked at İkmen and said, 'What do you think, Inspector?'

İkmen shrugged. 'It's your case, Mehmet. Personally, I'd be inclined to at least try and locate this hacker, if that is possible.'

'Well, is it?' Süleyman looked across at Çöktin.

'I can try . . .'

'Then do so,' Süleyman replied.

'Yes, sir.'

Just the thought of it made Çöktin feel sick. He shouldn't have mentioned Mendes and yet, with so many apparent mysteries contained within these machines, what else could he do?

Demir Sandal didn't have an office.

'I have a warehouse,' he said to Jak Cohen as he plunged one hand into the enormous holdall at his feet, 'but I don't advertise its location. A man can't be too careful.'

'No.'

The two men had, as they'd arranged, met outside the KaVe coffee bar in the little pasaj opposite the top of the Tünel funicular railway. This, the quieter end of İstiklal Caddesi, was perfect for discreet meetings – all the better if one could hide oneself in amongst numerous tall green plants. And for what the corpulent Demir had in mind, plenty of cover was essential.

'Look at this,' he said as he pulled a sequin-and-satin-thread-encrusted ensemble from his bag. 'You'll like this.'

Although the bra and skirt the pornographer held were far more ornate than anything Jak had ever seen before, that wasn't quite what Demir was drawing his attention to. As he pushed the many metres of satin away from the spangled knickers beneath he said, 'Look, Jak Bey, knickers split at the crotch.' He leaned towards him. 'When they dance you can see everything.'

'Mmm. Nice.'

'I can sell as a set or just the skirts alone if you want your girls to go topless.' Demir licked his lips. 'I have sequins for the nipples too – all sizes.' He laughed. 'I had this girl once, Jak Bey, nipples like finger cymbals – which I can supply too by the way. But this girl,' he leaned forward yet again, treating Jak to a strong blast of body odour, 'beautiful. Men would come from all over just to touch those big nipples. One of those women you replay screwing in your head, you know?'

Jak just smiled. In the last hour he had been treated to many stories from Demir Sandal's past, including his experiences of sodomy. Dealer in smut he might be, but Jak wasn't and had never considered himself a pervert – unlike Demir Sandal who, he had to admit, his brother had been right about.

'What sort of quantities can you supply, Demir Bey?' he said as he gently touched one of the skirts.

'What? The skirts and the bras or—'

'I like them as a set,' Jak said, 'and besides, my girls aren't going to be wearing them for very long, are they?'

'No,' Demir laughed, 'you want them off, Jak Bey, because "off" means money for you, right?'

The pornographer nudged Jak in the ribs and laughed again. But Jak only smiled. Maybe it was living in England for so long that made him so reserved, but maybe not. His father had always made a lot of noise, drunk sounds, frequently accompanied by violence. And then there were his brothers – Leon, a drunk just like his father, and Balthazar, so like this Sandal character it almost made Jak weep.

'I've got three clubs,' Jak said simply as he attempted to bring the conversation back up to a recognisable business level. 'I want Middle Eastern nights twice a month in each club during the winter period, and so . . .' he paused to look down at the notebook in his hands . . . 'I'll need forty-five full costumes.'

'Plus accessories?'

'Plus finger cymbals and, say, three veils, the heavy ones you showed me earlier, per costume.'

Demir Sandal shrugged. 'I can do that.'

'Good.'

'I can do anything you want, Jak Bey,' the pornographer continued. 'I can even supply some things I know in my heart you will never have seen, Jak Bey.'

'The costumes are what I came for, Demir Bey.'

'Ah, but you have shops too, Jak Bey, I know. I've seen the shops in England.' He raised his arms upwards in a gesture of appreciation. 'Everything to help a man have sex! Everything! Except,' he moved in closely yet again, 'the thing I have or will have here in our own humble third world country.'

'I'm not interested in anything illegal.'

'No, of course not!' Demir suddenly looked offended. 'Not a gentleman like you, Jak Bey.'

'My brother used to be a police officer.'

'Yes, I know,' Demir said soothingly, 'but you are, as I have said, Jak Bey, an honourable man. In my mind I can't even picture you standing in the same room with those evil sons of Satan.' He lowered his voice. 'You know even now some of them come to my places, fuck like madmen – all for free!'

Jak believed him. In spite of the fact that the Turkish police force had had to clean its act up considerably in recent years, things like this still went on. In fact, Balthazar had probably been part of such things when he'd been well. Not everybody was like Çetin İkmen or that nice Mehmet Süleyman who Balthazar was so friendly with. Jak just couldn't understand why Çetin wasn't delighted that his Çiçek was so taken with that impressively cultured man.

'What I have, what I will be getting, Jak Bey, will make you very rich. Even in England.'

Jak, roused from his temporary reverie, looked up.

'Oh?'

'Beyond belief,' the pornographer leered, 'if you ask for my worthless opinion.'

Jak was used to this. There was always some new and wonderful sex aid that was going to make everybody millions of pounds. They never did. The last 'magic item' he'd seen had been so ridiculous, he'd laughed out loud. But on principle he never passed anything by and so he said that he was interested.

'You won't regret it, Jak Bey,' Demir said as he took down notes about the quantities and colours of costumes required. 'I will call you when it is ready. You will be amazed.'

'I'm only here for another twelve days, Demir Bey.'

'Oh, that's plenty of time,' the pornographer said breezily, and then fixing Jak with a rather more steely glance than before, he continued, 'Now the price per costume, Jak Bey, giving due regard to the workmanship involved . . .'

Chapter 7

The girl Sırma Karaca was, Süleyman felt, typical of modern, over-privileged youth. Grudging in her agreement to come into the station to answer his questions, she now sat before him, all in black, pouting. Her mother, who was about the same age as Süleyman, was pleasant if a little nervous.

They'd established that Sırma and Gülay used to be best friends and that the dead girl would sometimes stay over at Sırma's house.

'But all of this stopped about six months ago,' Süleyman said.

Sırma rubbed some sweat from her forehead with one of her long, black sleeves. 'Yeah.'

'Why was that?'

'I think that Gülay moved on, as it were, Inspector,' Mrs Karaca said with a knowing smile.

'Mum!'

'What do you mean, "moved on"?'

Sırma sighed heavily. 'She left the scene. Got fed up with the music and the clothes.' She threw a disgusted glance at her mother. 'Grew up.'

Süleyman looked down at his notes. 'Gülay's parents, from what I can gather, were unaware of her interest in the Goth scene,' he said. 'Do you know why?'

'They didn't know much about her,' the girl replied with a shrug. 'She didn't want them to.'

Mrs Karaca, for some reason, put her hand on her daughter's shoulder and smiled.

'Her mum's into designer stuff,' Sırma continued. 'Gülay used to keep most of her clothes in my room. We used to get dressed to go out together.'

'I, of course, had no knowledge about this,' Mrs Karaca put in quickly.

'So Gülay would come to your home, change her clothes and you'd go out?'

'Yes.'

'Where?'

'Where we all go. To Atlas Pasaj. Sometimes we'd go and listen to bands at Kemancı. Gülay was really into Brain Dead.'

From which, Süleyman knew, she had not apparently 'moved on'. Kemancı again – where Fitnat and her black-clad friends were wont to go. He wondered if Sırma knew his ex-wife's stepdaughter.

'What brought your friendship to an end?'

'Gülay.' Sırma looked up into Süleyman's face, her own features grimly impassive. 'One day she said that she was fed up with it all. She wasn't going to come to Atlas with me and the rest of our friends any more. She said it was stupid.'

'So she did this suddenly, without any warning?'

'Yes.'

'Did any of your other friends notice anything odd about her behaviour around that time?'

'Only, like me, that for a couple of weeks before she left she was spending more time at her lessons and at home.' Sırma looked down at the floor. 'It was weird. Gülay hated extra classes – she didn't like learning and she didn't get on with her parents.'

'And the clothes she kept at your home?'

Sırma shrugged again. 'She said I could keep them, but they were too small and so I threw them away.'

So Gülay Arat the Goth had worn the right clothes, listened to the right music, moved in the right circles, and then . . . and then she'd just stopped everything except the music. Then she'd disappeared, or so it would seem, into a far more settled and contemplative lifestyle.

Süleyman leaned forward and smiled. 'Sırma,' he said, 'do you ever look up information on the Internet about the bands you follow? Do you maybe, contribute to newsgroups about them?'

'I go on the Internet sometimes,' Sırma said, 'to websites, but it's all a bit boring. I've seen the newsgroups.'

'And?'

'Full of weirdos who just want to "chat" about nothing all the time. Kids stuck at home with no life. Why?'

The policeman ignored her question and went on to the next item on his agenda. 'You've said, Sırma, that Gülay didn't get on with her parents? Do you know why that was?'

The girl and her mother exchanged a brief look before Sırma said, 'No.'

'Are you sure?'

'Yes.'

'Because if there's something you're afraid to tell me . . .'

'They're just never there,' Sırma said. 'They want her to be like them and do what they do, but they don't want to know what she wants – wanted.'

'But nothing more than that?' Süleyman said. 'Nothing you can think of that might have caused Gülay to take her own life?'

Sırma looked away, at her mother. 'No.'

'Very well.' Süleyman wrote down some brief notes and then said, 'And you didn't, after the break up of your friendship, see Gülay again?'

'Only once, about a month ago,' Sırma said, 'at Akmerkez. She was wearing what my mum would call a pretty dress.'

'Did she speak to you?'

'Yeah, said she was happy now.'

'Did she say why?'

'No.'

'Did you ask?'

'No.'

'Was she with anyone?'

'No.'

'So you just said hello, she told you she was happy, and you parted?'

'Yes.'

What a strange and stilted little conversation that must have been. But then tribes like the Goths were probably not very welcoming to those who had left their ranks. And Gülay Arat had apparently left completely – unlike Fitnat, who was playing at being 'normal' for the sake of her father and Zuleika. But then Fitnat, unlike Gülay, hadn't as yet found anything else to replace her adherence to the tribe. Not that Gülay had entirely broken with the scene. She had obviously still retained her interest in the music, but from afar.

Someone or something had prevented her from going out. Maybe her parents? There was a problem there, beyond the usual middle-class dysfunction, which Sırma and her mother knew more about than they were prepared to divulge. Maybe Çöktin was right that the answer to at least some of these questions lay within the girl's computer files. Or maybe another conversation with Gülay's brother, Nurdoğan, might prove instructive.

When the interview was over, Süleyman showed Sırma and her mother out. When he returned to his desk, his telephone was ringing.

He sat down and picked it up. 'Süleyman.'

'Hello, Mehmet, it's Çiçek.'

'Oh, hello.'

'Mehmet, I'm sorry to call you at work, but I have a bit of a problem,' she said.

'What's that?'

He heard her draw a breath, as if she were nervous. 'You know I share the apartment with another girl, Emine?'

'I knew you shared.'

'Well, it's her birthday tomorrow and I'm cooking dinner for her and her boyfriend and our other friend Deniz and her husband.'

'That's nice.'

'Yaşar, he's one of our stewards,' Çiçek was an air hostess, 'was going to come too because it's couples, but he's had to cancel. And so I'm looking for a man to sort of be my partner for the evening . . .'

'And you thought of me.' Süleyman lit a cigarette and then let the smoke out on a sigh. 'But, Çiçek, if Yaşar is your boyfriend—'

Çiçek laughed. 'Yaşar's gay, Mehmet,' she said. 'A lot of the stewards are. Didn't you know that? No, Yaşar was just coming along because he's good company and because I don't want my table to be unbalanced.'

'So you want me to balance your table?'

'Yes.'

'A policeman amongst what I imagine are all airline people.'

'Not exclusively, no,' she replied. 'Deniz' husband runs an antique shop. And, anyway, everyone knows about Dad and they're fine with it.'

72

'But haven't you a boyfriend?'

'No.' The clipped manner in which she replied told him that this was a sore subject. 'We won't talk about Turkish Airlines all evening, I promise.'

'Well . . .'

'Look, I'll just introduce you as a family friend. Everyone knows my family; they'll love you.'

Mehmet sighed. He wasn't really in the mood for socialising, but on the other hand he wasn't in the mood for staying in with his parents either. And anyway, even if the conversation wasn't glittering, it might help to take his mind off his problems for a while. Çiçek was, after all, a nice enough girl. He'd known her since she was a child – he was, he felt, a sort of uncle to her – and so it would at least be easy to be in her company. He might even be able to relax for a while.

'OK,' he said decisively, 'you have a date, Çiçek.'

'Great!'

'What time?'

After they had sorted out the details and spoken a little about Hulya and her quirky new home, Süleyman concluded the call. As he put the receiver down he frowned. His test results were due on the day following Çiçek's birthday meal – perhaps it would be the last time he'd be able to eat in anything approaching peace. Perhaps he ought to break his usual vow of abstinence and have a drink for a change.

İsak Çöktin just about made it home before he fell asleep. His mother, who wasn't keen on her son working through the night, fussed and fretted, but he hardly heard it. Fully clothed, he collapsed on to his bed, and crashed into a dreamless sleep immediately.

When, however, he woke to the sound of blasting Fasıl music from the apartment opposite, all of the worries that had clogged his brain back at the station returned. It was only 6 p.m., which meant that he'd still had only four hours' sleep – hardly enough to think rationally about what he might do now. He'd have to talk to someone about it. He picked his mobile telephone up off the floor and keyed in a number he knew by heart.

73

When the person at the other end answered, he said, 'It's İsak. You've got to come over. Something's happened.'

Of course, as soon as his cousin Kasım arrived, his mother insisted that he eat with İsak and his father too. And because there was no rushing his mother, İsak had to remain patient until the meal was over. As soon as it was done, however, he took Kasım out for a walk. A lot of rural immigrants like the Çöktin family lived in the Tepebaşı district of the city. A poor, ragged place, it was littered with people who envied the Çöktins their comparative wealth – people who, more importantly for today's activities, spoke their language too.

İsak and Kasım crossed the Tepebaşı dual carriageway and walked up into Beyoğlu.

'I know the doorman at the Armenian church,' İsak said as they entered the teeming Balık Pazar, with its fish shops, souvenir booths and great hessian spice sacks. 'He's a friend of our pathologist. He'll let us in so we can talk quietly.'

The two young men disappeared into what, to the uninitiated, looked like a cupboard in the wall. Behind this door, however, was a stone-flagged court and the unmistakable white façade of a church. Üç Horon was built in the nineteenth century for what was then a large Armenian minority. And although its congregation was now greatly reduced, the building itself was still the largest of its kind in the city.

The doorman, a thin and world-weary man by the name of Garbis, was only too pleased to let a colleague of Dr Sarkissian use a bench in the courtyard for a conversation with his friend. The Balık Pazar was like a madhouse in the evenings, especially in this late heat wave. Garbis even gave them an ashtray, and some small glasses of tea from his own samovar. As he walked away, the Armenian heard the men begin to talk in a language that was neither his own nor Turkish.

'My boss wants to use Mendes' expertise,' İsak said without pre-amble.

Kasım, who was a few years younger than his cousin, shook his head. 'How does your boss know about Mendes?'

'I told him.'

'You told him!' Wide-eyed and on the point of fury, Kasım said, 'Why? What were you thinking?'

İsak lit a cigarette and then looked down at the marble beneath his feet. 'The case we're working on – it involves vast amounts of electronic data.'

'Yes, but don't the police have experts—'

'Yes, but . . . look, Kasım, I can't go into detail. We need someone who can track people posting to newsgroups. We need someone who knows what has to be done to conceal identities.'

Kasım, one hand now up at his sweating brow, said, 'Are you mad?'

'No, I just want to help move my investigation forward, which will happen only if I can, somehow, get in contact with Mendes.'

'And if this boss of yours wants more information about Mendes? If he wants to know what other little things he's been up to? What then?'

'Inspector Süleyman won't ask about anything outside the scope of the investigation. Why would he?'

'Because he's a policeman!' Kasım snapped.

'So am I.'

'Yes, but you're different, aren't you, cousin?' Kasım said more calmly now. 'You are one of us first and a policeman second. This Süleyman—'

'Inspector Süleyman is well aware of what I am, Kasım,' İsak cut in earnestly.

'You told him!'

'No, of course not. But he knows.'

'How? Your identity card states that your religion is Muslim.'

'Yes, but Inspector Süleyman knows that I am Yezidi.' He shook his head impatiently. 'Why and how I'm not prepared to go into, but he knows.'

'So if he knows, why have you still got a job? You know as well as I do what people think about us.'

'Inspector Süleyman is different.'

'Not different enough to look the other way if he were to find out about your other "business",' Kasım said darkly.

İsak looked away, at some incomprehensible sign in Armenian. 'No. But we don't need to go into that.'

'Don't we? What if this Süleyman wants to know how we know of Mendes? No.' Kasım took a cigarette out of his pocket and lit up.

'Mendes must stay a secret.' He leaned in towards İsak, the better to press his point. 'Mendes set everything up for us, remember? If we do as he says, we cannot be found.'

'I know.'

'Mendes sympathises with us—'

'We don't know that, Kasım.'

'Well, he must because—'

'Mendes is a hacker,' İsak countered earnestly. 'He does these things for people because he, or she, enjoys the challenge. We don't, Kasım, know what Mendes is. As far as I'm aware, your friend has never met Mendes. Mendes could therefore be a Kurd or an American or a Korean—'

'Mendes' instructions were in our language.'

'Are you sure? What about your friend, Kasım, the one we set our system up through? Maybe he translated what the hacker had told him.'

'I don't know.'

'Well, you're going to have to contact your friend, or let me contact him.'

'No!'

'Yes, Kasım.' Çöktin put his cigarette out and took a sip from his tea glass. 'This is serious. People's, children's, lives could be at stake. I couldn't live with myself if I didn't do everything that I could . . .'

'It was a bad day when you joined the police!' Kasım spat.

Infuriated by his cousin's seeming lack of understanding, İsak said, 'I joined because I needed a job! What I do puts food on my parents' table!'

'You speak English – you could have got any job you wanted! You could go abroad!'

'And leave Mum and Dad?' İsak flung a dismissive hand to one side. 'Dad can't work, Kasım. Mum does her best, but . . . And anyway, I don't want to go abroad.'

'Why not?' Kasım moved in closer to his cousin's face. 'Is it because of that Turkish girlfriend you've got up in Balat?'

'Döne . . .'

'Yes, Döne – the one you'll have to leave anyway when your parents go back to the village to choose you a bride.'

Now red with fury, İsak hissed, 'Don't change the subject, Kasım! Are you going to go to your friend for me or not?'

'No.'

'Fine.' İsak stood up. 'Then I'll have to find him myself, won't I? Shouldn't be too difficult.'

'İsak!'

He bent down low to speak into Kasım's ear. 'I can have you followed, Kasım, as of this very minute. Think about it.'

And then, with grateful thanks to Garbis, he left. Kasım, alone now, looked down at what was left of his tea and sighed. He liked İsak. İsak was family and besides, he needed him to run the service. But to put the service at risk like this was reckless. Didn't he realise that if his boss did find out about their activities İsak could lose not only his job but his liberty too? Children in danger or no children in danger, that had to be too great a risk for anyone to take. On the other hand, if İsak wasn't going to help him run the thing then who was?

As soon as she'd put her employer's shopping away, Ülkü called him to say that Max Bey was out. Happily, Turgut must have been close by because it took him only a minute to get up to the apartment.

As soon as he was inside, she kissed him. It was difficult to know how much time they'd have together. She hadn't been in to see Max Bey go and so he could, theoretically, come back at any time. But Turgut didn't respond with great affection – obviously a bad day. They went into her bedroom and, after he'd gone back for a few moments into the hall to get his cigarettes from his jacket, he shut the door behind them. He sat down on the bed and unzipped his fly.

'Go on,' he said as he folded her hand around his penis and lay back against the pillows.

He always wanted this. Every time they met. But Ülkü did as she was told, looking away as she always did while her boyfriend grunted and gasped his way towards his climax. If he could, she knew, he'd have 'proper' sex with her. But like her, he was from some nowhere in the east of the country where women were virgins until they married and men went to whores or foreign women or got their girls to do what she was doing now. But one day soon, Turgut was always saying, they would marry and then all of this would change. Maybe that was why he was so depressed today – making the money they needed was all taking such a long time.

When Turgut had finished, she got up and went to the bathroom. Later, she would recall that she did hear what sounded like something falling in the study, but it wasn't loud, Max Bey was out and so she didn't pay it much heed. And anyway, Turgut was soon demanding her attention once again.

'Ülkü?'

'Yes?'

'You know I love you, don't you?'

She came back into the room, smiling. 'Yes.'

He was still lying on the bed when she returned, massaging that thing of his with his own hand for a change.

'I want you to suck my penis,' he said harshly, and then added, rather more softly, 'Please, it's the best thing a girl can do for a man and I'm so tense . . .'

'No!' Ülkü bristled. 'Only whores do that!'

'No,' Turgut said, 'nice girls do it too.' He smiled. 'Max Bey's students do it. Oh, Ülkü, it'll make me so happy.'

'But—'

'Ülkü,' he said, 'we don't get much time together. Please do this for me! A husband needs to know his wife will do anything he asks . . .'

Something bad must have happened, his eyes looked so wounded. If only she could talk to him about whatever was bothering him rather than do this – but then if this made him feel better . . . and so she did it. But unlike their other activities, it didn't take very long. And so, once Turgut had recovered, she did it again. He loved it so much and she so wanted to please him. Max Bey said that once Ülkü could read and write properly in English, she'd be able to do a lot better than Turgut. He didn't trust him, he said, and feared that Turgut was using Ülkü for some reason. But she was happy. Turgut was so handsome and even though she felt plain by comparison a lot of the time, she knew he loved her. Why would she want or need anyone else?

'Do you feel better now?' she said to him once she'd been to the bathroom again to wash.

'Yes,' he said, his eyes half closed. 'You're a good girl, Ülkü. You've made me very happy.'

Turgut got dressed and, as he was doing so, he said that he'd like a drink. She went to the kitchen to get water from the fridge. On her way back, however, she decided to go into the study to get her English textbooks. Turgut would have to go to his restaurant soon, and with Max Bey out, she would have a good opportunity to do some work.

She opened the door and reached around to the small table she knew she'd placed her books upon. What made her look into the body of the room she was never to know. But the sight of the blood all over the floor and up the walls caused Ülkü to drop her books to the ground and run screaming back to her bedroom.

Chapter 8

'What time did your employer go out?' The policeman, an Inspector İskender, was a small man with a big presence. Young, handsome and beautifully groomed, he had an iciness about his manner that the traumatised Ülkü found terrifying.

'I . . . maybe five o'clock . . . I'd been shopping. He wasn't in . . .'

'It was five,' a much more sure and certain Turgut said. 'Ülkü called me as soon as she got in. I was nearby anyway and I saw Max Bey leave just before she called. They must have missed each other by seconds. It was five, I know.'

'Was it necessary for Miss Ayla to be alone before you entered the apartment?' İskender said, his attention now solely on the rough-looking boy sitting in front of him. 'You were, after all, lurking out-side. Were you perhaps seeking to seduce the young lady?'

'No,' the boy responded coolly. 'Ülkü and I are, well, we are betrothed. I wouldn't dishonour her in such a way. But Max Bey doesn't like me. I have to "lurk" so I can get any time alone with her. He doesn't think I'm good enough for Ülkü.'

'And why should Max Bey care about the private life of his maid?'

Ülkü and Turgut shared a look before the former said, 'Because he is a kind man.'

Noise from the study next door indicated a flurry of activity around the scene.

'Excuse me,' İskender said as he motioned for two officers to come and guard the young couple.

As he went into the study, İskender could see several people including İkmen. Together with İskender's sergeant, Alpaslan Karataş and a couple of uniformed officers, they were studying the bloodstains closely. When İskender drew level with him, İkmen turned.

'Maximillian Esterhazy and I are old acquaintances,' he said. 'Max is a brilliant man.'

'What do you know about him?'

'In his fifties, an English national of Austrian descent. He gives private English language classes, does a bit of freelance writing and editing. Unmarried.' He looked up into İskender's face. 'I do hope this isn't his blood.'

'We won't know that until either we find his body or someone else's,' İskender said. 'Do you think he might be capable of violence?'

İkmen shrugged. 'Who isn't?'

'Is he homosexual?' İskender asked with that bluntness that was his trademark.

İkmen smiled. 'Unmarried doesn't necessarily mean gay, Inspector. Could mean that Max just has more sense than to marry. And, anyway, he's totally into his art; he has no time for such things.'

'What art?'

'Max is a magician.' İkmen felt rather than saw Alpaslan Karataş' head turn towards him.

'What do you mean? On the stage?'

'No!' İkmen lit a cigarette and sat down in one of Max's tattered armchairs. 'Max is a real magician. He is what they call in the West an adept: he studies magical systems; Kabbalah, Enochian magic.'

'So he's a charlatan?'

'Depends on your point of view,' İkmen replied with a shrug, 'but if Max wants something to happen, it generally does.'

'I've called for Forensic,' İskender said as he sat down beside İkmen and also lit a cigarette. 'Why did he come here?'

'He likes it here. I think it suits his essentially stateless nature,' İkmen said. 'He's written a few papers about Turkish magic, which were, I believe, well received back in his own country. I read one about the Yezidi. It was very good.'

'Yezidi?' İskender narrowed his eyes. 'They worship Satan, don't they?'

'No, that's a myth,' İkmen said wearily. He wanted to expand on this and tell İskender that a man he frequently ate and drank with, Çöktin, was actually a Yezidi, but he resisted the temptation and just said, 'Their practices are misunderstood. They're not bad people and they're definitely not Satanists. Max knows Satanists—'

'In İstanbul?'

'Yes.'

'So why didn't you get him to—'

'People like Max, Inspector,' İkmen said sternly, 'move to their own rhythm. Max, in his own way, sorted out Satanists and other assorted weirdos in his own unique fashion.'

'Until now.'

'Possibly.' İkmen shook his head. 'Depends what all this means, doesn't it? I don't know how I'm going to tell Inspector Süleyman.'

'Süleyman? He knows this man?'

'I introduced them,' İkmen said. 'They get on. Similar backgrounds.'

İskender looked confused.

'Inspector Süleyman comes from an aristocratic family and so does Max,' İkmen said. 'I think his father was a count. The Esterhazys left Austria and went to England just before the Nazis took over Vienna. They didn't hold with Hitler. I think that Max and Inspector Süleyman like to spend time talking about where they might have been and what they might have done had history been different. Life for peasants like us, my dear Metin, isn't complicated by the spectre of what might have been.'

The two men sat in silence for a few moments before Karataş, a large and, from the look of it, very old book in his hands, came over to them.

'This was open on his desk, sir,' he said as he placed the tome into İskender's lap.

'Well, if that isn't a representation of Satan, I don't know what is,' İskender said as he pointed out to İkmen the large illustration on one of the pages.

The older man briefly closed his eyes and then as he opened them again he groaned. 'In a sense, yes,' he said. 'The Goat of Mendes is what it's called. Not that Max's interest in it was for his own purposes.'

'Oh?'

'No. He was looking it up for me,' İkmen said, and then proceeded to explain why he had asked for the magician's assistance.

'So, do you think that this Goat of Mendes thing has anything to do with all this?'

'I don't know,' İkmen admitted. 'Maybe. I hope that soon we might be able to ask Max himself. What is certain, though, is that we are going to have to follow it up. Çöktin knows, or rather is aware of, a computer hacker who calls himself Mendes. I know that Inspector Süleyman wants to be put in contact with that person and perhaps so do I.'

'Or rather me,' İskender said, İkmen felt a trifle tetchily, 'because it is my case.'

'Of course,' İkmen put his head in his hands, 'of course it is.'

Another silence followed, time during which the officers in the room now awaiting Forensic listened to the absence of sound as the blood dried on to every hard and soft surface.

'But then again,' İskender said, his head now tilted thoughtfully to one side, 'I have to consider, assuming the absence of Mr Esterhazy, how far I might be able to get without any knowledge about "magic" . . . not far.'

İkmen looked up into hard and unfathomable eyes.

'And so if, Inspector İkmen, you'd like to take that side of the investigation over for me, I would be most grateful.' And then standing up quickly he added, 'I need to take a statement from the maid and her boyfriend.'

'Oh. Right. Yes. Of course, Metin.'

And then he was gone.

For a moment, İkmen looked across at Alpaslan Karataş who just shrugged. Metin İskender was a good man – clean, upright and unfailingly honest. But he was a strange character too. Stiff and rule-bound as so many of the men who had come from exceedingly poor backgrounds were, Metin was also the pampered pet of a rich wife who wanted nothing more than to get her husband to leave the police. She wanted him, so İkmen had heard, to explore his artistic side – wherever that might be. Not in tune with Maximillian Esterhazy and his ilk, that was for sure. But then, as soon as he heard about what had happened at Max's apartment, İkmen knew he would have to, somehow, become involved. Apart from anything else, İkmen and Max shared something that only they knew about. Wherever Max was, assuming he was alive, of course, and whatever he'd done, İkmen wanted to help him.

Twice he had tried to call the place he knew Zelfa and the baby were staying and twice someone had just picked up the phone and then put it down again. Süleyman was not, therefore, in the mood for any objections from this overweight bureaucrat.

'We know that the girl Gülay Arat was involved in the Goth scene,' he told Commissioner Ardıç as he paced agitatedly around his superior's desk.

'But that was some time ago, wasn't it?'

'About six months.'

Ardıç wiped a large amount of sweat from his brow and lit a vast, black cigar. A few years older than İkmen, he was a good example of what can happen to large men when they are confined to their desks. He moved his stomach from his knees and on to the lip of a drawer. 'So if she'd left the "Goth scene", as you put it, why should we be concerning ourselves with it now?' he said.

'She still listened to the music right up until her death,' Süleyman countered.

Ardıç yawned. 'And this computer evidence you say Çöktin has?'

'Newsgroups, yes.'

'Are they odd or Gothic in any way?'

'Some are odd, some are Gothic.' Süleyman sat down opposite his superior and sighed. 'The last person to communicate with her in this fashion used some words in a language we can't as yet identify. It seems that Cem Ataman was in contact with either the same person or someone else who also knows these words.'

'You think the boy's suicide and the girl's murder are connected?'

'I don't know,' Süleyman said as he took his cigarettes out of his pocket and lit up. 'Cem was a lonely, morbid boy – no one seems to know that much about his life. As far as we can tell, he wasn't actually a Goth, although he was certainly interested in diabolism, and he did cut himself, which is what a lot of those kids do. And, as I've said, he was involved in a newsgroup that has a connection, through this odd patois, to one that Gülay Arat used. Çöktin is looking into it.'

'He's very good with computers, isn't he?' Ardıç said.

'Yes. Although this newsgroup phenomenon is presenting him with some problems. I've authorised him to get some outside help.'

'What do you mean?'

Knowing that the use of the word 'hacker' would precipitate an explosion of unwanted questions, Süleyman said, 'A consultant with wide experience of Internet communication, sir.'

'I see.' Ardıç frowned. 'You know the Ataman boy's parents have requested the release of his body for burial?'

'I have explained to them—'

'Yes, I know, but I must admit that I can't see why you need to hold on to it now, Süleyman. The doctor has, I believe, gleaned everything he's going to glean from it. You may by all means retain the child's computer and other effects, but I feel the body must now go.' He coughed.

'I see. And my request to re-interview Sırma Karaca and gain access to Gülay Arat's other friends?'

Ardıç looked down at his desk, his eyes hooded and heavy. 'You can do that,' he said, 'provided you try not to upset too many people. I am told that these weird children who go to Atlas Pasaj are generally from the privileged classes. You will have to be,' he looked up pointedly at his inferior, 'gentle with them.'

'Yes, sir.'

'Notwithstanding the computer evidence, I'm still not entirely convinced that these two deaths are connected,' Ardıç said on a sigh. 'Young people do sometimes kill themselves and murders do happen.'

'The girl had also been sexually assaulted,' Süleyman said, 'in what Dr Sarkissian believes is a most bizarre fashion. And considering the dark interests of these children—'

'Yes, yes, yes!' He was getting tetchy now. Ardıç did when things were difficult like this. As İkmen so often said, Ardıç didn't respond well to crime that was not straightforward. Bar brawls, vendettas and the occasional death of a prostitute were things that he related to. Anything subtle or complex was entirely beyond both his capabilities and his patience.

'Look, Süleyman,' he said, 'by all means question these children, but take care. The Arat girl could have easily consented to the sex act Sarkissian detailed in his report. Her father, we know, runs a string of very dubious establishments where all sorts of things – drugs, porn, you name it – are rumoured to take place. Maybe she and some friends were re-enacting some awful porn movie . . .'

'During the course of which one of them stabbed her through the heart?' Süleyman shook his head. 'I don't think so, sir.'

'Well, don't rule it out,' Ardıç said harshly. 'There's some un-believably weird stuff on tape and video CD these days. People will do just about anything. Some of it, it is said, for Hüseyin Arat.'

'Yes, sir,' Süleyman said as he tried to banish the thought that Ardıç might have watched some of this material from his mind.

Süleyman left his boss's office soon afterwards. He'd got what he'd gone for – permission to interview Gülay's friends. He didn't need anything else. Except some sort of proof, in the real world, that he was doing the right thing. Gülay and Cem's deaths could, as Ardıç had said, be completely unconnected. The Goth scene and even the messages from Nika and Communion could be totally meaningless in the context of the children's deaths. After all, neither Nika nor Communion had said anything untoward to the young people – as far as the police could tell.

He was sitting in his office when the call came in from İkmen about Max Esterhazy. Where on earth could he be? And whose blood was spattered, as İkmen had put it, across his study? That Max had had a picture of the Goat of Mendes on his desk did, however, gal-vanise him. Like the connection between Nika, Communion and the two dead children, it might mean nothing, but the word 'Mendes' had cropped up in three different areas now – as a piece of graffiti on a church wall, as an almost mythical computer hacker and now in one of Max's textbooks, something he'd been looking up for İkmen.

Süleyman picked up his phone and called the Çöktins' apartment.

'I don't know how, from the amount of blood involved, a serious incident of some sort could take place in Mr Esterhazy's apartment without your noticing something,' İskender said, as he looked down coldly at Turgut Can. 'Miss Ayla, so she claims, telephoned you from the study just after she returned from her shopping trip. Just after, I imagine, you saw Mr Esterhazy leave.'

'She did.' The boy shrugged. 'Maybe Max Bey came back.'

'But if that were the case then you would have seen or heard him return, wouldn't you?' İskender replied.

'Not necessarily.'

'What do you mean?'

Turgut smiled. 'Well, I wasn't in his study . . .'

'No? So where were you, Mr Can?'

Turgut looked down at his hands, a vaguely sheepish expression haunting his face. 'In with Ülkü.'

'What do you mean?' İskender sat down at Max Esterhazy's long kitchen table and lit a cigarette.

'In her room.'

'Were you having sex with her?'

Turgut suddenly looked shocked. 'No!'

'Then what were you doing in her bedroom?'

'We were . . .' He glanced down again, that smile returning to his lips. 'I love Ülkü, Inspector,' he said, 'we were . . . she's a good girl, Ülkü, you know.'

'But?' It was so cynically asked that it even shocked İskender's sergeant, who was, after all, accustomed to his ways.

'She gives me some relief, if you know what I mean,' Turgut turned away, 'with her hand . . .'

'So, as soon as Mr Esterhazy was out of the way, you and your girlfriend went to her bedroom where she masturbated you.'

'Yes.'

'Don't you think that Mr Esterhazy, especially in view of his antipathy towards you, would have heard something had he returned to the apartment? I mean, you and your girlfriend must have made some noise.'

'Well . . .'

İskender turned to Alpaslan Karataş and said, 'Go and get Miss Ayla for me.'

'Yes, sir.'

İskender regarded Turgut Can sternly. 'And how long did that take you? The masturbation?' he said. 'You're a young and, obviously, lustful man.'

Turgut's face paled. 'What do you mean?'

The policeman smiled unpleasantly. 'I mean, Mr Can, that when

88

a girl starts pulling at a young man's cock it doesn't usually take him that long to get rid of his frustrations.'

Although outwardly suave, İskender did at times, like this, slip into the rough tones and patois of his youth. 'You entered this apartment at just after five, Miss Ayla called us at six forty-five – you must have spent an hour at the very least in her room. What were you doing?'

'I told you—'

'No, you told me part of it, Mr Can.' He looked up as the girl and Karataş entered the room. 'Ah, Miss Ayla . . .'

'Sir.' Her eyes cast down, Ülkü Ayla sat next to Turgut Can, her hands folded in her lap.

'I was just asking Mr Can here what you and he were doing while Mr Esterhazy's study was being decorated with blood,' İskender said.

Ülkü looked at Turgut, her face reddening as she turned.

'He says you were in your bedroom.'

'Yes.' It was more of a whisper than anything else.

'What were you doing there, in your bedroom?'

'We—'

'Ülkü did it again,' Turgut put in.

'What?'

'She wanted to . . .' He looked across at the girl and said, 'I'm sorry, Ülkü, I have to tell him.'

She started to cry.

'We finished and . . . Ülkü went to the bathroom and then when she came back we sort of . . . Ülkü gave me a blow job. I didn't ask her to,' he added quickly. 'She wanted it.'

'No!'

'I've never had one of them before,' Turgut continued, 'and so I thought I'd better make it last.' He smirked. 'You know how it is . . .'

İskender ignored him. 'Is this true?' he said to the girl. 'Did you first masturbate this man and then take him into your mouth?'

Ülkü, speechless, just shook her head as if she didn't understand.

'Well?'

'Y-yes, but—'

'So the two of you played with each other for an hour, did you?' İskender said contemptuously. 'You neither heard nor saw anything untoward during the course of that time?'

'No.'

İskender turned to Alpaslan Karataş and smiled. 'Must have been a good session, mustn't it, Sergeant?'

The younger man grinned nervously. 'Yes, sir.'

İskender raised his eyebrows. 'An hour?'

'I heard something fall when I was in the bathroom – I think it came from the study.' It came out in a rush, as if she had to get it out before something happened to stop her.

'And what time was this, Miss Ayla?'

'I don't know . . . maybe half-past five . . .'

'Did you go and check to see whether everything was all right?' Ülkü looked down again. 'No.'

'Why not, Miss Ayla?'

İskender could see that Turgut Can's face was tense.

'Because then Turgut called me to . . . he'd been upset, I was worried for him. He wanted me to do that thing with his . . .'

'To give him oral sex.'

'Yes.'

'No! It was her.'

İskender looked from the girl to the boy and frowned.

'It was her!' Turgut spat. 'She wanted it! She came out of the bathroom and went down on me! Sucking like a whore! Like that pervert Max Bey taught her!'

'No!' Ülkü looked across at İskender and said, 'Max Bey isn't like that, Inspector. He is like a father to me. He's never made me do anything bad.'

'So you never had oral sex with Mr Esterhazy?' İskender asked.

'No.'

'Did you have any other kind of sex with him?'

'No!'

'Yes, you did!' Turgut sneered. 'All that spooky stuff he did was all about sex! Those books of his are full of it! People fucking with each other and with animals!'

'It was his study!' She looked İskender pleadingly in the eyes. 'Magic. He never touched me! You have to believe it!'

'She's lying!'

İskender sniffed. This young man, the girl's so-called betrothed,

90

made him want to hit him. 'And yet knowing, as you assert, that Miss Ayla was having sex with Mr Esterhazy, you carried on seeing her?' he said. 'Further, you required her to service you too?'

'Yes.'

'I find that very hard to believe,' İskender said, 'unless, of course, you had some other motive in mind. If, for instance, you were using her to gain access to Mr Esterhazy or his property for some reason. There are lots of valuable things in this apartment.'

Turgut flushed. 'No! Ülkü sucked me! She's crazy for—'

'Sex? This – what did you call her – "good girl"? Your story, Mr Can, doesn't make sense,' İskender said as he moved his gaze from Turgut to Ülkü and back again. 'This afternoon when Miss Ayla heard something fall in the study, she, the housemaid, a girl devoted to her kind and generous employer, completely ignored it and offered to give you, Mr Can, a blow job instead.'

'If she says—'

'No, Mr Can,' İskender leaned forward and looked deep into Turgut Can's eyes, 'that is not exactly how it happened and you know it. Now let's have the truth, shall we, from both of you?'

Now that his father was dead, there was only Kasım and his elderly mother. Occupying three decaying rooms just around the corner from Çöktin's family apartment, Kasım's place was dominated by computers, screens, boxes of disks and electrical wires. His mother, who had long since given up hope of her son ever making anything of himself, readily let them in. And although she turned her face away from the stranger who had come into her home, she kissed İsak on both cheeks before shouting 'Kasım!' through a thin, plywood door and then retiring back to her own room.

İsak Çöktin didn't wait for a reply.

'I thought we'd said everything we needed to say at the church,' Kasım said as he regarded the sudden appearance of his cousin with contempt.

'Things have changed,' İsak said as he held the door open for a tall, grave-looking man in a stylish dark suit.

'Who's that?'

'This is my boss, Kasım, Inspector Süleyman,' İsak said. 'He needs to speak to you.'

Kasım pushed himself away from his keyboard and started to roll his chair back towards the window. His eyes were red from long sessions staring at the screen, and now they were also filled with fear.

Süleyman first looked around the small, paper-strewn room and then picked up a recordable CD from the pile beside Kasım's computer. 'I know all about this,' he said as he held it aloft. 'İsak has told me.'

Kasım looked across at his cousin, an expression of pure hatred on his face.

'But that's not why I'm here,' Süleyman continued. 'Subtitling films into your own language is your affair.'

'I can't believe—'

'Kasım, I had to tell him! I was in danger of getting lost in my own lies!' İsak sat down on his cousin's meagre bed and rubbed his face with his hands. 'Someone has disappeared, he may be dead.'

'A friend of mine,' Süleyman cut in, 'a very decent man – a foreigner.'

'There could be a connection between this man and Mendes, Kasım,' İsak explained. 'We need to contact him. You must tell us who your contact is.'

'I – I can't,' Kasım stammered.

'You must!'

Now that he'd told Süleyman about the little 'business' he and Kasım ran, subtitling films into Kurdish and then offering the results to known subscribers in the far eastern provinces, there was no going back. Of course, he hadn't had to. But a man had disappeared whilst apparently researching into the Goat of Mendes, which was, it was said, a Satanic image and so, suddenly, his way forward had become horribly clear. Explain to someone nominally sympathetic, like Süleyman, what the differences between Satanists and his people were and hope that he would understand. Süleyman, who, he knew, had always suspected what he and his family really were, now knew for certain. What Süleyman hadn't known was that he was also active within the illegal pirate community too. But then Mendes had instructed Kasım and himself to hide themselves well. Mendes was, after all, the very best. But if he were also involved in blood, possibly death, then that was a sacrifice İsak had to make – if he wanted to continue to live in peace with himself.

'If you don't co-operate, I will arrest you and charge you with offences likely to endanger national security,' Süleyman said coldly. And then turning to his deputy he added, 'And that will include you, Sergeant Çöktin.'

İsak lowered his head. 'Sir.' His boss was, he hoped, bluffing at this time, but retribution of some kind would come in the end. It had to. He as a serving officer had knowingly broken the law. Not even İkmen, let alone Süleyman, would or could just let that go.

Süleyman took his cigarettes from his pocket and lit up. He then offered the packet to Kasım, who, with a shaky hand, took one gratefully.

'I can understand why you might be reluctant to give us the name of the person who knows this Mendes,' Süleyman said a little more gently now. 'I suspect, as I know İsak does, that he or she is one of your fellows.' He leaned forward and peered, in a concentrated fashion, into Kasım's eyes. 'I have nothing against the Yezidi, Kasım; I'm not going to use what I know to harm your people. I just need to get a connection to this hacker. I need to find out why my friend's apartment is soaked in blood and why he has disappeared.'

Kasım looked from Süleyman's face to that of his cousin who said, 'Kasım! Please!'

'Mendes protects us! If anyone knew that it was me—'

'They won't,' Süleyman cut in sharply.

'I don't believe you!'

Süleyman grabbed the young man's collar firmly in his fist. 'Now you listen to me, Kasım Çöktin,' he said through angry, gritted teeth. 'You know nothing about me or any of the methods open to me. When I tell you I can guarantee that the fact your friend put us in contact with this Mendes is something no one outside of this situation will ever know, then you will believe me.'

'The inspector is a man of honour,' a slightly tremulous İsak added.

'Tell me and I will protect this person and you.'

'And if I won't?'

Süleyman let go of his collar and sank back down on Kasım's

spongy mattress. 'Then,' he said, 'I think that your career in the film industry may be in jeopardy.'

Kasım threw his cigarette butt down on to his bare floorboards and ground it out with his foot.

Chapter 9

'I started seeing Ülkü early last year.'

They'd moved Turgut Can from Max Esterhazy's apartment to the station. Ülkü Ayla they had sent to stay with a woman she knew from her native village. But not before she had talked at some length. About how Max had, on a trip to the eastern district of Mardin, effectively bought her from her impoverished mother, about how she'd come to İstanbul to be his maid and how he'd started to teach her English and sometimes he'd talked a little about his magical work too. But not very often. That was, Max had always said, something Ülkü had to make her own mind up about in the fullness of time. Turgut Can was something she, so Max had also said, had a choice about too.

İkmen and İskender regarded the young man in front of them with stony countenances.

'How did you meet?' the older man asked. Village kids like Turgut weren't exactly confident around girls, especially traditional ones like Ülkü.

'I'm a waiter,' the boy replied, 'at a small lokanta in Sirkeci. Ülkü would often pass by on her way to the Mısır Çarşısı – Max Bey always needed things from there. One day when it was very hot, she fainted. I picked her up and gave her a glass of water. Ülkü came from a village only four kilometres from mine.'

'So you started seeing each other?'

'Not immediately.' Turgut looked down at the floor. 'I left it a few weeks before I went back.'

'Why?'

'I didn't want Ülkü to think I was forward.'

'This from the man who made the girl suck his cock!' İskender said acidly.

İkmen ignored this comment. 'You were attracted to Ülkü?'

Turgut shrugged.

'So was there something else?' İkmen said. 'Something to do with Mr Esterhazy?'

'Ülkü told me he was a magician. I was interested.'

'Why?'

Turgut blushed. 'Well, I, er . . . look, I don't do that weird stuff myself. The truth is that he, Max Bey, he had some girls in his apartment. Posh girls . . .'

'Max's students,' İkmen said. 'So you wheedled your way into Miss Ayla's affections so you could leer at Mr Esterhazy's wealthy students.'

'No!' Turgut looked offended, almost hurt, 'No, I . . . look, that first time, the way he was talking to the girls, it seemed to me inappropriate and familiar.'

'What do you mean "inappropriate"? Was he touching them?'

'No, but all that stuff in his books. He has to be a pervert! Weird and unnatural!'

'But you can't have seen his books on that first occasion at his apartment, can you?' İkmen said. 'That you've seen them subsequently would seem to imply that you've taken a look since.' He turned briefly to İskender. 'Max would never let anyone except very old friends look at his books.' Turning back at the boy he continued, 'You went where you shouldn't, didn't you, Turgut?'

Turgut hung his head.

'You didn't go back for Ülkü,' İkmen said. 'You went back to try and get to know some of Max's students.'

'No! No, I like Ülkü. I want to marry her . . .' He looked down again and sighed.

'No luck with the students then?' İkmen said. 'Can't say I'm surprised, Turgut. You're a good-looking boy, but you are from the country and Max's students do tend to be wealthy.'

'I—'

'So instead you got some of your kicks from Mr Esterhazy's no doubt fascinating books and from fantasising about his students while the timid Miss Ayla pulled on your cock,' İskender said brutally. 'Mr Esterhazy did nothing—'

'No, I . . . Max Bey was inappropriate with those girls.'

'How?' İkmen asked. 'What did he do to them?'

Turgut cleared his throat. 'Well, he spoke and laughed with them in a familiar way.'

'Max is British,' İkmen said. 'His students are educated Turkish girls and boys. In both those societies, men and women have easy, platonic relationships.'

'Yes, but what about those books?'

'Max's life as a magician and as a teacher are mutually exclusive,' İkmen said. 'And, besides, if you thought that he was in fact seducing good Turkish girls, including your Ülkü, why didn't you come to us?'

Turgut looked down at the floor. 'I . . .'

'Well?' İskender said. 'Why didn't you come to us, Mr Can? Was it in fact because nothing inappropriate, beyond your own lust, was indeed occurring? Or were you perhaps planning to blackmail Mr Esterhazy at some point?'

'No!'

'So did you, in fact, ever see Mr Esterhazy touching or having sex with Miss Ayla?'

Turgut looked down again, 'Well, not . . .'

'No you didn't, did you?' İkmen said. 'You didn't like Max because he didn't like you, did he? What happened, Mr Can? Did he catch you trying to seduce one of his students or were you perhaps breathing heavily over one of his books?'

Turgut Can put his head in his hands and began to cry.

'Ülkü has told us how kind Max Bey has always been to her,' İkmen continued. 'But she says, although she can't understand why, that he doesn't trust you.'

'No!'

'Oh, yes. She disagrees, of course. She loves you. She's a simple girl, unaware of the fact, as I am, that Max's students and the fascinating pictures in his books were what you really went there for. Getting her to call you when he went out must have provided you with ample opportunity to view his literature.'

'But I didn't—'

'Maybe not on this occasion, no,' İkmen smiled. 'This time you just got down to business with Ülkü – if indeed that is what happened.'

Turgut Can looked up, sweating heavily. 'What do you mean?'

'What Inspector İkmen means,' İskender explained, 'is that we know from the kapıcı that Mr Esterhazy did, as you yourself suggested at the beginning of this process, re-enter the building. Fifteen minutes after you arrived.'

The boy's face drained of colour.

'He'd forgotten something,' İkmen said, 'and so he—'

'But that's not possible!' Turgut cried. 'I would have—'

'Yes, I agree. I think you would have probably heard him return,' İkmen said. 'Unless you were too busy with Ülkü. Maybe Max caught you forcing her down on you.'

'No!'

'We only have your word that you found the blood,' İskender said. 'Who is to say you didn't put it there?'

'But Ülkü—'

'Ülkü loves you, Mr Can,' İkmen said. 'She wants to marry you and believes that you want to marry her. She can't see that to you she's only something to shove yourself into. She likes Max, but I think she likes you more. I think she'd always do what you told her.'

Turgut Can, agitated, jumped to his feet. 'Yes, but what about the body?' he said. 'There's no body!'

'Not as yet,' İkmen said. 'But we've got men at the scene searching the air conditioning vents, the rubbish chute and the other apartments.'

'Yes, but I would have had to—'

'If you killed Mr Esterhazy fifteen or twenty minutes after you arrived at the apartment, you must have given yourself enough time to dispose of the body before you raised the alarm.'

'But how?'

'I don't know, Mr Can,' İkmen said. 'Perhaps you cut Mr Esterhazy up. There was a vast amount of blood.'

'But I didn't!'

'Then you won't mind giving us your clothes for analysis, will you?' İkmen said.

After Turgut Can left, the two officers sat in silence for a while. It was İskender who spoke first.

'You don't really think that that kid killed him, do you?'

'We don't know that Max is even dead,' İkmen said. 'But we have to rule Can and his girlfriend out. The boy's about as muddled and confused as you can get.'

İskender lit a cigarette. 'So do you think that Esterhazy is dead?'

'We won't know until the blood analysis comes back from the lab.'

'And even then we only have his blood group with which to compare it.'

İkmen smiled and then lit up a cigarette of his own. 'Max doesn't hold with doctors,' he said. 'There was always some potion or other that he used to cure himself of whatever. I must admit that I have no gut feelings on this, Metin. I can't imagine that Max has allowed himself to be attacked, but then if he hasn't . . .'

'He was, we think, in that apartment,' İskender said.

'And so if he isn't dead then why is he missing?' İkmen said on a sigh. 'We'll have to contact all the hospitals and doctors' practices.'

'And what about the blood?' İskender continued.

'Yes.' İkmen bit his lip nervously. 'If it isn't Max's, whose is it and how did it get there?'

Unbidden, the thought did briefly enter his head that maybe Max himself had 'put it there'. But if he had, then where was its previous owner and who was that person? Max, so he always said, so İkmen always believed, worked his magic alone. So accessing his world was going to be difficult. Unless, of course, the young girl, the maid, might be prevailed upon to recall something.

The man, who was in reality little more than a boy, turned to Çöktin and said, 'You know that if you get me into trouble my family will kill you?'

Dressed from head to foot in white, Hüsnü was a cross between a nerdish cyber-junkie and a late seventies gigolo. Like most of these full-time on-line types, he was independently wealthy – as evidenced by his amazing apartment in Cihangir – a Kurd, and a stranger to sleep. Indeed, in spite or maybe because of İsak Çöktin's status as a police officer, Hüsnü had been keen to impress the efficacy of amphetamines on his guests.

'If I sleep, I might miss something,' he'd said when he first ushered that Yezidi Kasım and his policeman cousin into his vast living area. He'd enjoyed the sight of the policeman's face as he attempted to take in the pure scale and power of his digital empire.

There were, Çöktin thought, probably six computers in that room, as well as a scanner, one television that never went off and another one that was silently playing a Video CD of the film *Hamam*. What was missing, as far as he could tell, was any sort of printer.

Hüsnü sat down at one of his machines and typed something into the keyboard.

'If you want to contact Mendes you'll have to be patient,' he said.

'Why? Does he go out a lot?'

Hüsnü laughed. 'He, if indeed Mendes is a man, never goes out,' he said with a good degree of arrogance in his voice. 'The dedicated hacker never leaves his post.'

'So why the wait?'

He turned to face İsak and said, 'Because, dear, of the way in which I have to contact him.'

'Which is?'

'Well, I'm not going to send him an e-mail, am I?' He laughed again. 'Mendes is a hacker, he breaks the law. If you recall, Sergeant, it was Mendes whom Kasım and yourself set up your little foreign language film company through. I helped, of course, but . . .' He looked hard at the screen and then grunted. 'No, I contact Mendes through an anonymous message site. I will leave him a message and he will, at some point, get back to me.'

İsak , who was now looking over Hüsnü's shoulder at what appeared to him to be a jumble of code on the screen, said, 'Well, why can't I just use the site myself?'

'Because Mendes doesn't know you. Because I'll have to establish whether he wants to have any contact with you.'

'You've never actually met or spoken to him?'

'Of course not!' Hüsnü turned to face İsak and said, 'Your cousin is such an amateur, Kasım!'

'Yes, I know.'

Stung, İsak nevertheless could do little but agree with them. Compared to this kid he was an absolute technological cretin – little better, in fact, than İkmen.

'I'll leave a message for Mendes to get back to me and then I'll have to call you,' Hüsnü said. 'Think about what you want to ask him before you come back here,' he looked at İsak's still bemused face again and added, 'because you will have to make contact from here. Mendes will trust me to control what goes on at this end.'

'Right.'

'He will also, if he wants to, pull out of the communication at any time.' He smiled. 'Depends largely on whether he's having any fun with it. Oh, and all communication, as far as you're concerned, will have to be in English. You do speak English?'

It was the way it was said, in that mocking tone the kid did so well, rather than the actual words he used that annoyed İsak. 'Of course I do!' he snapped.

'Well, write your questions out for me and I'll encrypt them for you.' He then turned back to his machine and began typing once again.

Not only in English but also rendered into number language, encrypted. Mendes obviously took very few chances. Not for the first time, İsak wondered how his boss, Süleyman, was going to respond to all this cyber-subterfuge. Kasım had felt that bringing him into Hüsnü's lair – for want of a better word – would probably prove counterproductive, but İsak was no longer certain. Maybe if Süleyman could see this bizarre set-up for himself he might be more under-standing. As it was, he was going to have to go back outside to where Süleyman was waiting in his car and attempt to explain it all to him. The unspecified delay in gaining access to Mendes wasn't going to please him.

'So if I leave it with you . . .'

'I'll contact you as soon as I hear anything.'

İsak reached into his pocket for one of his cards. 'You'll need my number . . .'

'Oh, please, no paper!' Hüsnü pushed the Yezidi's hand away from him, and then picked up his mobile phone. 'What's your number?'

As İsak spoke he keyed it into the phone, which he then placed down beside the keyboard.

İsak and Kasım made ready to leave. Just before they reached the door, Hüsnü turned and said, 'Remember me in your prayers, guys.'

'What?'

'You know, Satan?' Hüsnü said glibly. 'The Evil One? The one you guys worship?'

Infuriated, İsak made as if to go back into the room. 'It isn't like that! You know nothing!'

'İsak!' Kasım, his hand firmly on his cousin's shoulder, hissed into his ear. 'Leave it!'

'But—'

'Leave it!'

And then they left, Kasım pulling İsak after him to the sound of Hüsnü's keyboard and his eerily youthful laughter.

Just before dawn, Ülkü got out of bed and went to the window. The police car was still there, in the street, its lights out, only the glow from the officers' cigarettes indicating any sign of life. While it remained there, she couldn't leave.

Her feet bare, she padded her way down the hall towards the front door of the apartment and peered through the spy hole. There was no one there and so maybe she could just slip out and down the fire escape. But then, if she did that, what of Turgut?

What had happened at Max Bey's apartment had been a shock. She'd been so pleased when she'd come back to find him gone, because it meant that she could see Turgut in peace. Not that she looked forward to all that sex business, but as a future wife she had to do that for Turgut. There had been a few moments, a minute maybe at the most, when Turgut had first arrived and she had been in the bedroom while he had been in the hall collecting his cigarettes. Not surely enough time for Turgut to hurt Max Bey? But the police still had Turgut and so maybe they had found out about that – dragged or beaten it out of him.

Ülkü began to cry. Why had Turgut told the police all those lies about her and Max Bey? She had said nothing about him not being with her the whole time. And why had he said that she had offered to do that sucking thing with him? He'd begged her to do it! And now, alone with the police, what else was Turgut saying? What other lies was he making up and why was he doing it? Could it be that he was guilty of hurting Max Bey himself in some way? He had always been very interested in the Englishman's books, his students, and whatever he said and did. He always asked her about them, sometimes every day. Why was that?

Maybe she should tell the police the whole truth herself. But then Turgut would never marry her. No. Things were bad enough anyway. Until Max Bey returned, if he returned, she couldn't even go back to the apartment. Leyla had offered her a bed only for the night – tomorrow, when Leyla's husband returned, she'd have to go. She was homeless. Every option she explored was closed to her. Until she married Turgut she couldn't be with him, and going back to her mother was unthinkable. With so many other children to care for, her mother couldn't possibly feed her.

Slowly, Ülkü walked back into the living room where Leyla had made up her bed. Vaguely aware of a car pulling up outside some moments later, she lay silent and awake until the dawn call to prayer coincided with a sharp knock on the front door.

Rakı, the strong anise-flavoured spirit that is one of the staples of every Turkish drinks cabinet, is something it is impossible not to have enough of. One shot is plenty, two excessive and any more than that may be said to constitute a suicide attempt. For some hardened souls, however, rakı can be a way of life. Rauf Ünver, second-rate jazz saxophonist, on his way home from a gig in Beyoğlu was, as ever, full of the stuff.

Of course, staying on at the club after the gig was over hadn't been a very smart move. The two bottles he'd put away with a Greek trumpet player whose name now escaped him had been even stupider. Driving home now, just after dawn, or in fact at any time of the day or night, given his current state, was insane. Putting aside the very real danger of getting arrested for drunk driving, Rauf could also look forward to a beating from his wife, who was, no doubt, already picking out a suitable weapon for this purpose.

Rauf was just weighing up the relative merits of death by samovar attack as opposed to the slower, if no less painful, prospect of being force-fed the contents of the kitchen bin (she'd done this before), when something heavy hit the bonnet of his car. Somehow he found the footbrake, stopped the car and got out. Yediküle is not one of those 24/7 districts of İstanbul. Home to the Yediküle Castle, a fortress of both Byzantine and Ottoman construction, it is a district characterised by poor but respectable families living in closely packed Greek-influenced houses. So when Rauf got out of the car there wasn't a sound save that of his own feet on the road.

Swaying, he felt only slightly, Rauf stumbled around to the front of his vehicle, which, he could now see, was spattered with what looked like blood. Just the possibility that it might be blood made him vomit immediately. Then when he saw the body lying face down in front of his wheels, he had to stick his fist in his mouth to stop himself screaming. From the look of it, the body was that of a young girl – and he had killed her.

Rauf looked around wildly at what to him was a blurred environment and then ran back to his car. There was no one about, no lights had come on in any of the windows above and, although in his drunken blurriness he'd gone far too far south, he was still only minutes from home now. If he got caught, and the police found out how much he'd had to drink, they'd put him away for ever. Whereas if he went home, washed the car and said nothing, he might get away with it. Rauf reversed his vehicle away from the body and then drove off in the direction of Zeyrek and home.

He'd been gone about five minutes when Mustafa Yenilmez, leaving for his job as a porter at the Hilton Hotel, came upon the body and raised the alarm.

Chapter 10

By the time Mehmet Süleyman arrived at the scene, Arto Sarkissian had already seen the body.

'She's a young girl, maybe sixteen or seventeen,' he said wearily as Süleyman approached him. 'Stabbed through the heart – but no weapon as yet. She's also been hit by a vehicle.'

Süleyman first rubbed his face with his hands and then lit up a cigarette. Allah alone knew what Çiçek's friends were going to make of him at her dinner party. He hadn't intended getting up this early and he looked, he knew, like something out of a zombie movie.

'Suicide?'

'My first impression is that is unlikely. It seems the car hit her *post mortem*.' The Armenian shrugged and then, moving in more closely towards Süleyman, he said, 'I think she has been sexually assaulted.'

'Like Gülay Arat?'

'Maybe.'

The two men looked at each other for a moment, their faces frozen with tension. Around them, officers moved both to secure the scene and keep local bystanders away. It was already getting hot and people were anxious to get about their daily business before the heat overwhelmed them.

A young uniformed officer and a man in what looked like a hotel porter's outfit walked over to Süleyman. The officer saluted.

'This man found the body, sir.'

Süleyman looked at the man, whose face was still white with shock.

'Mustafa Yenilmez,' he introduced himself.

'What happened, Mr Yenilmez?'

'I was on my way to work. I live just over there,' he said, pointing towards a sagging, wooden building on the corner of the street. 'I came out and here she was. I called you immediately.'

'You didn't see anyone else in the vicinity?'

'No.' He looked down at the blood-stained dust at his feet before continuing, 'I heard a car just before I left the house.'

'But you didn't see anything.'

'No.'

'All right, if you'd like to give a statement to my officer . . .'

'Yes.'

Yenilmez and the officer made off in the direction of the former's home. Süleyman watched for a moment as forensic technicians began to take casts of the tyre tracks leading away from the corpse.

'We need to find that car,' he said.

'Yes.'

Süleyman took the doctor by the elbow and led him over to his car. 'Come on.'

Once inside Süleyman's great white BMW, the two men, now away from flapping ears, began to talk.

'So I've got one boy – a suicide – one murdered girl, now possibly two,' Süleyman said.

'Identical mode if not perpetrator of said deaths and no sexual assault on the boy,' Arto continued.

'And Max Esterhazy missing, his apartment soaked in blood.'

'Yes, I heard about that,' the doctor said, 'but I have no details. It would be better to talk to Çetin İkmen and Metin İskender about that.'

'There could be a connection,' Süleyman said, and then proceeded to tell the doctor about the hacker known as Mendes and the various connections that had been made to that name.

'Yes, Mr Esterhazy was doing some research into that image for Çetin,' Arto said. 'Hulya and Berekiah were shown a most disturbing drawing of this Goat of Mendes scrawled on to the wall of the Church of the Panaghia. Çetin said that Mr Esterhazy reckoned the image was inaccurate in some way, but I don't know how.'

Süleyman sighed. 'Yes, I know about it. But I don't know what Max thought about the image – I've not seen it myself – I'll speak to Çetin.' He then put his cigarette out and lit up another. 'This city seems to be experiencing a veritable festival of unexplained death.'

The doctor shrugged. 'This new girl has no ID,' he said, returning to the practicalities of the job at hand. 'Not that anyone's been able to find.'

'If she was thrown from a car—'

'If, yes.' Arto held a warning finger up to his colleague and said, 'She was hit by a vehicle of some sort but whether she was thrown from one, I don't know. Without wishing to tell you your job, Inspector, I would, if I were you, check out the houses in the street too.'

'I'll get Çöktin on to it.' When he arrives, Süleyman added silently in his head. The Kurd had experienced, if anything, an even later night than he had. His cousin's contact to Mendes had sounded like a very odd character and his way of communicating with the hacker paranoid and tortuous. İsak was, Süleyman knew, worried in case it didn't work out. Çöktin feared, he knew, that if it didn't Süleyman would take out his frustrations on him and tell their superiors about his film subtitling operation. It wasn't outside the bounds of possibility, and, in one sense, Süleyman felt that Çöktin did deserve it, not because it was against the law but because for a serving officer it was such a stupid thing to do. But a few minutes later İsak did indeed turn up and, despite his deathly appearance, began working with a will.

Later, just after the body was removed, Süleyman phoned in a description of the victim to be circulated to all departments.

They'd been with first the boy, Turgut Can, and then his girlfriend, Ülkü Ayla, all night. And although neither İkmen nor İskender fully believed that either of them had killed Max Esterhazy, they didn't think the couple were being entirely truthful either.

'I just don't get Can's seeming obsession with Esterhazy's books,' İskender said as he slipped some papers into his briefcase.

İkmen, who was sitting on top of Sergeant Karataş' desk, yawned. 'You've not had the chance to look at them yet, Metin. Some of the photos and illustrations are titillating to say the least.'

'But why couldn't the boy buy fuck magazines like a normal person?'

'Maybe because some of the practices in Max's texts turned him on,' İkmen said. 'The combination of ritual, even if one doesn't under-stand it, and sex can be very erotic. And these books are very rare. Even in England it's difficult to get hold of some of those titles. Max has an excellent collection – all the greats of the Western magical tradition. Very powerful in the right hands, extremely perverse in some people's opinions and worth a lot of money.'

'But it would seem that Can didn't actually steal any of them,' İskender said, 'so what . . . ?'

İkmen smiled. 'Why bother when he can have a look at the naughty pictures and then fantasise while his girlfriend sucks him off? And besides, we know that Can knows Max is a magician and so he'd also, presumably, know that stealing from him would cause him to curse the perpetrator. He'd be too scared. Max's power can be very frightening.'

İskender raised a sceptical eyebrow. 'But on a more mundane note,' he said, 'do you have any idea about where Esterhazy might have gone? You know him, after all.'

'If I did I'd be looking there myself,' İkmen replied. 'To be honest, Metin, Max kept all the discrete parts of his life very sep-arate. His magical life, his teaching, his old friends . . . I know he used to order his English teaching texts from Simurg. But I don't know whether he actually knew anyone personally in or around the bookshop.'

'Maybe we should check it out.'

'Yes,' İkmen sighed. 'There's a lot to do. I also need to find his address book, which may well help, and I want to get over to the Mısır Çarşısı too.'

'Ah.'

'Yes. The spice vendor Ülkü used to get sent to for various ingre-dients.' He looked down at the notes he had taken of his most recent interview with the girl. 'Someone called Doğa at Afrodite Pazarı. Apparently, he could always get whatever oddity Max was after. Maybe he is a magical practitioner of some sort himself.'

'Allah protect us!' İskender rolled his eyes heavenwards. 'I can't cope with all this unreality!'

'Then maybe you should busy yourself with obtaining the records of telephone calls to and from Max's apartment,' İkmen said. 'And if you can chase up that blood work I'm sure that Forensic will thank you for it. I always lose my temper with them.'

'Seems sensible,' İskender said as he opened his office door to let İkmen through. 'Now I'm going to go home, get a shower, have a rest and then come back and start again. Mr Can's lawyer is with him at the moment. Perhaps things in that quarter, and possibly with Miss Ayla too, will have changed by the time I get back.'

İkmen started to make his way back to his office, thinking all the while about Ülkü Ayla and how sorry he felt for her. Max had probably worked to educate and protect Ülkü, a young country girl, but not to excess. After all, Max was a liberal as well as a magician. People, Max had often said, must be free to follow their own will, even if that desire is flawed. Nevertheless, Turgut Can had obviously not been approved of. And if Max had thought for a second that he was forcing Ülkü to give him oral sex, he would have dealt with him. One thing he would never have done, though, was use Ülkü for himself. That was patently ridiculous. There had been, as İkmen – and he alone, he believed – knew, no one since Alison. But that wasn't something he wanted to bring up unless he absolutely had to . . .

'Çetin, do you have a few minutes?'

İkmen looked up into the sunken eyes of Mehmet Süleyman. Allah, but how his poor friend had suffered these past few months!

Forcing a smile, İkmen pulled the chair over from Ayşe Farsakoğlu's desk and motioned for Süleyman to join him.

'Please.'

'When is Sergeant Farsakoğlu due back from her vacation?' Süleyman asked, observing the even more dire than usual state of İkmen's office.

'İnşallah, on Monday.'

Süleyman smiled. 'Çetin,' he said, 'I think that you and I need to liaise about this Mendes connection. I know we've spoken before, but perhaps we need to think again.'

'Yes. Your hacker,' İkmen said, 'and my Satanic image.'

He bent down to open his desk drawer just as Süleyman's mobile began to ring. He didn't, as he put one of Max's books on to his desk, listen to the short conversation that passed between Süleyman

109

and Arto Sarkissian, but at the end of it he noticed that Mehmet looked even graver than he had done when he arrived.

'This is the actual Goat of Mendes,' İkmen said as he opened the book at the relevant page. 'It's not always represented in such a . . . a graphic fashion, shall we say, but this is the illustration that was open on Max's desk when we entered the apartment. The Goat in the act of initiating one of his acolytes.'

The picture, a woodcut, showed a man with a goat's head and hoofs, having intercourse from behind with a wanton and ecstatic-looking young woman.

When Süleyman didn't answer, İkmen continued, 'It says in the text that the Goat's penis is ice cold. Some acolytes describe it as metallic . . .'

'Çetin, another girl was discovered with a knife in her heart this morning. Dr Sarkissian has just told me that this second girl, like the first, was assaulted from behind with something he thinks might have been made of metal. He's just confirmed that the girl was murdered.'

The two men looked at each other for a moment, sweat running down their faces.

'Max told me that he'd recently had an altercation with some Satanists. He said he'd seen them off,' İkmen frowned. 'Maybe he only thought that he had.'

'Maybe. One boy has committed suicide with a knife, two girls have been murdered.'

'I don't know where suicide comes into it,' İkmen said, 'but then what do I know? The thing I asked Max to look at, the image scrawled on the wall of the Panaghia, was what Max described as atypical.'

'The one with thirteen penises?'

İkmen went into his drawer again and retrieved his Polaroid photograph of the drawing.

'Max had never seen anything like it before. Two penises, yes sometimes, but not thirteen. He was looking into its possible origins when he disappeared – or whatever.'

'Do you think he could have disappeared *because* he was looking into its possible origins?'

'I don't know,' İkmen sighed. 'So what of your Mendes, Mehmet? The hacker?'

'Not an easy person to contact,' Süleyman replied. 'I've left it with Çöktin. In light of what we've been talking about, however, I think I do need to reinstruct him. I know Çöktin doubts any Satanic connection to his hacker, but the name Mendes is a very unusual one. Maybe we need to ask Mendes why he uses it.'

'You need to be careful how you do that,' İkmen said. 'People involved in magic are very secretive – they look for double meanings in everything. And so if he is into Satanism and he does suspect you are on to him he will disappear. Not literally, of course, but—'

'I know what you mean, Çetin.'

'Conversely, there may be no connection at all between your hacker and either the suicide, the murders or Max. I mean, your actual aim in contacting him is to get help from him to trace those weird messages on the kids' computers.'

'Yes.' Süleyman did, for just a second, think about telling İkmen how and why Çöktin knew so much about Mendes, but then he thought better of it. Çetin was, he knew, far safer if he didn't know, both from their own superiors and what would be his own divided loyalties.

'So I'd do that,' İkmen said. 'What else are you doing?'

Süleyman went through a list of avenues he was currently exploring finishing with '. . . and although Gülay got out of the scene, I still want to talk to these Goths. I don't know why, but I feel that the Goth scene was, if not the cause, then the gateway to whatever the girl subsequently became involved with. And if this new victim was involved as well . . .'

'I'm not saying kids into Gothic clothes and black and everything are necessarily Satanists,' İkmen said, 'but I would go along with you about the gateway theory. After all, if you're going to recruit people to the cause of evil, why not do so from amongst the ranks of those who already wear the uniform and love the colour scheme?'

Süleyman smiled.

'So what are your plans for getting to these kids, Mehmet?' İkmen asked. 'They're not easy to access.'

'Gülay used to go around with a little group of friends. I've interviewed one already. I'm in the process of contacting the others.'

İkmen riffled in his pockets for his cigarettes and when he'd found them he first offered one to Süleyman and then lit up himself.

'Do you honestly think they'll tell you anything, Mehmet?'

'I don't know.'

'I think it's unlikely.' İkmen remained silent for a few moments, biting down on his bottom lip until he said, 'Have you ever considered sending someone in to these clubs, undercover?'

'I have but that takes time.'

'If only we had an "in" on the scene, eh?'

'Yes,' Süleyman replied, 'if only we did.' And then he leaned back into his chair and smoked in silence for a while. He was, İkmen felt, mulling over something, possibly difficult, in his head.

Before İskender returned, İkmen felt a visit back to Max's apartment was imperative. Whatever Süleyman might or might not be doing, it was important for him to try to track down Max's address book and find his friends – if indeed he had any.

İsak Çöktin entered the house in the middle of the block just before midday. An extensive search had been made of the other properties in the street, including the one outside of which the girl's body had been found. This one, however, number eight, had been empty for a number of years, which in such an overcrowded area struck Çöktin as odd.

'It is a place of mischievous djinn,' a local woman explained just before the officers entered. 'Sometimes at night you can hear them about their naughty ways.'

Or, Çöktin felt, the rather more likely scenario of kids getting in there to sniff gas and beat the place up. However, once he'd entered the upper storey of the property he quickly changed his mind. Whatever one might think of the street kids, they rarely actually killed each other, which is what must have happened in that room.

'There's blood everywhere, sir,' he said when he telephoned Süleyman.

'OK, we'll need a comparison with the blood of the victim. I'll order a full forensic examination.'

'Right.'

Once the call was over, Çöktin placed his phone back in his pocket. But it rang again almost immediately.

'Çöktin.'

'Mendes has just replied to my message,' a smooth, if slightly hyper voice said. 'He'd like to talk to you.'

'I assume you mean over the Net,' Çöktin replied.

Hüsnü laughed. 'I'm not even going to dignify that with an answer.'

'What do you want me to do?'

'It's up to you. I'm always here.' And then he cut the connection.

Man of mystery, Hüsnü, or at least that was what he wanted to be. Quite what he was, aside from a techno-junkie with money, Çöktin didn't know or even really want to be concerned about. But he would go out to Cihangir once he'd settled things in Yediküle – if indeed things could be settled. He'd seen some gruesome crime scenes in his time, but nothing quite like this. There had, it seemed, been a torrent of blood let loose in this creaking wooden room. Whoever had killed her must have thrown her body around in order to get this awful spattering effect. For some reason. Dr Sarkissian was, he knew, of the opinion that the girl, like Gülay Arat, had been sexually assaulted by someone. In addition, someone, probably her killer, must have thrown her body out of the window and into the street as the ledge was too high for her to have fallen without assistance. But why the seemingly wild distribution of blood? Anyone in the room with her must have been covered in the stuff. But then maybe that was the point of the exercise.

The not inconsiderable number of half-eaten limes that littered the floor were, however, rather less comprehensible.

İkmen had seen Max refer to his address book on many occasions and so he recognised it immediately. Old, black and held together with elastic bands, Max's book was, İkmen thought with a smile, exactly what one would have expected of him. What, however, was unexpected was the fact that he couldn't read it.

'Oh, Max,' he murmured as he turned over pages filled with what looked like random letters and numbers. 'What is this?'

That Max was a magician was something İkmen knew would complicate matters. If his understanding was correct, when one moved in higher arcane circles one was more likely to pursue secrecy in all aspects of one's life. But quite where a person might begin to unravel such a system or systems he didn't know. As well as being a Kabbalist, Max had also studied Enochian magic, Egyptian magic and was well-versed in the rites and rituals of pre-Christian England and Scandinavia. Max had once told him that some of the systems he used involved alphabets that were quite different from the Roman or Turkish alphabets. Not that the address book gave any evidence of those. Numbers, some of which were recognisable as telephone numbers, were listed alphabetically according to the Turkish system. So under S, for instance, there was a list of numbers all prefixed by, first, S, then a one- or two-digit number followed by either a foreign or domestic telephone number. There were no actual addresses at all, just more numbers, in groups that could, İkmen felt, be some sort of coded address. But how he could decipher such a thing without Max's mind to guide him, he didn't know.

There were code breakers. MİT had people who worked on codes all the time – shadowy people, dedicated to the protection of the state and therefore, of necessity, unknown and unknowable. İkmen had only ever, metaphorically, brushed against such people during the course of his career and he was quite glad about that. Intelligence agents were not people it was either wise or beneficial to be in contact with. And although İkmen had little doubt that these people could help him with Max's code, he was not going to give it to them. Apart from anything else, they'd ask why he was so interested in the book, which would lead to all sorts of explanations he didn't really want to get into. And anyway, with Max only officially missing, that was going a bit far. Maybe, he thought, I should just call some of these numbers that look local and see what happens.

But then maybe not. İkmen put the address book to one side and then took one of the big tomes down from Max's shelf. *Malleus Maleficarum* – the so-called *Hammer of the Witches*, a fifteenth-century treatise on how to spot witches and magicians and bring them to 'justice'. Not that İkmen could read this obviously old book. But he knew of it, and as he turned it over in his hands he reasoned that it was probably of nineteenth-century production. Still rare and probably obtained back in England as opposed to from the shelves at Simurg.

However, if Max hadn't obtained this book and others like it from

114

England, then where, locally, could he possibly have got them from? There was only one place and it wasn't Simurg or any other bookshop – İkmen could easily go there and then drop down the hill to the Mısır Çarşısı and the man known as Doğa. He moved over to the window and looked at the view of the Imperial Tombs that Max so much enjoyed. The Sahaflar, the book market, was only a few minutes down the road.

Zuleika had certainly improved her social standing since their divorce. Her second husband, Burhan Topal, was obviously deriving a very good living from his now established and respected media agency. As Süleyman walked through the gates leading up to the couple's Büyükada yalı, or summer house, he couldn't help but be impressed by the sight of several gardeners tending the very green lawn as well as ministering to the numerous flowerbeds. The view from the front of the property, of Heybeliada, floating majestically amid the deep blueness of the Sea of Marmara, in the summer was magnificent.

But then, as Süleyman observed while he waited for someone to answer the doorbell, Zuleika had been born and bred in the Princes' Islands. In fact her mother, his Aunt Edibe, still lived only ten minutes away down the hill on Çankaya Caddesi. As a child, he had often been brought out here to visit his mother's sister and her family. Like his mother, his aunt had married into a family connected, if in this case loosely, to the old Ottoman élite. His marriage to his cousin Zuleika, with whom he had never been close, had been at the instigation of these two powerful Anatolian women. It had been a mistake.

They were taking a long time to answer the door. He'd telephoned ahead. He'd spoken to Burhan Bey's daughter, Fitnat, and told her he was coming to speak to her father. On the street in front of the house a phaeton, driven by a gypsy and full of white-uniformed naval cadets, passed by on its way to the summit of the island's southern hill. No cars are allowed on the islands and so people have to get around by either phaeton, bicycle or on horseback. All laughing, their voices full of youthful arrogance, the cadets and their transport presented a particularly nineteenth-century tableau as they jogged past houses that had once belonged to luminaries in the old Imperial order.

There was and always had been an overpoweringly *fin de siècle* atmosphere in the islands. Perhaps that was why he still had a sneaking affection for them.

'Mehmet Bey.'

He turned round and smiled at the girl standing in the doorway.

'Hello, Fitnat.'

She was wearing something he felt might be more appropriate to a film set. The skirt, which was made up of several layers of black lace, hit the ground in a welter of ruched satin that matched the very tightly fitted bodice above. Pulled in via a row of laces at the front, this bodice, while accentuating much, didn't cover a great deal.

'Come in,' she said. 'I've set a table out by the pool.' She turned to look at him with undisguised appreciation. 'You don't mind being outside?'

'No. As long as that is agreeable to your father.'

She led him through the central sofa area of the yalı and out into the extensive gardens at the back of the property. Although Süleyman observed that the furnishings in the yalı were all very tasteful, they were far from contemporary. Zuleika hadn't, he thought, put her mark on it yet. But then, she'd only been married to Burhan for a year – barely enough time to get settled, really. And besides, to do too much too soon would not be politic in this case. Zuleika's husband, widowed only five years previously, was a lot older than she was and still, it was said, revered the memory of his first wife, Fitnat's mother.

The Topals' swimming pool was large and very clear. Very inviting, in fact, to a hot and tired policeman in a suit. Fitnat, or rather one of the little servant girls Süleyman had seen dotted around the house and out on the terrace, had set a table and two chairs under a willow tree at the top end of the pool.

'Would you like tea or a cold drink?' Fitnat said as she pulled one of the chairs out for Süleyman.

'Tea would be very good, thank you,' Süleyman said as he sat down.

'OK.'

She left to go into the house, her heavy skirts leaving a ridge in the grass as she moved. Having observed the ashtray on the table before him, Süleyman lit a cigarette and waited for his host to arrive.

But when the tea, borne on a tray by a girl several years younger than Fitnat, made its appearance, only Burhan Bey's daughter came with it.

'Where is your father?' Süleyman asked.

'Oh, Daddy had to go out,' Fitnat said breezily as she sat down next to him and then dismissed the servant with a silent wave of her hand. 'He had business in Taksim.'

Süleyman sighed. 'I came to see your father, Fitnat. You told me he was going to be here.'

'He had to go out,' she shrugged. 'Daddy's a very busy man.'

'Fitnat, it is important that I speak to your father.'

'Why?' She looked across at him with mildly amused imperiousness. 'Is Daddy in trouble?'

'No.'

'Well, then why—'

'I wanted to ask your father for some assistance,' Süleyman said as he took a sip from his tea glass and then placed it down on the table again.

'With what?' Fitnat leaned forward across the table towards him and smiled. 'Anything I can help you with?'

It was about Fitnat that he'd come. When he'd seen İkmen that morning, the older man had said what a shame it was they didn't have an 'in' on the Goth scene. It had come to him at that moment: Fitnat. Zuleika might like to get the girl pretty dresses and fool herself that the child was 'growing out of it' but Fitnat was still out and about with the Goths – as he'd seen with his own eyes up in Karaköy. However, if he was going to ask her about what she and her friends got up to in Atlas Pasaj he would have to obtain her father's permission first. But Burhan Bey was out and had been, he now suspected, when he'd called just over two hours before. Fitnat, as seemed to be her custom with older men, or at least with him, appeared to be set upon trying to seduce him.

'Oh, it's so hot, isn't it?' she said as she just very slightly loosened the laces of her bodice. 'I think I might have to have a swim in a minute.'

'And I think that I should go,' Süleyman said as he rose quickly to his feet.

'Oh, but—'

'Fitnat, I came to get your father's permission to ask you some questions.'

She looked up, her black-rimmed eyes wide with curiosity. 'Well, ask them,' she said. 'I'm a grown-up . . .'

'No . . .'

'Yes, I am!' She stood up to face him, her hands on her hips. 'And if Daddy were here he'd agree with me.' Then dropping her voice slightly she smiled. 'Ask your questions, Mehmet Bey, and I will decide whether or not I am prepared to answer them.'

He should just go. Young and, as he suspected, inexperienced as she was, someone like Fitnat could be dangerous. But then again, she might provide him with useful information, and he had come a long way, across the Marmara, on a ferry, full of day-trippers . . .

'All right,' he said as he sat back down again, 'all right, if you want to help me, I'll—'

'Just ask for what you want, Mehmet Bey,' Fitnat said, 'whatever that may be.'

At first she looked quite disappointed when he said he wanted to talk to her about her interest in Gothic fashion and music. But then as she warmed to what was a very interesting topic for her, her seductiveness returned and, this time, he responded to it in a far more humorous manner.

'So why don't you tell me what it's like in Atlas Pasaj?' he said.

She looked him in the eyes and smiled. 'It's loud, it's always full of people and the clothes are very, very Dracula,' she said.

'So,' he said, groping really for ways to get at the information that he felt he needed, 'how does a person get to be part of the scene?'

It seemed, from what she told him, that most people came to Atlas Pasaj via their friends.

'You get the odd person who comes on their own,' Fitnat said, 'but they're usually the real weirdos, you know. Like people who think they're really vampires.'

Süleyman frowned. Only two years before he'd come across a boy who thought he was a vampire. He'd been – for he was dead now – English. Süleyman remembered thinking at the time how strange and exotic this young man had been. Now, apparently, his way of life had come to İstanbul. How quickly things changed in the city these days!

'But I don't hang out with people like that,' Fitnat continued. 'My friends and I like the music and the clothes but we don't go in for all that devil stuff.'

'Devil stuff?'

'Zuleika gets scared that I might be associating with people who worship the Devil,' Fitnat laughed. 'It's why she wants me to stop going to Atlas and start wearing pretty dresses. Personally, I think that the Gothic look is very pretty. What do you think, Mehmet Bey?'

He smiled. 'I think you should tell me about the devil stuff, Fitnat.'

Annoyed that he had evaded her question, Fitnat shrugged. 'I told you, I don't have anything to do with that. It's stupid.'

'What's stupid about it?'

'Oh, everything. Their stupid cutting – they cut their arms and legs sometimes – letting blood for the Devil.' She rolled her eyes impatiently. 'And their stupid language . . .'

'Their language?' Süleyman felt himself tense.

Fitnat threw a disinterested hand into the air. 'Just words, really,' she said. 'They put them into their conversations and only they can understand them. It's pathetic.'

'So you can't . . .'

'No, but one of my friends can understand some of it.'

'A friend involved in devil stuff?'

'İlhan? No!' she laughed. 'That's all much too masculine for him. No, he spent some time with a boy who was into it about a year ago.'

'İlhan and this boy were . . . ?'

'They both shared a love of women's clothes, if you know what I mean,' Fitnat said. Then leaning in towards Süleyman she added, 'That's why İlhan is only my friend, you see, Mehmet Bey. He isn't a real man.'

'No.' Süleyman cleared his throat nervously. This girl was giving him some really illuminating information. The language some of these kids used was of particular interest. Maybe if this was the same as that used by the mysterious Communion and Nika they might be getting somewhere. 'Do you think that your friend İlhan would be willing to speak to me about this language?'

119

'No.' Her face suddenly dropped into a straight, almost prim expression. 'No, he wouldn't.'

'Why not?'

'Because all of that stuff is upsetting for him.'

'Why?'

The thin branches of the willow that enclosed them rustled gently in the very small, hot breeze.

'Fitnat?'

'The boy he got to know, the one who used to like women's clothes – İlhan heard that he stabbed himself. He died.'

Süleyman felt his face go pale. 'When?'

'When we went to Atlas for İlhan's birthday.'

'No, when did this boy—'

'I don't know,' Fitnat said. 'İlhan hadn't seen him for a long time. They don't hang around Atlas for too long, not those real intellectual devilly types. I think they must go somewhere else.'

'Where?'

'I don't know.'

'Do you know this boy's name? This friend of İlhan?'

'No.' She put a hand on to his arm. 'You're very interested in all this devil stuff, aren't you, Mehmet Bey?'

He smiled. Could it be that this İlhan's dead friend was Cem Ataman?

'Fitnat, I will have to speak to İlhan.'

'Why?' She was drawing circles on his arm with one long, black varnished nail.

'I can't tell you that.'

'Why not?'

'Because it – look, Fitnat, I just can't . . .'

She looked up into his eyes and smiled. 'But, Mehmet Bey, how can I ask İlhan to help you if I don't know what you want help with?'

İlhan, Süleyman knew, could very easily be induced to tell him everything that he knew. But, seemingly mesmerised by this girl's seductive antics, he hesitated.

Fitnat took her hand away from his arm and then placed one of her fingers in her mouth. She made great play of savouring this digit before saying, 'Your suit tastes very nice, Mehmet Bey.'

'Fitnat . . .'

'You know, I've seen the way my stepmother looks at you and I don't think that she should be doing that,' Fitnat said as she took one of his hands and began moving it up towards her breast. 'She's a married woman . . .'

'Stop it!' Süleyman hissed as he pulled his hand away from her.

'Stop what?'

'Stop slandering your stepmother and stop trying to get me to touch you!' He stood up. 'Because I'm not interested,' he said. 'I came here to speak to you about aspects of your lifestyle that may prove instructive in relation to an investigation.'

'I don't know whether my daddy would believe you,' Fitnat said with a seductive pout. 'Coming here, to a girl on her own . . .'

'Don't threaten me!'

The girl's face darkened. With her jaw set in anger she suddenly looked most unattractive. 'Don't you dare reject me!' she spat. 'My friends saw me talking to you the other evening. They'll tell my father you made suggestions to me. Who do you think he'll believe?'

'I need to speak to İlhan, Fitnat. People's lives could depend upon it!'

'Then you'd better do as I ask,' she said as she twined one of her arms around his neck. 'Daddy's going to be out for hours.'

'Yes, but I'm here.' The voice was female. Both Fitnat and Süleyman turned towards it.

'Zuleika!'

'Go to your room, Fitnat. I'll deal with you later.'

Fitnat released Süleyman and then ran over to her stepmother. 'Zuleika, he tried—'

'Go!'

Her face red with either fury or frustration or both, Fitnat ran crying back towards the house. 'Slut!' she screamed. 'You're not good enough for my father!'

When she had gone, Zuleika sighed. 'I'm so sorry about that, Mehmet,' she said.

'You heard?'

'Enough, yes,' she said. 'Since her mother's death, Fitnat has been quite out of control. I don't know why you're here but I know it was for an honourable reason.'

'I need to contact her friend İlhan.'

'And she said she'd give you his details if you slept with her?' Zuleika smiled. 'She thinks it's a way of getting at me. I'm so sorry that you got involved.' She moved towards him and put her hands around his face. 'Still so handsome. It's such a curse. I'm so glad we're only friends now.'

He smiled.

'If you want to contact her friend İlhan, I'll give you his details,' Zuleika said as she moved away from him again.

'You know this boy?'

'No,' Zuleika said, 'but I follow her on occasion. She's a nasty spoiled little brat, but I am afraid for her, Mehmet. She goes to some bad places. I have to protect her, for Burhan's sake. If anything happened to her, it would destroy him and I couldn't take that.' She looked grave. 'I care for Burhan, Mehmet – he's my very best friend. If anything happened to him I don't know what I'd do.'

Chapter 11

Fortunately for Çöktin, the address Süleyman had given him was very close to Hüsnü's place in Cihangir. This meant that once he'd spoken to İlhan Koç, he could just walk over to the hacker's high-tech apartment. He'd have to dispense with the two uniforms he had with him now, of course, but that wouldn't be a problem – depending, of course, on what the Koç boy had to say.

The name Cem Ataman was familiar. They had, İlhan said, been no more than friends. Cem, who İlhan described as a 'straight' boy, had been more interested in his clothes than anything else. Although not what Çöktin would have described as a transvestite, İlhan was certainly a boy who enjoyed the pleasures of women's clothing and make-up. Wearing a red silk Chinese-style blouse over very tight-fitting jeans, İlhan Koç was sexless rather than effeminate. Although wearing carefully applied lipstick, eyeliner and mascara, his hair, which was styled upwards in sharp points, lent an almost aggressive masculinity to his tall thin figure.

'I think he got in with me because he thought I was something I'm not.' İlhan looked over at the two straight-faced uniforms sitting across from them and then leaned in towards Çöktin. 'Some of the, you know, the real nutters down at Atlas like to dress like I do,' he said. 'Very flamboyant. Particularly in the Hammer.'

'Which is a bar?'

'Yes. My friends and I don't go there,' he said, adding darkly, 'it's too much.'

'What do you mean?'

'I mean that I like the clothes and the music and everything, but all that perverse stuff isn't for me.'

'Perverse stuff?'

İlhan moved still closer and whispered, 'Sexual confusion. Men dressing as women, women beating them. They all cut each other in the Hammer and there is talk of devil worship.'

'Which Cem Ataman was interested in?'

'Yes.' İlhan looked down at the floor, his face straight and sad. 'Or rather he was interested in learning the words they all use down there – which I taught him.'

Çöktin raised an eyebrow. 'Words?'

'The Hammer people use the same secret words as the trans-sexuals,' he said. 'I have a friend of that . . . persuasion, a transsexual, who taught me.'

'When you were maybe considering becoming a transsexual your-self?' Çöktin asked.

İlhan looked away. 'I'm not prepared to answer that.' And then turning his head back to face Çöktin again, he said, 'All you need to know is that some people in the Hammer also use the same words. It's how they pass messages between them they don't want others to understand.'

'But you do, right?'

İlhan sighed. 'Yes.'

'So you know that people in the Hammer are actively worshipping the Devil?'

'No.'

'But you just said—'

'I know that they want to,' he said, 'but whether anything other than sex actually goes on, I don't know. There are a lot of people there who just, I think, play about with the idea. I said that to Cem when he asked, but he still wanted to learn the words anyway. Cem was a bit, you know, intellectual. He knew, I think, a lot about devil worship.'

'And so he wanted to meet others of his kind?'

'Yes. Although I don't think that the Hammer provided him with anything.'

'Why not?'

'Because he didn't stick around for very long. I met him a couple of times and we talked, and then I think he went to the Hammer maybe once or twice on his own, and then nothing. I can't have seen him for eight months or so. I was very shocked to hear that he'd com-mitted suicide.'

'Have you heard of any others interested in diabolism who have gone on to kill themselves?'

'No.'

'So Cem's death and his interests could be unconnected?'

'Yes,' İlhan looked down at the floor again, 'and no. Some of the things they do in the Hammer are pretty odd. The cutting and the beating and everything. Like I'm always saying to my friends, if you get mixed up in those things . . .'

'These secret words,' Çöktin said. 'Give me an example.'

İlhan had been surprisingly accommodating up until this point but now he drew the line.

Çöktin, who had taken the precaution of returning to the station after Süleyman's call, took a piece of paper out of his pocket and looked down at it.

'So if I were to say the word "madi" to you, or maybe "haş gagi" . . .' He could see İlhan's face pale beneath his thick, pancake make-up. 'Words used, we think, to maybe communicate instructions to Cem and possibly others over the Internet . . .'

'You mean devilish things?'

'Maybe.'

And so, with a sigh, İlhan told Çöktin what the words meant. '"Madi" means ugly,' he said, 'and a "haş gagi" is a real woman.'

'What do you mean, "real" woman?'

'Not a transvestite, someone born a woman who has had sex with a man – not a girl, in other words.'

Çöktin frowned. The unknown person called Nika had referred to Gülay Arat as someone about to become a haş gagi. Nika, therefore, must have known the girl was about to have sex. But did Nika know with whom?

'Do you have any idea about the origins of these words?' Çöktin asked.

İlhan shrugged. 'My friend says it's a mixture of Armenian, Ladıno and gypsy, but I don't know.'

'Do you know anything about people using these words in news-groups?'

'No,' İlhan replied. 'Or rather, I don't have any direct experience myself. I know people do that, but I don't.'

125

'What people?'

İlhan, aware that this conversation was going in a direction he felt he didn't like, said, 'I'm not prepared to name anyone, you know. My friends are quite innocent.'

'You'll do what you have to,' Çöktin said softly. 'And that means telling me what I need to know.'

The Sahaflar, the courtyard of booksellers, can either be entered from Beyazıt Square or from inside the Grand Bazaar. This tranquil square of bookshops, based around a bust of İbrahim Müteferrika – the man who in 1729 produced the first printed book in Turkish – has an impressive pedigree. Built on the site of a Byzantine book and paper market, the Sahaflar sells books, both new and second-hand, of all sorts. It is a favourite haunt of students who come, mainly, to buy second-hand textbooks, of tourists, and of the generally curious on the lookout for ancient copies of the Koran or 1950s editions of Ambler, Greene and Amis classics.

Many of the booksellers, it is said, are dervishes, Islamic mystics who practise musical and dance-based rituals in order to achieve spiritual enlightenment. Like mystics of all hues – like Maximillian Esterhazy – dervishes are usually very informed about the mysticisms of other faiths and are frequently well read. If, as İkmen hoped, Max was wont sometimes to purchase books from the Sahaflar, maybe he got into conversation with the learned vendors too. It would have been typical of him.

The only problem İkmen had now was where to start. He knew a few of the men by sight, mainly through his friendship with Berekiah's employer, Lazar Bey. But it was one thing to nod to a man occasionally and quite another to ask him about a foreign magician who was currently a missing person. After all, if he wanted to get anything useful out of these men, the heavy policeman stance wasn't going to help him. So what position should he take?

İkmen was just scanning his eyes across a pile of what looked like early twentieth-century religious texts when he noticed something very bright shimmer up in front of him.

'Hello, Inspector.'

The voice, which was dark brown, bordering on black, was as

instantly familiar as the wild profusion of colours and jewels that were distributed across and around her body. Gonca the gypsy, smiling, put her cigar back into her mouth and reached out a large hand towards İkmen.

'I enjoyed your daughter's wedding enormously,' she said. 'Such a beautiful couple!'

'Thank you,' İkmen smiled. 'You did a very good job, Gonca.'

The gypsy shrugged. İkmen had employed her to read cards for the wedding guests which, together with champagne drinking, was a duty she had performed with plenty of enthusiasm. But Gonca was far more than just a card reader. She was a visual artist too, and one whose work, much of which incorporated magical themes, was greatly in demand amongst the chattering classes. Not needing to buy any-thing second-hand any more, she'd obviously come to the Sahaflar for her own amusement.

'So what are you looking for today?' Gonca said. 'Some treatise maybe on the Kabbalistic symbolism of tarot?' She smiled. 'You know, your eldest daughter has a very natural relationship with sym-bolic . . .'

'You are not the only person who thinks that my Çiçek is a tal-ented young lady,' İkmen said. 'Can I buy you a glass of tea?'

They went to the tea garden in Beyazıt Square. As usual, it was full of students as well as the odd peripatetic Eastern European selling trinkets from whatever 'old country' he or she came from.

When they'd got their tea, İkmen said, 'I came down here to speak to the book men about magical volumes.'

'Then you came to the right place.'

İkmen lit a cigarette and then cleared his throat. 'Look, Gonca,' he said, 'I have a bit of a problem. A friend of mine has gone missing, a magician . . .'

'Oh, that's out of my league, I'm afraid, Inspector,' she said. 'Magicians are quite beyond the knowledge of a humble gypsy.'

'What do you mean?'

'I mean that if this friend of yours is a real magician there is no way someone like myself can help you. If he or she is missing then there is probably a very good reason for that – even if it is some-thing you or I may never understand.'

'Well, to be honest, I'm not talking to you because I think you might be able to help,' İkmen said. 'But on the basis that my friend may have used the Sahaflar in order to purchase books I thought I might engage one of the vendors in conversation . . .'

'And, when you saw me, you thought that perhaps I may be able to help you find the right person,' she smiled, and then turning a little to her left she pointed to a very small, bespectacled man sitting alone at a table underneath a tree. ' İbrahim Dede specialises in esoteric texts,' she said. 'He is very learned.'

İkmen apologised profusely for disturbing the old man's leisure, but he just waved this away with one impatient hand. Any friend of Gonca Hanım was, he said with a serious expression on his face, a friend of his. Without actually naming him, İkmen described Max's interests, his lifestyle and said, without going into detail, that he was missing. As it turned out İbrahim Dede didn't need names to know exactly what İkmen was talking about.

'Maximillian Esterhazy has purchased books from me for nearly thirty years,' İbrahim Dede said, with a mischievous twinkle in his eyes. 'You know he studied under Rebbe Baruh?'

'Who?'

İbrahim Dede threw his hands up in surprise. 'Rebbe Baruh! An unparalleled Kabbalist,' he lowered his voice to a whisper, 'a man whose eyes had looked upon the face of the Almighty! Maximillian has his knowledge and is therefore capable of most things.'

'What do you mean?' İkmen asked.

'Kabbalists, real Kabbalists,' Gonca said, 'not stumbling amateurs like me, can do things that, to most people, would seem to be impossible.'

'If Maximillian doesn't want you to find him, then he will be able to disappear,' the old man said. 'He could very well still be in his apartment; he could even be watching us now.'

İkmen instinctively turned round but there was no one except a group of the ubiquitous university students to be seen. 'Yes, but why . . . ?'

'I don't know,' İbrahim Dede shrugged. 'Maybe he is working to restore the balance in this city. It has become very dark of late.'

'Dark?'

'Places of worship have been desecrated. You must know of this?'

'I know of one,' İkmen said. 'I consulted Max about it. Are there others?'

'Oh, yes. Ignorant and dangerous images fouling the light,' he smiled. 'These create a lack of balance between what you would call good and evil. I have observed similar phenomena several times over the years. They tend to occur at dangerous times, like now.'

'You mean, I assume,' İkmen said, 'this conflict between Saddam Hussein and the Americans.'

'Indeed. So many questions, so many threats. Does Saddam have these chemical weapons of which George Bush speaks? Does Iraq harbour terrorists? And, most importantly for us, which way is our government going to jump? Will we go to war too?'

İkmen, for whom, through his soon-to-be-conscripted son, these concerns were very current, lowered his head. 'But the image that I have seen,' he said, 'on a church – it was, so Max said, inaccurate.'

'The Goat of Mendes is a powerful negative image,' the old man said gravely. 'Even if some renditions do possess too many organs of generation.'

'You know . . .'

'Of course I do! Foul images like that have been appearing for some weeks. The forces of destruction are gathering in this city. I must, like any right-minded person, like Maximillian, do what I can to restore the balance.'

İkmen, who was becoming a little tired of such oblique conversation, said, 'Look, İbrahim Dede, I know that you mean well, but I need to find Max.'

The old man shrugged. 'I don't know where he is, Inspector.'

'Well, is there anywhere you think he might be? I mean, in order to counteract this "darkness" you speak of.'

'There are many possibilities,' İbrahim Dede said as he crossed his hands in front of himself on the table. 'If he knows who is pouring this negativity into our city, then he may well be pursuing them. If he doesn't then he may be enacting countermeasures.'

'What do you mean?'

'Performing rituals designed to redress the natural order of things. Maximillian is a great lover of İstanbul.' He looked across at Gonca.

'Who knows? Maximillian is a Kabbalist, I am not.'

'I don't suppose this Rebbe Baruh is still alive, is he?' İkmen asked.

'No. Maximillian is, as far as I am aware, the only ritual magician in this city now.'

'So what you're saying is that finding him is going to be well-nigh impossible?'

İbrahim Dede sighed. 'I think that without some knowledge about Kabbalah you are going to find it difficult. To the outsider the Kabbalistic system of symbolic and numerical correspondences can seem impenetrable.'

İkmen took Max's address book out of his pocket and opened it up on the table. 'You mean like this?' he said.

The old man peered down at the book through the lower half of his glasses. 'I have no idea what this might mean,' he said. 'I am, as I've said before, no Kabbalist.'

Gonca, who had been looking down at the book also, said, 'Maybe you could try and call some of these numbers and see who you get.'

'Yes, I've thought of that.'

'This page, A,' she said, 'could be a lot of people called Ahmet, Ayşe, Abdullah.'

'And the digits in front of the telephone numbers?'

She shrugged. 'Correspondences of some sort? Like İbrahim Dede says, for Kabbalists everything is about correspondences. Each day of the week and then every hour of the day is ruled by a planet. Each planet corresponds to a Sephira, which is a characteristic of both God and man that come together in the central image of Kabbalah, the Tree of Life.'

'Everything is interconnected.'

'Yes! Each Sephira has its correspondent tarot card, zodiac sign, angels, demons, jewels, food, perfumes associated with it. As above, so below, İkmen,' Gonca said. 'That which is in heaven and that upon earth are one and the same and are completely interchangeable.'

'Which is exactly what a magician does, isn't it? He substitutes things, one for another, thereby manipulating matter via media like cards, visualisation, ritual.'

'Indeed,' İbrahim Dede smiled. 'And when my fellows and myself turn in the sacred sema ritual of our founder the beloved Rumi, we on earth emulate the celestial spheres, become them indeed as we reach towards union with the universe and Allah. Maximillian could be anywhere in this world – or another.'

İbrahim Dede's eyes twinkled again and, just for a moment, İkmen had the feeling that he was being drawn, as if mesmerised, into their depths. And so, thanking the tiny old man and the bright gorgeous woman, he left and made his way down towards Eminönü and the far more temporal charms of the Mısır Çarşısı. As he walked through the main entrance into the bustling market, his sense of smell was assaulted first – by oregano, cumin, henna, coffee and the sweet aroma of hibiscus. To what celestial bodies and attributes, he wondered as he searched the stalls lining the great vaulting hall for one known as Afrodite Pazarı, does hibiscus correspond?

When Süleyman arrived back at the station, Çöktin reported his conversation with İlhan Koç and the gist of the message he had left for Mendes.

'I've asked him to tell me where I might go with regard to finding out the identities of Communion and Nika,' he said. 'I've asked him to reply to my e-mail address at home.'

'Do you think that he will?' Süleyman asked.

'There's no reason why he shouldn't, sir. If he's as good as I think he is, I think he'll route his replies through Hüsnü's system anyway.'

'OK.' Süleyman rubbed his face with his hands and sighed. 'Now this Hammer club, bar, whatever it is –' he said – 'we need to get in there, İsak. I want to hear people using this language and I want to get to the bottom of exactly what this Theodora's Closet thing is.'

'İlhan Koç said he thought it was almost certainly a transvestite site.'

'Yes, but he didn't *know*, did he?' Süleyman replied. 'I mean, why would Gülay Arat go on to such a site?'

Çöktin shrugged. 'Well, it is dedicated to the life and "works" of the Byzantine Empress Theodora, sir. She is, I'm told, something of an icon for such people. Maybe the Arat girl was an admirer, or maybe she just had some transvestite friends. After all, if you look at what she's posted, it is all rather camp and she was only talking

131

to Nika about sex – it couldn't have been anything else.'

'Maybe, but we still need to check the Hammer out.'

'Raid the place.'

'No. No, we, or rather some of our officers, need to go in there, have a drink and talk to a few people without attracting attention. As I said, I want our people to hear this language and get close to those who use it.'

'Amongst a load of Goths and cross-dressers?' Çöktin smiled. 'Sir, if I might be frank, I cannot think of even one man who could or would be willing to dress like that.'

Süleyman, although usually grave in most situations, smiled too. 'I agree,' he said. 'Which is why I'm going to ask Commissioner Ardıç to allow me to use female officers. Who knows, İsak, perhaps some of our ladies will enjoy the chance to dress in outlandish clothes?'

'Maybe, sir.'

Süleyman looked at his watch. 'I've got to see Ardıç in five minutes,' he said. 'Hopefully we can think about going tomorrow. Any movement on the dead girl from this morning?'

Çöktin shrugged. 'Not yet, sir. Although I understand that Constable Yıldız has been in contact with a man whose sister has been missing since yesterday morning. I don't know any details.'

'All right. Keep me informed,' Süleyman said. 'And let's get any connections to Atlas Pasaj, newsgroups, et cetera, established sooner rather than later, this time, now we know what we're looking for.'

'But if we don't find it, sir?'

Süleyman, who was now busy gathering papers up for his meeting with Ardıç, said, 'If we don't find it, then we think again, İsak! These killings may or may not be, as I believe, of a ritualistic nature. One must keep an open mind.'

'Sir.' The younger man lowered his head in deference, but not so low that Süleyman couldn't see the miserable expression on his face. Still obviously worried about his own usurpation of the law, the Kurd was probably wondering what was going to happen next.

But Süleyman, who hadn't made his mind up about that yet, simply said, 'Once I've finished with the commissioner, I have to go on to a private appointment. However, I do need to speak to Inspector İkmen in the very near future. I'd like you to arrange that for me,

İsak. Tomorrow morning, provided that is convenient for him. I believe he's still in the building.'

'Yes, sir.'

Süleyman picked up his paper, checked his pockets and then made his way towards the door of his office.

'I'll see you in the morning, İsak.'

'Yes, sir.'

For someone who quite obviously knew why Max Esterhazy bought his goods and speculated about what he did with them, Doğa Kaş was a very unfazed individual.

'The girl comes for him every week with a list,' he said. 'Can be anything – rosemary, cardamom, mint, cloves – sometimes essences – rose, musk.'

İkmen looked down at the large sacks of herbs and spices stacked against the front of the stall. Little cubes of lokum on silver platters sat on some of the sacks, succulent inducements to curious tourists.

'Before I met Max Bey, I always thought that people like him used cats' blood and dead toads in their potions,' he shrugged. 'But then maybe he does. Maybe he gets those from other places.'

İkmen smiled. Doğa Kaş, spotting a very obvious tourist, thrust one of the platters under his nose and said, 'Turkish delight, yes please!'

İkmen's mobile phone began to ring and so he turned aside to answer the call.

'Hello?'

'It's Metin,' İskender's clipped, professional voice replied. 'Thought you'd better know that Mr Esterhazy's neighbours are reporting sounds coming from his apartment.'

'Don't we have a man outside?'

'Yes, but only at the front. We sealed the back. Sergeant Karataş and I are going over now.'

Remembering what İbrahim Dede had told him about the alleged talents of magicians, İkmen said, 'Well, be careful.'

'What of?'

But İkmen didn't really know. Max? Someone at odds with or jealous of Max? 'Just be careful.'

'Oh, and the blood work is back. Group A positive,' İskender said, changing the subject rapidly, as was his wont, 'the same as Esterhazy's.'

'Ah.'

'But that's only the blood found around the desk,' he continued. 'That over by the window is AB negative.'

İkmen frowned. 'So Max, maybe, and another . . .'

'The blood around the desk was also older – it had dried into the carpet – than that over by the window.'

'So shed, maybe, at another time.'

'Possibly. Look, I'm just entering Esterhazy's building now. I'll speak to you later.' And then he cut the connection.

İkmen turned back to Doğa Kaş, who had just been roundly ignored by several tourists, and said, 'So, anything else you can tell me about Mr Esterhazy?'

The merchant looked both ways up and down the market before replying. Then, leaning in towards İkmen, he said, 'I think he has seen happier times, financially.'

'What do you mean?'

Doğa Kaş shrugged again. 'Max Bey has always been a very good payer. I give him credit, but he's never abused that – not until this year.'

'So what's gone wrong?' İkmen asked.

'I don't know,' the merchant replied. 'But he doesn't pay regularly any more and for big orders like his . . .' he threw his hands up into the air. 'I tell you, Inspector, if he wasn't such a nice man and if I wasn't afraid of what djinn he might let loose in my business if I upset him, well . . .'

For reasons that İkmen couldn't really articulate, there was something disturbing about the notion of Max being in financial difficulty. Perhaps it was because he was a magician. After all, if those who could manipulate both spirit and matter couldn't sort their finances out, what hope was there for the rest of mankind? And, further, Max had lived in the city for almost thirty years now, never with any sign of financial difficulty and always fully employed. What could have happened? And could his disappearance be connected to this in any way? Had he perhaps been killed because of debts he had to others?

If he had, then he had obviously, from what İskender had to say, wounded his assailant or whoever at the same time. Except, of course, that Max's blood – if it was indeed his blood – had been shed before the other blood type. His blood had dried into the carpet.

İkmen, deep in thought, left the Mısır Çarşısı just as the merchants were closing up for the night. And although a young boy did thrust a bottle of something that declared itself a 'Sultan's Aphrodisiac' in his direction just before he walked back through the main entrance, he resisted the temptation and went home to his wife empty-handed.

They'd been talking about emigration from the countryside to the city. So many people, frequently pious peasants from the eastern provinces, came to work these days that a lot of İstanbulus complained that their city was no longer their own. It was a view that Mehmet Süleyman, now several glasses of Villa Doluca into the evening, could sometimes sympathise with.

'And yet we are all peasants at root,' the young man, Omer, husband of Çiçek's friend Deniz, said with some passion, 'except, of course, you, Çiçek.'

Çiçek İkmen laughed. 'Well, not entirely,' she said. 'My dad's family, way back – I think his father's grandfather – came from Cappadocia. One of Dad's aunts still lives there, in Göreme.'

'Oh, the Fairy Chimneys!' Çiçek's other friend Emine exclaimed delightedly. 'How lovely!'

'Yes.'

Cappadocia, with its strange lunar landscape, fashioned by wild natural upheavals in the earth, was indeed a beautiful and magical place. Characterised by tall conical structures known locally as Fairy Chimneys – many of which are and always have been used as homes – the area is famous both for its ancient rock churches and for the fact that the current inhabitants openly believe in fairies. It was, Süleyman always felt, very fitting that the İkmen family should originate from such a ghostly place.

'Mehmet's family are real İstanbulus,' Çiçek said as she smiled at the unaccustomed sight of Mehmet Süleyman in drink.

'Only on my father's side,' Süleyman corrected. 'My mother was born in Adana.'

'Ah, like my father,' Attila, Emine's boyfriend, said as he poured himself and the other two men more wine. They'd all eaten their main course some time ago and were having a long, leisurely, very Turkish break before the presentation of the dessert.

Çiçek lit a cigarette and then turned to Süleyman. 'Your father comes from the city, though, doesn't he?'

'Oh, yes,' Süleyman smiled. 'I can honestly say that my father is about as İstanbul as you can get.'

Either the wine or the thought of the appointment he had at Krikor Sarkissian's clinic the following afternoon had loosened his normally very tight rein on his personal details. But then what did it matter if these really very nice people knew a few things about him? They, like Çiçek, were educated grown-ups. They wouldn't, surely, hold his connection to the old Ancient Regime against him?

And so, for the first time ever in his life, he just said it. 'My grandfather was brought up at the court of Sultan Mehmed the Sixth,' he said.

'Oh, so your family served—'

'No, my family were the served,' Süleyman said.

'Mehmet was born in a palace,' Çiçek, who'd never seen him as easy and relaxed as this before, said excitedly. 'Was it Yeniköy?'

'Just outside Yeniköy,' he said, and then smiling at the others around the table he added, 'but we don't live there any more. My father gave the house up a long time ago. Couldn't afford it.'

'And so you became a policeman,' Omer said. 'An educated, Ottoman policeman.'

There was a kind of sneer behind Omer's words that Süleyman didn't particularly like.

'We all do what we feel is best,' he replied. Under the influence of the unaccustomed wine he wanted to tell the truth – that originally joining the police had been a form of rebellion against his parents – but he stopped himself. That might require some explanation about his parents and their lifestyle, which was somewhere he knew he didn't want to go.

'I can't see that it's "best" to be part of an organisation that represses and beats those it should be serving,' Omer continued.

'My dad doesn't beat people up, Omer,' Çiçek said spiritedly. 'You like my dad.'

'Çetin Bey is different,' Omer said as he flung his napkin down on to the table and rose to his feet. 'Please excuse me.'

And then he left, presumably for the bathroom. When he was out of earshot, his wife rather nervously turned to Süleyman.

'I do apologise for Omer,' she said. 'He doesn't know what he's saying.'

'Omer's brother was on a march recently, protesting about all this business with Iraq,' Çiçek added. 'He was arrested in Taksim.'

Süleyman reached across for his cigarettes and lit up. He had hoped that this meal would not descend into the usual slanging match that accompanied meeting people who didn't know him or what he did. But it had and so he felt compelled to explain.

'I know it's scant consolation to your husband,' he said to Deniz, 'but I don't personally have anything to do with anything political.'

'Well, no, of course . . .'

'Like Çiçek's father, I work in homicide. Occasionally something of a political nature might impinge upon what we do, but only in relation to a death or deaths that are unlawful anyway.'

Deniz smiled nervously. No doubt worried, Süleyman thought, that he might report what her husband had said to someone in authority. What a joke! If she knew what he just let pass, who he allowed to work alongside him . . .

Out in the hall, Çiçek and Emine's telephone began to ring.

'Excuse me,' Çiçek said as she rose from the table and left the room.

Emine's boyfriend, Attila, who was both younger and more light-hearted than Omer, began talking about the difficulties of flying into and out of the former Soviet Union. A Turkish Airlines pilot, Attila was producing the sort of conversation Süleyman had anticipated and feared would come to dominate the evening. As he listened to both Emine and Deniz ask sensible questions and make coherent comments, Süleyman felt his mind begin to drift. Silent, he remained like that, until Çiçek, her face suddenly grave, reentered the room and walked over to him.

'Mehmet, I'm sorry,' she said as she placed a hand on his shoulder. 'My dad's on the phone, he wants to speak to you.'

'OK.'

He made his excuses, walked out into the hall and picked up the receiver. 'Hello, Çetin.'

'I'm sorry to disturb you, Mehmet,' İkmen said. 'I've already apologised to my daughter, but I feel that I ought to tell you that Metin İskender has been shot.'

'Allah!'

Süleyman sat down heavily in the chair next to the phone. Çiçek, who was, he noticed, looking at him from the door of the kitchen, furrowed her brow.

'He's alive,' İkmen continued, 'but it's not good.'

'Where is he? Where are you?'

'We're at Taksim Hospital. He's in surgery.'

'I'd better get over there,' Süleyman said.

'There's no need,' İkmen replied. 'There are hordes of us down here – relatives, colleagues, friends . . .'

'I want to be there, Çetin.'

'All right.'

And then without another word, Süleyman put the phone down. He put his head in his hands and attempted to calm his now laboured breathing. Metin İskender – shot? How and why had that happened?

A very light touch to the back of his head made him look up. 'What's wrong?' Çiçek said. 'Dad wouldn't tell me anything. Is he OK?'

'Your dad's fine.' Süleyman managed a small smile. 'But there is something else, Çiçek, and so I'm afraid that I'm going to have to go.'

'Oh.'

'I'm sorry.'

He went back into the living room to retrieve his jacket and make his excuses. Çiçek then escorted him to the front door and thanked him for coming.

'I've had a very nice evening, Çiçek, thank you,' he said. And then with one formal shake of her hand he was gone.

After she had shut the door behind him, Çiçek leaned back against the wall, her eyes full of tears. Emine, who had just come out of her bedroom after retrieving her camera, walked over to her friend and put her arms around her shoulders.

'Oh, poor Çiçek,' she whispered, 'you love him, don't you?'

Chapter 12

He'd eventually managed to see the body at 8 p.m. Some female junior pathologist, together with the young policeman, Yıldız, attended with him. Apparently the senior pathologist was off duty. It was all very unsatisfactory.

Not that it mattered a whole lot really. It was her, Lale, as no doubt had been written. And so he said that it was her, and gave them her full name and age. Lale Tekeli, sixteen years old. His sister. His only living relative.

The boy, Yıldız, wouldn't tell him how she'd died. 'You'll have to speak to Inspector Süleyman,' he said.

'Then get him for me,' Osman Tekeli said as he fought to control the tears that were welling up behind his eyes.

'I'm afraid you won't be able to see him until tomorrow morning, sir.'

'So I'm just left with it, am I?' Tekeli said bitterly. 'My sister is dead and I don't know how or why . . .'

'It's not straightforward, sir,' Yıldız said. 'Inspector Süleyman will have to explain it to you.'

'But I want to see him now!'

'I'm afraid that isn't possible, as I said—'

'But I can't wait until tomorrow!' Tekeli cried. 'I want to know now!' Then even closer to tears than he had been before, he said, 'Constable, I am a Muslim man. I teach at an İmamHatip lisesi. If my sister has died then I want to bury her body.'

Yıldız looked across at Dr Mardin.

'Mr Tekeli,' she said, her eyes averted from his down to the floor, 'burial at this stage cannot be approved.'

'What!'

'Sir, because of the nature of your sister's death it is subject to criminal investigation. The senior pathologist will not release her body until he is satisfied that he knows everything there is to know about how it occurred.'

'Was she . . . ?' He couldn't go on and began to cry. He was a small man and obviously a lot older than his sister had been. 'She was murdered, wasn't she?' he said when eventually he managed to recover himself. 'Well?'

'Sir . . .'

'Oh, but who would do such a thing?' He sank down towards the floor, tearing at his face as he went. 'She was such a good girl!'

Süleyman eventually found İkmen in the midst of a crowd outside the intensive therapy department. Someone, presumably a member of staff, had opened a side door in order to allow the smokers to do what they had to out in the open air.

Apart from İkmen, there were some faces that he recognised: Alpaslan Karataş sitting, head down, his shoulders covered with a blanket; Metin's mother and father, the latter, asleep on the concrete outside, stinking of rakı; a couple of uniforms he knew by sight. However, the rest of the group, presumably relatives, were men and women characterised by cheap, peasant clothing – shiny suit jackets, flat caps, flowered headscarves almost covering the women's faces.

'What happened?' he asked when he drew level with İkmen.

İkmen took a deep breath before he replied. 'Metin and Karataş went over to Max Esterhazy's apartment earlier this evening,' he said. 'The neighbours had heard noises coming from inside.'

'And so?'

'All we know is what Alp Karataş has told us,' İkmen said. 'Which is that they entered the apartment, he went into the study while Metin went into Max's bedroom. Alp heard a shot, ran into the bedroom and there was Metin – on the floor, bleeding. As far as Karataş – who was, it has to be said, rather more concerned with calling an ambulance and keeping Metin alive at the time – could see, there was no one else in the room or fleeing the scene. The bedroom window was closed.' İkmen shrugged helplessly. 'Fucking invisible gunmen!'

'So what's the prognosis?' Süleyman asked as he moved closer to İkmen and lowered his voice to a whisper.

'He took the shot in the gut,' İkmen said gravely. 'He's lost a lot of blood, there's extensive damage and he's been unconscious ever since it happened. He's in surgery now.' And then uncharacteristically he added, 'All we can do is pray.'

Süleyman looked at the assembled crowd around him and said, 'Where's his wife?'

'On her way back from Germany,' İkmen said. 'She'd gone on business.'

İskender's wife, Belkıs, was a very successful publisher and was frequently out of the country for one reason or another.

'She'll be devastated,' Süleyman said, and then lowering his voice to a whisper again he said, 'They are a most devoted couple.'

'I know.' İkmen shrugged. 'What can you do? Kismet.'

They stood in silence for a few moments until Süleyman said, 'Are all these people Metin's relatives?'

İkmen smiled grimly. 'Metin's veneer of sophistication is pervasive, isn't it? Yes, these are his relatives. Peasants have a lot of children, don't they?'

'His father is—'

'Drunk as usual, yes,' İkmen said. 'I've spoken to his mother, though. She's shocked and upset, but I think she's coping. I think she's used to facing up to most things without support from her husband.' He shrugged. 'I'm actually more concerned about Karataş at the moment.'

They both looked across at the seated figure of the usually large and imposing Karataş, seemingly shrunk down into a thin grey blanket.

'He just refuses to leave,' İkmen continued.

'Was he given any medication?'

'Oh, yes, he's tranquillised,' İkmen said. 'As well as the shock of the actual shooting, he had to endure Metin nearly dying in the ambulance. I think he'd be better off at home where his mother and sisters can look after him.'

Süleyman looked down at the motionless, grey face poking out from inside the blanket and said, 'But then maybe it's important to him that he stays.'

'I suppose it must be,' İkmen said, and then taking Süleyman by the elbow he led him towards the door leading out of the hospital. 'Come on. I need a cigarette and we have to talk.'

They eventually found a deserted corner over by the dustbins. Mercifully, Süleyman felt, they seemed to have been emptied in the not-too-distant past.

İkmen, once he'd got a cigarette in his mouth, came straight to the point. 'That blood we found in Max's apartment,' he said. 'It was the same group as his, or rather some of it was. Two individuals are involved, which could mean they may have fought. However, the blood that corresponded to Max's type had been there significantly longer than the other one.'

'So where can Max be now?'

'I don't know,' İkmen replied. 'But if the blood is Max's he might be hurt. I know he's not been admitted to any of the city hospitals – I've had them checked out. If he is still alive then someone could be caring for him.'

'A friend?'

'Maybe. The problem is, Mehmet, that I don't know any of his friends, and his address book is, as yet, indecipherable.' He then went on to tell Süleyman about the conversation he'd had with İbrahim Dede and the problem that Max's status as a Kabbalist might pose. 'As far as I'm aware,' he concluded, 'if one is totally involved with Kabbalah, it does order and dictate every aspect of one's life. I'm thinking that if I could understand it a little better I might be able to predict where Max may have gone and why.'

'But if he's lost blood,' Süleyman said, 'then surely anything beyond getting some help will be irrelevant?'

'If indeed it is his, yes. Mehmet, I know you didn't meet Max that often, but did you ever get the impression he was in financial difficulty?'

Süleyman crossed his arms over his chest and sighed. 'He never said anything. But ... I suppose, now I come to think of it, his no longer patronising La Cave was a bit odd.'

'The wine shop in Cihangir?'

'Yes. My father goes there.' He rolled his eyes in momentary despair. 'They're real wine lovers at La Cave. Max favoured French wines like Châteauneuf-du-Pape, Gigondas. But I suppose in the last six months or so I've only ever seen bakkal-standard Çankaya or Villa Doluca on his table.'

İkmen smiled. Although Süleyman rarely drank alcohol, it was significant of his background that he should notice a man's change in circumstances via the quality of his wine.

'Are you thinking,' Süleyman said, 'that Max might have disappeared on purpose? To escape from creditors, maybe?'

'I don't know.' İkmen shrugged and then added darkly, 'All I do know is that, with Max, anything is possible.'

Süleyman frowned.

'Don't ask,' İkmen said. 'Not now. Anyway, how is your own investigation going? What about that second girl you found this morning?'

'Yes,' Süleyman said. 'Again, young, naked. But murdered indoors this time by someone Çöktin thinks was probably eating fruit at the time. That or the girl had been. There were apparently loads of limes all over the floor. I don't know much about this latest victim yet, although apparently a man has been over to the mortuary for a possible ID. I'll be interested to see whether she was a Goth or just had Gothic-style interests, like Cem Ataman.'

'You're still going with that angle then?' İkmen said.

'Yes. Via various sources I will not bother you with now, I have discovered what might be a kind of inner circle of these kids who are, we are informed, very interested in Satanism. Whether they practise it or not is another matter. But there is a bar in Atlas—'

'You know the Panaghia is not the only place of worship to have been daubed with a diabolical image,' a very serious İkmen interrupted. 'The dervish İbrahim Dede is of the opinion that the city itself is under attack from what he describes as "dark" and "unbalancing" elements. He thinks that Max might be out there trying to put it right.'

'Well, I don't know about that,' Süleyman said, 'but I will take the attacks on the religious institutions seriously. Why don't they report these things? Anyway, I've asked Ardıç for permission to send a pair of female officers into a bar called the Hammer.'

'That's where these "Satanic" kids meet, is it?'

Süleyman told him about how Cem Ataman might have become

143

involved through the Hammer and about the seeming appropriation of the transsexual patois that certain patrons used.

'It's the same as that used by Communion and Nika on those newsgroups the kids were involved in,' he said. 'And yet if you translate what they say it's only about sex of, seemingly, the ordinary kind. The Hammer, however, is, I think, something else. From what I can gather it might be a starting point for the recruitment of young Satanists. I don't think anything actually happens there . . .'

'No.'

'Both the girls, Gülay Arat and this new one, were sexually assaulted prior to and just after their deaths,' Süleyman said. 'I'm finding the notion of something ritualistic increasingly pervasive.'

'Well, if that is so,' İkmen said, 'then whoever is manipulating them is going to be dangerous. Allah, but Max surely knew something! If only he'd talked to me!' He shook his head in irritation. 'If only I could get in contact with people in his world. I tried what looked like a recognisable number in his book when I got home, but it came up unobtainable.'

'Perhaps some of the numbers in the book are old.'

'Maybe.' And then İkmen smiled. 'The Hammer,' he said. 'You know I was looking at one of Max's books today, a very famous work called *The Hammer of the Witches* or *Malleus Maleficarum*, as it's known in the original Latin. Be interesting to find out whether that is why "the Hammer" is so named.'

They stood in silence for a few moments then until Süleyman said, 'So what are you going to do now then, Çetin?'

'I'm going to base myself at Max's place from now on,' he said. 'Try to immerse myself in his books and papers in an attempt to find out what might have been going on. I'd rather you let me contact the religious organisations, if you don't mind.'

Süleyman shrugged. 'OK.'

'I think that Max's maid, Ülkü, and her odious boyfriend can safely be ruled out now,' İkmen said. 'Their clothes were clean. Certainly they have no involvement with what happened today – they've only just left us. Mind you, I almost wish the boy, Turgut Can, were implicated.'

'Why?'

'Because, and I know this is personal, but I can't stand the way

144

he keeps on bad-mouthing Max. I know a lot of Max's books are salacious, to say the least, but the boy seems to be obsessed by the idea that Max is some sort of demonic pervert. It's lack of understanding, I know. To the simple mind magician equals diabolist.'

'Like the Yezidi,' Süleyman said.

They both, for just a brief moment, shared a look.

'Yes.'

Then in response to the sound of crying they looked across at the nearest group of İskender's relatives. But it was only his sister, Meral, finally giving way under the strain of her anxiety, as opposed to any news from the surgical team.

'Poor woman.'

'Yes,' İkmen said, but then, perhaps not wishing to dwell upon what might or might not happen to Metin İskender he changed the subject. 'Did you have a nice meal with Çiçek and her friends?'

'Yes. It was excellent,' Süleyman said and smiled. 'They were all younger than me. It was like going to dinner with a favourite niece.'

'You see Çiçek as a sort of a young relative then?'

'Yes,' Süleyman said. 'I suppose it's because I remember her when she was a kid.'

'Mmm.' İkmen put his cigarette out and then lit another. 'You know I think she sees you in an altogether more romantic light.' He held up a hand to silence what he felt might be protestation. 'I know you've not encouraged her. I'm just alerting you to it, Mehmet.'

Süleyman, shaking his head, said, 'But why?'

'Because she's lonely, you're cultured, handsome and, most importantly, safe,' İkmen said. 'Çiçek had a crush on you when she was a teenager. Now she's thirty, unmarried and, I think, becoming nervous about dating men she doesn't already know.'

'But I'm married!'

İkmen shrugged. 'I know. Çiçek won't do anything, Mehmet. She's a good girl. I'm just letting you know so that if anything should ever crop up in conversation you can let her down gently. Honestly, children!' He frowned. 'Even when they're adults they conspire to drive you insane.'

'Estelle! Estelle!'

'What . . . ?'

Berekiah Cohen turned over and stroked his wife's sleep-sodden face. 'It's all right,' he soothed. 'It's only my dad. Go back to sleep.'

He then threw himself back to look at the clock he'd been contemplating when his father's cries had shattered the silence of the night. Three fifteen. Still nearly another three hours before he needed to get up for work.

'Estelle!'

His father, as usual, was in the living room, propped up in that chair of his, surrounded by telephones and bottles of pills. Berekiah's mother had either not heard or chosen to ignore his cries. Well, he wasn't going to sleep, anyway . . .

Berekiah got up and, closing his bedroom door gently lest he wake Hulya, he made his way into the living room.

Squinting against the fierce neon light from the strip on the ceiling, he said, 'What is it, Dad?'

'I've run out of cigarettes,' Balthazar snapped. 'There's more in the kitchen.'

Berekiah went into the kitchen and retrieved two packets of Marlboro for his father. 'There you are.'

'Your mother should have got up,' Balthazar said grumpily as he lit one and breathed in deeply. 'Why aren't you in your bed?'

'I couldn't sleep.' Berekiah took a cigarette from one of his father's packets and then borrowed his lighter.

'Why not?'

Berekiah shrugged.

'Well, you must know!' his father said. 'A young man just recently married goes to bed for only two reasons. If you're not doing it then you should be exhausted.' He frowned. 'Everything is all right with Hulya . . . ?'

'Of course!'

'I only asked!' Balthazar said as he held up his hands defensively. 'You're my son; I have an interest.'

Rather too much of an 'interest' to Berekiah's way of thinking. Balthazar knew full well that Berekiah and Hulya were just fine. He did, after all, sleep in the next room. He just wanted to talk about sex. Perhaps, Berekiah thought, he should mention to Uncle Jak about getting his father some sex films and books before he returned to

England. Maybe that would cure him of his seemingly insatiable need to know how many times he and Hulya made love in an 'average' night. God, the sooner they moved out into their new house the better – or not.

That graffiti on the wall of the Church of the Panaghia haunted him. So crude and unpleasant. A rutting thing with women impaled on its many penises. It looked as if it were killing them. And that church wasn't the only one to have been visited by this 'artist'. It was, in truth, another chance meeting he'd had with Brother Constantine that was really keeping Berekiah awake. Jak had been up in Fener all day and Berekiah had gone over after work to join him. He'd met the monk on his way from the Greek Boys' School where he worked, to the local shops. In hushed tones Brother Constantine had told Berekiah that other terrible images had been found at the Ahrida Synagogue and at the Koca Mustafa Paşa Mosque.

'Desecration!' he'd whispered to Berekiah. 'Almighty God under attack from the Devil himself! Here in Fener and Balat, the Evil One comes to attack our souls!'

When asked to elaborate about the images and discuss what other divines might be doing about them, Brother Constantine had been reticent.

'Has anyone told the police about it, Brother Constantine?'

'No. We don't want them involved. The Patriarch has spoken to the Chief Rabbi, I know – and the Muslim clergy. It's most disturbing for everyone.'

Berekiah said he thought that someone in the police should contact them. 'I know that my father-in-law, Inspector İkmen, would be interested,' he said. 'He's very worried about what he saw at your church. I'm sure that if he knew about these other—'

'I know that you mean well, young man,' the monk said kindly, 'but I think this is something we need to sort out for ourselves. The police can't, after all, protect us from demons, can they?' and with that he continued on his way down to the shops.

But Berekiah wanted to tell İkmen. That the ugly drawings were proliferating was something that he felt his father-in-law would want to know. And besides, he and, more importantly, Hulya, had been upset by the experience. Jak was bringing in a different workman

147

every day to do something nice to the house, but the area, if not the property itself, still felt tainted. Something about that image was striking at a place very deep within his psyche and he didn't know why. Telling İkmen about the desecration of the other places of worship would, he knew, be breaking Brother Constantine's confidence, but on balance he felt that he had to. Something bad had crept into Fener and if someone didn't act to stop it, there was a possibility it might take root.

But now Jak, woken as he had been by Balthazar's cries, entered the room and yet another conversation about sex began.

'Are you going to see Demir Sandal again soon?' Balthazar said, without preamble, to his weary-looking brother as he entered.

'In a few days, yes,' Jak said as he raked his fingers through his hair, smiling as he did so at Berekiah. 'I can't understand why you are so perpetually awake, Balthazar.'

'Maybe it's because I'm so bored!'

'Then do something.' Jak threw himself down into a chair and lit a cigarette.

Berekiah, sensing that an argument was brewing, left the room.

As soon as he had gone, Balthazar leaned forward in his chair and said, 'If you would get me a girl, from Demir Sandal—'

'Balthazar!'

'All she'd have to do—'

'Look, he's going to give me some "new product" or other that's supposed to be really erotic and I'll get you some magazines,' Jak said wearily. 'But you'll have to organise how and when you use them. Think of Estelle, for God's sake!'

'What other woman do I have to think of?' Balthazar replied bitterly.

She'd thought that İlhan would probably never speak to her again. But he had – sort of. She'd run straight to the ferry stage after Zuleika had humiliated her in front of Mehmet Süleyman. If she hadn't turned up, Fitnat would have got him to fuck her for sure. Not that it mattered now. Now there was another, better man.

A policeman had been to see İlhan, but she didn't know what had been said. İlhan wouldn't tell her. What he did say, however, was

148

that he wasn't going to go down to Atlas for a while. He didn't want to talk about it and he'd still be her friend, but he just didn't feel it was right at the moment.

She had been angry at first and had gone straight down to Atlas, drunk several vodkas and then gone into the Hammer. She didn't go there often, but in such a black mood as she was, full of resentment towards her overcautious stepmother, it seemed somehow perfect. Full, as usual, with the customary selection of freaks with false fangs and big-breasted women with scars up their arms, she'd been surprised to find someone like him in there. Tall, dark, handsome and about the same age as Mehmet Bey. A man – interested in her – or so it seemed.

'Are you a virgin?' he asked as he laid her down on the bed and began to untie the laces of her bodice.

'Yes.'

His sharp intake of breath told her that this had excited him. That he was fiercely attracted to her had been evident when they'd met at the Hammer. Talking, about her mainly, had quickly led to a kiss that had then become the feel of his erection against her belly. She'd gone back with him, at first rather more to spite her stepmother, who had to be worried about her by this time, than anything else. But now that she was here, in this great big Beyoğlu apartment, overlooking the Golden Horn, stylish and expensive – well . . .

He had a good body. She wanted to give him her virginity, even though she knew that she shouldn't – even though she knew that she did need to wait. But for how long? She wanted it now! However, although he was excited this man proceeded slowly. Until the sun came up he teased both her and himself in ways she would never even have imagined. Without ever once coming close to penetrating her body, he made her feel things that brought her alive. And, when she did finally leave to the sound of the ferries making steam down at Eminönü, it was with a picture in her head of a bed battered and stained by orgasms created with hands, lips and breasts.

'Call me,' he said as he kissed her goodbye at the door. 'I want to take you further.'

Fitnat, her hand clutching tightly the card he had given her, knew that she would.

149

Chapter 13

Mehmet Süleyman was really too tired for this. Despite İkmen's suggestion that he should, he hadn't yet been home. The surgeons hadn't finished operating on Metin İskender until 5 a.m. and at that point going home had seemed like a waste of time. Besides, although Metin was still alive, he was far from out of danger. The shot, as well as shredding part of his intestines, had also damaged his spleen to such an extent that it had to be removed. His wife, the normally cool and stoic Belkıs had, apparently, screamed like a peasant when she'd seen him for the first time just after Süleyman and İkmen had left. And now here was Mr Tekeli, brother of Lale, the latest victim, possibly, of what could be some sort of ritual killing, wanting answers.

'She was stabbed through the heart,' Tekeli said slowly, as if trying to get the facts straight in his mind. 'But if you know this then why can't I take her for burial?'

'Your sister's death is part of an on-going investigation into the rape and murder of young girls.'

'She was raped . . .' He said it slowly, as if to himself.

'As I told you, sir, yes,' Süleyman said. 'I'm so sorry – for your loss and for the distress this is causing. I know how hard it must be to have one's beliefs tested in this fashion but unfortunately I cannot release your sister's body to you and, further, I must ask you to allow us access to her possessions.'

Tekeli first shook his head and then said, 'What possessions? What do you mean?'

Süleyman looked across at Çöktin, who just simply shrugged. In a sense and in light of information Çöktin had just that morning received from the hacker Mendes, even if Lale Tekeli had a computer and had been involved in any of the sites that the other youngsters had been, it was doubtful anything concrete could come of it.

As Çöktin had suspected from the start, there was no way of tracing either of the target contributors to the two newsgroups they had identified. Although local in origin, the source, as far as it could be traced, was in Argentina, where it was extremely doubtful any logs or records would have been kept. There was, however, some virtue in seeing whether Lale Tekeli conformed to the pattern so far.

'We need, specifically, to look at any computer equipment your sister may have possessed,' Süleyman said.

Tekeli looked up, his eyes red with barely contained tears. 'She only used her computer for her academic work,' he said.

'Did she have Internet access?'

'Yes, but she viewed only Islamic sites,' he said. 'I know, I monitored her. Lale was very studious, very pious. She even had extra tuition for some of her subjects.' He began to sob. 'Raped! She was always covered!'

'Mr Tekeli—'

'She wasn't one of those closed at the top and open at the bottom girls!' Tekeli said hotly, referring to the way that some Turkish girls cover their heads while wearing skirts slit to the thigh. 'Some of her turbans were pretty – from the Tekbir shop, you know – but—'

'Mr Tekeli, I know that this is going to be difficult for you to answer,' Süleyman said, 'but did your sister have any interests outside of learning and her religious obligations? Any friends—'

'No. No, she was a good girl. You know, she wanted to be a teacher . . .'

They all sat in silence for a few moments until Tekeli spoke again. 'If you think that looking at Lale's computer will help, then you may have it,' he said.

'Thank you, Mr Tekeli,' Süleyman said. 'My sergeant, if he may, will accompany you home to do that.'

'Whatever you think is for the best.'

And so Çöktin left with Tekeli while Süleyman prepared for the meeting Ardıç had called with İkmen and himself. But nagging away at the edges of his mind was something else too. Today was the day he had to go to see Krikor Sarkissian and get his test results. As he assembled all the information he needed for his meeting, he was disturbed by just how much his hands shook.

'One of my officers is fighting for his life,' Ardıç said as he looked from İkmen to Süleyman and then back again. 'In addition, a foreign national has gone missing and, to my way of thinking, we're not putting our backs into it. Care to explain?'

Although seated, softly spoken and outwardly calm, Commissioner Ardıç was holding on to his smouldering cigar as if his life depended on it. Those who knew him well, like İkmen and Süleyman, would know that he was in a very dangerous state.

'Sir,' İkmen began, 'it's complicated . . .'

'It always is with you, İkmen.' Deep brown eyes almost hidden beneath thick black eyebrows surveyed İkmen with some malice. 'But the fact remains that İskender is still critical, he cannot speak and so we cannot ask him who attacked him. Until we can, or until some evidence to the contrary comes to light, I feel that the necessity to speak to this Maximillian Esterhazy is paramount. I am therefore issuing a warrant for his arrest.'

'But, sir,' İkmen said, 'what could be Max's blood was found in his study the day he disappeared.'

'Yes, I know all about that,' Ardıç said. 'Dried-up, old stuff. I know about the other blood too. What I also know, however, is that the only prints found in the study came from Esterhazy himself, his maid and her boyfriend.'

'Neither of whom has type AB negative blood,' İkmen said.

'No, but beyond the fact that the AB blood exists there is nothing else in that room to suggest the presence of its owner,' Ardıç said, and then added caustically, 'Are you sure İkmen, that your magician friend didn't sacrifice small children? Sorcery, may I remind you, is still nominally a crime in this country.'

'Sir!'

Ardıç pointed a thick finger at İkmen. 'I want him found, İkmen,' he said. 'He was a teacher, I understand; get in touch with his students.'

İkmen then explained how he had tried to do this and why he had failed. Ardıç's face appeared to grow redder with the telling.

'Allah preserve us!' he said under his breath as İkmen finished. 'Well, we'll have to put something out in the media then, won't we? Why haven't you come to me before about this?'

'Well, sir—'

'And you, Süleyman?' he said, turning his attention now on the younger of the two officers. 'What about these dead girls?'

Süleyman gave his superior a résumé of what had happened since they last spoke. 'It seems to me, sir,' he said, 'that in spite of the rather disappointing lack of evidence from the children's computers, Atlas Pasaj and its inhabitants are going to be worth what we plan for tonight.'

'You've officers lined up?'

'Yes, sir. However—'

Ardıç looked up sharply. 'What?'

'This new victim, Lale Tekeli, as far as we are aware, had no connection to Atlas Pasaj and no "dark", shall we say, interests.'

'Not as yet.'

'No, sir. Miss Tekeli was a very studious girl and a devout Muslim.'

Ardıç leaned back in his chair and sighed. 'Well, maybe she was just better at hiding her "dark" interests than the others. Not that I believe in any of that nonsense myself,' he said. 'Bring the poor deluded kids at Atlas in by all means, but you won't find Satan or any of his demons with them – except, of course, their wealthy parents. So as I've said before, Süleyman, caution.'

'Yes, sir.'

Ardıç turned back once again to İkmen. 'Oh, and by the way, İkmen, it has recently come to my attention that at least one other place of worship, apart from the Church of the Panaghia, has been daubed with disturbing images. Maybe your magical Englishman—'

'I went to Max to get help with that, sir!' İkmen cried. 'He didn't understand the image in that form any more than I did!'

'It is much more likely to be connected to things we suspect may be happening at Atlas Pasaj,' Süleyman put in. 'If Satanic practices are coming from anywhere it's there.'

'Well . . .' Ardıç shrugged and then dismissed them.

Once outside Ardıç's office, they both lit cigarettes.

'I know this is going to sound bad, Çetin,' Süleyman said, 'but I've got a real fear about this Lale Tekeli.'

'About her not conforming to Gülay Arat's profile?'

'Yes. With Cem, although he did certainly kill himself, and Gülay, there is a connection via Atlas Pasaj. But with Lale . . .'

'Maybe they're all connected in other ways we don't yet understand,' İkmen said, and then looking down at his watch he added, 'I must get over to Max's. I'm meeting Karataş over there.'

'Going over what happened yesterday again?'

'Yes, and also he has been seconded to me for a few days,' İkmen said. 'I think he should be at home, but . . .' he shrugged. 'Anyway, he'll be useful to do the labouring work, fetching and carrying while I look through Max's stuff. I don't know whether this media idea of Ardıç's will work.'

'Why not?'

'Max's students are well off – rich parents. Would they want the aggravation of their children being associated with someone wanted in connection with a shooting? After all, you can always get another English teacher, can't you?'

'Maybe.' Süleyman frowned. 'What about Metin? Are you going back to the hospital?'

'After duty, yes, And you?'

He lowered his eyes. 'Yes, but only after –' he turned away just a little – 'I have to see Krikor Sarkissian tonight . . .'

'Ah. Well.'

Süleyman forced himself to look round at his friend and then also forced a smile.

'İnşallah everything will be all right,' İkmen said and then, after just a moment's awkwardness, he moved forward to take his friend in his arms. 'Now go home and take a few hours' rest,' he said.

Süleyman, his head on İkmen's shoulder, squeezed his eyes shut against the tears that were gathering behind his lashes.

The Tekeli apartment was small and very neat. Situated above a religious bookshop in the holy village of Eyüp, which is almost at the far northern tip of the Golden Horn, it was a very fitting place for the pious Osman Tekeli to live.

'Are you going to visit the holy shrine while you are here?' Tekeli asked Çöktin as he placed the cup of apple tea he'd made for him down beside his sister's computer.

Çöktin, who had been looking intently at the screen, turned to him and smiled. 'I don't know, sir. It does largely depend upon time.'

'I see.' It wasn't outright disapproval, but Tekeli obviously felt that Çöktin should make time. The latter, as he often did in situations like this, wanted to say that he was under absolutely no obligation to visit the shrine of Eyüb Al-Ansari or any other Muslim saint, but as usual he held his tongue. Eyüp village possesses a lot of old-world charm, and the tomb for which it is both famous and sacred, that of Eyüb Al-Ansari, the Prophet Muhammed's standard bearer, is one of the holiest sites in Islam. It is therefore a very quiet and contemplative place – not the sort of area where one would wish to disturb the inhabitants with what might seem like an aggressive statement of one's difference. Once Tekeli had returned to the kitchen, Çöktin took a quick sip from the cup and then turned his attention back to Lale Tekeli's computer.

There were no games in evidence and, as far as he could see so far, no involvement in either chat rooms or newsgroups. What there seemed to be a lot of was school-work – essays in Turkish, English and German on subjects ranging from accounts of aspects of Islamic theory and practice to a geographical description of the Marmara region and essays entitled 'Everyday Life in Britain'. Lale, it seemed, unlike Cem Ataman or Gülay Arat, didn't have any 'Gothic', musical or just plain weird interests of any sort. And as Çöktin looked around the dead girl's modest bedroom, he spotted what he thought was another difference too – money. Cem and Gülay came from rich families whereas Lale, it seemed, didn't. But then the Tekelis were not poor either. Osman Tekeli was a school teacher and possessed a considerable library of mainly religious texts. He drove a very recent model Mercedes and the two of them were enthusiastic hadjis, which meant that they went to Mecca on the annual pilgrimage. All this took money, if not the vast amounts that the Atamans and the Arats exhibited.

However, there was something even more fundamentally different than money and which really did bother Çöktin. And so he made his way into the living room to speak to Tekeli again.

'Sir,' he said as he looked down at the small, grey man contemplating the blank wall in front of him, 'if we are to apprehend Lale's murderer, we need to know as much about her as we can.'

'Why?'

To Çöktin, schooled for a number of years now in the still rather radical methods of both İkmen and Süleyman, this seemed like an odd question. But then for someone only accustomed to traditional police methods or, as he suspected in this case, no knowledge of the police at all, it had to seem a little strange. To many people, even some inside the force itself, the psychology of the victim and even the perpetrator was largely irrelevant.

'Because, sir,' he said, 'the more we know about Lale, about what she thought, where she went and who she mixed with, the more chance we have of identifying where she might have met the person who ended her life.'

'I've told you everything you need to know about Lale. She studied at my school – I took her and brought her home. We went everywhere together.'

'Except when she went to meet her killer,' Çöktin said.

Tekeli looked up. 'She left this apartment without either my knowledge or permission,' he said.

'Yes, which means she must have done that for a reason,' Çöktin said. And then he sat himself down in the chair next to Tekeli's and smiled. 'Look, sir, I know this must be hard, but I can't see any sort of personal items in your sister's room.'

'She had none.'

'No?'

Tekeli's face pinched into a scowl.

'Everyone has personal bits and pieces,' Çöktin said. 'Bits of broken jewellery, old watches, photographs, letters.'

'My sister was a most pious girl,' Tekeli said. 'She didn't have photographs.'

'Well, letters and other things then!' Çöktin said. 'Mr Tekeli, I know you must, as I would myself in your position, want to protect your sister's memory as the blameless thing I'm sure it is. But she must have had some stuff that was at least mildly embarrassing. Some soft toys or—'

157

'All right! All right!' Tekeli held a hand up to stanch the flow of Çöktin's words and then rose to his feet. 'If you must,' he said, 'if you must, I will give you what I have.'

'Thank you.'

Max was a genius. İkmen had, of course, always known it, but being in his apartment, almost alone with his books and papers, only served to underline this fact. Tomes and volumes on every subject, some of them written by Max himself, graced the vast bookcases lining his study. And not just in one or two languages – so far İkmen had identified French, Latin and Hebrew as well as the to be expected English, German and Turkish. A Renaissance man, Max, versed in literature, science, the arts and magic. İkmen had been looking at a couple of what he hoped were not too complicated treatises on Kabbalism in English when he'd idly shuffled through a drawer in the desk and found Max's passport.

Standard United Kingdom EU passport, it told İkmen nothing he didn't already know – except, of course, the bit at the back. Funny, but İkmen had never thought about Max having 'relatives or friends who may be contacted in the event of accident', but then he, extraordinary as he was, had to have some family somewhere. Although quite how Mrs Maria Salmon was related to him, İkmen couldn't know. A sister maybe, or a cousin? His parents, those noble Viennese who had sought refuge in Britain just prior to the Second World War, had to be dead now.

Well, there was only one thing to do and that was to call the number underneath the London address for this woman and see what happened. Max obviously hadn't left the country but if Mrs Salmon was indeed a close relative he might have told her something about his movements. Given the nature of Max's supposed disappearance, İkmen doubted this, but he punched the number into Max's keypad anyway and then waited for an answer. While he waited, İkmen looked at a representation of the Kabbalist Tree of Life in a book by a woman who claimed to be Britain's foremost Kabbalist. What Gonca had called Sephira – plural Sephiroth – were represented as circles connected by lines called paths. There were eleven Sephiroth, which apparently represented what the writer called 'characteristics of both

God and Man'. The paths he couldn't make out, but what he did already know was that the Tree of Life also symbolised both Adam Kadmon – the heavenly, macrocosmic man and the ordinary human or microcosmic man. Just like Gonca had said, with Kabbalists it is all about that above and divine being essentially the same and interchangeable with that below or in the world.

'Hello?' It was a woman's voice, English and slightly tremulous.

'Hello, Mrs Salmon?' İkmen asked.

'Yes. Who is this?'

İkmen explained who he was and why he was calling. And, although he was quite truthful when Mrs Salmon, who it transpired was Max's sister, asked him about what had happened to her brother, İkmen didn't go into detail.

'I haven't seen my brother for, oh, it must be fifteen years,' she said. 'I don't think I've spoken to him since Christmas.'

'That was, I take it, a seasonal greeting?' İkmen said.

He heard her just gently smirk at his formality. He spoke English very well – his father had drummed the language into him and his brother at every opportunity – but he was, he knew, still rather more formal than most UK citizens of the twenty-first century.

'Oh, I wished him a Merry Christmas, yes,' Mrs Salmon said. 'But he needed to speak to me about something else too.'

'What was that?'

'Well, look, it is rather personal actually,' Mrs Salmon said with that vague English stuffiness Max himself could sometimes exhibit. 'It concerned our parents, Maximillian's and mine. I know you say you are at my brother's flat but do you have an official number that I could call you on? Your police station? So I can verify you are who you say you are?'

'But of course.' İkmen gave her the station number with instructions on how to ask for his office. Mrs Salmon was obviously as cautious as her brother.

'Your parents must have been very extraordinary people,' İkmen said just before the conversation ended.

'What do you mean?'

'Getting out of Vienna, taking none of their fortune with them, just to get away from the horror perpetrated by the Nazis.'

'Is that what my brother told you?'

There was something very wrong here, he could detect that from her voice. 'Yes.'

He heard her sigh at the other end of the telephone. 'Then you and I really do need to talk,' she said. 'In about an hour?'

'That will be perfect.' And with that İkmen replaced the receiver.

After that it wasn't easy getting back into what he'd been doing. What did that 'Is that what my brother told you?' mean? That Max had been lying about his past? If he had, then why?

Karataş, his face still strained from his all-too-recent violent experiences, entered the room carrying a box.

'Sir, this food is going off,' he said. 'It's beginning to stink.'

'What is it?'

'Fruit and vegetables.'

'Well, we can't dispose of anything yet,' İkmen said. 'Unless, of course, it's meat. Leave it on the draining board for now.'

'Yes, sir.'

İkmen glanced at his watch. It would take him only a few minutes to get back to the station from here and so he temporarily resumed his studies. Malkuth, the lowest Sephira, was representative of the earth and of matter. Because it was at the bottom of the tree, it corresponded to the feet. Its element was, of course, earth and the angel associated with it – they all had angels, demons, planets and 'things', just as Gonca had said – was something called Sandalphon. Then there were lists of gems, in this case rock crystal, virtues – discrimination – even perfumes; for Malkuth it was Ambergris. The magician, when working on, whatever that meant, a particular Sephira was supposed to surround himself with as much of this stuff and cultivate as many of these attributes himself as he could.

But in terms of finding Max, with such a very basic knowledge of something the magician had spent his entire life cultivating, was İkmen actually achieving anything here? He looked up and put his chin in his hands. Knowing that Max organised his life in line with this system wasn't helping. One just simply became mesmerised by the various correspondences – looking, as it were, for one's favourite animal or fruit amongst the lists and seeing what it meant in Kabbalistic terms.

160

He lit a cigarette. Sometimes, when looking for a missing person, İkmen could get some sort of sense about the likelihood of that person being alive or dead. But not in this case. Even though he knew Max, even though they had, in a way, come almost as close as any two men can, he still couldn't tell. Something or someone, maybe even Max himself, was blocking his vision.

Chapter 14

Fitnat didn't wake up until lunchtime. Well, she hadn't got home until nine. But it had been worth it; in spite of her stepmother's fury it had been worth it. There were no regrets, and next time, she knew, it would be even better. Next time she'd have no fears about taking control, slipping him inside her body. She had, in truth, been a little too timid for that last night and anyway, she knew she really shouldn't. What they had done had been enough – for now. She closed her eyes and briefly recalled what just the touch of her breasts against his penis had done to him.

Oh, how she wished she could see him again tonight! But that wasn't going to be possible. Tonight was a class night and so she knew she'd have to at least look over her notes before she went. That it all seemed, compared to him, so unimportant, almost silly, was aggravating but unavoidable.

Fitnat reached underneath her bed for her folder and then stopped as she remembered so many other things about him. How good he'd tasted! How big! How he'd wanted her to have pleasure, touching every tender part . . .

'Fitnat!'

The voice was her father's and so she hurriedly pushed the folder back under her bed again and assumed an innocent smile.

'Coming, Daddy!'

But then maybe she'd go to Atlas tonight and see him anyway. She had his number, after all. Maybe . . .

Çöktin held the little model aloft and showed it to Osman Tekeli, who sniffed and turned aside when he saw it.

'I don't know where she got that from!' he said angrily. 'Abomination!'

Çöktin shrugged. 'A friend who visited Egypt?' he said.

'I don't know! I took it away from her!'

'And how did Lale respond to that?' Çöktin said as he put the model of the Egyptian god Anubis the Jackal on Osman Tekeli's sideboard.

'She cried.'

'But she didn't say where she got it from?'

'It is immaterial,' Tekeli snapped. 'I didn't ask!'

'You just took it away and—'

'She took it back once,' Tekeli said as he sat down and then put his head in his hands. 'But I retrieved it.'

'How?'

Even though his head was in his hands he turned aside to make his next utterance. 'I beat her!'

Not a few men would have been openly proud and feel fully justified in beating their own female relatives. But Tekeli, even though he had done it, wasn't happy about it. Now, at the mention of it, he was crying.

There were other sad little things in the sad little box. A hairgrip with a butterfly on it, a piece of red, sparkly material, a photograph of an elderly man and woman – very secular-looking – Çöktin wondered whether they were Lale and Osman's dead parents. After all, quite a few of the new religious types came originally from secular families. And then there was a postcard. It was a picture of the twelfth-century Ulu Cami in Urfa. On the back of the card, which was addressed to Lale, were the words 'Having a lovely holiday!'

'Who's this from?' Çöktin asked.

Tekeli looked up and shook his head. 'One of her teachers.'

'A nice religious picture, sir,' Çöktin said. 'Why did you confiscate this?'

'Because it's from a man.'

'What, a male teacher?' Çöktin frowned. 'At your İmamHatip lisesi? I would have thought he would have known better.'

'No, no, no! It's one of her tutors.' Tekeli shrugged. 'She had extra lessons for certain subjects.'

'And this man?'

'English,' he said. 'Maximillian Esterhazy – a very good teacher.'

164

'Maximillian Esterhazy?' Çöktin sat down. 'Sir, did your sister ever go to meet this man on her own?'

'Only here or in public places,' Tekeli said haughtily. 'I would take her to a public place, like a çay bahçe, and they would have their lesson. Then I would return to pick her up. Mr Esterhazy, after this first little error, understood completely. He is a most intelligent and sensitive person.'

'Our father, Inspector, was indeed a titled person,' Maria Salmon said, İkmen thought wearily. 'His name was Count Frederick Esterhazy and his father had been an aide to the old Emperor Franz Josef. Frederick, however, in later life, became a Nazi. And before you say anything about what Maximillian may have told you, that is the truth.'

'Mrs Salmon—'

'I don't say it lightly, Inspector,' she said. 'If my brother were not missing I wouldn't be saying it at all. It is a terrible admission. Our father was in the SS. I don't think I need to elaborate about that, do I?'

'No.' İkmen raised his head from his hands to light a cigarette.

'In 1945, when it was nearly all over for Hitler, my father put myself and my mother on a train going west. With the Russians advancing from the east and the British and Americans from the west, my father felt that my pregnant mother and I stood more of a chance of survival with the latter. This proved to be true, and my brother, Maximillian, was indeed born in London.'

'So why did Max lie?' İkmen said. 'That was his father . . .'

'Yes,' she said, 'it was. And for years we thought he was dead. I'll be honest with you, Inspector, I prayed that he was. But then suddenly my mother started getting letters, which I saw her hide – from places very far away in Brazil and Panama. Not only was my father alive, he was also making a lot of money – much of it for us. I left home at that point and I never went back. I would never, you understand, have told the British authorities about my parents, but I had to go; I couldn't take his filthy money. Maybe my silence was wrong. My husband, Inspector, knows nothing of this.'

'I understand.'

'But to get to the point, with regard to my brother,' she said,

'Maximillian was brought up in some style by our mother. She told him the truth about our father – he must have been about ten at the time. But he kept that secret even then.' She sighed. 'He also enjoyed the money. I tried, as time went by, to get him to think about where the money came from and to question his own relationship with it. But Maximillian always reasoned it thus: "If I always do good with it, then it's no longer dirty." But as far as I can tell he's never done anything much with it except live some sort of hedonistic expatriate life in your country.'

'Many people, Mrs Salmon, end up washed up on our shores,' İkmen said. 'There is something, some people call it a poetic ennui, that can detain many foreign people of a romantic nature in this city. You know that Max has always taught English since he came here?'

'I understood he did something,' Maria Salmon said. 'But I never knew what. Now, though, he's going to have to work.'

'Why is that?'

'Because our father died last year,' she said. 'In Panama City, I believe. His Panamanian wife took everything he had and Maximillian was left without an allowance. The call I mentioned last Christmas was from him to me, asking for money.'

'You refused?'

'I don't have any money, Inspector. Both my husband and I are retired. We have children and grandchildren. And besides . . .'

'What?'

'Look, I don't think that my brother is a bad person. Please don't think that I do,' she said. 'It's just that . . . as soon as we knew that my father was alive, my mother started talking about the "old days" again, you know. About how well off we were under Hitler and how the philosophy behind Nazism was so romantic and . . . Maximillian read every book on the subject he could get his hands on. I tried to tell him the truth! And he would listen. But then he would say that there were things one could take that were good from National Socialism – he said that one day he would use those things to help people – all people, Jews, Gentiles . . .'

Magic. Even I, an uninvolved Turk, İkmen thought, know that Hitler was fascinated by magic.

'If my brother is missing, I can't help you,' she said wearily. 'I

166

have no idea where he might be or who he could be with. He's never spoken to me about any of his friends over there. The only person I ever remember him talking about was Alison.'

'Alison?' Even all these years on, just the name made his heart jump.

'Yes. Some backpacker, I understand. Left him for a Turkish chap.'

Oh, no, İkmen thought, no, Max, that's a lie and you know it.

'Mrs Salmon, I appreciate your candour,' he said. 'I am so sorry to have revived what I can tell are painful memories for you.'

'If Maximillian is missing you need to know as much about him as you can, don't you?' she said. 'Even I know that. And I do care . . .'

'Mrs Salmon, one last thing.'

'Yes?'

'Magic.' She would probably think that he meant stage show tricks, but . . . 'Was Max ever interested in magic?'

'What, you mean tricks? I believe he was in some conjuring society at Oxford.'

'Ah . . .'

'I hope you do mean tricks . . .' There was something of a threat in her tone, a hardness that made İkmen pause. 'Because if you mean what I think you mean, then you'd better be very sure of your facts. Hitler, as I'm sure most people now know, was very interested in the occult. Much of what he did was informed by astrology and the dark arts. I would hate to think that my brother was involved with such practices. They are very dangerous.'

İkmen let out a stream of smoke on a sigh. 'Well, Mrs Salmon,' he said, 'I would love to disabuse you of that notion . . .' And then he went on to tell her about her brother's interests, tempered with his own still sincerely held belief that Max only ever employed his knowledge and skills for good.

'I've no idea how he got into that,' she said when İkmen had finished his exposition. 'God knows! Maybe he wasn't just conjuring at university. But then he did sometimes do those card tricks, you know.'

'He was a student of a rabbi, an apparently famous Kabbalist here in İstanbul, for many years,' İkmen said. 'Maybe his interest began after he left England.'

167

'Or maybe our father had a hand in it,' she responded bitterly.

'Your father was involved in the occult?'

'I don't know,' she said. 'Not for sure. But he did know Hitler well and so he must have at least had an awareness of what the Führer was doing with regard to astrology and magic. You know, Inspector,' she continued, 'it chills my blood to think of Maximillian as student to a rabbi. Hitler not only sought to exterminate the Jews, he also wanted to take their wisdom from them and use it for his own purposes.'

'But Max is a good person.'

'I do hope that you are right,' she said.

'Yes . . .'

Shortly afterwards, with a promise to contact her as soon as he found out anything, İkmen brought Maria Salmon's call to an end.

As he put one cigarette out, so he lit another. Rather than providing any answers to the enigma that was Max Esterhazy, his conversation with the man's sister had only served to raise more questions. Of course, he could see why Max had lied about his family. Although entirely innocent, even the children of known Nazis wouldn't be exactly welcomed in most parts of Europe. That was understandable. But the fact that Max, given his true background together with his connection to his father, was involved in the occult was disturbing. And then, of course, there was Alison . . .

Again, just the thought of her made İkmen shudder. Alison had been his friend. Nothing more. He'd been in uniform at the time and Alison – well, just as Maria Salmon had said, she'd been a backpacker. On her way to India, he'd met her in the Kapılı Çarşışı, all long blonde hair and big pink boots. Alison had made him laugh and because of that, and because she was English too, he'd introduced her to Max. She'd liked him a lot. However, things didn't remain exactly civilised between the three of them for long. Max, just as he had with Çiçek, had been keen to introduce Alison to his world. But she'd been scared. A Catholic by upbringing, she'd seen Max's arts as something dark and dangerous. İkmen supported her decision not to become involved, but this hadn't gone down well with Max. The two men had, in fact, fought verbally over Alison, who left soon afterwards, without ever speaking to İkmen, at least, ever again. Much later she did turn up, but this time as a missing person last seen in Kayseri. İkmen, who in spite of his love for his wife and children had been silently in love with Alison too, had been devastated. But then so had Max, which was why it was so strange that he had told his sister Alison had gone off with a Turkish 'chap'. He could only mean İkmen himself, and that again just wasn't true. His relationship with Alison had only ever been friendly and respectful, even though it had hurt him considerably to keep it that way.

İkmen had his head in his hands again when the phone rang at his side. It was İsak Çöktin. As he listened to what the Kurd had to say, he put his hand in his pocket and took out Max's small, black address book.

As soon as he'd left İkmen, Mehmet Süleyman had had to spend some time briefing the two female officers for the observation at the Hammer bar that night. Ayşe Gün had been, as was her wont, completely professional about it, even if young Muazzez Çelik was rather more excited about wearing large amounts of black lace than she should be. But, he reminded himself, the women were only, at this stage, observing and so the principal thing was for them to blend in. He and Çöktin would be on hand in the evening – which was why he had so wanted to get some sleep now. But fate, it seemed, had taken against him. Çiçek İkmen had arrived bearing what she claimed was a packet of cigarettes he had left behind on her dining table.

'I thought you might need them,' she said with a nervous smile.

'Thank you.'

She put the packet of Winstons down on the telephone table and then said, 'Well . . .'

Even his father, who was normally asleep somewhere in the house, was out. Mehmet was therefore entirely alone with someone he had, until late the previous night, regarded with fatherly affection. However, in the light of what İkmen had said about his daughter, he now had to treat Çiçek with extreme caution. The pretext she had used to gain access to his house had, after all, been extremely flimsy. But Turkish hospitality being what it is, he couldn't just throw her out without so much as a glass of tea. And so they took their refreshments in the garden.

'I didn't realise that your house was next to a church,' Çiçek said, pointing towards the small dome topped by a cross that could just be seen over the top of the ancient wall to her left.

'Yes,' he said as he placed the tea glasses down on the table before him, 'quite a few Greeks live in the village. There are even several tavernas which are worth a visit.'

'Oh.'

He sat down opposite her and attempted a smile. He was both over-tired and worried about his up-coming visit to Krikor Sarkissian's clinic.

'You're very fortunate to live here,' she said, he felt a trifle nervously. 'Where I was brought up it's mad, but then you know that!' She laughed.

'It is certainly quieter here in Arnavutköy,' he said as he looked up at the back of his parents' rather shabby wooden villa.

'It's lovely.'

He shrugged. 'Better if one can afford a yalı on the waterfront.'

Or even better, a palace, he thought to himself. Little wooden houses in tiny village backstreets were things, he knew, most of the population couldn't even dare to dream about. But the family's old palace at Yeniköy had, it was said, just been sold yet again – this time, again it was rumoured, to someone whose wealth came from dubious sources. But that was life . . .

'You know,' she said as she leaned towards him, her face just a little flushed from the heat – or something, 'when I was little, my dad always used to tell me that when I grew up I'd live in a yalı.'

'I bet he said you'd pay for it yourself too,' Süleyman said with a smile.

'Oh, yes,' she laughed. 'Dad, as you know, doesn't believe that a woman's only route to wealth is through her husband.' She looked down at the floor and then added, 'Unlike Mum.'

'They both have their points.'

'I guess so.'

Çiçek then dug into her bag and produced her cigarettes and lighter. Mehmet, his head back now, looked up towards the sun.

'Mehmet . . .'

'Mmm?'

'Mehmet, I . . .'

Hearing the nervousness in her voice he moved his head to look across at her. 'What?' She was, he couldn't help but notice now, as red as a tomato.

'No.' She put her cigarettes and lighter back into her bag and then quickly sprang to her feet.

'Çiçek?' He rose too. 'Çiçek, what is it?'

'No. No.' She shook her head distractedly as she made her way back towards the house. 'I should never have come here.'

With a sinking feeling in the pit of his stomach, Mehmet moved quickly to catch up with her, and when he did he took one of her wrists in his hand.

'What is it, Çiçek?'

She was crying. Poor kid. İkmen had said that she was struck on him but neither Mehmet nor, he imagined, the young woman's father could have known it was this bad. 'Çiçek?'

'Oh, just let me go!' she said as she tried to pull her wrist out of his grasp.

'Not until you tell me what's the matter.'

She turned, her features now reddened and stained with tears, and then she said, 'You obviously don't know, do you?'

Well, he did, but how could he say anything without betraying İkmen's trust?

'About what?'

She pulled her wrist free from his grasp and ran into the house. With a shrug, Mehmet followed.

'Çiçek!'

She'd opened the front door and was almost in the street before she turned to him and said, 'You don't know how I feel about you, do you? Oh, I've made such an idiot of myself!'

And then she ran down the steps and tore along the street, just like he'd seen her do many times when she was a rather wilful teenager.

Mehmet went back indoors and heaved his tired body up the stairs to his bedroom. Poor Çiçek, but then poor me too, he thought. After all, it wasn't her he wanted, was it – it was his wife, his child and his health. He would also, he thought as the bright sunlight about him

171

began to fade to grey, enjoy an end to the deaths of these children in the city. That, too, would be very nice . . .

By the time Çöktin arrived back at the station, İkmen had worked it out.

'As above, so below,' he said to the young man as he entered his office and sat down.

Çöktin frowned.

'It was Lale Tekeli's number that gave me the key,' he said, and placed Max Esterhazy's address book down in front of Çöktin.

'If you look here,' he said, 'all the numbers are in pairs. So you've got the four-digit area code for İstanbul, followed by the seven-digit subscriber number.'

'Yes.'

'What Max has done is arrange all of the numbers in pairs and then swap the last two digits of the subscriber number with the paired number above it.'

Çöktin looked confused.

'The last two digits of Lale Tekeli's number come from the phone number above. The one above hers comes from *her* number, which is below it. See?'

Çöktin pulled a face. 'Yeah. But why?'

'What, the need for secrecy or the method employed?' İkmen asked.

'Well, both.'

'The word magician sums it up well enough, İsak,' İkmen said, and then noticing that the look of confusion had not left the younger man's face he added, 'I won't bore you with it. Just accept that it just is.'

'Yes, but, sir,' Çöktin said, 'how can Lale Tekeli's number be listed under S? And what are these other numbers in front of the area code?'

İkmen leaned back in his chair and sighed. 'Well, that I don't know, İsak,' he said. 'I've called the number paired with that of Miss Tekeli, which it turns out was the number for Aygaz which, however hard you may try to juggle with the words "gas" and "canister", will not add up to anything resembling the letter S. In addition, quite what Max does when he gets a number he cannot pair with another, I don't know. I don't even know whether knowing that Lale Tekeli was one of Max's students is actually any help to you and Inspector Süleyman.'

'I'm going to see whether either of the other dead youngsters went to him,' Çöktin said.

'Well, if they did, do give me their numbers to check out, won't you?'

'Yes. Sir, that this man was, as you call it, a magician . . .'

'İsak, I barely understand what "magic" is myself,' İkmen said as he rose wearily to his feet. 'As you know, my mother practised a form of "magic", for want of a better word. But from the little I know of it, what Max practises, Kabbalah, is a very high, powerful art, far removed from simple card layouts, coffee grounds and precognition. This is conjuration, ritual – the active pursuit of angels and demons by the practitioner.'

Çöktin automatically looked away. 'Sounds dangerous – for those who believe in such things.'

'In the wrong hands it is,' İkmen said as he gathered his books and papers into a not altogether sanitary carrier bag. 'I don't think . . .' He was about to say 'that includes Max' but then in light of his recent conversation with Maria Salmon he paused. 'In ritual the magician surrounds himself with those earthly things that correspond to the divine. As I said when you came in, as above, so below.'

'Sir?'

'As the digits interchange at the end of the phone numbers so things that represent other things may be interchangeable within magical ritual.' Seeing that Çöktin was still confused, İkmen said, 'For instance, if you want to work with a certain angel you get hold of as many of the things associated with that angel as you can. I don't know – words, colours, bits of equipment . . .' He paused briefly in order to light a cigarette. 'I don't honestly know where I'm going with this, İsak. I know so little about Kabbalah and yet I seem to be compelled to look for Max within its mysteries.'

'One of which does seem to have paid off, sir.'

'Yes . . . mad old fool that I am,' İkmen muttered. And then, looking up and smiling again, he said, 'I'm going back to Max's now for a while, İsak; reverse some of those numbers and see who I get. I'm also going to try to get some slightly more expert advice too. You don't know whether Constable Yıldız is about, do you?'

'No. Why?'

İkmen smiled. For some time now Constable Yıldız had been, occasionally, 'seeing' the gypsy Gonca, and although İkmen knew where she lived he didn't have her telephone number on him. Yıldız, young and probably very, very grateful, should, İkmen reasoned, have it with him somewhere.

'Oh, no matter,' he said as he led Çöktin out of his office and made his way down the stairs. 'Keep in touch, won't you, İsak?'

'Yes, sir.'

It was, Çöktin recalled, Inspector Süleyman who had used the word 'ritualistic' when talking about the murders of the two young girls. Maybe the association that had, in fact, broken down – or seemed to have done so – with Lale Tekeli, was not via Atlas Pasaj but through this magician. But then it was possible he was dead and anyway, hadn't Osman Tekeli said that his sister never ever met Max Esterhazy on her own? He went back into the office that he shared with Süleyman and called Gülay Arat's mother.

Not only could the woman, who was yet again so obviously drunk, not recall anyone by the name of Maximillian Esterhazy, she could barely remember the name Gülay. Çöktin lifted the receiver and punched in the Atamans' number.

Chapter 15

At just before four o'clock that afternoon, Metin İskender regained consciousness. İkmen was very quick to allow an eager Karataş the chance to go to see him.

'Don't push him, but just see if he remembers anything,' he said as the big man left the apartment.

Fortunately Alpaslan Karataş was accustomed to the sort of scene that was happening around his superior's bed. A pale, post-operative figure attached to several pieces of equipment was surrounded by a swirl of relatives, all talking at once and offering each other and the patient items of food and drink. It was difficult to distinguish one relative from another under these circumstances, and even though Karataş knew that his boss's wife was a much more cultured and stylish woman than any of the other İskenders, he couldn't immediately recognise her. She, in the end, pushing roughly past Metin's rakı-soaked father, found him.

'The doctor says that Metin needs rest,' she said anxiously. 'But with all of these people, what can I do?'

Karataş said that he'd go to look for the doctor and see what, if anything, could be done about the crowd. And so weaving past still weeping – and sometimes smoking – female relatives, he made his way to the nurses' station. Two middle-aged female nurses were talking to a haggard-looking man who Alpaslan recognised from the previous night.

When asked whether İskender was fit to be quizzed about the incident that had landed him in this place, the doctor said, 'Yes, that's OK. But I don't know whether what, if anything, he tells you is going to be of any use. The brain can behave erratically after trauma and his memory of the event may be either temporarily or permanently impaired.' Then he smiled. 'I'll come and move some relatives out of the way for you.'

After about ten minutes they managed to get most of İskender's family out into the car park. Only his wife, mother and sister remained – his father, having now woken from his drunken stupor, had disappeared off in search of more alcohol.

Belkıs İskender sat down beside the bed and took her husband's pale hand in hers. She then stroked his head while saying, 'Metin, darling, Sergeant Karataş is here to see you. Look.'

İskender opened his eyes to find Karataş' large face before him. 'Sir.'

'Karataş . . .' He reached one hand out to touch the face and said, 'You are OK?'

'Yes, sir.' Karataş sat down on a chair beside Belkıs İskender. 'I'm so sorry . . .'

'What for?' The normally hard eyes now softened by drugs looked almost friendly.

'For not being there to protect you, sir.'

İskender smiled. 'I don't know what happened,' he said. 'Yesterday has gone.'

'What, nothing?'

İskender very slowly shook his head. 'I just remember lines,' he said.

Karataş frowned.

'On a piece of paper, strange lines, nonsense.'

'And this piece of paper, sir, it was—'

Belkıs İskender, fearing that her husband was becoming distressed, said, 'Metin . . .'

'Sssh,' her husband soothed. 'I'm OK, Belkıs.' Then turning to Karataş he said, 'I'm sorry, Alp, I don't know what it means. Just these lines . . . I think the piece of paper was near or on that man's bed, you know the man . . .'

'Mr Esterhazy, sir.'

'Yes, that's it.'

Karataş looked down at İskender's hands, one of which bore a cannula for a drip. Then he took his notebook and pen out of his pocket and placed them on the bed.

'Sir, do you think you could draw these lines?'

Belkıs İskender shot him an outraged look.

'Yes,' İskender said. 'But it's only a pattern.'

Karataş handed him the notebook and pen and then watched as İskender, with painful slowness, drew a figure that zigzagged backwards and forwards across the page. As he did this, Karataş imagined İkmen's face when he saw this nonsense. But then maybe he'd make more of it than the obviously annoyed Belkıs İskender. After all, as Karataş was only too aware, İkmen was investigating some very odd things back at the Esterhazy apartment. Just before he left some gypsy drenched in jewellery had turned up. İkmen, he noticed, had greeted her with obvious enthusiasm.

He didn't think he'd be like this, gabbling on like a fool.

'You see I have to meet my sergeant at six, and so I really don't have a great deal of time,' Süleyman said as he nervously paced the room in front of Krikor Sarkissian's considerable desk. 'So if we may, Doctor,' he said, 'conclude this business . . .'

'Once you've sat down, we will,' the Armenian said. 'Please take a seat, Inspector. My chairs do not bite.'

Dr Sarkissian looked grave. That combined with his insistence that he sit down could only mean one thing. He had AIDS. Wringing his hands compulsively, Süleyman wondered how he might retain any sense of dignity in the face of such a thing.

'Doctor—'

'Sit down!'

It was an order. How dare he? Süleyman looked down at the small, elegantly dressed man behind the desk with undisguised fury.

'Please,' Krikor Sarkissian then added gently. 'Please sit down, Inspector.'

And almost before he could think about what he was doing, Süleyman found himself sitting in the chair in front of Krikor Sarkissian's desk, his head down, ashamed, like a naughty school child brought before his disapproving teacher.

'Now I have your test results,' Krikor said, 'and I'm delighted to be able to tell you that you are clear of HIV infection . . .'

Where the tears came from he didn't know, but it must have been a big place because there were so many of them. This, he thought as the tears just kept breaking across him, is not in the least bit dignified

– and he felt ashamed. But he was also completely helpless in the face of such a release of tension, which is what this was. Aware only later of Krikor's hand on his shoulder, his entire body shook for a good ten minutes after the doctor's short but, to him, world-changing, statement.

Only when he had managed to retain his composure enough to raise his head from his hands did the Armenian speak to him again.

'Now can you see why I wanted you to sit down?'

Süleyman, through sobs, smiled.

'Even when it's good news, people need to be looked after,' Krikor said. 'No one, whichever way the test results go, is ever prepared for this,' he smiled. 'Now I'm going to ask Matilde to make you a cup of coffee and then we're going to talk.'

'Yes, but I—'

'Just five minutes,' Krikor said as he held a hand aloft to silence him. 'I think you owe me that.'

He'd only told him things he knew already, but as Mehmet Süleyman walked out of the doctor's office and made his way towards the station, he knew why Krikor Sarkissian had done so. In future, and if he ever wanted to have any sort of second chance with his wife, things would have to be different. But then the past few months had, if nothing else, taught him that he could control his baser urges. Odd really, he'd been a master of self-control when he was younger. What had happened to change that he wasn't really sure. But he knew that in the future he would have to revert to his former mode of behaviour again – which was no bad thing.

This didn't, of course, mean that he couldn't have sex, however. And when he went to see what Gün and Çelik had come up with as regards 'costumes' for the evening he felt that he probably needed it rather more than he had imagined he would. Çelik, with her long blonde hair tied into a messy bun at the back of her head, looked particularly stunning in her black lace ball gown.

But as soon as the women had gone, Süleyman, now partnered once again with Çöktin, resolved to keep his mind on the job at hand. Tonight, with any luck, they might get some sort of idea about what was going on at the Hammer and, if they were even more fortunate, who was doing it.

*   *   *

So far, Max Esterhazy's address book had yielded his barber, Simurg bookshop and the home of a young girl who had once taken lessons from him, but was now at university in America. And when Çöktin did finally call İkmen back, on his way out to Beyoğlu, it was with mixed news.

'Cem Ataman, the suicide, was one of Esterhazy's students,' he said. 'But he stopped his lessons just over six months ago.'

'And the other girl?'

'I've yet to contact someone sober at the Arat house,' Çöktin responded gloomily.

'OK.'

İkmen replaced the receiver and looked across at the exotic figure of Gonca the gypsy, lying amid numerous tomes, atop Max's old leather Chesterfield. When she felt his eyes on her, she looked up and smiled. Momentarily dazzled, İkmen looked away. All breasts, glitter and teeth, no wonder young Yıldız kept going back for more. At nearly fifty, it seemed Gonca had lost none of her appeal to the opposite sex. But how much of this was due to her self-confessed sexual appetite as opposed to looks and outright sorcery, İkmen wasn't sure.

He picked the telephone receiver up and dialled yet another number. The woman who answered sounded vaguely familiar. But he went into his usual routine of introducing himself – until she stopped him.

'You work with my ex-husband,' she said.

And then he remembered. Zuleika Süleyman. Allah, but what a life she had led poor Mehmet all those years ago! Always buying things, forever, just like his current wife, suspicious of his every move.

'Zuleika.'

'Yes, now Zuleika Topal.'

'Congratulations, Mrs Topal.'

'So how can I help you, İkmen?' she said, resorting to the high-handed tone she had always used with him when she was married to Mehmet. 'And how did you get this number?'

İkmen told her about Max and how he had possibly disappeared.

'Well, that's very odd,' she said.

'Why is that, Mrs Topal?'

'Because my stepdaughter, Fitnat, has a lesson with Mr Esterhazy tonight. She's on her way, or rather she told me she was on her way to his apartment now.'

'You know for certain that she had a lesson with him tonight?'

'Yes. Well, I believe so,' she said. 'Mr Esterhazy telephoned her yesterday.'

'Did you take the call?'

'No, Fitnat did.' There was a pause during which he thought he heard her smack those disapproving lips of hers. 'Oh, unless . . .'

'What?'

'Fitnat likes to hang around with all those weird Goths at Atlas Pasaj. She knows I disapprove, but—'

'Mrs Topal, does Fitnat have a mobile telephone?'

'Of course! If she's doing something she shouldn't, it will be switched off, though.'

'Can I have the number anyway? I really do need to track Mr Esterhazy down.'

'Yes.' She looked the number up and gave it to him. 'Will you let me know if you manage to get hold of her?'

'Of course,' İkmen said. 'I may even meet her. I'm at Mr Esterhazy's apartment myself.'

'But what about if she's gone to Atlas?'

İkmen knew what Süleyman had planned for the Hammer, but he didn't mention that to her. 'I'm sure that if she's there without your permission, we can pick her up,' he said.

'I would be very grateful, Çetin,' she replied. İkmen, holding back the laughter her unaccustomed use of his first name caused, said that he would do what he could and then, as soon as he'd put the phone down, he tried to call the girl's mobile without success. And so it was then that he contacted Süleyman.

He'd wanted to speak to him anyway.

'What did Krikor Sarkissian have to tell you?' he said, coming straight, and rapidly, to the point.

'I'm clean, thank you, Çetin,' his friend replied. 'Thanks be to Allah.'

'Yes, indeed.' İkmen agreed. Though in no way a religious man, he had secretly said one or two prayers for Süleyman. He'd also, as he was doing now, shed one or two tears for him too, although this time his silent tears were of relief rather than anxiety.

'Is there anything else?' Süleyman asked. He was obviously unaware of the effect this news was having on İkmen. But then, when it came to his private life, he could be somewhat closed off even with intimates like İkmen. The latter cleared his throat. 'The name Fitnat Topal mean anything to you, Mehmet?'

'Oh, yes, I know Fitnat,' his friend said with more than a touch of disdain in his voice. 'A little flirt.'

'Did you also know that she was one of Max's students?' İkmen said. He then went on to report his conversation with Zuleika.

Süleyman was shocked. 'But if she heard from Max yesterday . . .'

'*If* she did,' İkmen corrected. 'Fitnat took the call herself and so until we speak to her, we won't know. Zuleika thinks she may well have gone to Atlas Pasaj.'

'Well, we'll soon find out, won't we?' Süleyman replied. 'Gün and Çelik have just gone in.'

'Tell them to keep a lookout for her,' İkmen said. 'And if and when you find her I will need to speak to her.'

'OK.'

İkmen replaced the receiver and then looked across at Gonca once again. This time she was deep inside the books, scribbling her findings down on a pad of paper.

'Problems?' she asked, not looking up as she spoke.

'Complications,' İkmen replied.

Gonca laughed. It was a deep, throaty sound. 'What do you expect of a magician?' she said.

'I don't know.' He lit a cigarette and then leaned back in the chair and looked up at the ceiling. 'You know, Gonca, I've been a friend of Max Esterhazy for thirty years and yet I've not known him at all.'

'İbrahim Dede told me that the Englishman was the only pupil the old Kabbalist Rebbe Baruh would ever take,' she said.

İkmen shook his head. Knowing what he now did about Max's past, that seemed incredible. What had Max done? Had he, like Hitler before him, sought to rob the Jews of their magic by force? He couldn't imagine it and yet . . . There had, he recalled, been a violence in Max that day they had argued about Alison. He'd accused İkmen of all sorts – wanting the girl for himself, meddling in things he didn't understand.

Gonca, as could be her wont, suddenly lost patience with what she was doing and threw one of the books to the floor.

'I could go on with these correspondences for ever,' she said. 'Meaningless unless we know what your magician might have planned. And as for this . . .' She held the drawing that İskender had made in the hospital aloft for İkmen to see. 'When I first saw it I thought that maybe it was the Lightning Flash.'

'What?'

'Oh, it's the way the practitioner draws divine light down from the top of the tree, the God-head, into his own material body at the bottom,' she said. 'Kabbalists can't work without doing that – I think. It's very complicated, all this, you know, İkmen. I'm just a simple gypsy . . .'

At that moment, Karataş, who had been making coffee for them all, came in from the kitchen.

'If anyone comes to the door, I want to answer it,' İkmen said as he watched the big man place a cup in front of Gonca. 'It may be one of Max's students.'

'Yes, sir.'

'So, Gonca, look, if you don't think the thing İskender drew was this Lightning Flash then what is it?'

But Gonca, true to her nature, was rather busy looking at Karataş.

'Allah!'

Only when he had left them did she return to their previous conversation.

'I think it's a sigil,' she said. 'A written or drawn talisman. Magicians use them to capture the essence of something or someone. If you have someone's sigil you can, so they say, control that person. I don't know what they mean and even looking through these books isn't helping.'

'But if Max came back to the apartment to get this . . .'

'Sigil. Maybe he wants or needs to have control over that person,' Gonca said. 'But then do we know that it was Esterhazy who came here and shot your colleague?'

'No.' İkmen sighed. 'No, but if Max is dead then surely I would feel – something . . .'

'Would you?' she smiled. 'By your own admission, you don't know him as well as you thought you did. There's a lot of power in this place, you know, İkmen,' she said. 'Trust me.'

And then she got up and started walking towards the door.

'Where are you going?'

She shrugged. 'To the kitchen.'

İkmen raised his eyes heavenwards and said, 'Please leave Sergeant Karataş alone, will you, Gonca? For me? He's had a very bad couple of days and he needs to keep his mind on his job.'

But Gonca just kept on walking, her long red skirts swishing seductively around bare ankles encircled with jingling bracelets. But then what, really, did İkmen expect? As his wife was always saying, 'If you will always engage these outcasts to help you, you can't expect them to be reliable.' Which was true. Over the years he'd worked with a variety of people 'on the edge' as it were – transsexuals, gypsies, soothsayers, beggars. And sometimes they'd helped and sometimes they'd hindered. But what they had always consistently done was their own 'thing'. Whatever the problem he needed help with, whatever the urgency of the information required, these sorts of people – those most like him, in reality – had always done whatever it was to the beat of their own drum. Not unlike Max. He'd gone for help to Max. He had sought him out over that Goat of Mendes image – the desecration of the holy places. Something, İkmen thought, the Nazis had done. But Max? No, Max wanted to do good. His sister had said so; İkmen himself had always believed it. But then, yet again, he thought, how well do I or did I know this man?

İkmen picked the piece of paper bearing the sigil up off the floor and looked at it. Utterly, as Gonca had said, meaningless. Just a squiggle in biro. And they didn't even know whether it had anything to do with whoever came into the apartment and shot İskender or not. Maybe it was just a pattern – an innocent, zigzag doodle İskender had spotted somewhere in Max's bedroom just before he hit the floor. İkmen put the piece of paper in his pocket and then scowled when he heard Gonca's deep laughter coming from the kitchen.

Chapter 16

The atmosphere, as well as the décor, inside the Hammer wasn't what they had expected. There were no artificial tombstones, no fake cobwebs, not even a dark corner in which to be miserable. And although the clientèle was almost entirely made up of people in black clothes, with black make-up and heavily scarred arms, the harsh neon lighting gave the place more of a modernistic, Huis Clos feel than something Frankenstein's monster might find familiar. Looking around now that they'd had a chance to get drinks and find a banquette on which to sit, the two officers admitted to each other that they felt overdressed. These Goths, or so it would seem when they compared the Hammer to other establishments in the Pasaj, were both super cool and serious about what they did – or didn't. Getting to talk to people was, they both felt, going to be very difficult unless, of course, someone came to talk to them first.

'That doesn't seem very likely,' Gün said as she tried to stare without hope into the depths of her mineral water.

'Does seem to bear out the idea that this might be the place to come to get into more serious stuff, though, doesn't it?' Çelik replied.

'I've seen no evidence of Satanism, have you?' Gün, who was older and more experienced, responded.

Çelik looked down. 'No . . .'

'No, so don't make any assumptions.'

The heavy trance music that had, until just a few moments before, thundered through every fibre of the building started up again. Çelik, who quite liked trance herself, started to move her head to the beat. Gün, on the other hand, shook her head in despair and then signalled to her colleague that she was going to try to find the toilet. The girl at the bar, a thin, drugged-out-looking individual with a spectacular scar at her throat, pointed Gün in the direction of the basement.

Down there, surprisingly, it was as bright as it was up in the bar and as she walked down the bright white corridor towards the toilet, Gün felt as if she were going into an operating theatre. Pictures lined the walls – some, like the doctored reproduction of that famous shot of Marilyn Monroe standing over an air vent, made her laugh. Marilyn with fangs and a tail! But then there was another of what looked like a genuine dead man that made her cringe. The one that really caught her attention, however, was a simple framed line drawing. She took her mobile phone out of her handbag and called Süleyman immediately.

Gülizar had been making money on the side like this for several years now. Her father drove a phaeton, taking trippers and sometimes naval cadets up to the monastery, but that didn't earn him very much. And although her family had only the meanest sort of shack on the water-front, there were fourteen of them and so extra money was always welcomed. What Gülizar did, therefore, was both useful and justi-fied. Not that she was actively looking for work when she met him. It was dark and she'd just gone out to get some water when she saw him walking down the hill from the direction of the monastery. Thinking of anything but work, she walked over to see what he was doing. It wasn't, after all, usual to see someone coming away from St George's at this time of night. It very quickly became obvious what he wanted.

'All right,' she said. He gave her the money and she pulled him behind the nearest tree.

'Not here!' he said as he shoved her hand away from his crotch.

'Why not?'

'Up at the monastery.'

Gülizar frowned. It was quite a long climb up there, and deserted too.

'Why?'

'Because it's what I want!' he hissed. 'Now are you coming or—'

'I'll need an extra ten million,' she said, 'for the time and trouble.'

'All right! All right!'

It wasn't a long climb, but it was steep and she was too breathless to speak even if she'd wanted to. But then men in his condition – she'd felt he was already hard – didn't usually want to talk – only sometimes they wanted her to when she did them.

When they reached the walls of the monastery, he told her to take her clothes off. Gülizar didn't like this. 'I told you,' she said force-fully, 'that I'm not doing the lot – only pulling you off.'

All this fuss just for a wank! She should have known . . .

'Get your clothes off!'

Something in his tone told her that she should really do as she was asked. And so she removed her clothing and, ragged as it was, she piled it neatly on the ground beside her. Strangely, she felt very exposed and almost ashamed. Naked wasn't something she was accus-tomed to being, most of her customers settling for just some quick, fumbling relief.

'Come here,' he said.

She went, afraid now – although quite why, apart from the vul-nerability her nakedness made her feel, she couldn't say. He reached inside his jacket and took a small bottle out of one of his pockets.

'Use this,' he said.

She took the lid off and sniffed. It was musty and sweet. He unzipped his trousers as she poured a little drop of what looked like oil into her hand. This too was weird, but if it was what he wanted . . .

'Come on!'

Without looking down she rubbed the oil into his penis, watching his face as his stern mask closed its eyes upon her. And then sud-denly there was nothing.

Later she would have the impression of hands upon her, of a feeling inside somewhere between pleasure and pain and of light too – all around, white and harsh and startling.

This was real strong-arm policing. Armed officers swarming all over the bar – the whole of Atlas sealed off by further groups of men and women in full riot gear. Controlling them all – Süleyman, marching up and down, threatening, demanding. Those youngsters who weren't actually shaking were clinging to each other for support. İkmen would have been appalled.

But Süleyman had had enough. 'I want to see everyone's ID card and all foreign passports,' he said to the large group of people in the bar. 'I will then be asking you some questions and showing you some photographs. You may not leave until I say so.'

There was a murmur of dissatisfaction amongst the black-clad masses, but there was also a feeling that all they could do was bow to the inevitable.

Süleyman seated himself at a table in an alcove and waited the few minutes it took Çöktin to return from the station. He'd gone back to get a picture of Fitnat Topal that Zuleika had faxed over. So far the girl hadn't turned up at either Atlas or Max's place, and Süleyman wanted to know whether anyone present had seen her. He began with the bar staff. There were four of them – two boys and two girls. He checked their ID cards and then lit a cigarette.

'What do you know about this?' he said as he took the picture Gün had discovered in the basement from the banquette behind him.

One of the boys shrugged.

'Well?'

The other boy and one of the girls, the one without the scar at her neck, looked at each other. 'I know it was a gift,' the girl said. 'To the owner.'

'Who is?'

'Beyazıt Bey,' she said. 'Beyazıt Koray.'

'And where is Beyazıt Bey at the moment? Do you know?'

She shrugged. 'He doesn't come in very often.'

'Well, do you have a telephone number for him?'

'Hakan does.'

The younger of the two boys gave Süleyman a mobile number, which he passed to Çöktin with instructions to call the man and get him down there. He then showed the staff photographs of Cem Ataman, Gülay Arat, Lale Tekeli and Fitnat. One of the boys said he thought he'd seen Cem before, but he wasn't sure.

'What do you know about the people who come here?' Süleyman asked.

'What do you mean?'

'I mean, what type of people come here and why?'

The scarred girl, an expression of disbelief on her face, said, 'Well, as you see.'

'What?'

'People who like skate punk and trance. People who like to wear black.'

He leaned across the table and took one of her hands in his, turning the arm as he did so. 'People who like to cut themselves.'

After first looking down at her arm, she flicked her eyes up to his face and said, 'A lot of people cut themselves for many different reasons.'

'And what is your reason, Miss . . .' he looked down at her ID card to remind himself of her name, 'Özbek?'

She put her hand to her throat and looked down once again. 'I have my own reasons.'

'A lot of you young people involved in this scene do it.'

'Maybe we do it out of frustration,' the unscarred and seemingly older girl said. 'Maybe it's like a protest.'

'Against what?'

'Where do you want me to start?' she said.

Süleyman smiled. 'Have you ever heard,' he said, 'of the American actor James Dean?'

Hakan laughed.

'So this,' Süleyman flung his arms in the air to express his lack of language for this phenomenon, 'this movement you have here is all about the disaffection of youth, nothing more.'

'I guess . . .'

'And so that couple over there –' he pointed to a large, long-haired man standing beside an extraordinarily made-up woman, both of them very obviously middle-aged – 'are just simply anomalies, are they?' He paused. 'I've seen at least three men and probably as many as ten women who are probably older than I am since I've been here. What's going on?'

The older girl, who was called Soraya, said, 'Well, you obviously have a theory about it so why don't you just come out and ask us about that?'

Impressed by her boldness, Süleyman first smiled at her and then said, 'OK. Satanism – tell me what you know about it.'

*   *   *

İkmen didn't get home until nearly midnight. A combination of no sleep the previous night combined with an overload of information about Max, his interests and past, had finally brought him to a standstill at just after eleven. So after he'd first rescued Karataş from Gonca's attention and then taken the gypsy herself home, he'd headed for his own place and hopefully a little sleep.

As he walked into the clean but shabby living room, he saw that his son Bülent was still awake, watching CNN on the family's new satellite service.

'I thought you'd be plugged in to MTV,' İkmen said as he threw his briefcase down on to the floor and sat down.

'Dad, do you think we'll go to war?'

He'd never really said much about the mounting tension between the United States, Britain and Iraq before. Indeed, for most of his short life, Bülent had concerned himself with very little apart from enjoying himself. But he had been worried about his call-up to the army for a time when he was younger and now, with that call-up imminent, he was concerned once again.

'I don't know,' İkmen said. 'İnşallah we'll be spared.'

'I don't want to fight.' Bülent said it quickly, head down, obviously ashamed of this admission.

'I know,' İkmen sighed. 'Do you remember we talked about it some years ago? I said then that I could understand your feelings, Bülent, and that still holds good today. But, unfortunately, this current situation is one that we just have to watch and wait to see what will happen.'

'I know.' And then he went back to looking at the TV again.

Everyone was concerned, most of them in a quiet, accepting sort of a way. İkmen himself was worried – mainly for Bülent. But he was trying hard not to show it. After all, what did he or anyone else really know? It was thought, in fact the Americans and the British based their call for war on it, that Saddam Hussein had weapons of mass destruction – whatever that meant. Chemical and biological agents had, they said, been stockpiled by the Iraqi leader for many years. A rather cynical English reporter his brother knew said they knew this because they, the British, had sold them to him. But whether he still had them and, further, would actually use them against an

190

enemy was difficult to guess. He'd heard, like a lot of other people, stories about the issuing of gas masks and possible vaccination programmes against things like smallpox for those living near the Iraqi border. But if he were honest about it, he tried not to think along these lines too often. Max, he knew, had been extremely worried about the prospect of war. Like İkmen himself, he was of the generation that had managed to avoid conflict. In İkmen's case, too young for Korea, too old for any involvement in the Gulf or Afghanistan.

Bülent switched off the television and yawned. 'Çiçek was looking for you earlier,' he said.

'She could have phoned me; she's got my number.'

Bülent shrugged. 'I think she wanted to see you,' he said. 'She looked a bit, you know, agitated. When you didn't come home she just left.'

More problems, no doubt! İkmen couldn't help thinking it. Just as he got one child settled, so another one seemed to 'agitate', as Bülent put it. He hoped this wasn't about Mehmet Süleyman, though his gut feeling was that it probably was. If only some nice young man would just appear in Çiçek's life and make it all better for her! But then, as he knew only too well, life was rarely like that and even if one did try to manipulate it to be so, like a Kabbalist, there were terrible dangers. What was Max Esterhazy doing? Or what had he already done? Whatever it was, and notwithstanding what Max's sister had told him, İkmen couldn't shake the belief that what he was doing had to be to the good. That Max was dead was unthinkable – and yet that blood . . .

'I'm going to bed now,' Bülent said as he dragged his long, tired body out of the room.

Alone now, İkmen closed his eyes. Alison's face, her skin white as paper, came into his head, smiling. With hindsight, she'd patronised him horribly – calling him 'sweet' and 'dear' and feeding him pistachios with her fingers. But there had been a moment, just once. On the stairwell at her flea-bitten backpackers' pansiyon, it had been early but already hot. He'd taken her in his arms and he'd kissed her with a passion that had frightened him. He was a married man with three small children at the time, but he'd kissed that girl and she had responded to him. She'd wanted him to make love to her, she'd even used those words 'make love'. Not sex, not a fuck, making love. But, of course, he hadn't; even then he just didn't do that sort of thing and probably for the best. After all, look where that sort of behaviour had landed Mehmet Süleyman. Or not. Happily, as he now knew, his friend did not have HIV and so, for the moment, he had got away with it.

But the tendency towards illicit liaison had still to be inside him, didn't it? Like the old *Arabian Nights* story of the djinn in the bottle, once out such things would only cause chaos. A door once opened, never closed again ... Of course, İkmen himself had never been unfaithful to his wife. But if just that one illicit kiss were anything to go by then that which was forbidden was a fearsome drug. Even now he could see every detail of it in his mind as clearly as if he were watching a movie. The taste of her mouth, the feel of her breasts against the front of his uniform, that terrible rush of animal desire that had caused him to pin Alison to the wall with his body.

And, although he tried to distract himself by lighting a cigarette, when İkmen opened his eyes he broke down completely and wept.

'It's called the Goat of Mendes. This lot like this sort of thing.'

'I know what it is, Mr Koray,' Süleyman said harshly. 'It's where you got it that interests me.'

'One of my customers drew it,' he said. Probably in his mid-thirties, rich and obviously unimpressed by policemen, Beyazıt Koray was taking it all very casually.

'Who?'

'You want his name?'

'Yes.'

'Hüsnü.'

Süleyman looked across at Çöktin, who raised his eyebrows.

'How do you know this man?'

'As I said, he's a customer,' Koray replied. 'He also helps me out sometimes with my computer system.'

'Is he a hacker?'

'I don't know. He's odd,' Koray added. 'But then most of those Internet obsessives are odd, aren't they? He doesn't come in that often because he's always got something to do on his own system.'

'Why did he give you the drawing?'

'I don't know,' he said. 'Maybe he thought it would look good in here. He's like the rest of them – you know, on about demons and suchlike all the time. That picture of Marilyn Monroe was done by another customer. They like that sort of thing. This is one of the few places they can express that.'

'Are you aware of the fact, Mr Koray, that images like this have been used to desecrate places of worship?'

'No.'

Süleyman leaned closer in towards him across the table. 'Are you also aware of the fact that this establishment has a reputation for being a meeting place for Satanists?'

Koray sighed and shook his head. 'Just because the kids wear black . . .'

'No!'

'Look, Inspector,' he said, 'I sell these people drinks and somewhere to meet. What they choose to do beyond that is not my business. So they like copies of old horror film posters, wear black nail varnish and talk in flat voices – it's a phase with most of them anyway!'

'Even the ones who are forty-five?'

'I'm not in the business of telling people what to do!'

'You know they communicate in their own peculiar language?'

'Some of the kids like to copy the transsexuals! They think it's cool. What of it?'

'Rumour has it that some of these disguised conversations concern devil worship,' Süleyman said. 'We think people meet here and then go on to other, secret locations where foul rites—'

'I don't know anything about that,' Koray said emphatically. 'Anyway, what do you want me to do? Tell them they can't go elsewhere to worship the Devil? How am I supposed to police that myself?'

Süleyman turned to Çöktin and said, 'You'd better go and get Kasım's friend.'

'Yes, sir.'

'Take a couple of the men with you.'

When Çöktin had gone, he turned back to Beyazıt Koray and handed him the photographs of the three dead youngsters and Fitnat.

'Do you know or have you seen any of these people, Mr Koray? Three are dead and one is currently missing.'

Almost aimlessly he shuffled through the pictures until he came to the one that made his face blanch.

Süleyman narrowed his eyes. 'Mr Koray?'

Beyazıt Koray looked down at the floor and then said softly, 'Ah.'

By three o'clock in the morning, the cells and some of the interview rooms were alive with what looked like a plague of ghouls. If anything, Süleyman's desire to get answers to the questions that surrounded the recent deaths of the young people had increased. Specifically he wanted to come down hard on both Beyazıt Koray and Hüsnü Gunay. However, before he could question Koray he had to get his facts straight with Fitnat Topal.

'Did Mr Koray rape you, Fitnat?' he asked.

'No.' She was rumpled and a little drunk too. Her lipstick and eyeliner had slipped down her face and bled into her white foundation cream.

Constable Gün, still resplendent in black silk, said, 'But you were in Mr Koray's bed?'

'Yes.'

'But he didn't penetrate your body?'

'No.'

'So what were you doing in his bed, Fitnat?' Süleyman asked.

She tried hard not to think about it, just in case she smiled, and then said, 'Sleeping.'

Süleyman, with a sigh, raised his eyes up towards the ceiling and then lit a cigarette.

'All right, Fitnat,' he said. 'Let's leave Mr Koray for a moment and go back to the story you told your father, which was that you were due to have an English lesson with Mr Esterhazy at his Sultanahmet apartment. Is this true?'

'Well . . .'

'Is this true, Fitnat? Did Mr Esterhazy indeed speak to you on the telephone the day before yesterday to arrange this appointment with you? It is very important that I know the truth and only the truth about this subject.'

Fitnat looked down at her hands and sighed. 'Well, it's sort of true,' she said. 'I mean, yes, Mr Esterhazy did call me.'

'Are you sure?'

'Well, of course I am,' she said a little more aggressively now. 'I've been going to him for years! He called me and asked whether I would mind if we had our usual lesson at my place instead of his.'

'At your home?'

'No, at Hamdı Baba,' she said, naming a restaurant on Büyükada. 'He's done it before, in the summer. He said that because we're having such a fine September he wanted to make the most of that if I didn't mind. I said yes.'

'But you didn't meet him, did you?'

Fitnat lowered her head. 'No.'

'So what did you do instead?'

'You know what I did.'

'I want you to tell me.'

She looked up now, holding her head erect in a seeming show of defiance. 'I went to see Beyazıt.'

'What for?'

'You know . . .'

'Did any kind of sexual activity occur? Did he make you do any-thing—'

'No he didn't!' she said through gritted teeth. 'I told you, we slept.'

'All right! All right!'

He got up and, after instructing Gün to watch the girl while he was away, he went out into the corridor, put one cigarette out and immediately lit another. Burhan Topal and Zuleika would be arriving soon to take the girl away, which was a mercy. He leaned against the wall and blew out smoke in rings until he saw Çöktin coming up from the cells below.

'According to two members of his staff and a customer, Beyazıt Koray occasionally likes to take young ladies home,' the Kurd said when he drew level with his boss.

'Really.'

'Nothing Satanic, apparently,' Çöktin said. 'Clever, though, Mr Koray,' and he smiled.

'What do you mean?'

The Kurd moved his head closer in towards Süleyman. 'Apparently, he never penetrates them,' he said. 'No evidence, if you like, for fathers, brothers and sweethearts to act upon.'

'And so . . .'

'It is said, sir,' Çöktin said still with a smile, 'that Mr Koray is a very skilled individual.'

'I see. Well.' Süleyman cleared his throat. 'However, all of this is really a side issue, is it not, İsak? What we really need to do now is interview Mr Gunay.'

'Yes, sir.'

Süleyman caught sight of the familiar figure of his ex-wife and her husband coming down the corridor towards him.

He turned again to Çöktin. 'I'd like you to do that with me, İsak,' he said, 'after I've spoken to Mr and Mrs Topal.'

'Yes, sir.'

'Oh, and İsak, could you call Inspector İkmen for me?'

'It is nearly four o'clock in the morning, sir.'

'Yes, I know, but this is important.' He moved a little closer to Çöktin. 'It concerns Maximillian Esterhazy,' he said. 'It would seem that he really is still alive.'

Chapter 17

Sometimes events can overtake even the most important items of information. And so it wasn't until İkmen was on the launch, headed out towards Büyükada, that Süleyman had a chance to tell him about Hüsnü Gunay.

'Unfortunately Öz is his advocate,' he said, citing one of the city's most expensive lawyers. 'And so proving that he and the hacker Mendes are one and the same is going to be tough. He maintains that Mendes drew the image and e-mailed it to him.'

'Is it a print? I gathered it was an original,' İkmen said.

'I thought it was at first,' Süleyman replied. 'But yes, it is in fact a printout.'

'But why did this Gunay give it to the bar?'

'Because he thought Mendes would find the notion amusing,' he said. 'Gunay is an occasional presence in the Hammer – in tune, it would seem, with all that Gothic stuff. Apparently his "friend" Mendes finds all of that highly amusing and produced the artwork as a sort of a joke. He's not prepared at this time to say any more than that. Just like he's not prepared to discuss the peculiarities of the image . . .'

'The thirteen . . .'

'Quite.' Süleyman looked behind him at Arto Sarkissian and smiled. 'Which he claims was Mendes being ironic and so he couldn't possibly comment.'

'But you think he actually is Mendes?' İkmen said.

'I think it's very odd that Mendes, who finds things occult so amusing, should use an obviously demonic name,' Süleyman said.

'Maybe it's foreign,' İkmen replied. 'After all, we don't know where Mendes comes from or even what he or she is, do we?'

'No. But aside from that there is something else too,' Süleyman said with a frown. 'A complication. But we can't talk about it now. Maybe later.'

'Why not now?'

Süleyman held up his hand. 'Just trust me on this, Çetin.'

The older man shrugged. 'OK.'

The complication Süleyman was talking about hadn't actually arisen during the course of Gunay's interview. That had come later, when his lawyer, Adnan Öz, had had 'a word' with Süleyman afterwards. The word in question was Çöktin's name and the implication was that if Hüsnü Gunay had a day in court then so would the film-dubbing Yezidi. Öz had been, quite patently, angling for a deal.

As the great bulk of Büyükada came into view, Arto Sarkissian turned to İkmen and said, 'I understand this latest victim is a gypsy girl.'

'That's what the local officers say, yes,' İkmen replied.

'Do we know how old?'

'I don't think they're entirely sure,' İkmen responded gloomily. 'What does it matter anyway? Someone murdered her. She's dead when she shouldn't be.'

And, he thought, Max was supposed to be on the island yesterday. Max was alive and he was a connection too – to Cem Ataman, Lale Tekeli and, although only for the last few months, he had, so they'd learned just that morning, tutored Gülay Arat too. So what, if any-thing, was his connection to this gypsy?

As the launch pulled in to the side of the ornate Ottoman landing stage, İkmen experienced a feeling of intense loneliness. Because he and Süleyman had been working on different cases in different parts of the city, İkmen hadn't had time to tell his colleague everything he had discovered about Max Esterhazy. Not to mention Alison. But then no one, apart from Max, knew anything about her. And maybe Max knew even more about her than he had divulged to İkmen. Maybe Max even knew where she was.

Although part of Süleyman wanted desperately to go home and contact his wife about his test results, he had waited this long and so a few hours more would make little difference. Besides, at present he needed to be here on this beautiful, if slightly sad, little island. It was İkmen who went back to the city, needing to return to the pursuit of the still elusive Max.

The gypsies, the girl's family and friends, just stood at the bottom of the hill, their faces set and emotionless. Gülizar, so the local constable told him, had been 'well known' to men both local and from further afield. Poor and illiterate, if she had ever been off the island it would only have been to beg in the city. What did all this mean? If anything?

Gülizar had been stabbed through the heart and sexually assaulted, just like the other two girls. But unlike the others there wasn't or didn't seem to be any sort of connection between her and them. She wasn't and never had been part of the Goth scene, Max Esterhazy hadn't ever taught her and she was by no means affluent. The only tenuous link that existed was the notion that Max had been on Büyükada the previous evening. Although there wasn't, as yet, any evidence to support this. No one, certainly at Hamdı Baba, remembered seeing him, and yet if he'd asked Fitnat to meet him there, surely he must have looked in to see if she was about? Maybe he'd done that from a distance. It had to have depended, Süleyman supposed, upon what he was planning. Just the thought of it made him shudder. Had Max, as İkmen had almost shame-facedly suggested, intended to kill Fitnat, only lighting upon the unfortunate Gülizar when his student failed to show up?

But why would he do that? Why would Max, his friend, a kind and generous man in his experience, perform such evil deeds? İkmen had told him about how Max had lied about his past and Süleyman could, in part, understand that. But just because his father had been a Nazi didn't mean that Max was too. And İkmen concurred with this. The connection between Max and these murders was through his students and via Süleyman's own feelings about a ritualistic element inherent in the killings. Apparently Max was a much more powerful practitioner than had been previously thought. But that didn't necessarily mean that he was involved with killing anyone. Hüsnü Gunay – Mendes, if indeed that was what he was – hadn't responded to any of his questions about Max Esterhazy. Did he know or had he known Max or not? And what of the blood İkmen and İskender had found at Max's apartment? Was the older blood Max's, and where on earth had the other blood come from?

*   *   *

199

Demir Sandal hadn't wanted to go down into Karaköy, particularly seeing as that involved meeting Balthazar Cohen. But Jak Bey had insisted, and besides, it had enabled Demir possibly to gain a little more profit out of the enterprise. Balthazar was crippled and, according to his brother, in need of some erotic aids.

'Of course it depends upon your taste,' Demir said as he spread a vast swathe of books, magazines and videos before the eyes of the Cohen brothers. 'It's all here, Balthazar Bey – straight stuff, lesbian, bondage – everything you could want.'

Jak, who hadn't wanted the pornographer to come to the apartment, watched the door nervously against Estelle's return.

'What I want is a real woman!' his brother said tetchily.

'Well . . .'

Demir Sandal placed his large behind down in the chair next to Balthazar's and said, 'Now, Balthazar Bey, as you know, I don't provide women myself. But I do have – contacts. Now let us see, what is it that you require . . . ?'

'Oh, for God's sake!' Balthazar exploded. 'I know you've got tarts, Demir! You've got a record for pimping illegals! And as for what I want . . .' he leaned towards Sandal and shouted into his face, 'I want a girl prepared to have sex with me. She doesn't have to be pretty, young or even interested. She's just got to do it!'

Jak's feelings on the subject were that if Balthazar were a little kinder to Estelle, she might volunteer – maybe she even wanted to get closer to her husband herself. But Balthazar was adamant that wouldn't work. He was, he claimed, addicted to illicit sex and he hadn't had a 'fix' for nearly three years.

'Well, I will ask around and see what I can do,' Sandal said, and then, drawing Balthazar's attention back to his wares, he added, 'Now books, magazines . . .'

'Anything with lesbians,' Balthazar said dismissively.

'So a book, a video, a—'

'Everything,' Balthazar snapped, and then throwing a vicious look at Jak he said, 'My brother will pay. You can put it on his bill.'

Sandal looked across questioningly at Jak, who just shrugged his assent.

'Oh, what it must be to have a generous brother,' the pornographer said.

Jak managed a smile, but only just. Balthazar was now trying his patience to its very limit and so once Sandal had given him what seemed to be a huge selection of books and videos, Jak took him to one side to make payment.

'You'll need tea if you're going to do business,' Balthazar said. 'But the woman is out.'

'This won't take long, Balthazar,' Jak said.

He'd already made up his mind not to haggle. The costumes weren't expensive by European standards and besides, he was far too anglicised to be bothered with something he now saw as an unnecessary bore. Demir Sandal found it all highly amusing.

'Oh, Jak Bey,' he said, 'what have the English people done to you? Please, please, let us start again, this isn't right!'

Jak placed two large wads of banknotes down on the table and walked away. 'Take it or leave it, Demir Bey,' he said. 'I am very pleased with the workmanship of the garments you've sold to me and I am more than happy to give you what you ask.'

For a few moments, Demir Sandal just shook his head in disbelief. Then he clicked his tongue and said, 'Oh, Allah, what a great man! Jak Bey—'

'Thank you, Demir Bey.'

Jak wanted him to go now, before Estelle returned. He didn't want her seeing what he'd just purchased for her husband nor did he want to witness yet another of their rows. Demir Sandal pocketed the cash with lightning rapidity. Then he stood up.

'Ah, well, Jak Bey, I must be on my way,' he said. 'A lot of business to do in this city. A man can so rarely take his rest—'

'Don't forget about getting me a woman!' Balthazar interjected.

'Oh, no, Balthazar Bey. I will bend my mind to your problem immediately.' He stooped to shake hands with Balthazar and then turned to Jak and said, 'Ah, and, Jak Bey, but of course I promised you something else, didn't I?'

He put his hand inside his jacket and produced a videotape that looked as if it had seen much happier times. Minus a case, it was dusty and, probably by virtue of being in Demir's pocket, not a little greasy.

'Absolutely new and unique,' he said as he pressed the tape into Jak's rather unwilling hand. '*Women with Sea Snakes*,' he whispered. 'New frontiers have been set in this remarkable video, Jak Bey. In England they will love it, I promise you. I can make as many copies as you like, only twenty dollars, American, each.'

Somehow, Jak managed to usher him out of the apartment and, when he'd gone, he went back into the living room and tossed the video into a waste-paper bin. He'd been so happy to be back in İstanbul at first, but now he'd had enough – of Balthazar and his constant complaints, of Estelle's deep unhappiness, of the traffic, the bartering and of the way his nephew and his wife had become the objects of his brother's salacious speculation. What Berekiah and Hulya did to and with each other was their affair. He sat down opposite his brother and looked with distaste at the sight of Balthazar slavering over a magazine. Jak picked up the telephone directory and looked up the number for the British Airways office. Can my flight be brought forward somehow? he wondered.

'İkmen.'

He turned, only to be momentarily blinded by what looked like a cloud of purple and silver.

'Gonca?'

She walked over and threaded one of her arms through his. How long, he wondered, had she been lurking outside the station waiting for him?

'Now let us go to the apartment of the magician and let us talk,' she said.

'The keys are in my office,' İkmen replied.

'Then let us go and get them.'

He looked at her doubtfully and she laughed. 'OK, I'll wait for you outside,' she said. 'But if you're not out in ten minutes . . .'

'What do you want, Gonca?'

Her face assumed a serious expression. 'One of my people died last night,' she said. 'The daughter of a phaeton driver of the islands.'

'How do you know?'

'Ah . . .' She looked purposefully mysterious.

But İkmen wasn't easily taken in. The gypsies of the islands, though poor, had similar priorities to those in the city.

'An amazing thing, the mobile phone,' he said, and she smiled.

'All technology emanates from the creativity of man, İkmen,' she said. 'And that is magic.'

He went and got the key and the two of them then walked, arm in arm, towards Max Esterhazy's apartment. The sun was still unusually strong for the time of year and Gonca turned an appreciative face up towards it.

'So how, apart from the obvious, does this death on Büyükada concern you?' İkmen asked, hoping with every fibre of his being that his wife didn't see him arm in arm with Gonca.

'I was visited last night,' she said, 'by someone you know, a very nice boy . . .'

'Gonca!' İkmen stopped in his tracks and turned to look at her. 'Do tell me you didn't seduce Sergeant Karataş!'

'No, no, no, no, no!' she laughed. 'No, my "involvement" with the police hasn't increased of late, I can assure you, much as I would have liked it to have done. But—'

'So you saw Constable Yıldız.'

'Oh, no names, please,' she said. 'A person came to see me, troubled by death, you understand. One suicide, two murders. He used, this person, the word "ritual", copying, he said, his superior. Young people, killed around the city; young students maybe of a magician. I thought what a strange way for such similar modes of dispatch to be distributed – such disparate parts of the city . . . and then this morning—'

'Gonca, we are quite aware of the fact that these deaths are probably connected, possibly by Max.'

'We need to know some details about these dead children, İkmen, before we can proceed,' she said.

'That isn't my case, Gonca.'

'Oh, well then,' she said. 'Perhaps we ought to speak to Inspector Süleyman.'

'He's over on Büyük . . .'

'Wasting his time.' Gonca looked into İkmen's eyes with a fierce intensity. 'You know I've always wanted to meet him properly,' she said. 'I've heard many things. That he's extremely handsome, I know – I saw him once. But is he needful too, I wonder?'

She held İkmen's mobile phone, seamlessly lifted from his inside jacket pocket, up to his face, and said, 'Call him.'

'What details do you want, Gonca?' İkmen said, as he punched Süleyman's number into his telephone.

'I want to know if anything was found with the bodies,' she said. 'Flowers, fruit – things like that. Oh, and I'll need to know when they were born too.'

'I thought you said you weren't a Kabbalist,' İkmen said slightly sourly.

She led him into the front entrance of the apartment block and began to walk up the stairs. 'Oh, I'm not,' she said. 'But now that we have four we have a pattern – even I know that.'

Chapter 18

For once İkmen was genuinely baffled. There was a young man in the room that Gonca wasn't flirting with. It was most strange. But then maybe she was annoyed that Süleyman hadn't attended himself but had sent Çöktin over with the information she required. Or maybe it was because the Kurd's attitude was somewhat hostile.

'Cem Ataman committed suicide,' he said. 'Why do you want to know about him?'

'He died with a knife in his heart,' she said.

'Yes, which he did himself.' Çöktin turned to İkmen. 'Sir, I'm not happy about this method of procedure . . .'

'İsak, just tell her what she wants to know,' İkmen said wearily.

There was a moment of silence while Çöktin took his notebook out of his pocket.

'Cem Ataman,' he said, 'born July the first 1984.'

The gypsy wrote this down on a piece of paper and then said, 'And the two little girls . . . ?'

'Sir!'

'For the love of Allah, Çöktin, just do it, will you!'

Çöktin, his chin set in anger, looked down at the book again and muttered, 'Lale Tekeli, twelfth of December 1985.'

İkmen raised his eyebrows: the same date – if not, of course, year – as his own birthday.

'And?'

'I'm getting there!' Çöktin said. 'Gülay Arat, first of January—'

'OK, OK. Now tell me exactly where each of these children was found,' the gypsy said. 'Come on, blue eyes, hurry up!'

Oh, so that is it, İkmen thought, she doesn't like his blue eyes. She fears the misfortune they may bring. Although quite why, he couldn't imagine. Gonca, like a lot of deeply superstitious people, was

205

covered in the traditional blue boncuk beads, said to protect one from the malign influence of 'the eye'.

Çöktin, still not happy around the gypsy, told her anyway, and then she turned to İkmen. 'Now this girl, not the gypsy, the one the magician was supposed to meet on Büyükada, when was she born?'

'I have no idea. Why?'

'Well, find out, İkmen.'

'Not until you tell me precisely what your point is,' İkmen said. 'I assume astrology is involved somewhere . . .'

'Not just astrology. Look.'

She drew what appeared to be a very rough map of İstanbul – basically three blobs, one representing the old city, one the new and another Asia.

'The boy died in Eyüp, here,' she said. 'At the top of the Golden Horn, west of the city.'

'Then the girl over at Anadolu Kavağı,' Çöktin said. 'What is your point?'

'Anadolu Kavağı, the north,' she said, 'then Yediküle,' she marked its approximate position on her rough map with a cross, 'south.'

'But the gypsy girl—'

'The gypsy girl was murdered in the east,' Gonca said. 'And I need to know whether the girl your magician was going to meet was born under either the sign of Gemini, Libra or Aquarius.'

'But why?'

'Because if she was,' the gypsy said, 'then we will know exactly what your magician is trying to do.'

'Which is?' İkmen asked.

'Performing a grand ritual,' Gonca said. 'All the more powerful for being opened with human blood.'

Turgut had disappeared. The police had apparently released him without charge and now he had gone. Her friend Leyla's husband had, however, returned and so Ülkü was now effectively homeless. She was also, almost, broke. There certainly wasn't enough money for her to get back home to her mother, even if she'd wanted to. Ülkü had never felt so frightened and alone in her life.

If only she was able to go back to the apartment and get the rest of her possessions! But every time she'd gone there she'd seen policemen coming and going from the place and so she'd been too frightened to go in and ask. That minute, at the most, when Turgut had gone to get his cigarettes on the day that Max Bey disappeared, haunted her still. What if, somehow, he had done something bad during that time? It was unlikely, and surely she would have heard him do it? But what if she hadn't? She should have told the police. But now it was too late. Now they'd be angry with her if she told, maybe even beat her for her trouble.

Ülkü leaned her head against the wall she was standing in front of and closed her eyes. If only Max Bey would come back – if, that is, he were still able to do so. She liked him so much. He'd always been so kind, and although he did sometimes do things that she found rather odd, that didn't make him a bad person. Even having those books, full of pictures that quite frankly frightened her, didn't mean that he was evil himself. As he had told her mother when he took her from her home, he was in the business of fighting dark, bad things. He was a good magician and one day he was going to make her, Ülkü, a wealthy and cultured woman. All he'd ever asked was a little domestic help and her commitment to learning. He'd never made her do anything sexual – not like Turgut.

What was she going to do? She couldn't hang around the apartment block for ever and besides, she was hungry. Ülkü opened her eyes and watched as people in cool, smart clothes passed by clutching guidebooks and drinking from cans. Tourists. Turks too, hurrying from place to place, many of them carrying trays of food destined for tourists. Perhaps she could beg? Further down towards Aya Sofya there was a clutch of women beggars from Anatolia. And although they would, she knew, be most averse to her joining them, she could emulate their methods elsewhere. After all, she was young, thin and now not particularly clean either. If she went down there and listened to what the women said, maybe she could use the same line?

She was about to go off and do just that when a familiar face flashed in front of her eyes. For a moment she could hardly take it in. He'd looked at her and then completely ignored her! Why had he done that when he must know she had to be looking for him? Ülkü shouldered the few possessions that she had and then ran to follow the retreating figure down the hill.

They had a proper map now upon which İkmen had marked the four murder sites.

'You see, it's the little things that mean so much,' Gonca said to Çöktin as she replaced one of Max's books on his desk and sat down. 'The fact that the girl in Yediküle, a southern district, was murdered amongst lime fruit, for instance. Lime corresponds to the Kabbalistic Sephira Hod, which is ruled by the Archangel Michael, the guardian of the southern quarter. The girl was a Sagittarian, a fire sign, the element governed by Michael and that which exists in the southern quarter and can be accessed through that portal.'

'Portal?'

'When a magician wants to perform a ritual, he must do so within a safe place,' Gonca said. 'So he creates a magic circle in which to work and he opens the four portals, north, south, east and west, and invokes the aid and protection of the guardians, the angels of each quarter. To aid him in calling these beings down to our plane of existence, he also surrounds himself with as many things connected to them as he can.'

'The correspondences,' İkmen said.

'Yes. Lime is a southern, Michaelean fruit. The northern portal is earthy and so the crystal you discovered holding down that girl Arat's clothes was absolutely right for that portal, which is controlled by the Archangel Sandalphon.'

Çöktin shook his head slowly. 'I understand all that, kind of,' he said. 'But the fact remains that Cem Ataman did take his own life and he didn't have any stuff with him. Also the gypsy girl doesn't conform to your pattern. According to you she should have been born under either the sign of Gemini, Libra or Aquarius. But she wasn't – no one knows when she was born.'

'But Fitnat Topal is a Gemini,' İkmen said, 'and so if we assume that she was the one originally marked for death . . .'

'And maybe some of the "stuff", as you call it, is mutable,' Gonca said to Çöktin. 'Maybe he used the appropriate perfume for the gypsy girl. It has now evaporated . . .'

'Yes, but the fact remains that Cem Ataman killed himself and he, unlike the others, was male. There was no sign of sexual assault with him either,' Çöktin said. 'The only connection between Cem and both of the other girls is that they all, at one time or another, went to Max Esterhazy for English lessons.'

İkmen lit a cigarette and then sat down next to Gonca. 'He has a point, you know,' he said. 'But assuming that this rather skewed circle you've identified does in fact exist, Gonca, what does the magician do with it once he's got it?'

'He performs a ritual,' she said. 'In the centre of the circle.'

'What kind of ritual?'

'It depends on what he wants to do. There are lots of them, rituals of cleansing, rituals to protect, to attack, to attract good or bad fortune. You'd have to ask the magician himself. All I do know is that by encompassing what is the whole city he intends whatever he is doing to affect İstanbul. If I'm right he's used places of great spiritual power in which to open the portals – Eyüp, Yediküle Castle, St George's Monastery, Yoros. Islamic, Christian and pagan. And he's used blood to open them,' she said darkly. 'Blood sacrifices. There is nothing more powerful than human flesh.'

İkmen looked down at the map and rubbed his face with his hands. 'Not really a circle, is it?' he said. 'Where's the centre? If there is one it looks to me as if it's in the Bosphorus.'

'Then maybe that's where it is,' Gonca said.

'Yes, but he'd need a boat.'

'So he needs a boat?' she smiled. 'He's a magician, İkmen, his power boosted by blood. And anyway, this is a maritime city; getting hold of a boat is easy.'

'Maybe. But then this ritual in the centre, does that require blood too?'

Gonca shrugged. 'As I said, it depends what he wants to do,' she said. 'I don't know enough about it to be able to say. But if he's raising malign or extremely powerful forces then maybe. He's a foreigner, isn't he?'

'English.'

'Well then, whatever he does may depend upon the magical traditions in his country.'

Or countries, İkmen thought gloomily. Max was English, but he was also something else too, or could be. Quite how extensively he had been influenced by his father's politics and possible beliefs was impossible to tell.

'You must find this man, İkmen,' Gonca said. 'He could cause great harm. For a large working like this, be it good or bad, he'd have to conjure demons as well as angels just in order to keep the balance. I dread to think what he might be about to unleash.'

'If you're right he's already done so,' İkmen said. 'But we are looking for him, as you know. Not that we've had so much as a sniff of him.'

Gonca smiled.

'So far he's always used students, lured them to him somehow,' Çöktin, who had been thinking very deeply about this, said. 'Maybe we could get to him through them. I think that we should at least contact everyone in that address book to warn them.'

'Yes,' İkmen said. 'Get on to that now, will you, İsak?'

Çöktin picked up the address book and then said, 'A few people came forward after the newspaper appeal. I'll just check them out first.'

'OK. Just go through reversing the last two numbers,' İkmen said. 'I still don't know what the codes at the beginning of each number mean, but just get on with it.'

'You know, I noticed one thing,' Gonca said, 'that numbers are only listed under certain letters.'

'Well?'

'The twelve signs of the zodiac,' the gypsy continued. 'They're the right letters. Your man must have asked all his contacts when their birthdays were. How sweet!'

Çöktin positioned himself by the phone and lifted the receiver.

İkmen put one cigarette out and then lit another. 'Well, there's another mystery you have solved,' he said with a smile, 'maybe. You know I do appreciate your help in this matter, Gonca. You must have far better things to do.'

'Possibly. But if this man means harm to the city—'

'Oh, I don't think that he does,' İkmen said, frowning. 'If this is indeed all about Max Esterhazy, as opposed to just some madness you and I have slipped in to, then that isn't possible. He loves İstanbul – or rather I always thought that he did.'

'Then maybe he is trying to protect it,' Gonca said. 'Actually when we spoke to İbrahim Dede, he, I remember, concurred with this view. İbrahim Dede is a very wise man. Maybe your friend is responding to these recent desecrations and, more importantly, to the threat of war.'

'Allah, but what a way to do it!'

Gonca placed one large hand on his knee. 'Ah, İkmen,' she said, 'but the ends justify the means, do they not?'

He looked across at her, a little shocked. 'You can't believe that, surely?'

She shrugged. 'Right and wrong, black and white – these are meaningless concepts in the scheme of the universe. Balance and the maintenance of balance are the only real facts. Your mother was a witch, İkmen; surely you must have some sort of grasp.' She laughed. 'Just now you thanked me for helping with this problem and, so far, I do this freely for you. But what if I said that I would only continue to help you if you made love to me?' She leaned a little towards him and added, 'I know you are faithful to your wife.'

'Well, I . . .'

'It's difficult, isn't it, İkmen?' She paused to light one of her black and reeking cigars. 'Means and ends,' and then she laughed. 'Oh, don't worry, I was speaking hypothetically. I like young men, as you know, and if and when I demand payment for my services I will take it with one far more beautiful and infinitely less interesting than you.'

He had, of course, surmised that she was only making a point, but he was nevertheless relieved at what she'd said.

'So how do we proceed then?' İkmen said. 'If we assume that this ritual may be happening? Or maybe it's happened . . .'

'Oh, I don't think it's happened yet,' Gonca said. 'If we don't know what he's doing we can't know when the most propitious time for him to perform the ritual can be.'

'But he's always worked at night before.'

'Right. And even in the middle of the Bosphorus it is easier to perform a ritual or a crime or both at night. And, İkmen, if he has opened those portals he is going to want to perform his work soon otherwise he will lose power.'

'I had better go and talk to my superior,' İkmen said, and then as the full force of what he had just said hit him, his face sagged. 'Although what I'll tell him . . . Ardıç is going to think that I've finally gone mad.'

'Then why don't you go with that handsome Süleyman, the Ottoman?' she said. 'Surely Ardıç will listen to someone as proper and upright as they say he is. And anyway, if he comes here first it will give me a chance to meet him.'

İkmen regarded her with a cynical eye. Gypsy or no gypsy she didn't seem to know too much about Süleyman, beyond, of course, his legendary physiognomy.

'Keep your hands off Süleyman, Gonca,' İkmen said. 'He's a married man.'

Gonca laughed. 'And I'm a married woman,' she said, 'so that's perfect, isn't it? Black and white, good and bad, only different faces to the same coin, İkmen.'

What malleable morality! And yet he'd heard such sentiments expressed before and always by those who involved themselves in the unseen and mysterious. His mother had been the same – in fact, all that side of his family were what probably those of a conventional stamp would call amoral. Not bad. But then surely raising demons had to be bad. Max, İkmen always felt, was against such practices. But then if this balance Gonca spoke of was at risk . . . Max, if indeed this was all about Max, couldn't possibly have done such a thing, could he?

The Sea of Marmara was so unusually still and blue it was almost as if some ancient god had swept his hand across it, commanding the waters both to calm and become wholesome once again. That Süleyman, like everyone else, knew there was oil, rubbish, jellyfish and any number of untold horrors in its depths was immaterial. Today, for the transport of the gypsy Gülizar's body to the city of Constantine, the weather was warm, fine and the sea was a gorgeous jewel.

He was struggling with the idea that Max Esterhazy was involved with such a terrible thing. And indeed, no one knew that he was. No one answering his description had been seen on Büyükada, although, as İkmen had said when he'd called, he could have hired a boat for the purpose. Maybe Max was going to use this boat again if İkmen was right about what his next move might be. Rituals and spells – it all sounded like something from the fifteenth rather than the twenty-first century! What Ardıç thought about the manpower İkmen was employing to scour boatyards and police the shore, he couldn't imagine. But it was happening, which meant that İkmen must have said something. Lying, or rather being economical with the truth, was something the older man did very well.

Soon he would be able to make that call to his wife and tell her the good news about his test. And although he had wanted to do this ever since he'd been to see Krikor Sarkissian, he now realised that part of him was holding back. What if the result made no difference to her? Until he knew for certain that he was clear, he could still think about his marriage as being 'on hold'. But if Zelfa rejected him now, that would mean that it was most definitely at an end. Suddenly, as if by magic, his mobile phone began to ring.

Knowing that it almost certainly wasn't his wife, he nevertheless pressed the receive button with a shaking hand.

'Süleyman.'

'Hello, Inspector.' It was the smooth and unmistakable voice of Adnan Öz, Hüsnü Gunay's lawyer.

Süleyman, nervous about what the man might have to tell him about İsak Çöktin, nevertheless went on the offensive immediately. 'Why are you calling me, Mr Öz? What do you want?'

'I want to tell you that my client, Mr Gunay, is willing and indeed eager to undertake a handwriting test to prove that he couldn't pos-sibly have either produced the picture in the Hammer bar or dese-crated the walls of the Church of the Panaghia.'

'Well, that's very good, Mr Öz . . .'

'My client hopes that by taking such a test he may finally lay to rest any notions you may have about the hacker Mendes and himself being one and the same. A speedy resolution to this matter will also have the result that the officer we spoke of will not need to seek legal advice on his own account.'

In other words, if Süleyman played the game and found that Gunay and Mendes were in fact very different people, Çöktin's involvement in the Kurdish film industry would remain a secret. And although Süleyman was very keen to protect his sergeant, Öz's high-handed manner had irritated him and he said, 'Don't threaten me, Mr Öz. I will arrange for an analysis to be performed as soon as I am able, but if your client is a hacker and has desecrated places of worship, he will go to court.'

'Well, it's a good thing that Mr Gunay is innocent then, isn't it?'

'Let us see what the expert says, shall we?' Süleyman said, and then with a scowl on his face he cut the connection.

The Hammer and its inhabitants seemed so very far away. And yet, until the early hours of this morning they had been uppermost in his mind. Now, however, things were different. Max Esterhazy had entered the equation and not in a way that Süleyman could easily understand. All this magical stuff was OK for İkmen, but he didn't even pretend to understand it – a fact underscored by his memory of Max, who had rarely spoken of such things to him. But then proving that the magician had killed the three girls was quite another matter. So far there was no DNA evidence and no witnesses. İkmen, if that was his intention, was going to find it difficult to proceed with what was only circumstantial evidence. Max had taught all but one of the four youngsters and there was some reason to believe that rituals of some sort had been enacted at the murder sites. But there was no certainty and without asking the maid, Ülkü Ayla, about Max's whereabouts on the nights when the three girls died there couldn't even be any safety in placing him at any particular scene. He'd tried to contact the girl at the home of her friend, but apparently Ülkü Ayla had gone – her friend didn't know where.

Süleyman, his head full of his wife, Max, Ülkü Ayla and Çöktin, replaced his phone in his pocket and lifted his face up to the warm Marmara wind.

Chapter 19

Without even thinking about it, people make assumptions regarding how certain encounters might proceed. And although İkmen wasn't usually given to fantasies of high drama, he had imagined, maybe because he knew what Max Esterhazy was, that his next meeting with him would come about in a dangerous fashion. He would never have dreamed that he would have almost walked straight past him.

At the Eminönü end of the Galata Bridge, there is an underpass that extends the pathway along the shore on both sides of the structure. It isn't an entirely salubrious place, playing host as it does to some very unpleasant public toilets and, at night, not a few drunks. By day, however, it is bearable and, indeed, İkmen, were he honest, did go there occasionally to the stallholders under the bridge to purchase a cheap lighter or even the odd packet of fake Marlboro cigarettes. On this occasion, however, he was just simply getting from one side of the bridge to the other. Having observed activity around the Bosphorus and Üsküdar ferry stages he was now, with Constable Yıldız, on his way to see what was happening at the Golden Horn terminus. There were always quite a lot of private boats over there. Strolling in silence, İkmen was thinking about what he'd had to make up in order to get Ardıç to sanction so many officers on the waterfront, when suddenly there was Max. Smaller somehow and, strangely for such a striking man, almost invisible in the crowd, but it was definitely him. With a nod towards Yıldız, İkmen reached out his arm and clamped his hand around Max's wrist.

'Max.'

The magician turned and in turning it was almost as if he became himself again – tall, foreign and obvious to all around him.

'Çetin!' There wasn't a flicker of anxiety, only delight at seeing his friend.

215

Yıldız, positioned behind Max, placed one hand on his gun holster.

'Max, we've been looking for you,' İkmen said, reverting, as he usually did with Max, to English. 'Everyone's been very worried.'

'Have they?' the magician smiled. 'Why's that then, old chap?'

'I think that we need to talk,' İkmen said. 'I have my car here.'

'Oh, but that's lovely,' Max replied. 'However, I am a bit busy at the moment . . .'

'This isn't a social invitation, Max,' İkmen said.

The magician looked into his eyes and then shrugged his shoulders helplessly. Hikmet Yıldız put his hand on the magician's other arm and together with İkmen he led him out of the underpass and on to the path.

İsak Çöktin cleared his notes off the magician's desk as soon as İkmen, Yıldız and Max Esterhazy entered the study.

'So far I've found three students, all of whom have had lessons cancelled,' he whispered as İkmen, still with his eyes firmly on Max, ushered the sergeant into the living room.

'OK.'

İkmen quickly returned to the study where Hikmet Yıldız was giving an account of what they had found there after he'd left.

'Blood, you say?' The magician rubbed his chin thoughtfully. 'God!'

'Some of it we thought was yours,' İkmen said. 'Well, it was the correct blood group, at least.'

'Well, it clearly isn't mine,' Max said as he moved to go and sit behind his desk.

'I would rather you sat here, please,' İkmen said, indicating one of the nearby leather armchairs. He wanted, he felt, to keep Max's hands where he could see them. 'Max, where have you been?' İkmen too settled himself down into an armchair. 'What have you been doing all this time?'

'Oh, this and that, you know . . .'

'No, I don't,' İkmen responded sharply. 'What I know is that we were called to this apartment by your maid on Tuesday. You had gone, there was blood in the study. The last sighting of you, Max, was by the kapıcı who said he saw you re-enter the building

216

approximately fifteen minutes after you left your apartment.'

'Well, the kapıcı must be mistaken.'

'I don't think so.'

'Çetin, I didn't come back and haven't been back here since five o'clock on Tuesday evening,' Max said. 'I left, I've been ... elsewhere.'

'Where?'

Max leaned forward in his chair and smiled. 'Çetin, you know what I do ...'

'Yes, I do,' İkmen said. 'But if you were about magical business then why didn't you tell Ülkü Ayla, your maid, where you were going?'

'Because she was out at the time and because she, like you, didn't need to know.'

'Ah, but she did, Max,' İkmen said. 'Because when this apartment became a crime scene then Miss Ayla had to move out.'

'But I didn't know some nutter would come in here and throw blood about, did I?'

'Did I say that blood was thrown about?'

'Spattered, what—'

'Maybe someone was killed in here,' İkmen said.

'You mentioned nothing about a body. I assumed—'

'Correctly, as it happens,' İkmen said. 'But be careful what assumptions you make, Max.' And for just a second he fixed him with his eyes before continuing. 'Now, while I respect your right to privacy with regard to your business, Max, I do have to ask you to tell me where you were and who you were with on the Tuesday night after you "disappeared", Wednesday and last night.'

'Why?'

'Just answer the question, Max.'

The magician knitted his long fingers underneath his chin and then smiled. 'Now, Çetin ...'

'Please don't even think about either dissembling or appealing to our friendship, Mr Esterhazy,' İkmen said. 'One of my colleagues was shot in this very apartment, while in pursuit of this investigation. Just answer my question and answer it now, please.'

For the best part of a minute, Maximillian Esterhazy sat in absolute stillness and silence. Nothing moved, not even his eyes, which bored into İkmen's with what could have been fury. However, at the end of this period, which was heralded by a huge, amiable smile, Max spoke quite normally. 'Oh, well,' he said. 'I suppose I'd better get on to old Sevan.'

'Do I take it you mean the advocate Sevan Avedykian?' İkmen asked.

'Yes, that's the chappie,' Max said with a chuckle in his voice. 'Excellent fellow.'

İkmen reached across to Max's desk and retrieved his hands-free telephone.

'There you are,' he said. 'I think it is probably best that Mr Avedykian meet us down at the station.'

Max Esterhazy took the phone from him with a shrug and then looked about him for his address book. İkmen, without a word, went in to Çöktin and retrieved it for him.

The news that Max Esterhazy had been found travelled fast. And although İkmen hadn't specifically requested Süleyman's attendance, in view of the fact that there was little he could do for Gülizar the gypsy until after the autopsy, he made his way back to the station. As he walked down towards the front entrance, he noticed two women – one coming into and one leaving the station. The older and more flamboyantly dressed of the two stopped when she saw the younger woman, who was Çiçek İkmen, and engaged her in conversation. Süleyman, hoping that perhaps he might be able to get past Çiçek without being seen, did try to do this, but without success.

'Ah, Inspector Süleyman, I presume,' the older woman said as she pushed a ring-and-bracelet-encrusted hand out towards him. Just briefly her eyes flicked towards Çiçek's now crushed and reddened face and she said, 'You and I have some business, Inspector, together with a mutual friend.'

'How do you know me?' he said, and then almost as an after-thought he bowed stiffly to Çiçek.

'I am a gypsy; I know almost everything,' Gonca laughed. 'And for anything I don't know I have this young lady's father. And besides, I don't have to be a witch to know that once I've found the handsomest man in İstanbul I must have located Mehmet Süleyman, do I?'

'I . . .'

'I came to see my dad,' Çiçek said, as she looked beyond the gypsy and up into Mehmet Süleyman's face. 'But he's busy, so I've left a message.'

'Ah, right. You know . . .' He wanted to say something about what had passed between them when she'd come out to his parents' house, but what with the gypsy and his own awkwardness, he just couldn't find the words. 'Fine. Good. Yes.'

Çiçek, smiling if on the verge of tears, shrugged. 'OK then,' she said. 'I'd better be going . . .'

'Yes . . .'

She was such a nice girl. He had such a lot of good memories about her. When she'd been a teenager he'd sometimes bought her sweets – much to her chagrin at the time. They'll make me fat, big brother Mehmet, she'd always said, you're very, very naughty! But she'd always laughed – then. And even though all those long years ago he'd known that she had a crush on him, it had been just that, a crush. But now that she was older, that had changed and what he saw before him, though still beautiful, was a deeply unhappy and lonely woman. He also saw someone he knew he could only ever love as a sister.

'I'll see you later, Gonca Hanım,' she said, and then turning to Süleyman she bowed. 'Mehmet.'

'Çiçek.'

And then she left just as the gypsy twined one of her big long hands around Süleyman's arm.

'She likes you, that girl.'

'What do you want with me?'

The gypsy laughed. 'Oh, what do I not want with you?' she said lasciviously. 'But unfortunately I've come to see İkmen on this occasion.'

'So have I.'

'Oh, then we will go in together, I think,' Gonca said. And so, somewhat reluctantly, Süleyman allowed himself to be escorted into the station by her.

İkmen was waiting in his office when they arrived. Surrounded by paper, cigarette ends and books, he was, unusually, without his jacket and looked more like a flustered academic than a police officer.

'Ah, good, you're both here,' he said as he looked up and very briefly smiled at them. 'Max Esterhazy is currently down in Interview Room number 1 with Sevan Avedykian.' And then, seeing the look of confusion on Gonca's face, he added, 'His advocate.'

'Ah.'

'Sit down.'

They both, somehow, found chairs. İkmen then went on to tell them how he'd found Max and what had happened subsequent to his discovery.

Süleyman, frowning throughout, sighed. 'I'm not happy about this,' he said. 'With the maid gone and no forensic evidence.'

'I know, but what can I do?' İkmen said. 'He wouldn't give me a straight answer with regard to his whereabouts.'

'He will,' Gonca put in, 'twist and turn like a fish.'

'I know! I know!'

'He is much more knowledgeable than any of us,' the gypsy continued. 'He may laugh if you tell him of the connections you have made.'

'He may well be right to do so,' Süleyman said acidly and then, turning to İkmen, he continued, 'You know I still have this hacker in custody as well as two men from the Hammer who have previous records for sexual assault? I am still pursuing that line of enquiry.'

'Yes,' İkmen sat down, 'and I think you're right to do so. But I also know that Max is hiding something, he must be. And I'm not prepared to let him go until I know what it is.'

Süleyman shrugged.

The gypsy beside him, and still in possession of his arm, smiled. 'Well, we'll soon know, won't we?' she said. 'As time goes on and the magician becomes evermore anxious.'

'Why should he be anxious?' Süleyman asked.

'Well, darling, it's like this,' she said, and then proceeded to tell him about how a magic circle is created and specifically about the four now, supposedly, open portals.

In response he just put his head in his hands despairingly.

'Inspector Süleyman has a few problems with this,' İkmen said. 'Which I can appreciate.'

Gonca looked at the younger man and frowned sympathetically. But then she suddenly turned her entire attention on to İkmen and said, 'But if you are to do this then you will need to do it correctly, so listen and learn, İkmen. Magical people are tricky and ritual magicians are the cleverest of all tricksters known to man.'

'Jak! Jak!'

Not again! Not now that he'd only just managed to get into his book for the first time in a week!

'Jak, come quickly!'

With a low growl of suppressed fury, Jak Cohen hauled himself out of his chair and walked into the living room. Why the hell he was bothering to try to get the latest *Harry Potter* under his belt in this madhouse he couldn't imagine.

'What now?' he said as he regarded his brother's indignant face over the top of the TV remote control.

'It's this video,' Balthazar said indignantly. '*Women with Sea Snakes*? More like women with rubber snakes!'

'Oh God.' Jak raised his hands up to his head and said, 'Did you get that out of the bin?'

'Yes. *Women with Sea Snakes* . . .'

'Why? Why did you get it out of the bin, Balthazar?'

'Well, I—'

'Christ Almighty!' he said in English before reverting back to Turkish. 'You don't honestly think that they put girls in with real sea snakes, do you?'

Balthazar, squinted at the strange, watery images on the screen and said, 'Well . . .'

'Of course they're rubber, Balthazar. Real sea snakes would kill them, especially given what they're doing with the poor bastards!'

'Yes, but—'

'Oh, watch it if you must!' Jak said with a sigh. 'But please, don't moan.' He looked wearily at the screen and pointed, 'Look – that girl there, she's nice. Imagine she's giving you a blow job or something.'

But then as he looked at the screen, it suddenly went blank.

'Or maybe not,' Jak said. 'What rubbish!'

He'd just moved to eject the tape from the machine when a picture of sorts appeared on the screen. In the middle of it was a girl, naked and on her knees.

'Leave it! Leave it!' Balthazar said as he tetchily waved his brother away from the screen. 'This looks good.'

'Christ!'

Jak, his concentration as well as his patience well and truly at an end, sank down into a chair to join his brother in appreciating whatever degraded rubbish this might be.

A dark shape, which appeared to be a man, moved behind the girl and then, just for a moment, she was entirely still, eyes staring straight at the camera. Only when she began to move did his hands reach around, take her breasts and move her up and down against him.

'This looks real to me,' Balthazar said appreciatively.

'The quality's awful,' his brother said, 'and it's quite, well, creepy in a way . . .'

'Mmm. Good, though.'

They watched for a while – the sex, the genuine at first fear and then pleasure that seemed, from what they could see, to be in the girl's eyes. That, Jak said, was unusual. Porn actresses were, in his experience, generally dead in the eyes. But then something else happened that made them both sit up. It happened very quickly and so they had to play and keep on playing that part of the tape many times over before they could work out absolutely what it was. When they did, however, Jak took the tape out and laid it down on the floor in front of the television. Then they both just stared at it for a time while Balthazar tried to work out what one might do in a situation like this.

'On Saturday night I did what I usually do, which means that I had dinner at Four Seasons in Beyoğlu and then went to visit a friend.'

'What friend?' İkmen said sharply.

Max Esterhazy smiled. He appeared to be perfectly at ease in this stuffy little room with its tiny window and numerous cigarette ends. Even the mirror, which everyone in the room knew was of the two-way variety, failed to disturb Max's seemingly natural sang-froid.

'A lady,' Max said. 'Her name is Gül Özpetek – she's divorced and lives in Şişli. And yes, I can and will give you her details and yes, I did stay with her all night. I usually do, Ülkü will tell you.'

'If we could find Ülkü that would be most compelling,' İkmen said. 'But we couldn't let her back into your home, a crime scene or so we thought, until we had either found you or a dead body.'

'Of course.'

'Unfortunately Miss Ayla appears to have moved on from where she had been staying, however,' İkmen looked up. 'What about Tuesday's events, Mr Esterhazy? Your disappearance . . .'

'My client didn't disappear, Inspector İkmen,' Sevan Avedykian slid in smoothly. 'He left his apartment at five p.m. and, since that time, has been staying with a Mr İrfan Şay, a gentleman, I believe, with an interest in Mr Esterhazy's area of expertise.'

Sevan Avedykian was, as İkmen knew of old, a pragmatic sort of man who was probably not easy around words like magic.

'Why didn't you tell your maid where you were going, Mr Esterhazy?'

'Mr Şay, a respected businessman, is anxious to keep his interest in things of an occult nature to himself,' the lawyer said.

The subtext behind this was one that İkmen could understand. After all, officially, 'sorcery' was still a crime in the Republic and so people, particularly of a 'respected' nature, might well want to keep their interest in it to themselves. However . . .

'Yes,' İkmen said. 'I can understand that, but it still doesn't account for the fact that your client failed to tell his maid that he was going to be absent. He could at least have left a note. I mean, when, Mr Esterhazy, were you planning to return to your home?'

Max Esterhazy shrugged. 'I don't know, old boy. One gets into conversation . . .'

'And yet you cancelled at least three of your tutorial sessions,' İkmen said. 'You also rescheduled Miss Topal's session to take place not at your home but on Büyükada. Why was that?'

'Fitnat and myself have frequently had our sessions out on the island,' he smiled. 'It's so very pleasant out there when it's hot. Unfortunately, I couldn't make it in the end.'

'Did you let Miss Topal know?'

Max shook his head and sighed. 'No, and I know that was appalling

223

manners, but İrfan and myself, well, we got involved, if you know what I mean. He is a very demanding student, eager for knowledge. I should, in retrospect, have just cancelled Fitnat, but she is such a needy student.'

'So you didn't go out to Büyükada yesterday evening?'

'No.'

'Not keeping those around you apprised of your movements does seem to be a weakness of yours, Mr Esterhazy.'

For the first time since İkmen had discovered him, Max Esterhazy exhibited some displeasure. 'I'm not accustomed to having my movements proscribed by others,' he said. 'Ülkü knows I sometimes go off for several days at a time. I also, sometimes, cancel tutorials – sometimes I don't feel inclined to teach. It isn't unusual.'

'But large amounts of blood spattered over your study is unusual,' İkmen replied.

'I don't know anything about any blood.'

'So the kapıcı lied when he said he saw you re-enter your building on Tuesday afternoon?'

'I think he must have been mistaken,' Esterhazy said evenly. 'Maybe he confused me with one of the other foreign gents in the block. There are several of us, you know.'

'Yes, but you've lived there for over twenty years,' İkmen said. 'A space of time in which, I imagine, the kapıcı would have got to know your appearance very well. I don't think he was mistaken, Mr Esterhazy.'

Max Esterhazy shrugged.

'And besides,' İkmen continued, 'Miss Ayla said nothing to us about your "going off" for several days at a time.'

'Maybe she forgot.'

'If we knew where she was perhaps we could ask her,' İkmen said acidly.

'Well, unless she's with her ghastly boyfriend, I can't help you,' the magician replied. 'I know nothing about blood or Ülkü or her boyfriend. I've just returned from a somewhat protracted stay with my friend İrfan, I need to get on with my life and—'

'Where were you, Mr Esterhazy, on Tuesday and Thursday nights and on Wednesday evening?'

'I've told you, Çetin, I was with my friend İrfan who, I know, given the circumstances, will be very happy to verify what I've told you.'

'I'm sure.' Süleyman was probably looking him up now, back there behind the mirror with Gonca – may Allah protect him.

'Why are you asking about Tuesday and Thursday nights and Wednesday – whenever – anyway? What happened—'

'Two murders were committed, Mr Esterhazy, one on Tuesday night and the other on Thursday night. One of the victims, Lale Tekeli, was a student of yours. Then on Wednesday a colleague of mine was shot and wounded whilst going about his investigations in your apartment. Last Saturday night was also a time of tragedy for the family of another of your students, Gülay Arat.'

'Gülay and Lale?' Max Esterhazy shook his head in disbelief. 'No! Great girls, both of them. No! I liked them. You think *I* killed them?'

'You were missing . . .'

'In common with many others, I imagine,' Sevan Avedykian put in tartly. 'Please, Inspector—'

'We have reason to believe, Mr Avedykian, that certain aspects of these crimes reveal a connection to ritual magic.'

'Then why not tell us what they are, Inspector?' the lawyer responded calmly. 'My client would, I know, welcome the opportunity to refute them. If indeed he needed to do so. As he said on all the occasions that you named, he was with other people who are prepared to vouch for him.'

They all sat in silence for a few moments then, the lawyer and his client amid an air of self-satisfaction, and İkmen in order to gather his thoughts. Avedykian was, of course, quite right in his assertion that Max – provided his alibis checked out – could not easily be placed at any of the scenes, ritual magic or no ritual magic.

'Now, Mr Esterhazy, I should tell you,' İkmen said, 'that in the course of our investigations into your supposed disappearance, we did contact your sister, Mrs Maria Salmon.'

'Did you?' he smiled.

'Yes. And during the course of that conversation it quickly became apparent to me that certain details about your past were at odds with what you had led me to believe.'

225

'I take it that by this you mean my client's parentage,' Avedykian said gravely.

'Yes.'

'I put it to you, Inspector,' he continued, 'what would you have said to people if your father had once been a member of the Nazi party?'

'I think I would have said nothing,' İkmen replied. 'I certainly wouldn't have created an entirely fictitious background for myself.'

'But you are not in that situation, are you?'

'No.'

'Then you cannot possibly understand,' Avedykian said, 'the shame and horror that my client experiences on a daily basis. Mr Esterhazy dealt with his situation in the only way he knew how. If a little foolish, you will as I'm sure you have, Inspector, find that my client's "lie" is only one of omission. His father was indeed a titled Austrian and his family did indeed flee to England at the end of World War Two. Remember too that my client has never been either a member of or had association with the Nazi Party.'

'Your client took money from someone who was,' İkmen said.

For the first time in the interview Sevan Avedykian looked genuinely nonplussed. Max had, in a very short time, prepared him well but he had omitted to mention the money.

'Your father sent you money, didn't he, Mr Esterhazy?' İkmen said. 'From Panama.'

Max Esterhazy looked down at the floor and then murmured, 'Yes.'

'Every year until his death in 2001.'

'Yes.'

'A Nazi war criminal sent you money, which you spent in the full knowledge of both his offences and his associations.' İkmen leaned in towards Max and said, 'If you were so ashamed of him, why didn't you tell the British authorities where he was? Was it because you were greedy? Now that your work is your only source of income—'

'I was coaching İrfan for money,' the magician said as he raised his amiable head once again. 'It's why I cancelled all the kids' lessons – I admit it. İrfan's rich and he pays me well. The only offence I've committed is letting those kids down. Christ, Çetin, how was I to know some nutter would slosh blood all over my flat!'

'You have no reason, as far as I can see, to keep my client in custody,' Sevan Avedykian said firmly. 'You've presented no forensic evidence and my client can verify his movements on the days you have indicated.'

'And the kapıcı?'

'It is the kapıcı's word against that of my client,' the lawyer smiled. 'You know as well as I do how difficult such cases are to prove – in either direction.'

'Yes, but your client, Mr Avedykian, has already admitted to being a liar.'

'We have, I feel, dealt sufficiently and satisfactorily with the subject of Mr Esterhazy's past,' Avedykian said. 'And besides, quite why my client would deface his own apartment with human blood is something that I personally would like to know.'

'Then why don't you ask him?' İkmen said.

'Oh . . .'

'Çetin, I didn't do it!' Max Esterhazy laughed. 'Why would I? Quite apart from anything else, where I'd get human blood—'

'Maybe you sacrificed someone.'

'Oh, now this is becoming absurd.' Sevan Avedykian stood up. 'Come along, Mr Esterhazy.'

But Max Esterhazy didn't move.

'A grand ritual of some kind, that's it, isn't it, Max?' İkmen stared hard into the magician's unmoving eyes. 'Made so much more powerful by blood. You must be working on something very big.'

'Christ, Çetin, have I taught you nothing? I'm a good chap, I don't do evil things. Everything I do is for the best.' The magician stood up and joined his lawyer over by the door. They were just about to leave when İkmen spoke again.

'I know you've opened the portals, Max,' he said. 'I also know that they can't be left open for long. Now you must complete the work.'

But Max Esterhazy appeared to smile and shake his head as he followed his lawyer out of the room. However, a few moments later, when İkmen had gone into the adjoining room, Gonca had a slightly different take on Max Esterhazy's last moment in Interview Room number 1.

'Just for the smallest moment there was a look, of surprise I think it was,' she said. 'He had, or imagined he had, thought of everything.'

'You still believe in the ritual theory? It, like Max's version of events, possesses holes, Gonca,' İkmen said. 'Cem Ataman committed suicide.'

'I'm going to ask Çöktin to check out this Mr Şay and Mrs Özpetek,' Süleyman said. 'Şay, you should know, Çetin, is an electronics magnate. First came to the city from Edirne in 1997, and by 1999 he was living in a very nice yalı in Bebek. If Max has financial worries then Mr Şay could be helping to rectify that situation.'

He took his jacket off the back of his chair and logged out of the office computer system.

'Where are you going?'

'Hüsnü Gunay. I still have my own work to do, Çetin.'

'You must have the magician followed, İkmen,' Gonca said. 'See where he goes and what he does. If you can follow him.'

'What do you mean?'

'I mean that if he doesn't want to be followed then tracking him will not be easy,' Gonca said. 'Great magicians have the gift of invisibility.'

He knew what she meant. When he'd found Max in the underpass he'd only just found him. Smaller and far more 'local' at first sight, İkmen still didn't know quite how he'd managed to recognise him. But then maybe that had more to do with İkmen himself than with Max. Maybe that was his own 'magic' manifesting, as it sometimes did.

'I'll get on to it now,' İkmen said, and left the room quickly.

Gonca, alone again with Süleyman, licked her lips and then smiled.

Chapter 20

It took a while to organise surveillance on Max Esterhazy, and so İkmen arranged for the magician and his lawyer to be detained – Çöktin had to check out İrfan Şay and the woman Max had named – until his man was ready in position. Commissioner Ardıç, as ever the sceptic, would only give him one officer, Yıldız, for this duty, which was far from ideal. But İkmen could hardly follow the magician himself and so he grudgingly accepted what he was offered. Just before Max and Avedykian were due to leave he went out to one of the nearby kiosks in order to buy cigarettes. It could possibly be a long and tense time ahead and so he'd need all the nicotine he could get to sustain him. Max, a friend, whether guilty of murder or not, was not now the man he thought he had been and that saddened him.

Armed with sixty of his favourite Maltepe cigarettes, İkmen was just walking back to the station when he heard someone call his name. Looking back towards the small amount of tourist activity around the Hippodrome, İkmen saw Jak Cohen waving rather wildly at him.

Ten minutes later, İkmen was sitting in front of a TV and video recorder, smoking cigarette after cigarette.

'Balthazar says he thinks it's real,' Jak said.

'I would agree with him,' İkmen replied.

The girl, the only figure in the scene with an uncovered face, seemed at first to be enjoying what was happening. Only when the largest of the masked figures entered her, from behind, did the fear and pain begin to show. And although what was happening didn't seem to be part of a ritual, there were ritualistic elements to it. The masks, the robes, the way the man having sex with the girl kissed the knife just before it was plunged into her chest. It was only a fragment, four minutes at the most, but that, as İkmen knew only too well, was quite enough time to kill another human being.

229

'Where did you get this, Jak?' İkmen asked.

Jak told İkmen about Demir Sandal and he, like Balthazar, knew the man of old. Not that Demir had ever been involved in anything like this before. As far as İkmen was concerned Demir Sandal was just a grubby little pornographer with a reputation for employing girls with large breasts. Serious stuff, like this, was surely out of his league.

'I'll have to get Inspector Süleymen in here,' İkmen said. 'He may be able to identify the girl.'

It was unusual to request that an officer interrupt an interview, but in this case İkmen felt fully justified.

'If I didn't think it was imperative that you see this, then I wouldn't have interrupted you,' İkmen said as he walked along the corridor with Çöktin and an annoyed Süleyman in his wake. 'This may well change the way you proceed with your hacker.'

'I hope so,' Süleyman replied. The handwriting expert was taking his time analysing Hüsnü Gunay's artwork and comparing it to that of the supposedly elusive Mendes. Adnan Öz was becoming impatient.

As soon as they entered the room, Jak, who had now rewound the tape again, nodded in recognition of Süleyman and then played the video. After about thirty seconds, Süleyman moved closer to the screen.

'What is this?' he said.

'I think it's what they call a "snuff movie",' İkmen replied. 'Do you recognise the girl?'

Süleyman, eyes widened by what he was seeing on the screen, just stared.

'Isn't a snuff movie one where people actually get killed on screen?' Çöktin said.

'Yes.'

They all watched in silence until the final act took place. Jak, who had, some time ago, stopped feeling sick at the sight of it, looked up at the ashen faces that surrounded him. For several minutes nobody said a word. İkmen and Süleyman lit cigarettes while Çöktin just sat down and stared at the now blank television screen.

Eventually, Süleyman cleared his throat and then spoke. 'I think the girl is Gülay Arat,' he said. 'You can see that the action takes place out in the open – Lale Tekeli was killed indoors – and it certainly isn't the gypsy Gülizar.'

'So all this business with the Goths, the hacker and that Englishman is irrelevant,' Çöktin said. 'The youngsters were killed to make these snuff movies.'

'I don't know whether that is the full story,' İkmen replied. 'My own feelings are that there is a certain ritualism to the proceedings. However, if Inspector Süleyman has identified one of his victims in the film then he will have to decide whether to pursue this matter on that basis. Whatever happens we must find out who is producing this material and put a stop to it.' He turned to Jak. 'I know Demir Sandal hasn't got an office as such, but I assume you have a mobile number for him.'

'Yes.'

Süleyman shook his head. 'I can't believe this is Sandal's work,' he said.

'Jak got it from him.'

'*Women with Sea Snakes* is what he gave me,' Jak said miserably. 'Free! Said it was the most remarkable work of pornography I would ever see – the next big thing!'

'Well, he was right about that,' İkmen said.

'Yes, but I don't think it's for the reason he thinks,' Jak said. 'Like you, Çetin, I don't think that Mr Sandal would do anything like this.'

'We'll have to start with Sandal, though, won't we?' Süleyman sighed, and then he looked across at İkmen and said, 'I'll wrap this interview up as quickly as I can and then İsak and myself will get on to it. Thank you, Çetin.'

İkmen shrugged. 'Yıldız is following Max Esterhazy so I have to be around. Jak, can you call Sandal and tell him you want to meet in, what?' He looked across at Süleyman.

'Depends where you usually meet,' Süleyman said, looking down at Jak.

'İstiklal Caddesi.'

'In an hour?' Süleyman suggested.

'OK.' Then Jak frowned. 'But what if he won't come?' he said. 'I supposedly bade him goodbye yesterday.'

'Well, whatever you bought from him, say you need some more,'

İkmen said. 'I imagine Demir treated you like a foreigner and therefore ripped you off. I can't see him not jumping at the chance to lighten your wallet still further.'

Jak took his mobile phone out of his pocket and then called up Demir Sandal's number.

Maximillian Esterhazy said goodbye to his lawyer just outside the station and then proceeded to walk towards his apartment. For a man who had recently been questioned in connection with serial killings he seemed very relaxed. But then maybe he was innocent. Apparently when Sergeant Çöktin had checked out his alibis they had held up. Yıldız didn't really know why İkmen was persisting with this. But then he was just a constable so what did he know?

After buying a pouch of tobacco and some water from a small local shop, Esterhazy entered his block and disappeared up the stairs. Because the building had a fire escape at the back, this was where things became tricky. How to watch the man now that he'd gone inside was a problem, and one that having an extra body on the operation, particularly one that Esterhazy hadn't seen before, would have rectified. But there was only him and so Yıldız went up to the first floor where Esterhazy lived and looked around for any possible vantage points, which seemed to be zero. It was very frustrating. If he stood outside the building he'd have to choose whether to watch the front or the back – he couldn't possibly do both. Here on the landing he could only watch the front, unless, of course, he tried to hear whether or not Esterhazy was still inside. He was just about to put his ear to the door when it swung open sharply and Esterhazy, complete with a small suitcase, walked out on to the landing. Yıldız, his face pressed against the door of one of Esterhazy's neighbours, pushed the bell as casually as he thought he could and then watched the magician descend the staircase. As soon as he could no longer see Esterhazy's head, Yıldız followed. Fortunately no one came to answer the neighbour's bell.

'Don't fuck with me, Demir,' Süleyman said as he watched the pornographer sweat amid the lush green plants outside the KaVe. 'Tell me where you got this video here and now or I'll take you in and force the issue.'

'But, Inspector, I don't understand,' Demir Sandal, his face red with tension, replied. 'The women are just playing with rubber snakes, anyone can see that!'

'I'm not talking about the women with the snakes, Demir.'

'Then . . .'

'Look, I haven't got time to explain,' Süleyman said. 'Just tell me where you got this tape and I'll be on my way.'

'But, Inspector, for a man in my position, suppliers and distributors need to know they can trust me.'

'Then how about I don't mention your name, Demir?' Süleyman smiled unpleasantly at the large heap of man in front of him. 'How about I stop myself from beating you senseless where you sit too!'

'The inspector isn't playing games, Demir,' Çöktin put in over his boss's shoulder.

'But that doesn't give me any choice!'

'Correct.'

For a few moments the pornographer wrung his hands and appeared to wrestle with various thoughts in his head until finally he said, 'My name, you won't mention it?'

'No.'

'But my friend will know it was me! How else would you have got this tape? Where else will you have got his name?'

'Depends how many tapes there are, doesn't it, Demir?' Çöktin said.

'Yes, but—'

Süleyman, finally driven half insane by this prevaricating blob of a man, grabbed him by his large, slack throat.

'Tell me.'

Although known by almost everyone as a handsome man given to the finer things in life, like art, music and poetry, those who really knew Mehmet Süleyman knew that he also possessed a capacity for violence. It wasn't something that, in general, he was proud of, but it was a fact of his life and it did sometimes come in rather useful.

Demir Sandal looked down into the fierce eyes of his tormenter and said, 'Erol Burak.'

'Who is?'

'He works at Edirne Fotoğraf on Ankara Caddesi.'

'Sirkeci?'

'Yes.'

Süleyman pulled his hand away from the man's throat and took a deep breath in order to calm himself.

'They sell photographic equipment and electrical goods,' Demir Sandal said. And then unable, even under these circumstances, to stop himself selling, he added, 'If you want a VCD player, Erol will give you a very good price.'

İkmen had, for some reason that he could now no longer remember, assumed that Gonca had left the building. And so, when she wandered into his office carrying a mobile telephone, he got quite a shock.

'Put that down!' he said as he rose from his chair, waving his own phone as he did so.

'Why?'

'Well . . .'

She laughed. 'You think I've stolen it, don't you? But then why wouldn't you think that?'

'Gonca . . .'

'Actually, though, it is mine,' she said. 'I just called one of my daughters to tell her I'd be a while yet. A gypsy without a mobile phone, İkmen, is like a kapıcı without eyes – an entirely useless waste of flesh. You know you let the magician go far too soon, don't you?'

İkmen sat down in his chair again and nervously fingered his phone. 'I couldn't keep him. I don't know that anything we talked about is true.'

Gonca reached inside her voluminous plastic handbag and retrieved a packet of cigars. 'You know that sigil thing your İskender said he saw just before he was shot?'

'Yes . . .'

'You know I asked a few people about that?'

'Do they know what it means?'

'No. But İbrahim Dede, you know, he has a friend, a rabbi – I don't know his name – not a Kabbalist. But anyway, this rabbi knows a thing or two, and he says to İbrahim Dede that these sigils, you know, they take a long time to make.' She took one of the cigars out of the packet and lit up. 'To you and me it is just a few lines on a paper, but the work behind it is amazing – spells, incense, the right hour and time. Sometimes, you know, even some of the magician's own blood is shed in order to—'

İkmen's mobile began to ring and so he held up a hand to silence her.

'Yıldız – yes.'

He turned away in order to have what sounded like an intense conversation. Short and to the point, he finished it quickly and then turned back to Gonca.

'So maybe the blood on Max's floor that matched his group was his,' he said.

'It is a possibility,' Gonca agreed. 'Although if he did do that, I think he must have had some other sort of motive to allow the blood to stain the carpet. He must have wanted it to be there for some reason. However, now that he has gone . . .'

'You know I'm having him followed. That was my man now,' İkmen said. 'He's walking across the Galata Bridge.'

Gonca looked out of the smoke-grimed window at the now gentler late afternoon sunshine. 'Night is still a way away,' she said. 'He has time.'

'To do what?' İkmen asked.

Gonca shrugged. 'I don't know,' she said. 'Disappear, I suppose. Because if he wants to finish the ritual, that is what he'll have to do.'

'If,' İkmen held up a warning finger to her, 'if that is what he is doing, Gonca. We don't know. Max has alibis for all the time he spent away from his apartment.'

'What about all the blood that you found?'

'What about it?' İkmen said. 'Some of it, as we've discussed, may be his, but a lot of it isn't.'

'Have you tried to match it to any of the victims?'

'We're in that process now,' İkmen said with a not altogether pleasant smile on his face. This gypsy was getting rather too pushy for his liking. It made him wonder if indeed she had known Max and, maybe, disliked him for some reason. It was possible and, given Max's true background, it was also understandable. The Nazis had not, after all, had any love for Gonca's people. Someone had once told him that the exact number of gypsies killed by the Nazis wasn't known or even knowable. So 'low' were they, the gypsies didn't even merit a figure – they'd just killed them where they stood. He looked across at her and wondered what she might be thinking, and then realising that he couldn't even take a guess at that he changed the subject.

'Gonca,' he said, 'these portals you speak of. If you're right, they're open?'

'Yes.' She rearranged various layers of netting and chiffon around her hips. 'After the ritual has been completed he will have to close them.'

'Does it have to be him?'

'Every magical working is individual,' she said. 'This is his spell and so he is responsible for it. It won't work without him.'

'And the portals? What if he doesn't close them? What if someone else tried to do that?'

Gonca shrugged. 'I don't know,' she said. 'I'm not a Kabbalist. But I imagine that if he doesn't close them eventually the power within them will fade. As for another person, I don't know. I don't think that anyone else can do that. Maybe this is where we find these things out?' She smiled. 'When the demons he has summoned come pouring unfettered into this world.'

İkmen, for whom diabolism had always been an intellectual stretch, frowned. 'Is that possible?'

'I don't know. But if the magician is using human blood then he is working with some very powerful forces,' she said. 'And don't forget, İkmen, that even workings that are aimed towards the good of man are sometimes achieved via the intervention of devils. The truly great rituals involve the intervention of both angels and demons. One must do this in order to retain the cosmic balance. After all, how could we appreciate the goodness of our mothers without the lies of dictators to measure that against?'

It was a fair point and one that İkmen had heard before – from, he thought with a smile, his mother. Now long since dead, the witch of Üsküdar had taught him a thing or two during his all-too-short decade with her. Maybe, had she lived, Ayşe İkmen would have been able to advise him about other things he'd felt unable to speak to his father about. Maybe she might even have been able to talk to him about Alison. Given what he suspected about Max Esterhazy, it was becoming ever more difficult to shift Alison from his mind. Officially she had disappeared somewhere in the wilds of Cappadocia, although actually placing her there had been difficult. Not, of course, that İkmen had ever tried to do so. Alison had been someone else's case for the relatively short amount of time she had been actively sought. In the seventies, a lot of young Europeans turned up stoned and hungry, and not all of them made it to India or back to their various homelands. Alison had just simply drifted on to the 'hippy' missing list where, no doubt, she was doomed to remain.

İkmen phoned down for tea for Gonca and himself as a way of distracting his thoughts. They then sat and waited for the tea in silence, the hot afternoon sunshine clouded as it came into the window by the vast swathes of Gonca's cigar smoke.

They'd just had a consignment of new equipment in from Germany and so the shop was packed. Sleek young men, many of whom still shared sleeping quarters with numerous siblings and who had never ventured out of İstanbul, let alone Turkey, devoured tiny digital cameras and elegant video equipment with hungry eyes. Mobile-phoned to the hilt, these lads lived with the reality of satellite TV-infested slum housing and saw not a trace of incongruity in their situations. Mobile or food was a no-contest situation as far as they were concerned, and they were prepared to do whatever it took to secure Edirne Fotoğraf's products and thereby enhance their reputations.

Şerif and Kerim Burak, though probably no older than their enthusiastic customers, were somewhat cooler in their approach. They did, after all, sell this stuff and had, therefore, had time to accustom themselves to all the clever things that their photographic 'toys' could do. They were actually quite keen to carry on ignoring what looked to them like two rather less hip older guys when Süleyman, ID in hand, pushed his way through the crowds and forced the issue.

'I want to see Erol Burak,' he said to the older-looking of what was obviously a pair of brothers.

Şerif, immediately defensive, said, 'My father's done nothing wrong.'

'Where is he?'

237

The innocence stance didn't impress Süleyman; he'd experienced too much of it.

'He's in the back.' The young man flicked his head in the direction of the counter. 'My brother will take you.'

Kerim, his eyes hooded by suspicion, led Süleyman and Çöktin through into a room filled with cardboard boxes. There were, Çöktin at least noticed, three, maybe more, different kinds of digital camera, video equipment galore and, as Demir Sandal had predicted, some very smart-looking VCD and even DVD players. Like a lot of these little photographic and electrical shops, space was at a premium, especially for storage, and when Erol Burak was finally located he was squeezed between a cardboard tower block and what looked like a pre-Republican sink, which he was using as an ashtray. Small and somewhat downtrodden-looking, Erol Burak possessed the sort of middle-aged world-weary look that one almost instinctively attributed to those involved in the sex industry.

'I want to know where you got this,' Süleyman said as he held Demir Sandal's videotape aloft.

'What is it?'

'It's called *Women with Sea Snakes*,' Süleyman replied somewhat haughtily.

'What of it?' He wasn't obviously worried about it, which led Süleyman to suppose that he knew only of its official content.

'I want to know where you got it, Mr Burak.'

'Why?'

'That's my business.'

Burak looked up and shrugged. 'Look, this isn't my main business,' he said. 'Not the tapes. This shop—'

'I'm not interested in you or your shop,' Süleyman responded hotly. 'I just want to know where you got this.'

Burak put his cigarette out in the sink and then cleared his throat. 'The tapes are for the boss,' he said. 'He's a little nervous around some of these people in that sort of business. Religious family, you see. Where did you get it?'

'Never mind. Now this boss—'

'He owns the shop,' Burak said. 'I manage it for him. But he also does a bit of . . . film work, you see. Not anything strong, if you know what I mean. Girls and snakes – they're rubber, you know – girls and men and . . . none of it real, if you know what I'm saying . . .'

'Mr Burak, we are not here to investigate either you or your employer with regard to legitimate business. I just want to know who—'

'Mr Şay gives me the tapes and I distribute them to interested parties.'

Süleyman turned first to Çöktin, who raised an eyebrow, and then back to Burak once again.

'This is Mr İrfan Şay,' he said, 'electronics sultan?'

'Yes.' Burak coughed. 'Filming's an interest of his. It makes him quite a bit of money too. But the wife and kids can't know, if you know what I mean.' He smiled. 'The wife is very pious; she wouldn't like to see all of that on the screen.'

'All of what?'

He lowered his voice. 'Women's bodies. Not that it isn't tasteful, the way Mr Şay does it, but—'

'Do you have Mr Şay's telephone number?'

'Well, of course, but—'

'Right, I need to call him,' Süleyman said. 'He and I, I feel, need to talk.'

Erol Burak, although not entirely happy with what was happening, nevertheless bowed to the inevitable and led Süleyman and Çöktin through into his tobacco-and-tea-stained office. Mr Şay wasn't going to be too pleased when he got a call from the police, but Erol knew better than to try to oppose them. Mr Şay could be both vicious and unreasonable, but the police – well, in his experience they were quite something else. The police could shut you down, lock you up and threaten to throw away the key. All this over a pair of thick American tarts and a metre of rubber piping!

The nights were, Hikmet Yıldız felt, beginning to arrive a little earlier now. Although still hot and bright, it was now obvious when late afternoon had arrived and so he knew that it had to be about four without even looking at his watch. September, it was an odd month, and could just as easily have been as cold as it was now hot. Not that thinking about the weather was germane to anything except the passage of time. He'd been following Mr Esterhazy for hours now and had, as a consequence, visited some parts of the city he hadn't been to for some time. The walk across the Galata Bridge, with occasional stops to ask what this or that fisherman had caught, had then turned into a ride on Tünel, the underground funicular railway, up the Galata hill and into Beyoğlu. In and out of various shops along and around İstiklal Caddesi – including the gloriously named Ottomania rare books shop – it was obvious that Esterhazy, who had to have recognised him, knew he was there. It was just simply a matter of time – and will – in determining if and when Esterhazy escaped and if and whether Yıldız would be able to keep up with him. Looking at him as he jovially wandered in and out of shops, talking so easily with everyone that he met, it was hard to equate this man with the world of demons and devils. But if he was, in fact, a magician, then that was what he did – or rather that was what Yıldız, who had been privy to only some of İkmen's researches – understood to be so. But then maybe Gonca would explain more about that to him later.

Taksim Square was up ahead now, Esterhazy moving smartly towards the park around the Monument of Independence and its attendant crowds.

Gonca, Yıldız knew with all of his soul, knew everything. Her house was full of magical stuff and her mother, an elderly crone with no front teeth, read cards and oil with, it was said, amazing accuracy. 'You are here,' Gonca had said that first night he'd met her and then followed her back to her home, 'because I performed spells to make that happen. You cannot help but be here.' His first sexual experience had followed that remark – almost fully clothed, standing with his back against one of the gypsy's artworks – a collage. Later she'd taken him to her bed where she'd taught him things he'd never even seen in those magazines his little brother Süleyman bought. Gonca might be old but she was beautiful, and she certainly knew how to make him feel good.

Yıldız followed the magician across the park and into Cumhuriyet Caddesi. Apart from the Military Museum there wasn't much that Yıldız could think of to interest Esterhazy up here. But he drifted along, amid a small cloud of sexual memory and some attention, anyway. Maybe the Englishman wanted to do some shopping in Şişli

240

or Nişantaşı. People with money went up there to do that sort of thing and the Englishman had to have money just because he was an Englishman.

Yıldız continued to walk and drift. Now they were moving uphill it was fortunate that the Englishman didn't walk too fast. It was, after all, still hot. In fact he was actually moving really slowly now, which meant that Yıldız, as he had done on a few occasions before, should attempt to overtake him. So without too much effort he did just that. Pushing up to just beyond the museum it had been his intention to slip down Mim Kemal Öke Caddesi and then pick his quarry up again after he passed, but as he turned Yıldız looked at the man – and got a shock. It wasn't him! In fact it wasn't an Englishman at all but a tall, middle-aged Turk complete with moustache. Same jacket and trousers, yes . . .

Yıldız' heart began to pound. When and how had the Englishman metamorphosed into this tired-looking Turk? He'd not taken his eyes off him, not once, he was sure! Or was he? Wearily Yıldız put his hand in his jacket pocket and took out his mobile phone. This man, this Esterhazy, had to be some kind of super magician! He pressed the button for the station and, once he was through, he spoke to İkmen.

'I've lost him, sir,' he confessed. And then in response to the furious words from the other end, he added, 'I don't know where, sir, no. All I do know is that what was once an Englishman is now a Turk and I don't have a clue as to how he did it.'

When he did finally manage to replace his phone in his pocket, Yıldız discovered something that he didn't remember having been there before. At first he thought it was just a blank scrap of paper, but further inspection revealed that there was something on it – of sorts. For some reason that Yıldız couldn't really articulate, it made him feel slightly cold.

It was dusk by the time all the different members of the team managed to assemble back at İkmen's office. Messy at the best of times, İkmen's airless little room was now packed to capacity and was, consequently, very hot and cramped. Süleyman and Çöktin, who had just got in from their trip over to İrfan Şay's place in Bebek, looked particularly exhausted.

İkmen lit a cigarette and then said, 'Now look, gentlemen,' and then turning to Gonca he added, 'madam. I don't have any proof that Maximillian Esterhazy has committed any kind of offence. Furthermore, Commissioner Ardıç is extremely uncomfortable with what he considers to be little more than the product of an overactive imagination – mine.'

Several people laughed softly.

'And so what I am proposing to do tonight, namely to patrol that portion of the Bosphorus between Arnavutköy and Rumeli Hisarı on the European side and Kandilli and Anadolu Hisarı on the Asian side, is not something that has attracted much support. I have, however, with the aid of Inspector Süleyman's evidence we'll hear in a moment, managed to secure a launch to cover this side, but with regard to the Asian side we're going to have to rely upon officers on the shore. This means that, assuming that what I think may take place, does, we could easily miss it.' He sighed. 'It is therefore a thankless task and so, with that in mind, I am not going to force anyone to join me. I can enlist junior, uniformed officers if necessary.'

There were four other people in the room besides İkmen and Gonca – Süleyman, Yıldız, Çöktin and Karataş – none of whom moved or spoke in response to what İkmen had said.

'I take it then,' İkmen said, 'that this means you are all willing to move forward with this investigation.'

Various mutterings of approval followed.

'All right,' İkmen continued, 'then let's get down to looking at what we already know. Firstly, we have what I'm sure Mr Esterhazy would deem a coincidence. Inspector Süleyman?'

Süleyman cleared his throat before speaking. 'Esterhazy gave us the name of İrfan Şay as the person he had been staying with these last few days. We telephoned Mr Şay, who supported his story. This afternoon Sergeant Çöktin and myself came into possession of a videotape that, it would appear, is a visual record of the death of Gülay Arat – the girl we believe is the first victim of this ritualistic whatever it is. The interesting part of this story for us is that this tape leads us straight back to Şay who, we are reliably informed, enjoys making pornographic videos and produced this particular tape. Now when I phoned Şay this afternoon he expressed a willingness to talk.

However, when Sergeant Çöktin and I subsequently visited Mr Şay's yalı in Bebek a couple of hours ago, he was apparently out and about somewhere. We could, of course, have returned with authorisation to search his property. But if, as Inspector İkmen believes, one of these rituals is due to happen tonight I decided it would be more useful to try and catch him actually filming the event.'

'This video,' Karataş asked. 'The girl actually dies?'

'Yes. Some people, believe it or not, find that arousing. However, unfortunately no faces apart from hers can be seen because they're all wearing masks and even those are indistinct. It is a very bad print and, because no one in it can be identified, it couldn't be used in court unless it were supported by other evidence. At the moment we have to assume that what Şay is filming and what Esterhazy is doing are two different things.'

'But isn't this magician meant to be a good person?' Karataş said. 'I mean, why would he, if he really believes in all this magic, allow somebody to film what he does?'

'I don't know.'

'Esterhazy has been in trouble financially of late,' İkmen put in.

'Good point. Maybe money does come into it too.'

He looked at İkmen, at his frowning face and wondered whether he was thinking along similar lines to himself – namely that Max's art had always been much more important to him than money. But then he'd never needed money before and anyway, if İkmen were right, the way he'd got his money in the past had, it seemed, proved somewhat dubious.

Hikmet Yıldız, who had up to that point been silent, said, 'I don't know whether this means anything,' and he threw the piece of paper he'd found in his pocket down on İkmen's desk.

'What is it?'

The young man shrugged. 'Don't know, sir. Found it in my pocket just after I discovered that Mr Esterhazy wasn't Mr Esterhazy. It's a weird-looking thing. I certainly didn't have it before, or at least I don't think that I did.'

İkmen opened the paper out, looked at it, and then passed it over to Gonca.

'Is that a sigil?' he asked.

She frowned. 'Yes, it could be,' she replied. 'Although if it is, I can't tell you what it means.'

'Well, if it is then it must have some sort of meaning for whoever placed it in Constable Yıldız' pocket.'

The young man looked concerned. 'Is it a magic thing, sir?'

'Well . . .'

'Not like a curse?'

İkmen saw Yıldız' face turn white. A peasant by background, Yıldız was probably rather more susceptible to this type of thing than a native city dweller. For all İkmen knew, the sigil, if that is what it was, could represent a curse. But there was no point in frightening the poor boy, especially in view of the fact that no one really did know what this thing was.

'Oh, no, Yıldız,' İkmen said with what looked very much like confidence. 'It's not a curse, of that you can be sure.'

'Oh,' the young man breathed more easily. 'Well, praise be to Allah for that.'

'Indeed. Now,' İkmen said, 'arrangements . . .'

They spent a good half an hour talking about who was going to go where, with whom, and what action they might take should İkmen's suspicions be realised. At the end of the proceedings, when everyone else had gone off to obtain the equipment and refreshments necessary for a long night on the Bosphorus, Süleyman remained behind.

'Çetin,' he said as he offered the other man a cigarette and then lit up himself, 'what if Max does indeed perform some kind of ritual but without causing harm to anyone else? He is, after all, perfectly entitled to follow whatever faith or philosophy he may wish to.'

'Ah, but we still have legislation against sorcery,' İkmen said.

'Yes, but that includes prohibitions against praying at the tombs of saints and the practice of dervish rituals,' Süleyman said, 'all of which are allowed to happen now, Çetin. I think that you're on unsure ground with this, especially in view of the fact that both you and I know Max and what he does.'

'I'd only use it as a way of holding on to him,' İkmen replied. 'If no blood is spilled in his ritual tonight then appealing to elderly Republican legislation will maybe buy me enough time to really check his story out.'

'But if he is allowing someone to film his rituals for money, then he will spill blood, will he not?' Gonca had re-entered the room without so much as a whisper. Both men turned towards her with a start. 'After all,' she continued, 'why would you film anything as boring as a magical ritual without sex or violence? If this Şay is a pornographer that is what he will want.'

İkmen looked at Süleyman, who just shrugged.

'Gonca Hanım has a point.'

'Of course I do.' She took one of his arms between her strong hands and looked deep into his eyes. 'But what even I don't know is who his victim is going to be,' she said. 'Except, of course, that she will be a virgin.'

'Gülizar the gypsy wasn't.'

'Oh, yes she was,' Gonca said. 'She only ever gave pleasure with her hands and her mouth.'

'Really? Well, Gülay Arat and Lale Tekeli were virgins,' Süleyman said. 'But then what about Cem Ataman? Male, a suicide – he breaks all of the apparent rules. I'm still not—'

'Sssh!' Gonca placed one red-tipped finger over his lips and then, much to İkmen's amusement, moved in very closely to him. 'That mystery remains to be solved,' she said. 'Let us wait and see what develops out in the Bosphorus. Let us watch for the magician . . .'

'Who may or may not come.'

'As Allah wills,' she said. And then, laughing at her uncharacteristic ascent into piety, she left the room.

When she had gone, Süleyman said, 'I still can't accept it, you know, Çetin. Max – he's a friend. I can't believe that he would kill. I do hope—'

'That it isn't so?' İkmen smiled. 'So do I,' he said gravely. 'More than even you will ever know.'

Chapter 21

From the water the Bosphorus village of Arnavutköy can look pretty. But, as Mehmet Süleyman knew only too well, his home village was a little down at heel these days. And although the yalıs that lined the waterfront had once been some of the finest in the city, few of them now retained their previous gloss. It was something that for some reason the night-time seemed to emphasise rather than conceal. Not even, he thought bitterly, poor old Ali Ağa's yalı looked good these days. All sagging lintels and ruined boathouse, it was a disgrace and would have reduced his grandfather's old servant to tears had he still been alive. But the old eunuch had been dead for over thirty years now and Mehmet remembered him only dimly. Odd really that some-one of his age should have had any contact with such an anachronism anyway, but Ali Ağa had been very old and the only thing he could really recall about him was the pristine nature of his surroundings. It was, the old man had always said, unseemly for the servant of a prince to live in a state of disorder. Apparently he had worshipped the ground on which Mehmet's grandfather, Abdurrahman Effendi, had walked, which, given what the old prince and his ilk had done to people like Ali Ağa, was very puzzling. Gloomily, Mehmet looked down into the black waters of the Bosphorus and wondered how many eunuchs the empire had created and what a high price these emasculated crea-tures had been made to pay for their lives of relative luxury.

Although it had been quite hot in the day, the evenings were starting to get cold now, especially on the water. İkmen and Çöktin both wore coats, and even Gonca had a large dark wrap draped decorously about her shoulders. When she saw him looking at her, she smiled but didn't approach. She was a very lovely woman and one Mehmet knew he could possess whenever he wanted – if he wanted. Sleeping around had hardly done him any favours so far. But if Zelfa wouldn't answer any of his calls . . . He wanted so much to tell her that he was well, to beg her forgiveness yet again, and, of course, to be reunited with his son. But if he were honest with himself, he knew that wasn't likely. Zelfa was a proud, independent woman – why would she want a weak last gasp of a dead monarchy like him? Without even thinking about it, his eyes slid across to Gonca's ample form as she joked and laughed in low tones with the pilot.

'Sir?' A light young voice cut across his thoughts.

'İsak.'

The young man looked behind him before he spoke. 'Sir, about Hüsnü Gunay . . .'

'I'm still waiting on the handwriting expert,' Süleyman replied. 'But Gunay seems very confident that he isn't this Mendes character and so I'm expecting an end of it. Still leaves a question over who desecrated the places of worship, though.'

'Mmm. Maybe someone copied the picture in the Hammer.' He looked up. 'Sir, about Gunay—'

'İsak, if you want to continue with your career you're going to have to stop this film subtitling business.' Süleyman looked him hard in the eyes. 'I mean it. İnşallah, we will be able to get through this little crisis, but another? Another would finish you, İsak, whether I tried to protect you or not.'

'I know.'

And then they lapsed into silence. There was still a lot of movement on the great waterway – ferries, military craft, fishing boats and private vessels of various kinds. Not a good environment for someone to pursue strange and possibly deadly rituals – yet.

'What do you think about all this magical stuff, Sergeant?'

Alpaslan Karataş looked across at Hikmet Yıldız and shrugged. With the aid of a pair of binoculars he could see the launch heading out from Arnavutköy. Obvious to all what it was, a little too conspicuous to Karataş' mind, but then it wasn't either his decision or, at the end of the day, his problem. İkmen had chosen to circuit the whole of the designated area while he and Yıldız stood on the shore at Kandilli. It was easy enough, and quite why it was irritating him so much was stupid really. But it was, and while his boss, Metin

İskender, was laid up in hospital it was going to continue to bother him.

He must have played it over hundreds of times in his mind now – the moment when he heard the shot, the hopefully split second later when he responded. But had it been a split second or more? When he'd entered the room, the magician's bedroom, there hadn't been so much as a closing door to signify that anyone had been in there. Not a sound, not a movement, not even the rippling of a recently disturbed curtain. Just the Inspector, bleeding and unconscious on the floor – looking as if he'd been there for hours. Had he or had he not responded as quickly as he could?

İskender, rather oddly for him, had said that the fact that he was alive at all was due solely to what Karataş had done for him. Further, the last time he'd seen him, the inspector had said that he, Alpaslan, should put it behind him now and concentrate on his work. But the question continued to nag and he continued to be troubled, because neither way could he win. If he'd not acted immediately then what kind of person did that make him, and if he had, what kind of sorcery had spirited a person with a gun out of that room and into, apparent thin air? In light of this Yıldız' question was not one that he could answer even though he needed some sort of explanation very badly. But what could you do? Apart from descending into the myths and dark fears of your ancestors?

'I know nothing of this magic Inspector İkmen and the gypsy speak of, but djinn, well . . .'

'My mother once had a lot of trouble with djinn, back in our village,' Yıldız said. 'A corner of the kitchen was troubled, particularly at night.'

'Such spirits shouldn't be spoken of,' Karataş said as he felt a cold shiver run down his back. 'Not after dark.'

'No . . .'

Karataş looked around at the black water of the Bosphorus and thought about the gypsy on the boat with İkmen and Süleyman. A troubling woman: funny and coarse as the gypsy women could be, she was worrying for all that. She did, it seemed, know a lot about this magic the Englishman was said to practise. That a woman should know and talk about such things was something he was not entirely comfortable with. Did she, in fact, know too much? She did, it seemed to him, sometimes almost impose herself on İkmen and she was, or seemed to be, easy in the company of officers. As a gypsy that shouldn't, surely, be so? But then no one else had or seemed to have noticed this and so perhaps it was all right after all. But he wasn't really convinced by this argument and so he just gazed ahead of him and tried to clear his mind. Maybe nothing would happen this night – if they were fortunate. But then maybe it would and so he had to be ready. But ready for what? If a man could be shot out of thin air then what other surprises might be in store for them? Again he shuddered. Something dark and frightening could be out there now, watching him – something he knew he didn't and couldn't understand. Even djinn with their wicked, contrary ways would be welcomed as opposed to that – whatever it was.

The darkness was making İkmen's head swim. Maybe it was the effort of straining his eyes into the shadows, particularly now that there were so few other vessels around. In the summer the European stretch of this shore would be alive with music and dancing as the nightclub season took the city by storm. But not now. Now it was too late in the year and the clubs were silent, their *habitués* having moved on to other establishments in Taksim and Beyoğlu. For once he almost wished that he were one of their number. That he didn't like loud music and had rarely danced in his life didn't now seem to be that much of a bar to his enjoyment – especially if he were well provided with alcohol. There wasn't much he wouldn't do for a drink now, he suddenly thought with great gloom. His numerous barely controlled stomach ulcers would hate him for it, but he knew all about them and how to anaesthetise the troublesome things.

If only he and his men knew what they were looking for! Some sort of maritime craft. What did that mean? A yacht? A fishing boat? A raft? And based upon what premise? That some magical thing was being constructed? Something that necessitated the inclusion of a suicide victim? And Gonca. He looked across at her, talking to Süleyman, and frowned. She had, or at least he thought she had, been of great assistance to him, but why? She didn't know Max, or so she said – though she knew the dervish İbrahim Dede, who did know him. But then the dervish, surely wouldn't, if he knew, lie to İkmen about Gonca's involvement. And anyway, even if she did know Max, did that make her involvement now necessarily suspect? A tired brain plus straining eyes were making him think mad thoughts. Unhelpful.

İkmen momentarily closed his eyes and then opened them again. The small fishing boat in front of him had probably been there all the time; it wasn't after all that close. But someone had obviously put a light on somewhere that was illuminating the figure of a girl, who appeared to be dancing. To what he couldn't ascertain, as there didn't appear to be any music.

Süleyman, who had seen it too, came over and touched İkmen on the arm. 'What do you think?'

'I don't know.' İkmen turned to the pilot and said, 'How close can we get to that fishing boat without being obvious?'

'A hundred and fifty metres, maybe a hundred.'

'OK. Do it,' İkmen said. 'A girl prancing around on a yacht is one thing, but on a fishing boat . . .'

The pilot moved the launch forward as slowly as his low-revving engine would allow. İkmen, his body as well as his eyes now straining over the starboard bow, experienced a slowly creeping feeling that was distinctly unpleasant. Maybe it was due to the girl's hair, which was blonde and which flew behind her in a wild, almost joyous tangle? But then lots of girls had blonde hair – there was nothing odd in that. The pilot edged as close as he dare without attracting obvious attention. İkmen screwed up his eyes to take in the girl's voluminous hippy-style dress and then with dread he let his gaze drop down towards her feet.

'Alison.'

'All right, I know it can't possibly be her, not in reality,' İkmen hissed. 'Alison's got to be fortysomething now – that is, if she's still alive! But . . .'

'I don't understand why anyone would get a girl to look like a hippy you met in the nineteen seventies!' Süleyman whispered in return. 'Why would anyone . . . ?'

'Max. Max would.'

'But why?' Süleyman asked. 'She was a friend, you met her, it was a long time ago.'

'She went missing! She was full of life and she went missing!'

'But why would Max ... ?'

'Because,' a light touch on his arm caused Süleyman to turn and look down into the eyes of Gonca the gypsy, 'maybe there is some history between İkmen and this girl and the magician.'

'Well, of course there's a history!' İkmen spat. 'We both knew her!'

'And you both desired her,' Gonca smiled. 'You at least, İkmen. I can see it written in your face.'

Süleyman, who, like the rest of the world, believed that İkmen had never so much as looked at another woman, regarded him closely.

İkmen sighed. 'Nothing ever happened. Alison was just a good friend and I, I controlled myself,' he said wearily. 'I can't speak for Max.'

'But if the magician uses her to taunt you then he knows that you still feel,' Gonca said. 'It is, in you, a weakness he may exploit.'

'But how do you know it's this Alison or meant to be her?' Süleyman asked.

İkmen drew him back to the side of the launch and pointed. 'Army boots,' he said. 'Pink. Alison painted them herself.'

'But Doc Marten boots can be bought in many colours now.'

'No!' İkmen hissed. 'Army boots. Look at them! Huge! They were Alison's favourite thing; she loved them.'

And when he looked, Süleyman did indeed see what İkmen meant.

'So what do we do now then, Çetin?' he said. 'Assuming that Max is on that boat with that girl?'

'We hold back,' İkmen said, 'until we can see what is happening.'

'And if Max or someone else attacks the girl?'

'We hold back.'

And then he fell silent, his eyes pinned upon the small bright figure dancing in the middle of the Bosphorus.

It seemed like she danced for hours. On and on it went – the girl alone and seemingly performing to no external sound. But strangely, given her slight form and flowing hair, it wasn't graceful. There was something off centre about it, maybe an element of drunkenness or the influence of drugs. Had the officers been able to see her face, maybe they would have been able to tell, but she was still a long way off and her hair was frequently over her features. Karataş and Yıldız, still on the shore at Kandilli, had been informed about this development and, for the moment, were staying where they were.

'You don't think that this performance could be some sort of distraction, do you, sir?' Çöktin whispered to a grave-faced İkmen.

'I don't know,' İkmen said. 'I don't know.'

'Well, someone must have sailed the boat out here,' Süleyman said. 'I can't see her doing it, can you?'

'No.'

And so they watched and continued to wait. Only Gonca failed to display any outward signs of impatience. Maybe, İkmen thought, her poise stemmed from the accumulated experience of her people. Maybe that was what being 'other' taught a person: to wait – for food, for justice, perhaps even for a glimmer of understanding. She'd wait a long time. Unlike other groups of outsiders, gypsies were not either integrating or being welcomed into society. Oh, İstanbul was better in most respects, certainly than some of the Central European cities – but the gypsies still remained 'outside' and probably always would do. And maybe, from their point of view, with good reason. His father, who had taught modern languages at İstanbul University, had always been very interested in European history, particularly the Second World War period. İkmen still remembered what he'd said about Hitler's Final Solution as applied to the gypsies. 'You know, boy,' Timur İkmen had said one day, 'I used to wonder how the Nazis could think so little of the Jews. But at least the bastards killed them. But the gypsies? They weren't even flesh to the Nazis. Made them dig their own mass graves and then pushed them in. Buried them alive and then stamped on the earth above their heads. How does a people recover from something like that?' He'd swallowed hard after that little speech, choking back tears. And Timur hadn't even liked gypsies!

Idly, but in a slightly horrified fashion, İkmen began to wonder if Max's father had ever taken part in such appalling acts. If he had there was no way, surely, that even a son could countenance such a thing. Even a son would, for his own sanity if nothing else, have to distance himself from such a father. Unless, of course, that father had money. Cash changed things – cash made men film little girls dying amid strange rites and offered rich, idle minds a plethora of interests, both good and evil.

The girl suddenly stopped dancing and what looked like two men emerged from below deck. One tall, one of medium height, they both wore long robes, their faces obscured by what appeared to be masks. The smaller of the two carried something – possibly a table – that he set down at the back of the vessel. Gonca, now roused from her reverie, came to join İkmen and the others at the side of the launch. Squinting into the darkness, she said, 'I don't know why we can't use binoculars.'

'Because the light might catch the lenses,' İkmen said. 'What can you see?'

'Not much.'

The taller of the two men approached the table and laid something down upon it. Then he began to talk. None of the occupants of the launch could hear what he said, but that he bowed four times in four separate directions was, Gonca said, significant.

'He's acknowledging the four portals,' she said. 'North, south, east and west. He's not performing the rite to open them because they are already open.'

'So what now?'

'So whatever ritual he wishes to perform in the centre of the circle,' the gypsy replied. 'But on that table there will be a ritual dagger, I can tell you that without even seeing it. In the old days it was used to perform ritual sacrifice, now it is just symbolic – most of the time.'

İkmen looked across at the now motionless girl and then said to Süleyman, 'Tell the pilot to take us in.'

'But don't you want to catch him in the process . . . ?'

'I don't think that we dare wait that long,' İkmen replied.

'Very wise,' the gypsy muttered. 'I think.'

'What do you mean?' İkmen said.

As the boat's engines kicked into life Gonca sat down on the deck and lit one of her black cigars. 'Because I don't know what happens if you interrupt a magician during a grand ritual,' she said. 'Allah alone knows what forces he's already conjured. İnşallah, we will be able to control them when the time arrives.'

The tall man in the fishing boat turned towards the launch as its engines began to propel it forward.

İkmen had wondered whether the fishing boat would try to outrun the launch when the occupants saw it coming. But they didn't. The shorter man did, or so it seemed, toy with the idea of flinging himself into the Bosphorus but, in all probability, stories about the unpredictability of the waterway's currents prevented him from doing so. The tall man was, however, another matter. Until the launch came alongside he just stood, absolutely static, only moving to take the girl gently in his arms when the officers and the gypsy began to board.

İkmen knew it was Max. In spite of the long grey robes and the sinister goat-horned mask, he just knew. The girl, her face turned in towards the man's chest, just whimpered.

'What are you doing, Max?' İkmen asked as he watched the familiar eyes move uneasily behind the mask. 'I didn't think this was your style.'

'I am practising my craft,' the magician replied in the English that was more comfortable for him. 'There's no law—'

'Sorcery is still officially outlawed in this country,' İkmen replied in kind. 'Now please, Max, take the mask off and let's have an end to all this.'

The girl moaned a little now, which resulted in the magician tightening his grip upon her.

'But my ritual is incomplete. Forces have been invoked that now require just one more ceremony in order to achieve our ambitions.'

'Our ambitions?'

'I'm doing this for you.' The normally jovial English voice had taken on an altogether harsher tone. 'I'm protecting the city. It's a big job.'

'Protecting the city from what?'

'From war. From gas attack, from chemicals, from the ghastliness of ethnic cleansing. I've dedicated my life to working for peace.'

İkmen, in spite of himself, laughed. 'You think that Saddam Hussein would ethnically cleanse the Turks?'

'It can happen.'

'Yes, I know. I know we must all be vigilant,' İkmen said. 'But if you are trying to deal with your personal guilt through our misfortune, then it will not work, Max. This city does not need your help. We have an army, we have intelligence agencies, we are not the aboriginals I think you would like us to be.'

'I love this city! Why do you think I'm doing this?'

'Doing what?'

In the silence that followed, the girl, encircled by the magician's arms, began actively to struggle. She made noises too. Both the look of her and the sounds she was making were disturbing. Had she, İkmen thought grimly, been Max's intended victim? Was she to be sacrificed by the dagger that Gonca had said must be on that table – but wasn't. İkmen couldn't see it and, with the smaller man now positioned between Süleyman and Çöktin with his hands in plain sight, if it was anywhere it had to be with the magician. One limp girlish hand beat the magician's chest without too much volition.

'Who's the girl?' İkmen said as he lit up a cigarette and began to puff furiously.

'You know who she is.'

'No, I don't,' İkmen responded sharply. 'The hair is a wig, even I can see that now. Why have you made this girl look like Alison, Max? Is it to taunt me? If you knew that I was coming then why did you not attempt to evade me?'

'You may or may not have come. Your presence is irrelevant. She's Alison—'

'No she is not!'

'You know her.'

'No!'

'All women are Alison, in the end,' the magician said. 'You know her.'

'No, Max, no I don't,' İkmen said. He looked across at Süleyman who, he noticed, was standing with his hand inside his jacket. Silently İkmen prayed that he wouldn't act impulsively. This was, after all, Max Esterhazy, their friend.

'I think you'll find you do know her,' the magician said as he turned the girl around to face İkmen. 'There.'

256

Her face was slack as if she were drunk, and her eyes were almost totally closed. But for all that, she was instantly recognisable. İkmen, beyond words, drew in one long, unsteady breath. Çiçek.

'A working designed to raise power to cover a city demands only the finest sacrifices,' the magician said. 'Çiçek has all the right qualities. She is a natural adept, she is beautiful . . .'

'Then it seems a great pity to waste her.' Gonca the gypsy, her black cigar still between her fingers, smiled. 'You took a gypsy's blood, out on Büyükada, did you not?'

The magician, whose command of Turkish was good, nevertheless paused. Gonca's accent was thick and so he had to concentrate hard to understand her.

'Gülizar was a little whore,' Gonca said. 'Your ritual is tainted.'

'Give me my daughter, Max.' İkmen, now that the shock of seeing Çiçek in this situation had started to abate, spoke in a low, controlled voice.

But the magician just ignored him and continued his conversation with the gypsy. 'The Büyükada girl was not my first choice,' he said. 'Fitnat Topal failed to turn up.'

'So, as I said, your ritual is tainted.'

'No!'

'Max, if you give Çiçek to me, I swear I will—'

'Cut me a deal, as they say on American television shows?' The magician removed his mask for the first time to reveal a strained and greying countenance. Somehow he looked older, suddenly. 'I shot one of your colleagues, Çetin,' he said. 'If I hadn't, young Çiçek wouldn't be here now.'

'What do you mean?'

'I mean that foolishly I forgot one vital piece of equipment when I left my home on Tuesday . . .'

'That sigil,' Gonca said. 'You use it to control the girl?'

'Yes.' He looked back at İkmen. 'That's clever – how did you know that?'

But İkmen didn't answer him. 'You put another one in my constable's pocket today.'

The magician, just very vaguely, smiled. 'Yes, but that was just

257

by way of a joke,' he said. 'The one I prepared for Çiçek was serious. I used my own blood in its preparation.'

The fact that Çiçek was staring at him, apparently without recognition, while all of this was going on, only added to İkmen's fear. Even if he did get her back, would she be herself? Would anyone ever be able to rouse her from this fugue? He looked across at Süleyman and Çöktin, and the masked man who stood, breathing heavily, between them.

'Who's that?' İkmen said, flicking his head in the direction of the small, tense group.

'It's Turgut,' Max replied simply. 'Ülkü's boyfriend.'

Süleyman ripped the mask from the young man's face. He was very white and he was obviously terrified.

'But you're keeping me from what I have to do,' Max said, and he reached inside his robes. Something shiny glittered into the night.

'It's all about money, isn't it?' İkmen said as his thin chest rose and fell in time to his now laboured breathing. 'You sold yourself to İrfan Şay, you prostituted your art—'

'Çetin—'

'Your father's money stopped and so you looked around for other ways to support your lifestyle. You don't care about the city, Max! You care about yourself! But now it's over. You cannot escape. The ritual is at an end.'

The magician raised the long, curved knife up over his head and said, 'Oh, but it isn't, Çetin. It can't be. The portals are open and those who I have called to protect İstanbul must be rewarded.'

İkmen looked across at Süleyman, who had now taken his pistol out of its holster and was aiming it at the magician's head. 'Put the knife down, Max,' he said. 'I will kill you if I have to.'

'Yes, I know,' the magician replied, and then he raised his other arm, freeing Çiçek as he did so. Slowly, or so it seemed, she sank down his long body towards the floor.

'But virgin blood has to be shed,' Max said, and then he looked up at his upraised arms and smiled.

Everything happened very quickly then. İkmen dived forward to drag Çiçek towards him, while Süleyman, battling against the bilious movement of the boat, attempted to reach the magician. Max Esterhazy brought the arm carrying the knife back and then sliced it at his other upraised arm. The wrist and hand flew off into the Bosphorus and suddenly they were all plunged into a world of blood.

He was over the side before any of them could even draw breath.

'Get him!' İkmen yelled as he folded himself protectively around his insensible daughter.

Süleyman threw his jacket to the deck and plunged in after the magician. The pilot of the launch turned his searchlight on so that it illuminated the water around the boat. Çöktin flung the still trembling Turgut Can to the deck and stood over him, his pistol at his head. Only Gonca moved in a dignified fashion as she slowly bent down to touch the blood on the deck boards and then lift a small drop up to her mouth. After apparently tasting, she raised her eyebrows and then leaned against the side of the boat to look at what was happening in the water.

Süleyman, aware of what the currents could do to only adequate swimmers like himself, kept one eye firmly on the boat as he searched the waters. Max, surely, couldn't have got far. He had dived into the space behind where he thought the magician had fallen. But at the moment there was nothing to show either where he'd been or where he was. But then having sustained such massive injury, it was logical to assume that he must have gone down. Süleyman took in a large gulp of air and dived beneath the surface.

'He's extremely athletic, isn't he?' Gonca said appreciatively as she once again relit her cigar. 'I like that.'

'How you can think about anything at a time like this is beyond me!' İkmen said. 'Come, for the love of Allah, and help me with my daughter!'

Gonca turned and made her way over to İkmen and the unconscious girl.

'İkmen, there is always time for lust,' she said as she took Çiçek's head in her hands and slowly massaged her face. 'Your girl will be all right.'

'How do you know?'

'As I never stop telling you, İkmen, I'm a gypsy, I know everything.'

'Yes, Max is a magician and look where it's got him!' he snapped.

Çöktin, anxious at the length of time Süleyman had spent in the water, handed his gun to the pilot and leaned over the side of the boat. 'Sir!'

But no answer came from the now almost stilled water.

'Inspector Süleyman!'

'He made me do it!' Turgut Can said through teeth now gritted against the night-time cold. 'I don't know where that blood came from, I swear!'

'Shut up!' the pilot said. 'No one's interested!'

'Sir!'

İkmen, alerted by the desperate tone in Çöktin's voice, stood up and went to join him at the side of the boat.

'Sir, Inspector Süleyman has been under the water for too long!'

İkmen placed a hand on his shoulder. 'I know.'

And then seemingly unable to take it any longer, Çöktin threw his jacket to the deck and said, 'I'm going in after him.'

'No!'

'Yes!'

İkmen took hold of Çöktin's arm between hard, bony fingers. 'No! It's dangerous down there. I won't have you risking your life too! I should go, I told him to get Max.'

'Sir, with respect . . .'

İkmen removed his jacket and had just bent down to take off his shoes when Çöktin shouted, 'Here!'

Looking up sharply, İkmen saw what looked like two white smudges in the water about a hundred metres from the boat.

'İsak!' It was definitely Süleyman's voice. 'Help!'

'Now you can go in,' İkmen said as he replaced his shoes.

Çöktin dived in and, in what seemed like a long time, but actually was only a few minutes, he could be seen with Süleyman approaching the boat. What was more, they were not alone.

'Max is alive,' Süleyman gasped as İkmen pulled him back on to the boat. 'Allah preserve me, I've drunk I don't know what . . .' He spat on to the deck, clearing his throat as he did so.

Çöktin, still below in the water, began to move the seemingly unconscious magician into a position where İkmen could grab him.

'And he's got two hands,' he said as he pushed the man up into İkmen's arms.

'Yes,' İkmen grunted.

'Unless his blood were made of tomatoes he would have,' Gonca put in with a laugh in her voice. 'A very silly little illusion for such a big magician!'

Chapter 22

As soon as they had cleared all of the water from Max Esterhazy's lungs, İkmen and his officers got the magician, Turgut Can and Çiçek on to the launch and headed for the city. İkmen didn't, however, leave the magician alone during their trip. Still sneezing Bosphorus water, Max Esterhazy, shackled now to İkmen, was subjected to an onslaught from the furious inspector.

'What did you give my daughter, you bastard?' İkmen yelled as soon as the magician opened his eyes.

'Na . . .'

'What did you give her?'

'Na . . . Nothing . . .'

İkmen turned to look back at the still insensible Çiçek and then took the magician by the throat. 'Nothing!'

'Ha . . .' A moment almost of amusement passed across Max Esterhazy's face before he hauled himself up against the side of the boat and said, 'Çiçek?'

She made a small sound and her eyelids did briefly flicker.

'Çiçek, wake up, lovey,' Max said in English. 'Come on, it's only Max . . .'

'Only Max!'

'Steady.' It was Süleyman's voice and his hand upon İkmen's arm that stopped him going any further.

'If he's saying he hypnotised her—'

'She's coming round, İkmen,' Gonca said. 'Look.'

Çiçek's eyes were open now and, although they moved in a fashion that suggested they were unfocused, it was plain that some sort of change had occurred.

'Well, it's not exactly hypnotism,' the magician said, still amid the occasional cough of Bosphorus water. 'The sigil . . . I was in control some days ago – of her. She was lonely . . .'

'If you've touched her . . .'

The magician's eyes suddenly and alarmingly hardened. 'No,' he said, 'I haven't. I've never touched, as you say, anyone. She was to have been the first.'

'Oh, and what about the others?' İkmen said. 'What about Gülay Arat? What about the gypsy girl and that other one? What about Alison?'

Max Esterhazy shook his head. 'None of them,' he said. 'The girls provided at the portals were taken by things you wouldn't understand.'

'Oh, demons, I—'

'If that's what you want to call them, yes,' he smiled. 'When one attempts such a powerful ritual, one needs to evoke entities possessed of powerful appetites. The practitioner, myself, merely guides the ice-cold penis of the Goat entity into the supplicant. Only one, in reality, you will notice, Çetin.'

'And İrfan Şay,' İkmen said. 'He filmed these "entities"? Oh, please, Max, don't insult my intelligence.'

'Believe what you like.'

'I will. And mostly I will believe that all of this was about you and the profit you could make from giving Şay movies containing real death.' And then turning to Süleyman he said, 'You'd better organize transport for when we reach Eminönü.'

Süleyman took his phone out of his pocket and turned aside to make the call.

İkmen leaned in close to the magician now and said, 'So what about Alison then, Max? What was that performance with my daughter?'

The magician smiled softly. 'Alison was perfect,' he said. 'I loved her passionately.'

'What did you do to her?'

He shrugged. 'Nothing. That is my tragedy, Çetin. She came into my life and then she left, to go to Cappadocia.' He leaned in towards İkmen in order to whisper, 'She turned me down because she was in love with you.'

'She never—'

'You were married, of course she didn't tell you,' Max snapped. 'But she loved you, my perfect woman – over me.' And then his voice hardened again. 'Amazing, isn't it? I'm tall, good-looking and I want to make her my goddess, and she pines for a penniless little Turk! I've never forgiven you for that Çetin! Never! I've never been with a woman since . . .'

'What about your lady up in Şişli?'

'Only a friend!' he laughed bitterly. 'I can only have friends, Çetin. I wanted Alison and only her. I dressed Çiçek up to look like her because I knew it was the only way I could ever become aroused enough to—'

'Don't speak of my daughter like that!'

'When you came to me asking for help with that ridiculous scrawl, my ritual was already underway,' Max said. 'It was you, your presence, Çetin, that gave me the notion of using Çiçek. You denied her to me just as you had denied Alison. All the blood I poured over my apartment was for you, to confuse and punish—'

'Çetin, there's going to be a car waiting at Eminönü for us,' Süleyman said.

'OK. And Karataş and Yıldız?'

'They will meet us at the station.' He then looked down at the magician and said, 'You are going to have to answer a lot of questions, Max, not least of which concern Cem Ataman. I mean, you didn't kill him, did you?'

'I wasn't even there,' Max responded. 'He was a good student – of magic – the best one. I could talk to Cem about anything – my fears, my enthusiasms. He had a tremendous hunger for the mysteries – once, of course, I'd sorted him out as regards useless concepts like good and evil. He went willingly to perform the rite and he died. He gave me the western portal as a gift.'

'So you knew . . .'

'Of course I did! Cem and I planned it together.' He closed his eyes. 'But I'm tired now and disinclined to answer any more questions.'

'Well, you'll have to later!'

Max opened his eyes briefly and replied, 'I don't think so. I will tell you only that my grand ritual, using my own blood, as you saw—'

265

'That was tomato juice!'

'Get it tested and see,' Max smiled. 'My working is over and the city is safe. Gülay Arat was a willing victim – what a naughty place that Atlas Pasaj is, introducing young ladies to the Devil! Silly people looking ridiculous in black, as I told Gülay. It so delighted her when she learned what I did, what I could teach her. She wanted and welcomed what came into the world through me. But little Lale was a good Muslim and was very afraid; even when I attempted to reassure her she fought. It was very ugly to watch. The gypsy was, of course, a mistake. Foul blood. I knew I'd have to pay for it in some way, which is, of course, why you're here. But the ritual is nevertheless complete and that is the main thing. I'm telling you these details, Çetin, while I can,' he said. 'I'm sure you'll have fun beating the rest out of Turgut. I know you're on to İrfan Şay, but . . . Oh, and by the way, just for the record, Ülkü Ayla is a complete innocent in all this and, should you find her, I would like it if you could be kind to her. Poor little girl, I sacrificed her too in a way . . . Now if you don't mind . . .' He leaned back against the cabin of the launch and closed his eyes.

'What about the other blood, Max, the blood that wasn't yours?'

'Oh, that's so easy, Çetin,' the magician smiled. 'Where do you think I got it?'

'I, well . . .'

'Dad . . .'

İkmen turned round sharply to see his daughter's slightly raised face looking up at him. It was extremely white and there was a deadness in her eyes that was totally unfamiliar to him. İkmen looked down at the cuff around his wrist and said to Süleyman, 'Can you . . . ?'

'Of course.' He went over to Gonca and gently took Çiçek from her.

'Mehmet?'

'Yes, you're OK now, Çiçek,' he said as he smoothed the unaccustomed blonde hair from her face. 'I'm here, and your father. There's nothing to be afraid of any more.'

As the lights of the Eminönü docks and the imperial mosques and palaces behind them came into view, İkmen studied the apparently sleeping face of Max Esterhazy closely. How could he have known and yet not known this man so completely? And what had happened to make him, suddenly, take the action that he had? Was it the impending conflict in the region? Was he so afraid that it would change his life that he felt he had to kill in order to prevent it? Or had it all just been a purely commercial act punctuated by stupid costumes and sleight-of-hand parlour tricks? İkmen more than most knew that magic, whatever it was, possessed some power. In a way he knew he was relieved that Max had completed his ritual, because if he hadn't İkmen didn't know what that inconclusion might produce.

And what of Alison? He had never dreamed that she'd felt like that about him! And why had it affected Max so badly? Alison had been lovely, but she was just a girl like millions of others ... But then maybe that had more to do with Max's past than Alison herself; maybe the key to that lay in what the magician's father had been and the ambiguity that appeared to surround that. On one level, Max almost certainly did want to do good, to protect the city – maybe even make up for some of the dreadful things that, perhaps, his father had done. But there was also an element of fury there too. His woman had preferred someone he considered inferior and he'd never been able to get over it. Turks were maybe in their place as occasional friends and servants – which brought to mind Ülkü Ayla and the assertion of innocence Max had made for her. Was she truly innocent or was this yet another of Max's games? Time and some hard interviewing would, he hoped, produce an answer.

They pulled into the shore and İkmen and the pilot took an apparently sleeping Max Esterhazy to the waiting police car.

İkmen had Max and Turgut Can taken down to the cells while he took Çiçek to hospital.

'We'll interview them both in the morning,' he said to Süleyman as he took his leave of him.

'It is morning, Çetin.'

İkmen shrugged. 'When I get back then,' he said, and then added with a smile, 'You'd better go home and change, Mehmet. I think that suit is now beyond human intervention.'

Süleyman, who had up until now almost forgotten about his water-logged appearance, smiled.

When İkmen had gone, Çöktin turned to Süleyman and said, 'Sir, who is this Alison?'

'Oh, just someone,' Süleyman said wearily. 'The inspector and Esterhazy knew her years ago.'

'Oh.'

'You'd better go home for a few hours too, İsak,' Süleyman said. 'It's been a terrible night and we will, I am sure, have to listen to yet more horror later. Go home, clean up and I'll call you. Oh, and,' he placed his hand on his deputy's already retreating back, 'thank you for what you did tonight. You probably saved my life.'

Çöktin, as if embarrassed, put his head down. 'Sir.'

Süleyman watched him go and then started to make his way up to his office to complete the necessary paperwork. This had to be done and so the ruined suit and squelching shoes would have to wait for a while at least. If nothing else, he thought grimly, my appearance will give people something to talk about.

He'd just started to mount the stairs when he heard the commotion down below. Raised voices together with the sound of running feet made him retrace his steps a few paces. It sounded as if the noise was coming from the cells. Mentally he went over all the precautions he had taken to ensure that neither of the prisoners could harm themselves. They'd been very thorough. But then again what happened to prisoners once they were 'down there' was something he couldn't legislate for. Not everyone was like himself and İkmen, and Esterhazy, at least, was being held on suspicion of murder. He made his way down to the cells and pushed his way through what seemed like thousands of constables.

'What's going on?' he asked one of the men that he knew by sight.

'Prisoner's dead, sir.'

'Dead?'

'Yes.'

Even before he got to the door of the cell, he knew it was Max. On the launch there had been something strangely final in his manner. He didn't remember now what the magician had actually said, but then maybe it hadn't been to do with anything as overt as speech.

He pushed the cell door open and saw Max, motionless on the floor, a very young constable pumping half-heartedly at his chest.

'Have you called the doctor?' He squatted down beside the body and pushed the young man out of the way.

'No.'

'Well, do so! Now!'

'Yes, sir.' The young man stood up and ran towards the door.

Süleyman pinched the magician's nose between his fingers and blew into his mouth. He then pumped on his chest for several seconds before resuming his place at the man's head again. As he pinched his nose for a second time, Max's eyes flew open and for just a split second, Süleyman thought he saw a smile cross his blueing lips.

'Allah!'

But then in a blink of an eye the effect had disappeared and the magician was just like a great, blue and grey stone once again. Süleyman continued working on what he knew in his heart was a dead body until, after what seemed like a lifetime, the doctor arrived.

Çiçek İkmen was strangely animated, given her ordeal. She wasn't, of course, her usual lively self, and her father was insistent that she remain in hospital and submit to medical tests, but she wanted to talk and he felt it was important to listen to her.

'What was the fortune-teller doing on the boat?' she asked him as she gazed, now firmly, into her father's face.

'It's a long story, Çiçek,' İkmen replied. 'What happened to you, my soul?'

She saw the tears in his eyes and she squeezed his hand encouragingly. 'I don't know,' she said. 'I met your friend Max. We had a drink.'

'Where?'

'At the Kaktüs,' she said, naming a friendly, literary and arty bar just off İstiklal Caddesi.

'Why? Why did you go with him?' Now his guilt was beginning to manifest itself, making İkmen feel slightly sick. Max had said he 'wanted' Çiçek, that he admired her 'magical' personality. Why hadn't İkmen even considered this as a possibility?

269

'I was depressed,' Çiçek said. 'Dad, I made a fool of myself with Mehmet.'

İkmen's heart jumped. 'What do you mean?'

'Oh, I haven't done anything,' she said. 'I just went and told him how I felt.' Her eyes filled with tears. 'Didn't he tell you?'

'No.'

'Probably too embarrassed,' she sobbed. 'I don't know what possessed me to do it, Dad! He asked me why I was looking so down and so I told him. I don't know why.'

For some reason that İkmen balked at attributing to Max's sigil, Çiçek had behaved in an impulsive fashion that was not natural to her. Gonca had said that magicians put a lot of effort into these sigils and so they were very powerful at doing whatever the practitioner wanted them to do. Had Max really taken control of Çiçek, manipulated her into a position where she would confide in and trust him without thinking?

'What happened then?'

'Then nothing,' she shrugged. 'Then the fortune-teller on the boat and you and . . . and Mehmet . . . And there was hair too, on my head, blonde . . .'

'It was a wig, little pigeon.'

'Oh.'

The door opened and a small man in a white coat entered.

'Here's the doctor,' İkmen said. 'I just need to speak to him before he sees you.'

He then walked over to the small man and led him outside where he gave him a brief overview of events.

'It was as if she were hypnotised,' he said in conclusion. 'The man in question spoke to her and she opened her eyes.'

'But she now remembers nothing of the events on the boat?'

'No.'

The doctor shrugged. 'It is unusual for a person to recall nothing from their experience of hypnotic trance,' he said. 'I certainly have never come across such a thing. Maybe the trauma has caused temporary amnesia. I will examine your daughter and also perform a blood test.'

'For drugs?'

'Yes. Although the way she came round would seem to suggest that your daughter was in a hypnotic state, that could just be coincidental.'

'You mean he gave her a drug, knowing approximately when it would wear off?'

'Maybe. It seems likely from what you have told me that if a drug were administered to her, that happened in the bar. My guess would be that if she was given anything it was probably Rohypnol, which renders those ingesting it both pliable and at least temporarily amnesic.'

'I have heard of it,' İkmen said with a sigh. 'Men give it to girls and then . . .'

'Rape them, yes,' the doctor said very matter-of-factly. 'But I warn you that we may never know. Rohypnol clears the system very quickly and so I don't know whether the blood test will be very illuminating.'

İkmen let the doctor in to Çiçek and then went outside to have a smoke. Metin İskender was still recovering from his bullet wound somewhere else in the building. As his condition had improved, staff had moved him to another part of the hospital. İkmen had never visited – too busy. Terrible! Metin had almost died, but because Max had had them all whirling around in circles with his sigils and portals and books featuring goat-headed men, İkmen hadn't once been to visit him. Max had shot him, it seemed, because Metin must have interrupted him as he searched for Çiçek's sigil. Where had he got the gun?

Max had really planned all this. But had he done so before or after he'd come into contact with İrfan Şay? How, indeed, and where had he met Şay? Had he done so before or after he'd planned to execute his ritual? And what of the overendowed Goat of Mendes images on the places of worship? That, it now seemed, had just simply amused him and he could have just dismissed it to İkmen as the nonsense that it was. But he hadn't because İkmen's appearance had, it seemed, proved just too fortunate and tempting to miss. Revenge – thirty years on! Or was it? The surreal quality of his recent experiences on the Bosphorus coupled with his tiredness made İkmen question what was real and what wasn't. Alison had been on the boat but it hadn't been Alison, it had been Çiçek. Max had sliced off his own hand before his eyes – except that he hadn't. Magician and illusionist seemed to be a more accurate title for Max Esterhazy now – or maybe he was and always had been just the latter . . .

İkmen switched his mobile phone back on and waited to see whether he had any messages. He did, but only one, from Süleyman.

It was a bizarre sight. One man in robes, another, leaning against the cell door, his clothes reeking of seawater, and the third man, exhausted beyond craziness, shouting his every utterance.

'So Max caught you wanking over his books! What then?' İkmen said.

Turgut Can slumped still further down into his seat. Maybe, Süleyman observed, he was trying to get as far away as he could from İkmen's furious questioning. But with Max now dead they had to find out as much as they could in any way that was open to them and that included from Turgut Can.

'That was months ago. He threatened me, with magic. Max Bey frightened me.'

'He was a magician, it's what he did!' İkmen shouted. 'You shouldn't have got involved with him! Why did you?'

'I told you, he frightened me. And he offered me money.'

'How much and what for – exactly?'

'One thousand pounds – sterling.' Turgut Can looked up, his eyes bright with greed. 'Can you imagine?'

'Yes, and sadly like most people, I can only do that,' İkmen snapped. 'So how were you to "earn" this vast amount of money, Turgut?'

'At first all I had to do was throw some blood around Max Bey's study.' He paused briefly to take a cigarette from the packet on the table and light up. 'On Tuesday. He would go out and I would distract Ülkü while I did what he had asked.'

'How?'

'I took her to her . . . her bedroom and then I went alone, I said, to get cigarettes. But instead of going to the hall, I went to the study. Max Bey had left a covered bucket by the door and I picked that up to throw it when I saw him standing over by the window.'

'Who?'

'Max Bey. He said he'd had to come back because he'd forgotten something – some magical thing. I said he should go and he said that he would soon. I think when Ülkü heard a noise from the study that was probably him leaving.'

'So you didn't throw the bucket of blood at the walls?'

'No, he did. I couldn't, not with him there.'

'Do you have any idea, Turgut,' Süleyman said, 'where this blood might have come from?'

'No.'

'Did you ask?' İkmen said.

Turgut Can shrugged. 'No. I didn't like to; he frightened me.'

'So no curiosity about the provenance of a litre or so of blood?' İkmen sat down, lit a cigarette and rubbed his face with his hands. 'Don't answer that,' he said. 'I think the thousand sterling has already done that for you. What did you want the money for, Turgut?'

'I don't know. A car? There was a condition on the money too, which was that I was to leave Ülkü alone – maybe even get out of town.'

'Why?'

'Because Max Bey thought I was bad for Ülkü. He said he wanted for her to have a chance in life and with me around that wasn't going to be easy.'

'And you were all right with that?'

'I liked Ülkü, but . . .' he shrugged again, 'there are many girls . . .'

'When did you last see Ülkü?'

'This – no yesterday afternoon – on Divanyolu. She didn't know where to go or what to do, but how could I help her? Max Bey had told me to stop seeing her and so I just moved away from her.'

'And what did she do?' Süleyman asked.

'Well, she cried . . . and—'

'You left her,' İkmen said. 'Alone and homeless, you with your thousand sterling in your pocket!'

'No! No! No, Max Bey hasn't paid me,' the young man said bitterly. 'After the blood thing and once I'd managed to get out of here, I didn't see Max Bey until yesterday. That's why I was on that boat with these stupid clothes and—'

'You knew nothing of his activities between his disappearance and last night?'

'No! I swear! He met me, yesterday. I don't know how because I was just about to leave the city. But there he was at Haydarpaşa, waiting for me.'

'Why were you leaving the city, Turgut?'

'Because I was scared,' he said. 'You scared me. I didn't think you'd take me in – Max Bey said that you wouldn't – but you did and I talked a lot of rubbish, lost my nerve . . . I thought something might come back at me because of what I'd done, and I didn't, by then, think I'd ever get any money from Max Bey. I was going home.'

'But Max Bey offered you money to stay, did he?'

'Yes. He said that he needed help with a boat. The person who was going to help him had let him down and so if I did it he would pay me.'

The name İrfan Şay came unbidden into İkmen's mind. Could it be that the businessman turned film-maker had taken fright at Süleyman's sudden appearance at his home and gone off somewhere? There was a warrant out for his arrest; Süleyman had set that in motion already. Filming a murder did, after all, make one a confederate in that crime.

'Did Max Bey, at any time, give you the impression that he was going to kill my daughter?'

'No! No, I would never have agreed—'

'But you would have been OK with him having sex with her?' Turgut Can did not reply. 'So did he take you to this boat or—'

'I went to Eminönü with him – the western side of the Galata Bridge,' only a spit away from where İkmen had first found the magician, 'then he left and came back with the young lady later.'

'What time?'

'About seven.'

'And how was the young lady when you first saw her?'

'I thought she was drunk,' Turgut said. 'He, Max Bey, laid her in the bottom of the boat – I thought at first to sleep it off. But then later, when we were out on the water, he started undressing her and . . .'

İkmen, his face white with tension, said, 'And what?'

'And he put her in those funny clothes and that wig. He'd already dressed himself and me up for this ceremony, but she didn't look right for that with the blonde hair and big boots.'

No, but she had looked like Alison and, as the now late Max Esterhazy had told İkmen himself, she had to have that appearance if he was ever going to be aroused by her.

'Did Max Bey have sex with her?'

'No. But I know he was intending to do so,' Turgut said. 'He watched her dance about for ages. Then he said that he, and not the Goat, was going to have her. This time the Goat was going to watch – he said. But then he put that goat head thing on when you arrived and told me to cover my head with my mask. Then he called the devils.' He looked up and shook his head. 'When he cut his hand off like that I nearly fainted!'

'Yes, but he didn't cut his hand off, did he?' İkmen said. 'That was, it seems, something of an illusion, maybe even a joke, if you like.'

Turgut Can nodded his head. 'Oh, jokes, yes,' he said. 'Max Bey liked them – and puzzles. All that blood business in his apartment was a puzzle.'

Süleyman frowned. 'What do you mean?'

Turgut Can turned to İkmen. 'It was for you,' he said. 'Max Bey said he needed to "disappear" for a while and so he did that thing with the blood to give you what he said was "something to think about". I don't know why, but he mentioned you by name and said that, well, it almost seemed as if it was some sort of challenge he was setting you.'

'Max Bey wanted Inspector İkmen to believe that he was dead?'

'Not exactly, no. There was the blood and then there was also some of his own blood too. I don't know where that was. He said it was there somewhere. He just wanted to confuse everyone – even Ülkü! He didn't think about what he was doing to her!'

'Nor did you,' İkmen put in tartly.

Turgut Can lowered his head again. 'No.'

'And so do you know where Ülkü might be now?'

'No, not at all.'

'Because,' İkmen said, 'her possessions are still in his apartment. Also it may well be that some of Max Esterhazy's assets are due to Miss Ayla.'

Turgut looked up. 'Like what? What do you mean?'

'I don't know,' İkmen said. 'But I shouldn't spend any time thinking about that, Turgut, because they cannot, I promise you, have any relevance for you.'

'What do you mean?'

'I mean that you, at the very least, misled this investigation and will therefore need to serve time in prison.'

'But I—'

'You're going to prison, Turgut. You're not going to get any money.' He leaned in towards him maliciously. 'What a shame.'

'But I haven't hurt anyone!' Turgut whined. 'I didn't even throw the blood across the room in the end. I did nothing! Ask Max Bey, if you don't believe me!'

İkmen looked across at Süleyman, who now joined them at the table.

'I'm afraid that won't be possible, Turgut,' he said. 'Max Bey died shortly after he was brought into custody.'

Turgut Can's eyes flooded with fear. 'You killed him.'

'No. No, we found him dead in his cell,' Süleyman said. 'We don't yet know how he died.'

'So that's what all the noise was about.'

'Yes.'

'So now you only have me . . .'

'Yes, Turgut,' Süleyman said, 'which is why it is even more important that you tell us everything you know. That you tell us the truth.'

'I have told you the truth!' He raked one nervous hand through his hair and said to İkmen, 'It was about you, some of it. The blood, anyway. He wanted to confuse you. He had some thing, some feeling about you I didn't understand. But the rest of it? I don't know! I didn't know he'd killed those people! I would never have done anything—'

'We will see,' İkmen said, and folded his arms across his chest. He looked very grey now – almost ill. But then aside from the shock of what had happened to his daughter he did also have to contend with the fact that someone he had considered a friend was now dead. And Max Esterhazy, notwithstanding all the recent revelations, had been a friend – once. Quite what had made him into what he even-

276

tually became, İkmen didn't know. Maybe it had all started way back with Alison, and with a rejection that İkmen hadn't even known about. Alison had loved him – a little, poor Turk over what was, outwardly at least, a suave, handsome and educated Englishman. Except, of course, that Max wasn't and never had been an Englishman. By taking money from his father and by concealing that man's location he had, in effect, taken a stance against the country that had nurtured him. He had profited from its enemy and, as well as lying to and deceiving İkmen, he had dishonoured his own past too. But contrarily, and possibly typically for Max, he'd done it for apparently the best of reasons – to save the city – to spare the lives of boys like Bülent İkmen and his friends. Only time would prove whether or not all the bloodshed had been worth it.

Chapter 23

Dawn came, bringing with it, as it sometimes did, a clutch of bodies for examination. And, as the dawn call to prayer faded into the already thick air above the city, the mortuary attendants arrived for yet another day of hard physical labour. Lifeless bodies are typically heavy and often unwieldy too – one had to be fit in order to be able to heave them around. Hacer Mardin, who had worked as a pathologist for just over five years, was very glad that she didn't personally have to man-handle her charges. Her boss, Arto Sarkissian, was sometimes known to lend a hand in this way, but Hacer, being female, wouldn't have been allowed to do so even if she'd wanted to. Some man or other – old, young, fit or frail – was always rushing to her aid. It would have been nice if it had been because she was pretty, but Hacer knew it wasn't that. Men helped her because she was a woman in a man's world and that, Hacer often felt, was a statement about her abilities or lack thereof. She'd even shared her theory with Arto Sarkissian once, but he hadn't, she had to admit, had much time for it. Although he didn't say anything, he was, she imagined, placing her in the 'mad feminist' corner of his mind. But that didn't mean he didn't trust her. Today, as happened sometimes now, she was the only pathologist in attendance, which meant that together with her assistants she alone would pronounce upon causes of death, and order, if necessary, fur-ther forensic tests. Four cadavers had come in overnight from vari-ous sources and so the early start she had made had been justified.

Already on trolleys, the four bodies were still bagged. So, on the basis that it was better to see what she was up against as soon as pos-sible, Hacer unzipped the first one immediately. Even without looking she knew that whoever was in there had been dead for some time. Hacer, despite her expertise and experience, just briefly felt her early morning glass of tea rise in her throat. Corpses like this frequently came apart in your hands, as it were, and it wasn't something that was easily tolerated by anyone. Hacer zipped the bag up and went over to the second trolley.

'That came in from police headquarters, Hacer Hanım,' one of the attendants said. Whether the subtext was 'police equals brutality equals a very messy body' Hacer didn't know, but she nodded her acknowledgement to the man and unzipped the bag. As she stared into it, life as usual went on around her. People scrubbed up, cleaned out fridges, turned up the samovar in the corner and talked about football. Hacer, however, was in a somewhat different space.

'I hope this isn't someone's idea of a joke,' she said as she moved around the trolley to confront the all-male group.

'Hanım?'

'The police headquarters body,' she said. 'What's he done, escaped?'

'With respect, Hanım, what—'

'The bag, it's empty,' she said. 'Are you sure it was full when you picked it up?'

The two assistants who had collected the body looked at each other.

'Yes,' the older of the two said. 'Certain. Not three hours ago, Hanım.'

His friend nodded his agreement.

Hacer Mardin sighed. 'I'd better go and call the police,' she said, and left for her office.

The two men who had brought what they believed was the body of a foreigner into the mortuary went over to the bag and studied it in some detail, both inside and out.

That İrfan Şay hadn't, apparently, left the country didn't mean that he was any easier to find. However, his home, its occupants and contents were a good start and, at just after two thirty that afternoon, Süleyman and Çöktin returned with authorisation to search the premises. İkmen, for whom the disappearance of Max Esterhazy's body had been the final straw, had returned to his home to get some rest. Both physically and emotionally exhausted, it was the only time Süleyman could ever remember seeing İkmen refuse a cigarette. Seemingly, not even nicotine could console him now.

The only person at home when the police arrived was Şay's twenty-five-year-old son, Emir. As smooth as, Süleyman imagined, his country-bred father was rough, Emir Şay claimed to know nothing of either his father's business interests or his current whereabouts. But he didn't either object to or appear unduly worried about the search, which led Süleyman to wonder just what, if anything, the young man did know. When the officers began searching Şay's office, Emir sat himself down outside on the terrace with a large book that, it transpired, was a physics textbook.

But while outside was all studious calm, inside the yalı things were far from serene. Şay's office was small and cramped, and so working through his considerable paperwork wasn't easy. After all, officially, he was a businessman engaged in the sale of electrical equipment and so most of his paperwork pertained to that. But there were also cameras, conventional and video, and what seemed like vast amounts of attachments, add-ons and lenses. It took the police a while to find any actual tapes, but when they did it very quickly became clear that they hadn't been wrong about İrfan Şay.

'That looks like Lale Tekeli to me,' Çöktin said, pausing the tape on a frame of the girl's terrified face. 'It's in a wooden room like the one we think she was murdered in.'

Süleyman, slumped back into one of Şay's armchairs, said, 'Can you make out any of the other "actors" in the drama?'

'They're all wearing masks, sir,' Çöktin replied. 'Look.'

And he replayed the tape from the beginning. There were three other robed and masked figures in the film. Whatever Max had said about 'entities taking the girls' the tall one had to be him – but the others? If they believed Turgut Can then he wasn't one of them and so the others were a mystery. Şay would, of course, be involved either as a participant or as the cameraman. But who were the others? Süleyman watched as the tall figure produced either a metal dildo or a large metal sheath from the parted folds of his cloak. The other two bent the girl forwards to allow him to enter her. She screamed. But that didn't stop him thrusting hard into her, strange, unknowable words issuing from behind his mask as he did so. It was only when they'd finished watching the tape that they became aware of Emir

Şay's presence just inside the French windows. His eyes were genuinely wounded and his face was very pale.

'Did my father have anything to do with that?' he asked. 'Is that why you're here?'

Süleyman sighed. 'We think, sir, that your father may have had some involvement with the production of these videos.'

'Did they really stab that girl?'

'Yes, sir, I'm afraid—'

'Allah.' Emir Şay sank down into the nearest chair and put his hand to his chest. 'I'm so sorry,' he said. 'If I had known about this . . .' He looked up into Süleyman's face. 'Inspector, I'm sorry but I lied to you yesterday when I told you my father was out. He told me to – he told me you'd come because of unpaid taxes. After you left he went.'

'Where?'

'I honestly do not know,' Emir said. 'I was just glad that he'd gone.'

Süleyman sat down opposite the young man and lit a cigarette.

'My father and I don't get on,' Emir said. 'I'm grateful to him – he bought me a good education. But we are very different people and when he fills the house with whores I just can't stand it. You know my mother still lives in Edirne? He visits her once a year if she's lucky.'

'You don't think he would have gone there?'

'No. Inspector, that video, who would want such a thing? It's revolting.'

'You'd be surprised what some people will pay for, Mr Şay,' Süleyman replied wearily. 'You know, in America they call them "snuff movies", tapes of people really being killed.'

'A certain type of person gets sexually aroused by such things,' Çöktin put in.

'Mr Şay,' Süleyman said, 'do you know of an Englishman called Maximillian Esterhazy?'

'Max?' Emir smiled. 'Yes, he's just been with us for a few days. He's a very intelligent and witty man – I like him. Although quite what he finds to talk about to my father and his ghastly friends, I have no idea. You know, when Max is around, my father stops buying whores? I think he's a good influence.'

Süleyman looked across at Çöktin, whose face remained static. Back in Şay's office, more boxes of tapes plus some amateurish and extremely unpleasant magazines were being removed.

Constable Gün placed one of the boxes down on the floor in front of Çöktin and said, 'There are some outbuildings in the garden, Sergeant. Do you want us to—'

'Search wherever you like. My father has a dark room out there, so who knows what you may find?' Emir Şay said, and then he covered his face with his hands and appeared, just briefly, to weep. 'How could he? Twisted, unnatural man!' And then, as Gün left, he looked up sharply. 'You know who I blame for this? Ali and Christoph.'

'Friends of your father?'

'Ali Saka is my father's accountant. Christoph Bauer is just a . . . he does something up at the German Hospital. He is German or Swiss or something.'

'Did either of these men also know Maximillian Esterhazy?' Süleyman asked.

'Dad met Max through Christoph,' Emir replied. 'I don't know how. Max is a very spiritual man – he knows a lot about the dervishes. All Christoph ever seemed to want to do was get drunk and fuck prostitutes. I can't imagine how he and Max became friends, but they are.'

Çöktin, who had been taking note of the men's names, said, 'Do you know where these men live?'

'Ali lives, I think, in Kadiköy, but I don't know about Christoph. You'll find their numbers in my father's diary.'

Çöktin went into the office to search for it.

Emir Şay looked briefly out of the French windows at the shining Bosphorus water and then said, 'You can't imagine how it feels to discover something like this.' He looked now at Süleyman. 'I mean, I knew my father was no saint, but this . . . How could he? How could he dishonour me, my mother and himself in such a way?'

'For money.'

'But he has money! More than enough!' And then he sighed. 'You know, I think if it's OK, that I might phone Max Esterhazy now. He's a very sympathetic friend.'

Süleyman shook his head sadly before he launched into as much

283

as he could tell the young man about Max and his possible involvement with his father's business. When he had finished, Emir sank back into his chair and this time he wept quite openly.

'When those close to you betray you,' Süleyman said, 'it is very hard to bear.' And, he thought silently to himself, I should know. Max had, after all, been his friend too – in a way, if one could count as friend one who never shared the truth of his life with one. But then if he had, would Süleyman have wanted to be friends with him, the son of a Nazi, one, further, in receipt of Nazi money? Now he would never know. Max was dead, even if his body could not currently be located. Those morons at the station had probably messed up, knowing them. No doubt Max was in some cell somewhere, forgotten and by now probably smelling too.

'Sir . . .'

It was Gün in from the garden.

'Yes?'

'Sir, I think you need to come outside.'

'What have you found?' Emir Şay, suddenly roused from his weeping, rose to his feet. 'Not more filth, surely?'

'No, sir.' Gün looked at Süleyman. 'Sir?'

Süleyman rose to his feet and, followed by Emir Şay, he made his way towards the back door. However, as he drew level with Gün, the constable stopped him and whispered, 'Not the young man, sir.'

'Ah.'

'What?' Emir threw his hands up and shrugged.

'Let me just go with the constable and then I'll get back to you, Mr Şay,' Süleyman said.

'Yes, but—'

'I'm not asking you, Mr Şay,' Süleyman said sternly. 'Please wait here. I will return momentarily.'

And so Emir Şay remained. He sat down and while several uniformed men systematically took his father's office apart, he looked at the now blank television screen that had all too recently shattered his world.

İkmen couldn't sleep. He'd tried. But what with his son Sınan returning from the hospital with Çiçek, not to mention Fatma's tearful reunion with her daughter, there hadn't been much peace to be had. Then when Mr Gören and Mr Emin got going about the unfortunate Halide again, that just about finished him off. Arming himself only with two packets of cigarettes, İkmen set off into the backstreets of Sultanahmet, down into Cağaloğlu and across into the warren of tiny streets that surrounded the Kapılı Çarşışı. This area was, for him, a place of both safety and anonymity. Teeming with all manner of life – human, feline, canine, birds – even the occasional pony – there was always something to look at and, if one could stay still for long enough, enjoy. You could buy almost anything in this area – cheaply produced pots and pans, electrical goods of variable quality, leather in every form and shade imaginable. His cousin, in fact, the transsexual Samsun, lived with her leather dealer lover not two minutes from where he was now. But he didn't want to go and see Samsun now. She was there if he needed her, but for the moment, he just wanted to smoke, walk and try to make some sense of what Max had done to him – to all of them. He pushed past a couple of fat babushkas, women from the former Soviet Union filling their black bin sacks with cheaply purchased children's clothes, and found a vacant piece of wall against which to lean in order to light his cigarette.

Max had liked this area. He'd once said that he considered it one of the most truly Turkish districts of the city – whatever that had meant. In light of what was now known about him, it had probably meant that the place was chaotic and in places less than sanitary. But, at the time, İkmen had taken it to mean that it was lively and interesting. He pushed himself away from the wall and began his wanderings again. But no, that was unfair, Max had loved İstanbul – indeed, at least part of the motivation behind that crazy ceremony of his had been to protect the city. It had been arrogant and paternalistic but also deeply affecting too. Where was Max now? Although he knew it was stupid, İkmen couldn't think of him in the past tense. He had been pronounced dead by their own doctor and, indeed, Süleyman had known that he was dead when he was trying to revive him. But Max was a magician – Max was someone who could create the illusion of cutting off his own hand – Max was someone who could, seemingly, appear and disappear at will. Could he, was it possible for him to fake his own death too? Just the thought of it produced a deep sense of paranoia and as İkmen unwittingly entered the Sahaflar, he could almost feel unseen, mocking eyes upon him.

İbrahim Dede was sitting outside his shop enjoying the sunshine. And as a troubled-looking İkmen passed, he called over to him.

'Çetin Bey!'

Almost, but not quite lost inside his own head, İkmen looked up and frowned.

'Come, join me for tea,' the dervish said. 'You have the look of a man in need of conversation.'

And so İkmen went over to join him. After asking one of the young boys who worked for him to bring them both tea, İbrahim Dede took İkmen through to his little office at the back of the shop and sat down. As İkmen sat in front of him he noticed that the small cubicle was decorated with many drawings of tall, graceful dervishes, their skirts swirling about their ankles, turning in the sema or ritual dance. He hadn't intended to come here, even though he knew that Max and the dervish had been friends, but now that he was, he felt it only right that he share what he knew with the old man. After all, dervishes were spiritual people, traditionally accepting of the foibles of flawed humanity – and he knew also, because he trusted his instincts, that İbrahim Dede would not repeat anything that he told him. So İkmen began and some time later, he stopped.

When he had finished, İbrahim Dede crossed his arms in front of him on the table and shook his head sadly. 'Poor Maximillian.'

'Poor Maximillian! What about those poor children?'

'Such a lot of talent and good intentions,' he said. 'But perverted by the three-fold evils of money, envy and guilt.' He sighed. 'I, like you, didn't know about his past. But whether he took his father's money or not, his tainted lineage troubled him. I know this because Maximillian was a good man and only good men are so troubled.'

'He killed people, İbrahim Dede,' İkmen said softly. 'He encouraged a boy to take his own life and he killed three girls himself.'

'Or rather the entities he conjured did,' İbrahim Dede said.

'That's what Max said, yes,' İkmen replied. 'He first assaulted them with a metal penis, "the Devil's" own, apparently, and then he killed them. But it was Max himself in—'

'Reality?' the dervish put in. 'What is that, Çetin Bey? If a devil or a djinn takes possession of a magician in a ceremony and if that magician becomes that devil or that djinn, then who performs the ceremony? The man or the entity?'

'We call that madness, İbrahim Dede.'

'The police do, yes,' he said. 'But you are a little different to your colleagues, aren't you?' He smiled. 'If you were not then Maximillian would not have felt so wounded that you bettered him in love.'

'I didn't even know that I had!'

The dervish raised a hand. 'Immaterial,' he said. 'Maximillian liked and respected you and so the girl's preference for you hurt him. In addition, as we have said, love İstanbul as he did, he was only comfortable here when he could feel superior to us. His ritual, as well as saving the city, was also designed to prove that we needed looking after and that he was the only person capable of doing that. This girl you speak of, by expressing her preference for you, undermined his sense of himself as a good person.'

'Mmm.'

'And as for the trickery? Well, you know that a lot of those we call magicians and prophets are also conjurors too. There are lamas in Tibet who can go without food for many months and survive; there are fellows of mine who can reduce their own earthly desires to such an extent that they appear almost dead.'

'Almost dead,' İkmen said, 'yes. But Max was completely dead. Our doctor confirmed it.'

İbrahim Dede shrugged. 'I don't know. I was not there. All I can tell you is that I do not know, myself, where Maximillian might be. Gonca the gypsy I have seen, however.'

In the midst of everything that had happened, İkmen had almost forgotten about Gonca. She had, he recalled, slipped away just after they'd reached the station.

'And?'

'And she is essentially a good woman. But a gypsy girl did die for this ceremony of protection Maximillian created.'

'What are you saying?'

'I'm saying nothing,' İbrahim Dede replied. 'I give you only the facts; it is for you to make your conclusions.'

İkmen sighed. 'So what did Gonca tell you?'

'If I am to keep your confidences, then I must also keep hers,' İbrahim Dede said sternly.

'Ah.'

Then the dervish smiled. 'She told me nothing you have not done,' he said more gently now. 'You know that she of all of you could see that Maximillian had not really sliced off his hand. But then she knows a trick or two herself and so maybe she was expecting the illusion. You know that Gonca felt that something was wrong in the city a long time ago – before all this, before the foul images on the places of worship.'

'We still don't know who did those,' İkmen said.

'No.' He looked up. 'You should thank the gypsy, Çetin Bey. You should give her something she desires.'

İkmen, who instantly recalled Gonca's amused suggestion that he offer himself to her, also remembered that she had, thankfully, then declined his services. But then maybe whatever İbrahim Dede had in mind was of a rather more spiritual nature.

The old man finished the small amount of tea in his glass that had long since grown cold and said, 'Whatever the truth of what has happened to Maximillian might be, do not waste time pursuing him or even his corpse now. His ceremony is at an end – in spite of you and your fellows. And in victory he has proved himself the better man – in his own eyes. The girl's rejection was assuaged in that final act of self-sacrifice, whether indeed it was real or imagined.'

'Society needs to exact punishment, İbrahim Dede.'

'Indeed, and you will, I believe, discover those who were acting with Maximillian, who exploited his need for money. But Maximillian himself?' He smiled. 'He is beyond your power now. Let him go.'

İkmen sat in silence for a while and then he said, 'You know, I feel so guilty. That so much of this was about me.'

'Put that from your mind,' the dervish said. 'Please, Çetin Bey. After all, have we not seen what guilt can do to a man already this day?'

İkmen stared up at the images that looked down at him from every wall. Men whirling through space, eyes closed as they experienced the ecstasy of union with the divine. Free from desires, worries – even guilt. Though not a religious person, İkmen did appreciate the essential truths behind great faith and he took what he saw as a sign that perhaps he should do what İbrahim Dede suggested. And so he bowed down to kiss the old man's hand in recognition of both his wisdom and his own agreement with what had been said. The old man, well aware of what this meant, smiled.

The corpse of İrfan Şay, his head destroyed by a bullet from the gun at his side, had been a grisly and disturbing sight. His poor son, Emir, had just collapsed. To discover that one's father is, at best, an accessory to murder is one thing, and one does, naturally, express anger at that parent. But to then find that he has committed suicide is still a cause for grief. Şay, for all his faults, was still Emir's father and he had once loved him.

Şay's two confederates had been quickly tracked down after that and were both now in custody. Bauer wasn't saying anything although Ali Saka had started whining, in the car back to the station, about how İrfan Şay had made him take part in his film-making against his will.

'It is all down to Bauer,' he said, referring to his German so-called friend. 'He encouraged İrfan. He works in that hospital, yes, but his real passion is pornography. He knows how much these death movies can make. He knows people, ask him! And the Englishman – ask him too! Sick, the both of them, with their infidel ceremonies!'

'Which you took part in,' Çöktin had reminded him smartly.

'Only because İrfan made me,' Saka replied. 'I never provided the victims nor killed anyone. Bauer used to steal blood from the hospital to make the scenes even more gory. How bad is that! I was just a cameraman, unwilling and, well, trapped really.'

Saka had been quiet since then and, when they reached the station, he demanded to see his advocate. Tomorrow, Süleyman thought, as he wearily made his way over to his car, was going to be another exhausting day. So much involved in this case! So complicated – like, he imagined, one of Max's rituals.

He crossed the car park with his head down and so the sound of someone's voice as he reached his car came as a shock.

'Hello, Inspector.'

He looked up to see Gonca, resplendent this time in green and gold, leaning against his car, smoking one of her thin, black cigars.

'Gonca Hanım. What are you doing here?'

'Well, I am waiting for you to drive me home,' she said.

'But haven't you been home?'

Just for a moment he wondered whether in fact she'd been at the station since the early hours of the morning, but then he decided that that wasn't possible. If vaguely, he did remember her leaving.

'You know, what you need in your life is some fun,' she said. 'Harmless enjoyment that cannot impinge upon anyone around you.'

Süleyman frowned. The gypsy, seeing this, laughed. 'Oh, don't look so frightened,' she said. 'I'm not going to seduce you!'

With what sounded like a sigh of relief he opened his car door and bade her get inside.

'Of course I'll take you home,' he said as she slid into the passenger seat beside him.

As soon as she was seated she put her hand on his knee.

'But . . .'

'But I didn't say anything about you seducing me,' she said. 'Through the magic of condoms and my sworn silence you can have a lot of fun tonight and with absolutely no consequences for the future.'

That he even paused to think about it did appal part of his mind. But there was another bit of him that was, and had been ever since his test results came through, crying out for some sort of sexual contact. He had hoped it would be with his wife but, so far, she hadn't answered any of his calls. And anyway, hadn't Krikor Sarkissian said that as long as he was careful there was no reason for him to become infected with any sort of disease in the future? The gypsy, even by the thin light of the streetlamp above, was very beautiful. However, she was also giving herself, at times, to Constable Yıldız. Surely as a man of dignity he shouldn't follow, as it were, his inferiors?

But then the gypsy took one of his hands in hers and placed it into the folds of her blouse so that it touched the flesh of her breast. 'Fun,' she breathed as he began to move his fingers just very gently. 'Come and have some fun.'

There was no more talking or even thinking about what they had both been through that night. There was also, for Gonca, very little in the way of taking control too. Unlike the boys she frequently amused herself with, Süleyman was a man who knew both what to do and what he wanted. And when the morning came, she did what she rarely did for male visitors and brought him tea in bed. As he drank, she lay down beside him and moved her hand under the covers towards his penis.

'Why don't you stay?' she said. 'I can feel that you want to.'

Playfully, which was something of a new experience for Süleyman, he pushed her hand away. 'I have work to do.'

'Just once more,' she said.

'Look, Gonca,' he replied a little nervously now, 'I thought we agreed . . .'

'Some fun now and then never again – no names, no nothing? Yes,' she smiled, 'of course. But let me just do this . . .'

She took his half-empty tea glass and put it on the floor beside the bed. She then opened her silk robe to let her large breasts fall free and he felt himself stiffen. Taking control, just for this once, she mounted him and began to move herself against him. Looking at her like that, moving on top of him, her hands all over her breasts, was he thought probably the sexiest thing he had ever seen. And yes, he was having fun too – a lot of it.

When it was over she lay in his arms, smiling up into his face.

'You know it is going to be difficult for me to forget this,' he said as he kissed the top of her hair. 'You're a very skilful woman.'

'Ah, but you must,' she said. 'As we agreed.'

'I know.'

'Like you must forget the magician now too,' she said. 'His punishment is in hand.'

Suddenly Süleyman felt his whole body go cold.

'Gonca . . .'

She turned over and looked into his eyes. 'Out of evil has come good,' she said. 'We are safe and the illusions are at an end. The children will be avenged.'

'What do you mean?'

The look of horror on his face made her laugh. 'In the afterlife,' she said. 'In hell.'

'Oh.'

A little later he got up, washed and dressed. He then made his way to the front door with Gonca, still in her robe, following. Just before she opened the door she kissed him and then she said, 'You know, for gypsies in a place like this, the death camps the magician's people built in Europe mean very little. But when one of our own dies, well . . .'

'What?'

She opened the door and pushed him into the street.

'We make our own arrangements,' she said, and then she laughed before closing the door after him. Several barely dressed waifs flew to his feet begging 'Bey effendi' for small notes or coins. Some of them, he noted, were Gonca's own children.

Chapter 24

Ali Saka and Christoph Bauer eventually admitted to taking part in İrfan Şay's films of Max Esterhazy's ceremonies. Saka, who at some point had decided that saying he was being influenced by the Devil might help, was a particularly pitiful sight. There was no actual evidence, however, that either of them had actually taken part in the murders. They had been committed by the tall figure with its metal-covered penis. Max or a demon – it depended largely upon one's point of view and beliefs.

Bauer, a far more pragmatic individual, probably by virtue of his being a senior hospital official, admitted to stealing several litres of human blood from his employers. A Satanist, Bauer wasn't what would have normally been considered Max Esterhazy's type. Except that Max saw in Bauer and his perversions, plus his friendship with the amateur pornographer Şay, the chance to make money. Bauer claimed that Max had actively sought him out. He had, he'd said, been looking for one in touch with the Devil. Whether he had decided to do this in addition to saving the city by magical means or whether the money was the subservient motive was not and probably would never be known.

Two weeks later, İkmen and Süleyman met on İstiklal Caddesi for an evening drink. The weather had turned now and, although not cold, they did need to wear their jackets as opposed to carrying them across their shoulders. İkmen, who was rather fond of the James Joyce Irish pub – and its pints of Guinness – suggested they go there. But on their way to the pub they did just both pause at Atlas Pasaj. Groups of young, black-clad kids were already assembling for the evening – thankfully without that naughty child Fitnat Topal. She had been banned from the area in the wake of her assignation with the former proprietor of the Hammer.

293

'We became fixated on this place and its *habitués*,' Süleyman said. 'Quite wrongly.'

'You successfully identified a link from the dead youngsters to this particular zeitgeist,' İkmen said. 'They're very visible, these kids, and they wear their devilish associations with pride.'

'But they're not all bad.'

'No.' İkmen sighed. 'Silly and easily led, yes. But they're just young.'

'Like Çöktin?'

İkmen took his friend's arm in his and propelled him along through the early evening crowds on İstiklal Caddesi.

'You haven't managed to persuade him to stay then?' İkmen said wearily.

'No. He says he let me down, over his involvement with his cousin and the film subtitling.'

'It was stupid,' İkmen said.

'Yes, but it's not going any further,' Süleyman replied. 'Hüsnü Gunay is not this hacker Mendes, neither is he the author of the obscene images. Provided İsak doesn't do it again, it's over.'

İkmen stopped and raised a finger up to Süleyman's face. 'Provided it's over,' he said. 'And remember that the lawyer, Öz, knows about it too. Word gets out, Mehmet. I know it is sad and I will miss Çöktin myself, but I do think it is for the best. He's young, İnşallah, he will prosper. You know I wouldn't have been so lenient as you have been, don't you? He would have been gone by now.'

Süleyman shrugged. Sometimes İkmen could be extremely hard when one was least expecting it. After all, it wasn't as if he was political or anything, and in fact he had often expressed sympathy with Çöktin's people. But, Süleyman supposed, he was probably thinking of the department as a whole and the effect such a scandal would have upon it.

They walked in silence until they got to just past the Alkazar Sinema when İkmen said, 'So this hacker, Mendes, who is he?'

'We don't know,' Süleyman said. 'And according to both Hüsnü Gunay and Çöktin we probably never will. Something about routing data via South America – I don't know. But the newsgroups we wanted to track, although we know they are used by Goths and transsexuals, are relatively harmless and so, unsavoury as it may be, we must let them get on with it for the time being. We don't even know whether Mendes is local or not. Because of Max and his associations the word Mendes has demonic associations for us. But it is also a Spanish surname, you know.'

'That image, though,' İkmen said. 'The thirteen . . .'

'Mendes drew it as a joke for his, or her, friend, Hüsnü Gunay,' Süleyman said. 'Gunay apparently e-mailed or whatever at length to Mendes about his Gothic interests, his amused and cynical involvement in the Hammer scene. Mendes and Gunay must have found it hilarious to have a stupid and obscene drawing penned by the former in the place. Gunay, although a sometime customer up at Atlas, is very cutting about the club. Full of what he describes as "ignorant dilettantes" – by which I assume he means people not as serious about life, philosophy and computers as he is.'

'Mmm.'

There was a very pleasant smell of lamb on the air that, mixed with the cigarette smoke from various sources, almost made İkmen hungry. But he carried on walking. Guinness, so Mehmet's wife, Zelfa, had once told him, contains all the essential nutrients needed by humans and so best wait for his 'meal' at the James Joyce. 'I wonder how the image got from the club to the places of worship?'

'Unless we catch the person doing it, I don't suppose we'll ever know,' Süleyman said. 'Those Goth kids are very loyal to each other and their cause.'

'Such negativity!' İkmen said with furious upraised hands. 'But then I can't blame them. Poor kids. Living in a bizarre world of constant communication, horrific violence both real and fictional, and now the threat of all-out chemical warfare. The so-called "free" world we live in is manipulated by a man incapable of pronouncing common words in his own language. What hope is there?'

Süleyman smiled.

İkmen, seeing this, said, 'I sound like a mad old man, don't I?'

'A little. Even if you are right,' Süleyman said, and then changed the subject. 'I hear that Metin is going to be returning to work as soon as the hospital allows.'

'Yes. I spoke to his wife. She's not happy about it, but . . .' İkmen shrugged. 'Men like Metin, really poor boys, have so much to prove. The deprivation of Ümraniye still haunts him and, I mean, you saw his father. What a mess! It's difficult for any of us to escape from our pasts. Look at Max.'

'Yes. And he shot Metin, didn't he?'

'With İrfan Şay's pistol, yes,' İkmen sighed. 'Having failed to pick up Çiçek's sigil the first time he returned to the apartment he must have been desperate that second time. It's amazing to me that he forgot it in the first place. Max was always so organised. Perhaps the strain of doing what he did, the sheer complication of the operation, caused him to lose track of exactly what he was doing. You know, the last time we spoke, before the boat and everything, I noticed that his hands shook when he picked up his coffee cup. Makes one think. Maybe he was unwell too.'

'Or maybe you're just looking for excuses for him, Çetin?' Süleyman stopped to light a cigarette outside a pastane, its art nouveau window filled by a huge pyramid of sticky baklava. But when İkmen didn't answer he went on to a different tack. 'You heard from his sister?'

'Yes,' İkmen said. 'The Metropolitan police contacted her and gave her some indication about what had happened, but then she called me. Poor woman. I said "I wish I had a body for you to mourn and to bury" – I said I wished that Max hadn't died. You know, she told me what Max had studied at Oxford. Strange he never said. It was theology – destined for a career in the priesthood.'

'What changed his mind?'

'She doesn't know. Maybe it was the conjuring club he became involved with at university, maybe it was his father, maybe he didn't really change his mind until he came here and met Rebbe Baruh. I don't know. But, you know, even when, at one point, I thought that perhaps he'd killed our old friend Alison all those years ago, I still couldn't quite believe that he was totally bad. His sister said that she found an old diary of Max's from when he was about twelve. She read out to me a sentence he'd written on the first page. It said something like, "I'm moving to the light. I pray that God will not reject me."'

They started walking again, but silently for a little while now.

There really wasn't much one could say with regard to Max's childish pronouncement. What he had been and what he eventually became were, they both knew, only reflections of what he had experienced. The essence of Max remained the same.

'So how is Çiçek?' Süleyman asked.

İkmen smiled. 'She's fine,' he said. 'And you'll be very happy to know that you have resumed your place in her heart as a young uncle figure. You know, Mehmet, I really do wonder whether that spell, that sigil Max worked on Çiçek, did affect her. After all, if she hadn't been pining over you then she would have been far less susceptible to his suggestions.'

'They didn't find Rohypnol in her blood?'

'No. But then apparently it is notoriously difficult to detect. A lot like little Ülkü Ayla.'

'Still no sign of her?'

'No.' İkmen sighed heavily. 'Poor kid could be anywhere. I know she wasn't actually dumped, but it's not uncommon for people like Max to bring youngsters like Ülkü from the east to the city and then dispense with them. They don't work hard enough or their manners are too rough. Thrown out, they just drift. It's a shame because Max did, I think, really care about Ülkü in his own strange way.'

They reached the door of the pub and İkmen paused before going in.

'And what of Zelfa?' he said.

Süleyman sighed. 'Well, she has at least agreed to come back and talk,' he said. 'I don't know what will happen. I miss her.'

And he did. His one interlude with Gonca had been fun but, like a very rich chocolate, it aroused the senses without satisfying them. Also now it made him feel a little sick too. But then maybe that was because he, and he knew İkmen too, harboured some suspicions about her with regard to Max's continued disappearance. Whether Max were dead or alive, it was possible that Gonca could know his whereabouts. It was possible that Gonca could have killed him too. But, as the gypsy herself had told him, there was no point in pursuing the magician any further now. And perhaps she was right.

'Well, learning to drink Guinness properly will help,' İkmen said as he held the door open for his friend to enter. 'Come on, let me buy you a pint.'

Süleyman frowned.

'It's rather less than a litre and rather more than a half,' he said. 'According to an Irishman I once met in Karaköy – don't ask how – it is what God would drink if He had a human form. Enlightenment in a glass was how he described it.' He smiled. 'Maybe Max should have spent less time with his books and his spells and more time in the pub.'

Süleyman, smiling also, walked ahead of İkmen into the midst of the enthusiastic Friday night crowd.

Brother Constantine had become quite a regular spectator at the drama that was the Cohen house renovation. And although Berekiah and Hulya weren't always up at the site, they were on this occasion together with his mother and father – the latter sitting hunched up in his wheelchair in the middle of the still unruly garden.

'Mr Cohen?'

Both Berekiah and Balthazar looked down towards the gaping hole where once a grand entrance gate had stood. When the young man saw the monk he put down the hammer he had been using to nail back a rotted window frame and went down to greet him.

'Brother Constantine. How are you?'

'Better than I was,' the monk said.

'Good.' He had, Berekiah knew, been very distressed and disturbed by the desecration of the Church of the Panaghia.

'What does he want?' Berekiah heard his father say. 'Tell him to go away!'

'Father!'

'Christians!' Balthazar spat on to the ground. Estelle, infuriated, moved his chair into a corner of the garden, pushing him into a patch of briar.

'I'm so sorry, Brother Constantine,' Berekiah said apologetically. 'My father is a sick man, angry at the world . . .'

'Maybe he needs our prayers.'

Berekiah looked over his shoulder at his father swearing in the bush and shook his head. Angry, sexually frustrated and bitter, his

298

father was gradually alienating everyone. Uncle Jak, now back in Britain, had promised he would visit again – but only once Berekiah and Hulya's house was in a state to receive visitors. Another 'holiday' at the Cohen apartment in Karaköy would, Jak had said as he left, either result in his own suicide or Balthazar's murder.

'Anyway,' Berekiah said, 'what can we do for you, Brother Constantine? Would you like tea?'

'No.' The monk placed his hand over his heart and then smiled. 'No, thank you, Mr Cohen. I came simply to tell you that we have discovered who has been desecrating our places of worship,' he sighed, 'and sadly, it was one of our own.'

'A monk?'

'No. But one who used to be of our number,' he said. 'A young man – an acolyte once – now he moves amongst some very strange people up in Beyoğlu.' He leaned in towards Berekiah. 'Devil worship, you know.'

'So how did you find him? Have you told the police?'

'He was caught in the act,' Brother Constantine said, 'at the Aya Triada in Taksim. One of our own, Orthodox, churches. He was known and recognised,' he added somewhat menacingly.

'And the police?'

'There is no need,' Brother Constantine said. 'It is a spiritual matter. We will take care of him.'

'What do you mean?'

The monk sighed. 'I mean that when a person does such a thing it shows that his soul is sick. The poor boy is pursued by demons, his mind obsessed by this obscene picture he has copied, his every action dictated by the Devil.' He shuddered. 'We live in threatening times, Mr Cohen, and sometimes the way of evil can seem more attractive and less difficult than the way of God.'

'Do you not think he might need medical attention, Brother Constantine? I mean, as well as your own ministrations.'

'No. No, it is his spirit that wavers, Mr Cohen, not his mind.' And then the monk smiled. 'But I appreciate your concern. I also appreciate that Mrs Cohen's father is a police officer – but if we could just keep this to ourselves . . .'

Berekiah wasn't happy with this, but he agreed to keep the monk's counsel anyway. After all, provided the desecration had come to an end, there was no need to involve İkmen in what sounded like just a very sad story.

And so after a little discussion about the house and its progress Brother Constantine left. However, instead of walking back up towards the house and his family, Berekiah wandered out into the street for a while. It was just getting dark now and soon the sunset call to prayer would ripple across the city like a great wave of devotion, an entreaty to a higher beneficent power. Well, they needed something – Muslim, Christian, Jew – whatever. As the monk had said, they lived in threatening times and if they didn't appeal to something both good and powerful to come to their aid then what could they do? Descend like that poor acolyte into some sort of twisted perversion that poisoned the mind and frightened all those who came into contact with it? That, surely, had to be the route to chaos and they had enough of that to deal with as it was.

Berekiah looked up at the dome of the great Greek School and then sighed. What would war do to places like that? Would they and other, maybe even more important buildings, be bombed? Would people be gassed or poisoned? What was in the minds of people like Saddam Hussein and George W. Bush? Berekiah's own brother-in-law Bülent would join the army in the New Year – just as he had done himself once. He shuddered: chances were, he knew, that anything he had experienced in the army would be far worse for Bülent. And Bülent's sister, his wife? Hulya had told him only yesterday she thought there might be a chance she was pregnant. Very quick, but then she was very young – and excited. If only he felt the same. But Berekiah, in spite of the fact that he didn't show his wife this, could only feel anxiety and depression. A baby? Into this world? Berekiah looked up and down his silent, trouble-free street and then started to make his way back to his ruined old house. As he walked through the entrance the sunset call to prayer began and he watched as Hulya, beautiful, her eyes full of hope, came out into the garden to listen to it. And so, with a smile on his face at the sight of her, Berekiah went to join Hulya. What better place, after all, and despite everything, was there for him to be?

Author's Notes

The Turkish Republic

The Turkish Republic, which was created by its first president, Mustafa Kemal Atatürk, and his supporters, was formally declared on 29 October 1923. A democratic and secular system, the republic replaced the Ottoman Empire, an Islamic theocracy which, at its height, ruled the Middle East and much of Eastern Europe. Although the population of modern Turkey is ninety per cent Muslim, the republic remains secular, is currently a full member of NATO and is also an associate member of the European Union. Turks use the European calendar and take Sunday and sometimes Saturday too, instead of the traditional Friday, as their official weekend. Freedom of worship for all faiths, although enshrined within the constitution, does not extend to the practice of magic, which is still, officially, forbidden under laws designed to prohibit sorcery.

Kabbalah

Kabbalah is the magical system devised and practised by Jewish occultists. Although its actual genesis is lost in the mists of time, two of its key texts, the Sefer Yetzirah and the Zohar, are known to date respectively from the sixth and twelfth centuries AD. Study of Kabbalah was traditionally centred around certain learned men or rebbes, and schools of Kabbalah are known to have existed in Spain, Portugal, Italy and across the Ottoman Empire.

At the most basic level Kabbalah is a system of relationships or correspondences that, theoretically, open up access to the inner reaches of the mind. Based around a diagram called The Tree of Life, Kabbalah teaches that both man and the universe are one and the same and therefore interchangeable. Following the magical adage 'as above, so below', it is therefore possible to manipulate or influence the divine by using those corporeal forms (tarot cards, perfumes, colours) that correspond to whichever angel or demon may be asked for assistance in the unseen world. Although Kabbalah is neither strictly 'white' nor 'black' magic, the ultimate aim, which is union with the god-head, is perceived to be desirable. It is said that all the greatest Kabbalists do indeed eventually dispense with corporeal reality and literally disappear.

Glossary

Ağa	Term used in place of 'Mr' for local landowner, also used in Ottoman times as term of respect for eunuchs.
Akmerkez	American-style shopping mall in the Etiler district of the city.
Anadolu	Anatolia, as in Anadolu Kavağı – the Anatolian Fortress.
Bakkal	Grocery shop.
Baklava	Sweet, pastry and nut dessert.
Bey	As in Çetin Bey, an Ottoman title denoting respect, still in use today following a man's first name.
Caddesi	Avenue.
Çay Bahçe	Tea garden that serves tea, coffee and soft drinks, usually open-air.
Dede	Grandfather; also a respectful term applied to dervishes, as in İbrahim Dede.
Djinn	Evil spirits.
Fasıl	Urban folk music.
Hamam	Traditional Turkish steam bath.
Hanım	Lady, woman. Like the male Bey, it is a title denoting respect for an older, usually married woman. It follows the woman's first name, as in Fatma Hanım.
Haydarpaşa	Large railway station on the Asian side of the Bosphorus, the terminus for trains from Ankara and other Anatolian cities.
İmamHatip lisesi	Religious (Islamic) high school.
İnşallah	'God willing' or 'If God wills'.
Kapıcı	Doorkeeper. Blocks of flats have kapıcılar

	men who act as security, porters etc., for the apartment community.
Kapalı Çarşı	The Grand Bazaar.
Kariye	Otherwise known as the Kariye Mosque and the Church of St Saviour in Chora, north of Balat, a Byzantine church featuring exquisite Christian mosaics.
Kaymak	Clotted cream.
Kısmet	Fate.
Kokoreç	Grilled sheep's intestines.
Ladino	Language spoken by Turkish (mainly Sephardic) Jews, a mixture of Hebrew and Spanish.
Mısır Çarşı	The Spice Bazaar, also known as the Egyptian Bazaar.
MİT	Turkish Secret Service.
Pasaj	Arcade with shops.
Pastane	Cake and pastry shop. Cakes can be bought to take away or eat in, usually with tea or coffee.
Phaeton	Horse-drawn carriage.
Pide	Unleavened bread, served with toppings of meat, cheese etc., at small restaurants called pideci.
Rakı	Aniseed-flavoured alcoholic spirit.
Rumeli	European.
Rumi	Jelaleddin Rumi, a mystical poet and great Sufi master. Disciples of Rumi are known as Dervishes.
Sahaflar	Book bazaar.
Sema	Ritual dance of the Sufis (so-called Whirling Dervishes).
Sofa	Central downstairs room in a yalı.
Sokak	Street, alleyway.
Ümraniye	Impoverished district of İstanbul on the Asian side of the Bosphorus.
Üsküdar	Asian, working-class district of İstanbul, used to be called 'Scutari'.

Villa Doluca	A brand of local wine.
Yalı	Ornate Ottoman residence usually on the banks of the Bosphorus or on the Princes' Islands, generally constructed from wood.

Turkish Alphabet

The Turkish Alphabet is very similar to its English counterpart with the following exceptions:

- The letters q, w and x do not appear.
- Some letters behave differently in Turkish compared with English:

C, c   Not the c in cat and tractor, but the j in jam and Taj or the g in gentle and courageous.

G, g   Always the hard g in great or slug, never the soft g of general and outrage.

J, j   As the French pronounce the j in bonjour and the g in gendarme.

- The following additional letters appear:

Ç ç   The ch in chunk or choke.

Ğ, ğ   'Yumuşak ge' is used to lengthen the vowel that it follows. It is not usually voiced (except as a vague y sound). For instance, it is used in the name Ayşe Farsakoğlu, which is pronounced *Far-sak-erlu*, and in öğle (noon, midday), pronounced öy-*lay* (see below for how to pronounce ö).

Ş, ş   The sh in ship and shovel.

I, ı   Without a dot, the sound of the a in probable.

İ, i   With a dot, the i in thin or tinny.

Ö, ö   Like the ur sound in further.

Ü, ü   Like the u in the French tu.

Full pronunciation guide

A, a	Usually short, the a in hah! or the u in but, never the medium or long a in nasty and hateful.
B, b	As in English.
C, c	Not the c in cat and tractor, but the j in jam and Taj or the g in gentle and courageous.
Ç, ç	The ch in chunk or choke.
D, d	As in English.
E, e	Always short, the e in venerable, never the e in Bede (and never silent).
F, f	As in English.
G, g	Always the hard g in great or slug, never the soft g of general and outrage.
Ğ, ğ	'Yumuşak ge' is used to lengthen the vowel that it follows. It is not usually voiced (except as a vague y sound). For instance, it is used in the name Ayşe Farsakoğlu, which is pronounced *Far-sak-erlu*, and in öğle (noon, midday), pronounced *öy-lay* (see below for how to pronounce ö).
H, h	As in English (and never silent).
I, ı	Without a dot, the sound of the a in probable.
İ, i	With a dot, the i in thin or tinny.
J, j	As the French pronounce the j in bonjour and the g in gendarme.
K, k	As in English (and never silent).
L, l	As in English.
M, m	As in English.
N, n	As in English.
O, o	Always short, the o in hot and bothered.
Ö, ö	Like the ur sound in further.
P, p	As in English.
R, r	As in English.
S, s	As in English.
Ş, ş	The sh in ship and shovel.

T, t	As in English.
U, u	Always medium-length, the u in push and pull, never the u in but.
Ü, ü	Like the u in the French tu.
V, v	Usually as in English, but sometimes almost a w sound in words such as tavuk (hen).
Y, y	As in English. Follows vowels to make diphthongs: ay is the y sound in fly; ey is the ay sound in day; oy is the oy sound in toy; uy is almost the same as the French oui.
Z, z	As in English.